REGULAR SHOW™

WRASSLESPLOSION

ROSS RICHIE CEO & Founder • MATT GAGNON Editor-in-Chief • FILIP SABLIK President of Publishing & Marketing • STEPHEN CHRISTY President of Development • LANCE KREITER VP of Licensing & Merchandising
PHIL BARBARO VP of Finance • ARUNE SINGH VP of Marketing • BRYCE CARLSON Managing Editor • MEL CAYLO Marketing Manager • SCOTT NEWMAN Production Design Manager • KATE HENNING Operations Manager
SIERRA HAHN Senior Editor • DAFNA PLEBAN Editor, Talent Development • SHANNON WATTERS Editor • ERIC HARBURN Editor • WHITNEY LEOPARD Editor • JASMINE AMIRI Editor
CHRIS ROSA Associate Editor • ALEX GALER Associate Editor • CAMERON CHITTOCK Associate Editor • MATTHEW LEVINE Assistant Editor • SOPHIE PHILIPS-ROBERTS Assistant Editor • KELSEY DIETERICH Designer
JILLIAN CRAB Production Designer • MICHELLE ANKLEY Production Designer • GRACE PARK Production Design Assistant • ELIZABETH LOUGHRIDGE Accounting Coordinator • STEPHANIE HOCUTT Social Media Coordinator
JOSÉ MEZA Event Coordinator • JAMES ARRIOLA Mailroom Assistant • HOLLY AITCHISON Operations Assistant • MEGAN CHRISTOPHER Operations Assistant • AMBER PARKER Administrative Assistant

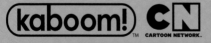

REGULAR SHOW: WRASSLESPLOSION, June 2017. Published by
KaBOOM!, a division of Boom Entertainment, Inc. REGULAR SHOW,
CARTOON NETWORK, the logos, and all related characters and
elements are trademarks of and © Cartoon Network. (S17). All rights
reserved. KaBOOM!™ and the KaBOOM! Logo are trademarks of Boom
Entertainment, Inc., registered in various countries and categories. All characters, events, and/or institutions depicted herein are
fictional. Any similarity between any of the names, characters, persons, events, and/or institutions in this publication to actual names,
characters, and persons, whether living or dead, events and/or institutions is unintended and purely coincidental. KaBOOM! Does not
read or accept unsolicited submissions of ideas, stories, or artwork.

BOOM! Studios, 5670 Wilshire Boulevard, Suite 450, Los Angeles, CA 90036-5679. Printed in China. First Printing.

ISBN: 978-1-60886-985-5 , eISBN: 978-1-61398-656-1

REGULAR SHOW™

WRASSLESPLOSION

CREATED BY JG QUINTEL

WRITTEN BY
RYAN FERRIER

ILLUSTRATED BY
LAURA HOWELL

COLORED BY
FRED STRESING

"THE COMEBACK"

WRITTEN BY
EDDIE WRIGHT

ILLUSTRATED BY
ELLE POWER

COLORED BY
LISA MOORE

LETTERED BY
WARREN MONTGOMERY

COVER BY
JORGE CORONA

DESIGNER
GRACE PARK

ASSISTANT EDITORS
SOPHIE PHILIPS-ROBERTS
& MARY GUMPORT

EDITOR
SIERRA HAHN

WITH SPECIAL THANKS TO MARISA MARIONAKIS, JANET NO, CURTIS LELASH, CONRAD MONTGOMERY, MEGHAN BRADLEY, KELLY CREWS, RYAN SLATER AND THE WONDERFUL FOLKS AT CARTOON NETWORK.

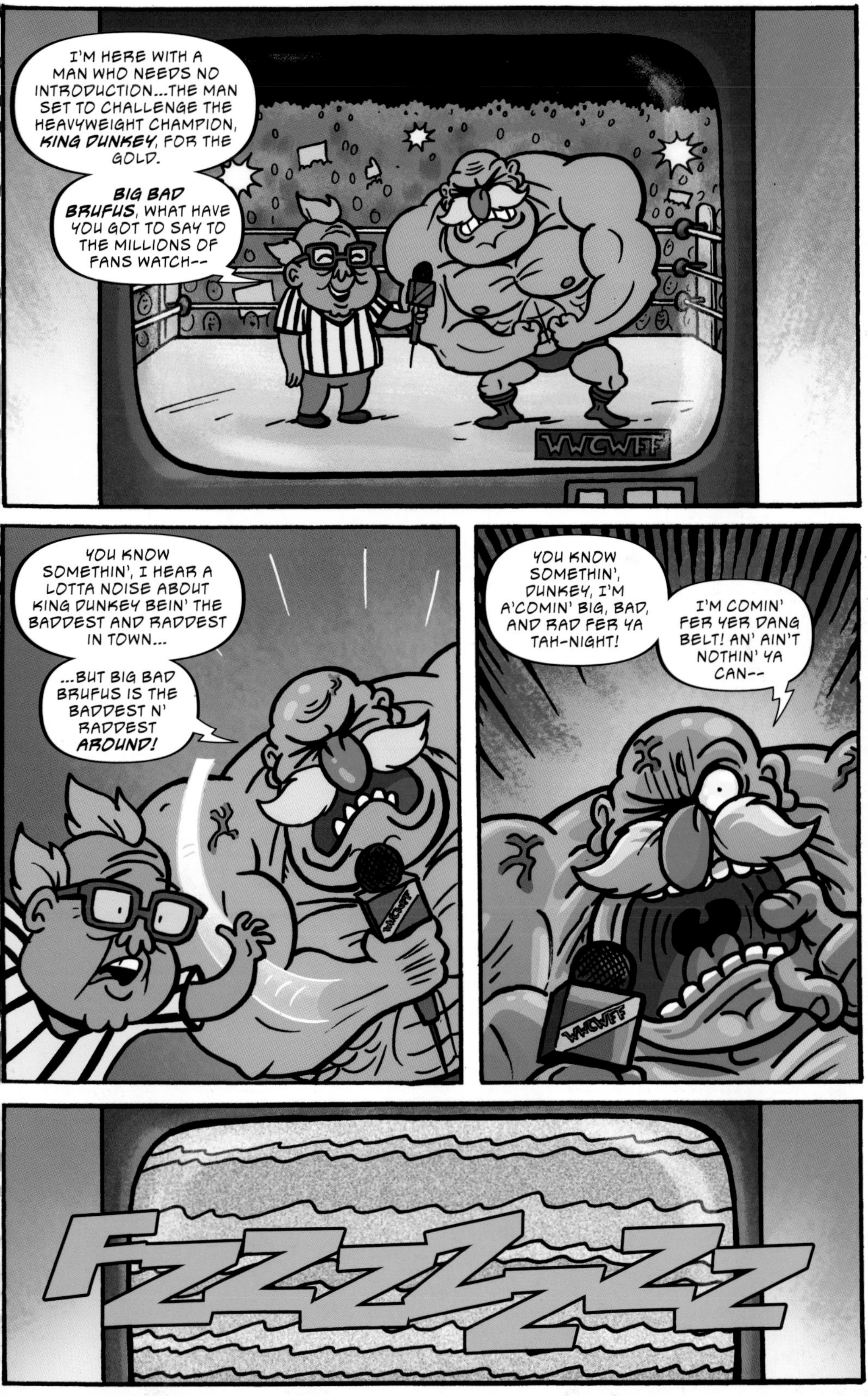
I'M HERE WITH A MAN WHO NEEDS NO INTRODUCTION...THE MAN SET TO CHALLENGE THE HEAVYWEIGHT CHAMPION, KING DUNKEY, FOR THE GOLD.
BIG BAD BRUFUS, WHAT HAVE YOU GOT TO SAY TO THE MILLIONS OF FANS WATCH--
WWCWFF
YOU KNOW SOMETHIN', I HEAR A LOTTA NOISE ABOUT KING DUNKEY BEIN' THE BADDEST AND RADDEST IN TOWN...
...BUT BIG BAD BRUFUS IS THE BADDEST N' RADDEST AROUND!
WWCWFF
YOU KNOW SOMETHIN', DUNKEY, I'M A'COMIN' BIG, BAD, AND RAD FER YA TAH-NIGHT!
I'M COMIN' FER YER DANG BELT! AN' AIN'T NOTHIN' YA CAN--
WWCWFF
FZZZZZZZ

UHHH... DUDE? WHAT HAPPENED TO THE T.V.?
FZZZZZZZ
NO. THIS CAN'T BE HAPPENING.
NNNNOOOOOOOO-UHH!
...GNARMAGEDDON IS THE BIGGEST WRESTLING PAY- PER-VIEW OF THE YEAR...
DUN DUN DUN
C'MONNN, YOU STUPID DUMB IDIOT PLEASURE FUN-BOX!
WHY WON'T YOU LET US GAZE UPON YOU?!
FZZZ ZZ ZZ

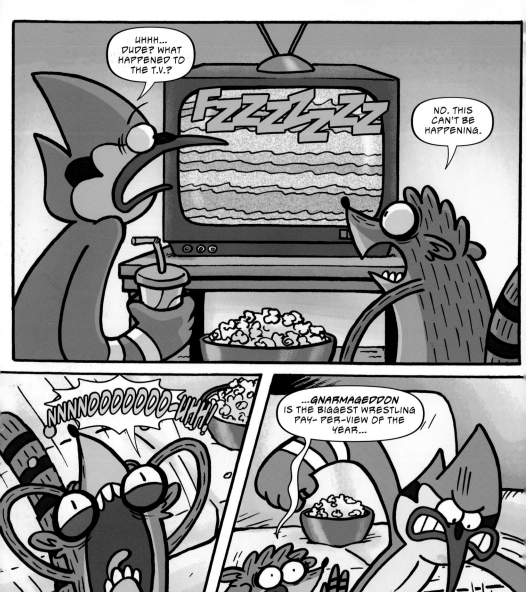

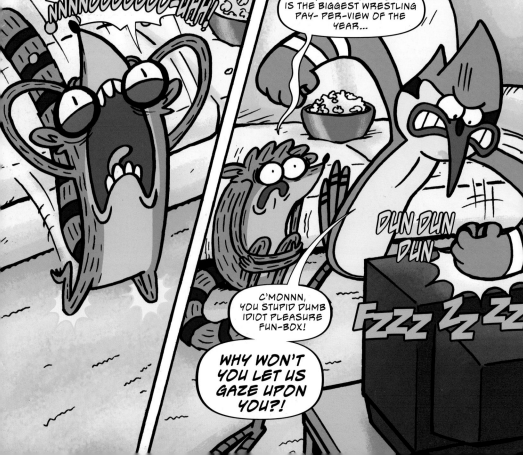

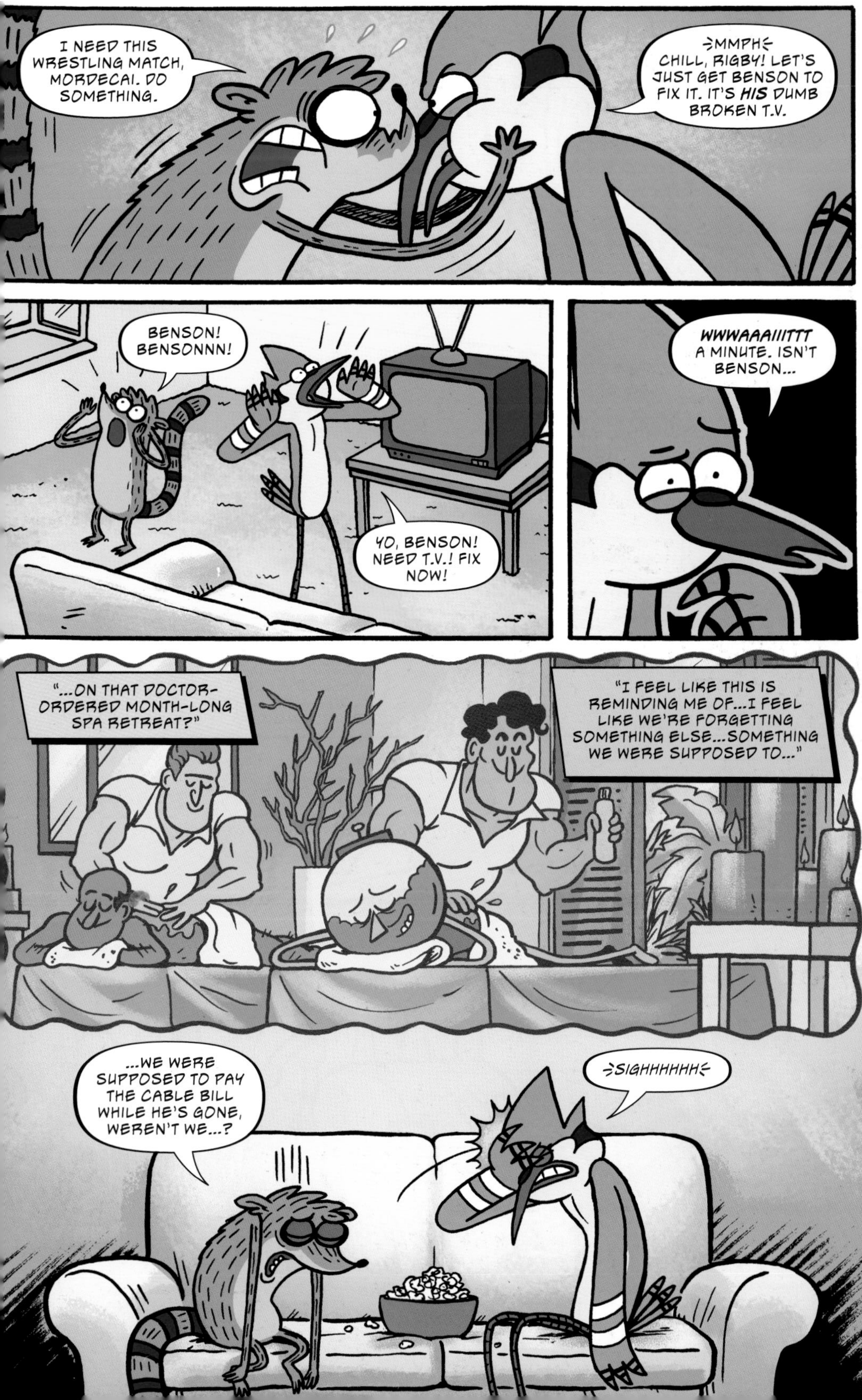
I NEED THIS WRESTLING MATCH, MORDECAI. DO SOMETHING.
≥MMPH≤ CHILL, RIGBY! LET'S JUST GET BENSON TO FIX IT. IT'S ***HIS*** DUMB BROKEN T.V.
BENSON! BENSONNN!
YO, BENSON! NEED T.V.! FIX NOW!
WWWAAAIIITTT A MINUTE. ISN'T BENSON...
"...ON THAT DOCTOR-ORDERED MONTH-LONG SPA RETREAT?"
"I FEEL LIKE THIS IS REMINDING ME OF...I FEEL LIKE WE'RE FORGETTING SOMETHING ELSE...SOMETHING WE WERE SUPPOSED TO..."
...WE WERE SUPPOSED TO PAY THE CABLE BILL WHILE HE'S GONE, WEREN'T WE...?
≥*SIGHHHHHH*≤

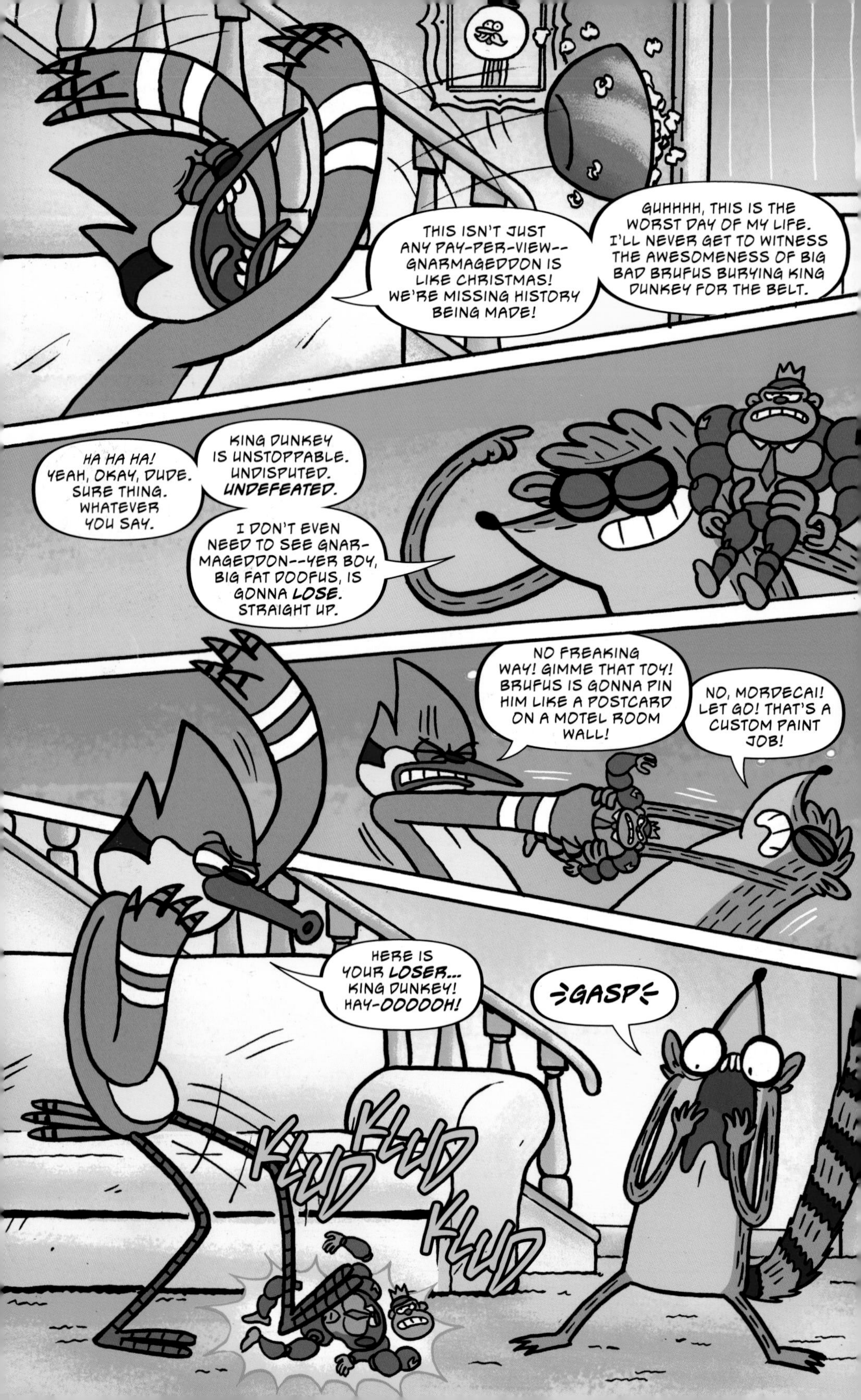
THIS ISN'T JUST ANY PAY-PER-VIEW--GNARMAGEDDON IS LIKE CHRISTMAS! WE'RE MISSING HISTORY BEING MADE!
GUHHHH, THIS IS THE WORST DAY OF MY LIFE. I'LL NEVER GET TO WITNESS THE AWESOMENESS OF BIG BAD BRUFUS BURYING KING DUNKEY FOR THE BELT.
KING DUNKEY IS UNSTOPPABLE. UNDISPUTED. *UNDEFEATED.*
HA HA HA! YEAH, OKAY, DUDE. SURE THING. WHATEVER YOU SAY.
I DON'T EVEN NEED TO SEE GNAR-MAGEDDON--YER BOY, BIG FAT DOOFUS, IS GONNA *LOSE.* STRAIGHT UP.
NO FREAKING WAY! GIMME THAT TOY! BRUFUS IS GONNA PIN HIM LIKE A POSTCARD ON A MOTEL ROOM WALL!
NO, MORDECAI! LET GO! THAT'S A CUSTOM PAINT JOB!
HERE IS YOUR *LOSER...* KING DUNKEY! HAY-*OOOOOH!*
GASP
KLUD KLUD KLUD KLUD

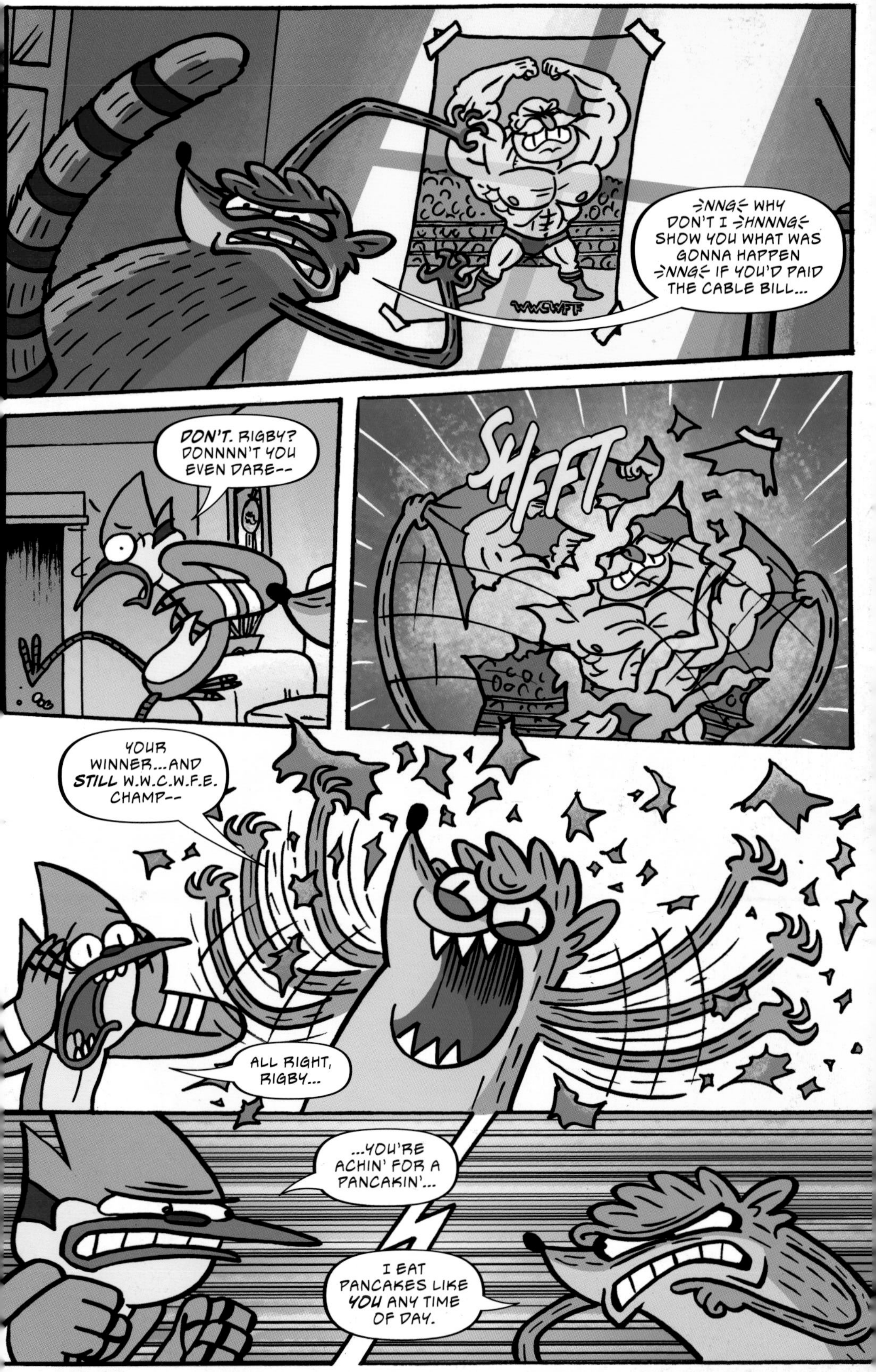

WWCWFE
=NNG= WHY DON'T I =HNNNG= SHOW YOU WHAT WAS GONNA HAPPEN =NNG= IF YOU'D PAID THE CABLE BILL...
DON'T. RIGBY? DONNNN'T YOU EVEN DARE--
SHFFT
YOUR WINNER...AND *STILL* W.W.C.W.F.E. CHAMP--
ALL RIGHT, RIGBY...
...YOU'RE ACHIN' FOR A PANCAKIN'...
I EAT PANCAKES LIKE *YOU* ANY TIME OF DAY.

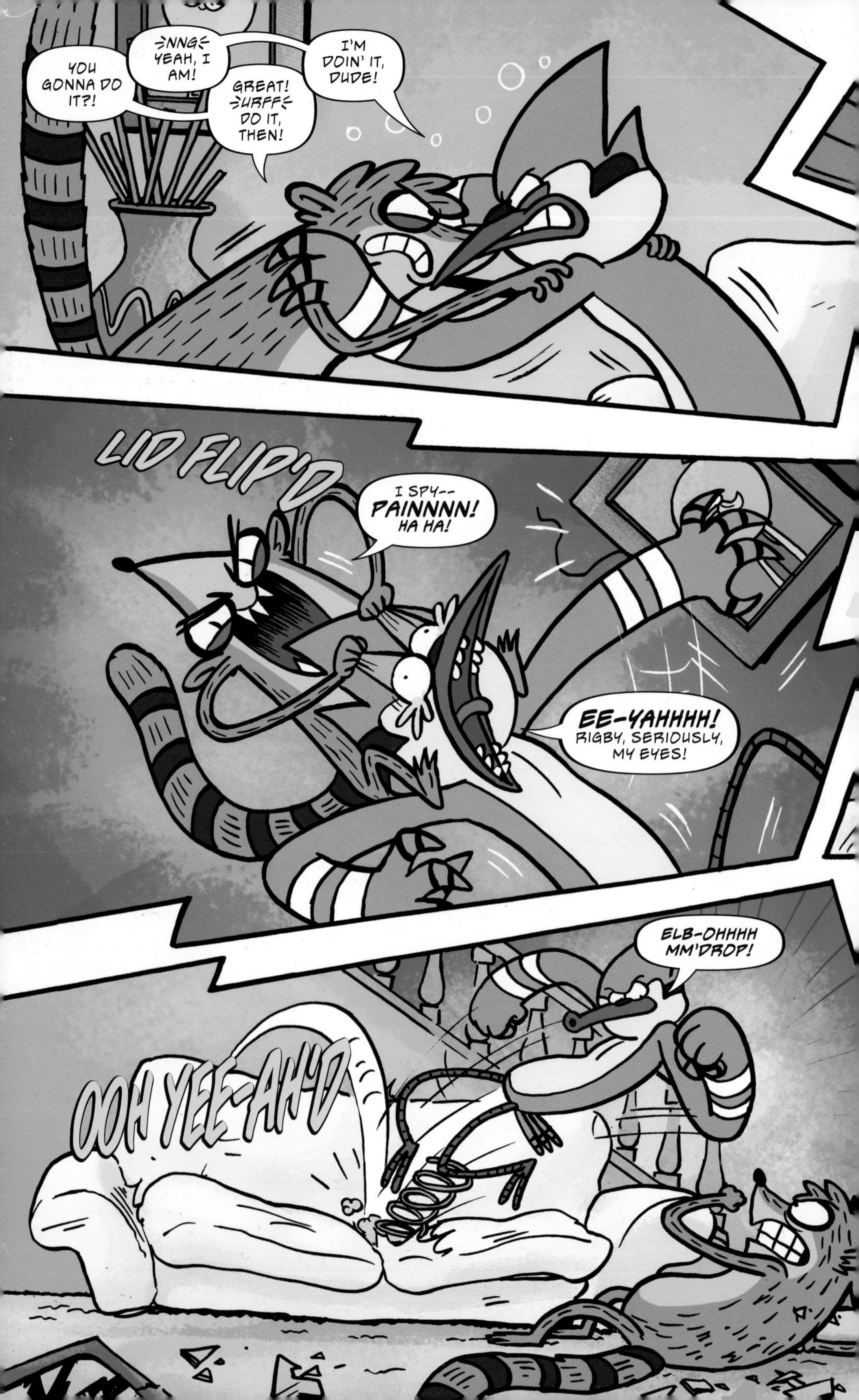
YOU GONNA DO IT?!
NNG YEAH, I AM!
I'M DOIN' IT, DUDE!
GREAT! URFF DO IT, THEN!
LID FLIP'D
I SPY-- PAINNNN! HA HA!
EE-YAHHHH! RIGBY, SERIOUSLY, MY EYES!
ELB-OHHHH MM'DROP!
OOH YEE-AH'D

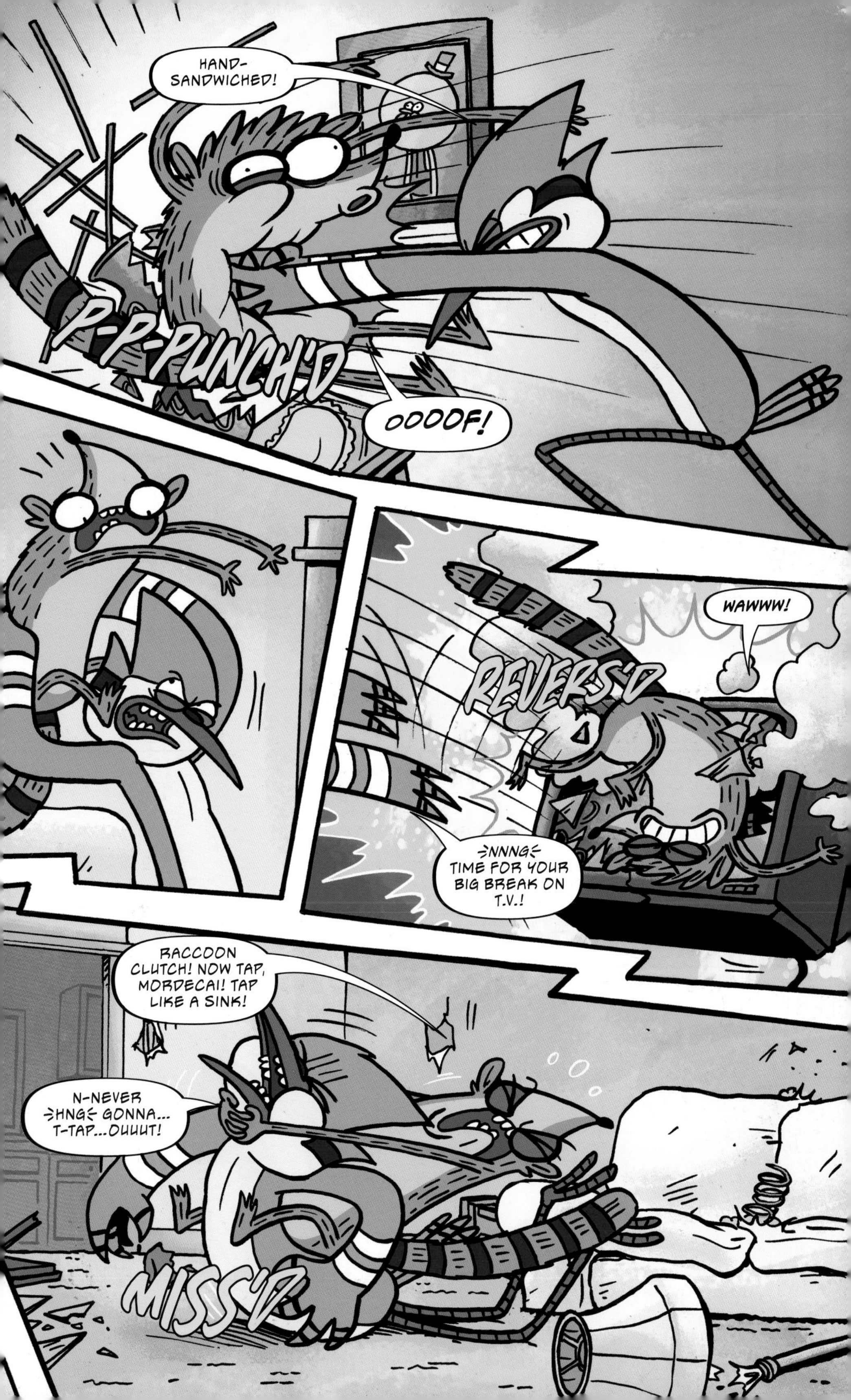
HAND-SANDWICHED!
P-P-PUNCH'D
OOOOF!
WAWWW!
REVERS'D
NNNG
TIME FOR YOUR BIG BREAK ON T.V.!
RACCOON CLUTCH! NOW TAP, MORDECAI! TAP LIKE A SINK!
N-NEVER HNG GONNA... T-TAP...OUUUT!
MISS'D

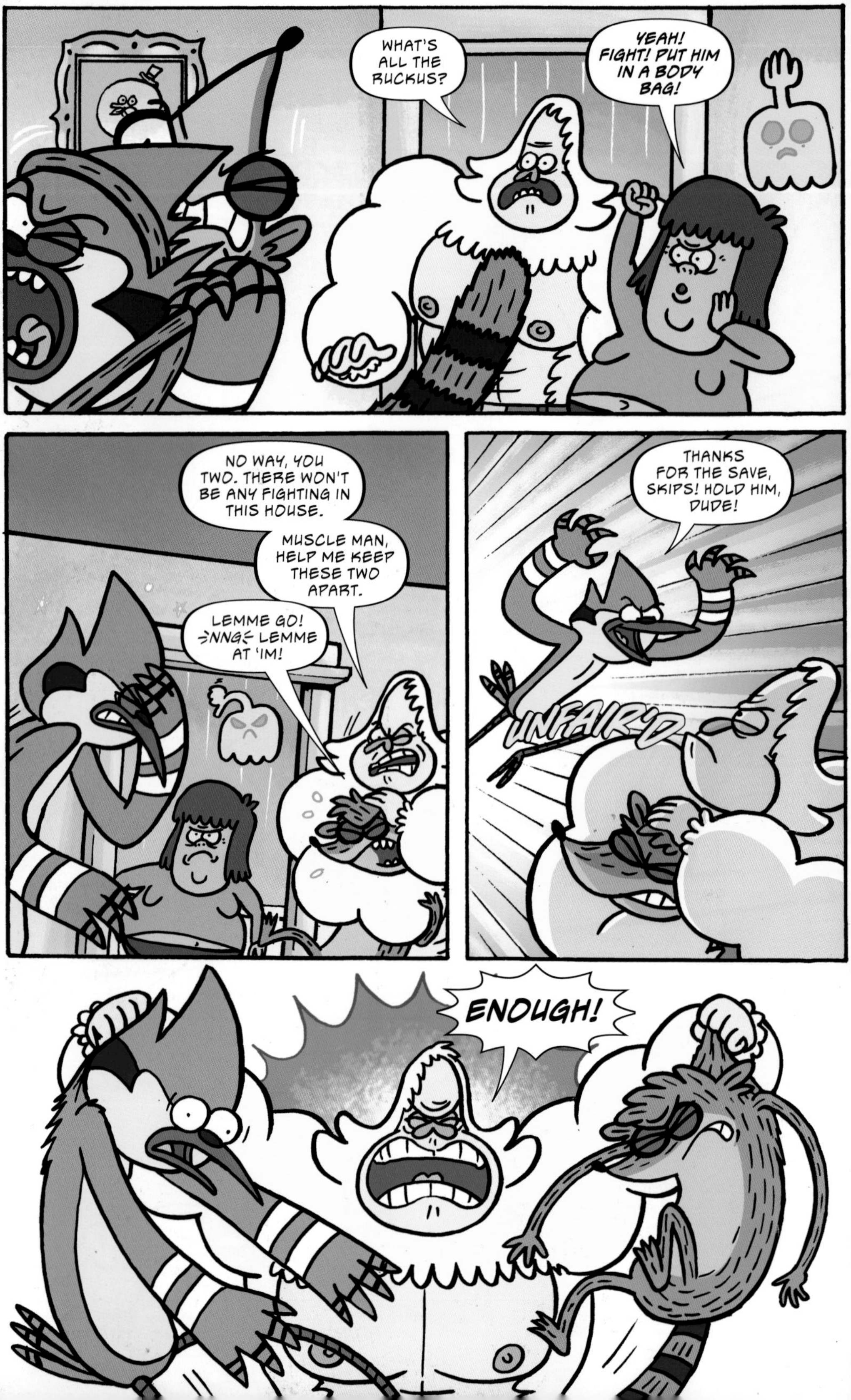
WHAT'S ALL THE RUCKUS?
YEAH! FIGHT! PUT HIM IN A BODY BAG!
NO WAY, YOU TWO. THERE WON'T BE ANY FIGHTING IN THIS HOUSE.
MUSCLE MAN, HELP ME KEEP THESE TWO APART.
LEMME GO! =NNG= LEMME AT 'IM!
THANKS FOR THE SAVE, SKIPS! HOLD HIM, DUDE!
UNFAIR'D
ENOUGH!

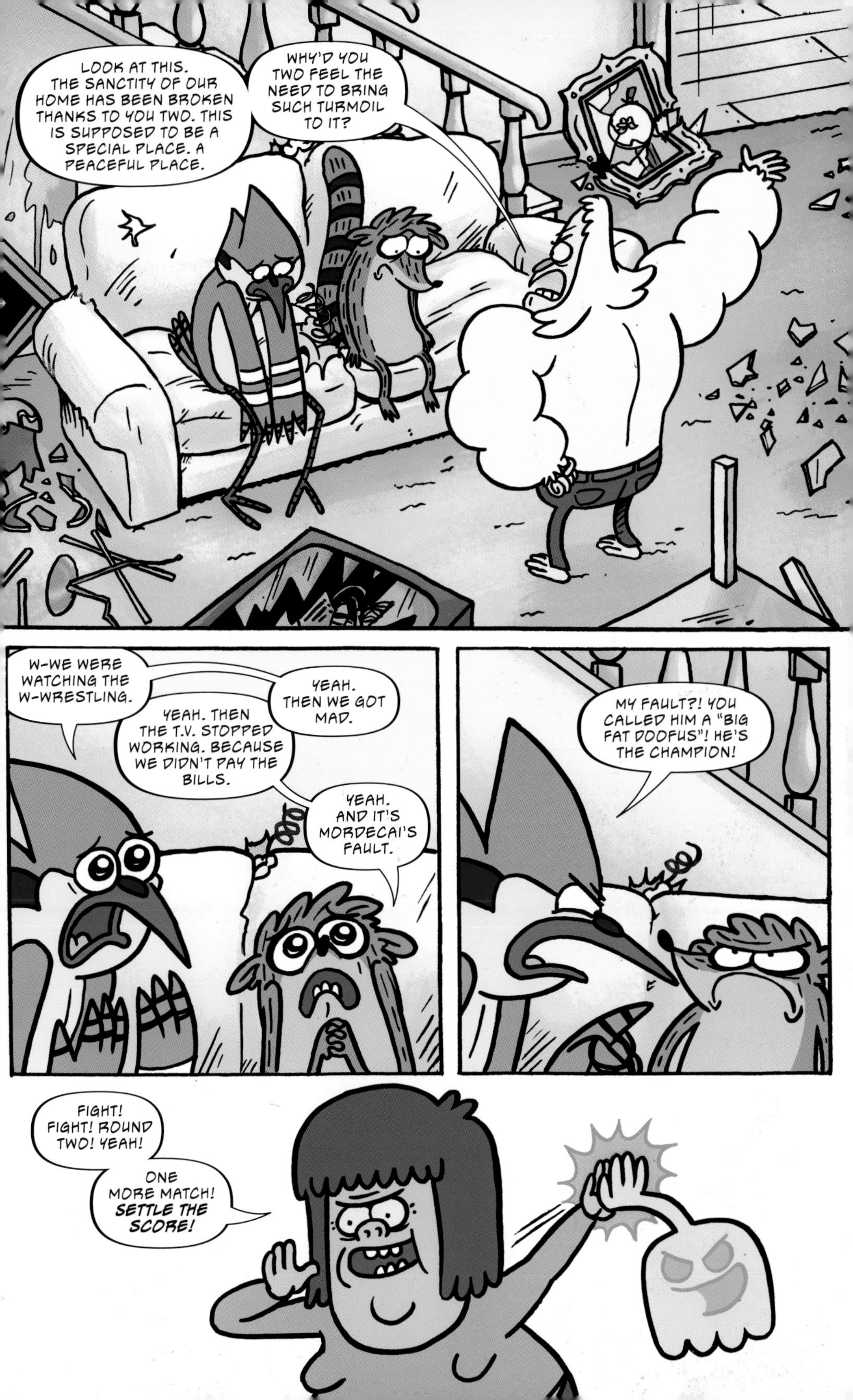
LOOK AT THIS. THE SANCTITY OF OUR HOME HAS BEEN BROKEN THANKS TO YOU TWO. THIS IS SUPPOSED TO BE A SPECIAL PLACE. A PEACEFUL PLACE.
WHY'D YOU TWO FEEL THE NEED TO BRING SUCH TURMOIL TO IT?
W-WE WERE WATCHING THE W-WRESTLING.
YEAH. THEN WE GOT MAD.
YEAH. THEN THE T.V. STOPPED WORKING. BECAUSE WE DIDN'T PAY THE BILLS.
YEAH. AND IT'S MORDECAI'S FAULT.
MY FAULT?! YOU CALLED HIM A "BIG FAT DOOFUS"! HE'S THE CHAMPION!
FIGHT! FIGHT! ROUND TWO! YEAH!
ONE MORE MATCH! SETTLE THE SCORE!

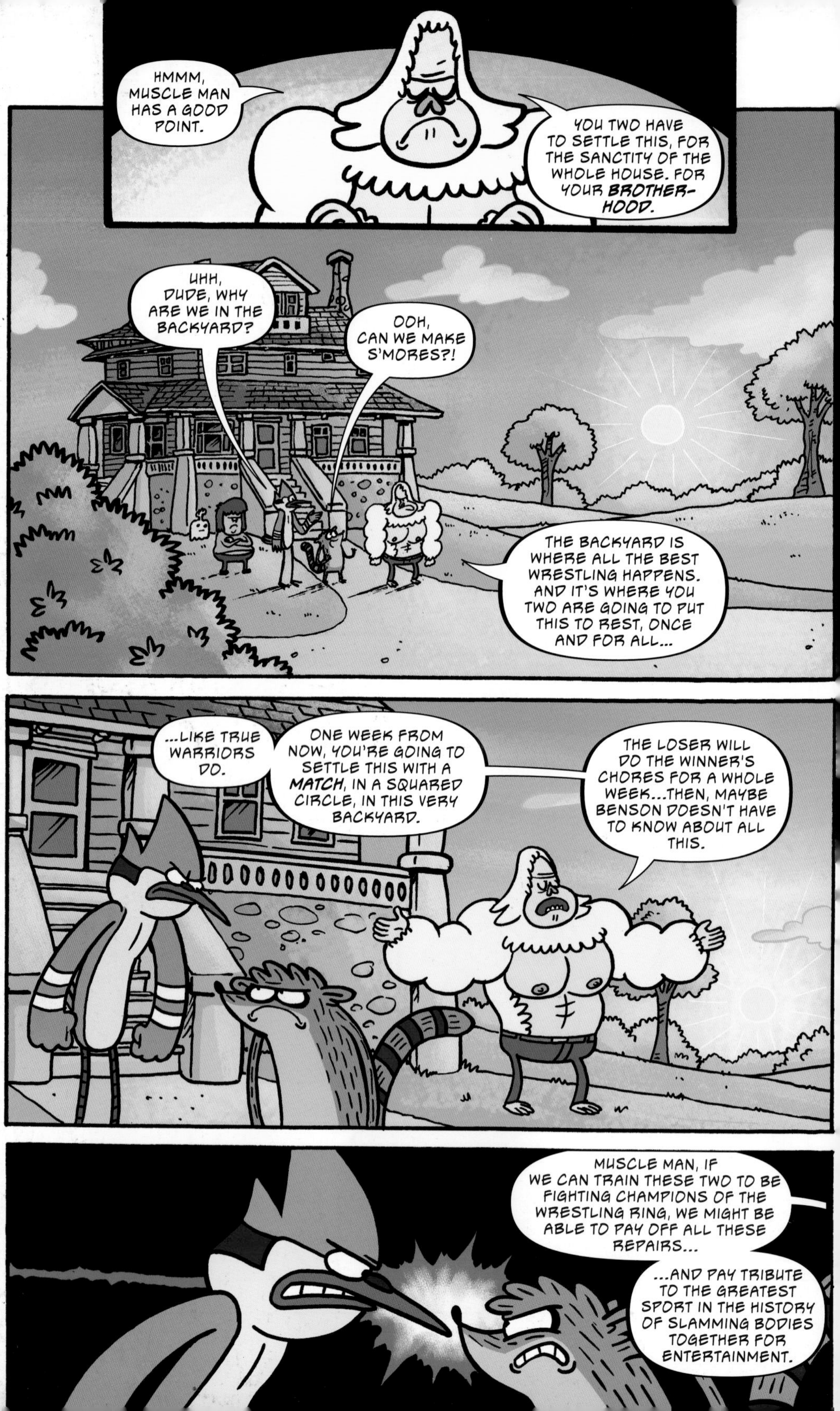

HMMM, MUSCLE MAN HAS A GOOD POINT.
YOU TWO HAVE TO SETTLE THIS, FOR THE SANCTITY OF THE WHOLE HOUSE. FOR YOUR **BROTHER-HOOD**.
UHH, DUDE, WHY ARE WE IN THE BACKYARD?
OOH, CAN WE MAKE S'MORES?!
THE BACKYARD IS WHERE ALL THE BEST WRESTLING HAPPENS. AND IT'S WHERE YOU TWO ARE GOING TO PUT THIS TO REST, ONCE AND FOR ALL...
...LIKE TRUE WARRIORS DO.
ONE WEEK FROM NOW, YOU'RE GOING TO SETTLE THIS WITH A *MATCH*, IN A SQUARED CIRCLE, IN THIS VERY BACKYARD.
THE LOSER WILL DO THE WINNER'S CHORES FOR A WHOLE WEEK...THEN, MAYBE BENSON DOESN'T HAVE TO KNOW ABOUT ALL THIS.
MUSCLE MAN, IF WE CAN TRAIN THESE TWO TO BE FIGHTING CHAMPIONS OF THE WRESTLING RING, WE MIGHT BE ABLE TO PAY OFF ALL THESE REPAIRS...
...AND PAY TRIBUTE TO THE GREATEST SPORT IN THE HISTORY OF SLAMMING BODIES TOGETHER FOR ENTERTAINMENT.

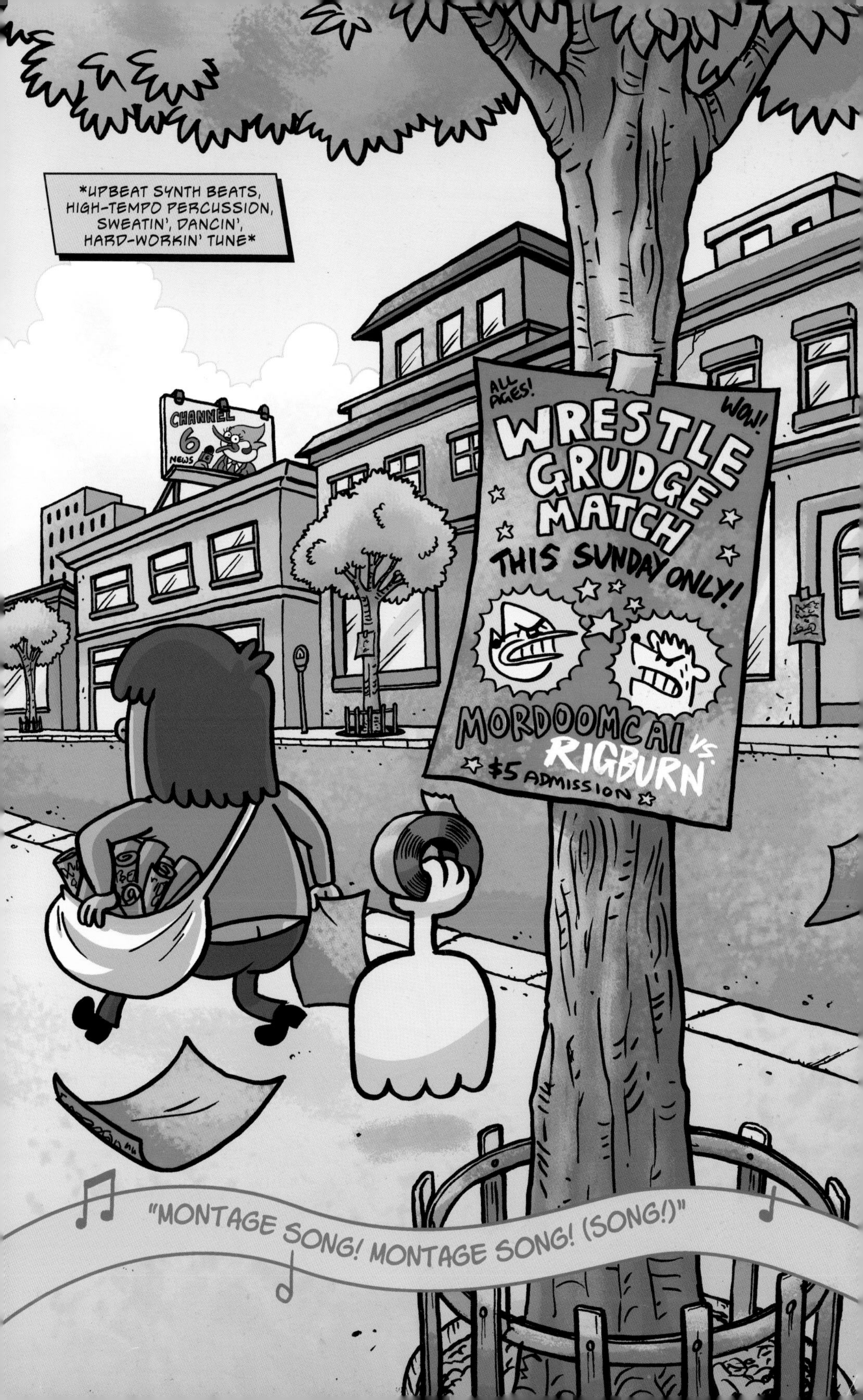
UPBEAT SYNTH BEATS, HIGH-TEMPO PERCUSSION, SWEATIN', DANCIN', HARD-WORKIN' TUNE
CHANNEL 6 NEWS
ALL AGES!
WOW!
WRESTLE GRUDGE MATCH
THIS SUNDAY ONLY!
MORDOOMCAI VS. RIGBURN
$5 ADMISSION
"MONTAGE SONG! MONTAGE SONG! (SONG!)"

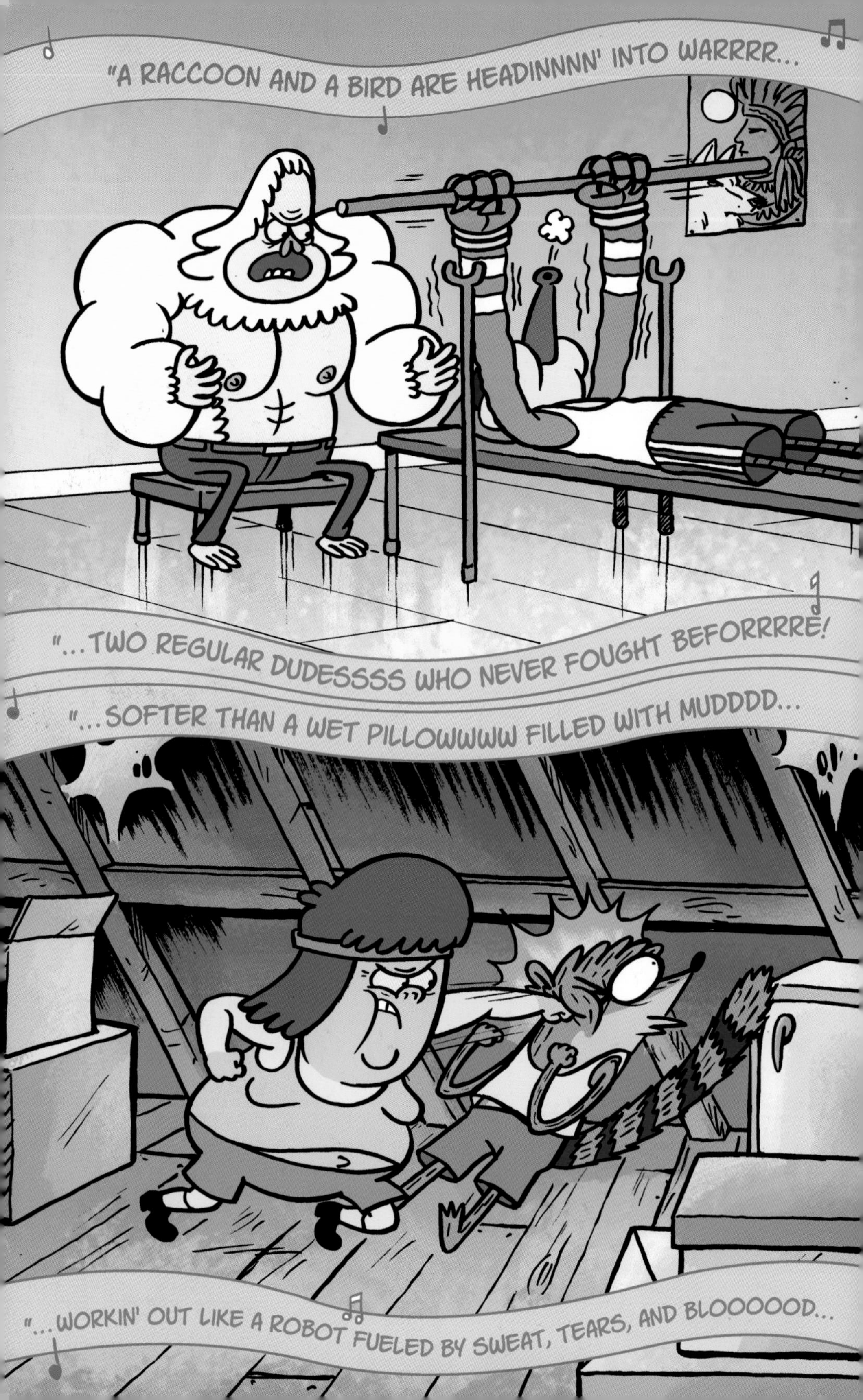
"A RACCOON AND A BIRD ARE HEADINNNN' INTO WARRRR...
"...TWO REGULAR DUDESSSS WHO NEVER FOUGHT BEFORRRRRE!
"...SOFTER THAN A WET PILLOWWWW FILLED WITH MUDDDD...
"...WORKIN' OUT LIKE A ROBOT FUELED BY SWEAT, TEARS, AND BLOOOOOD...

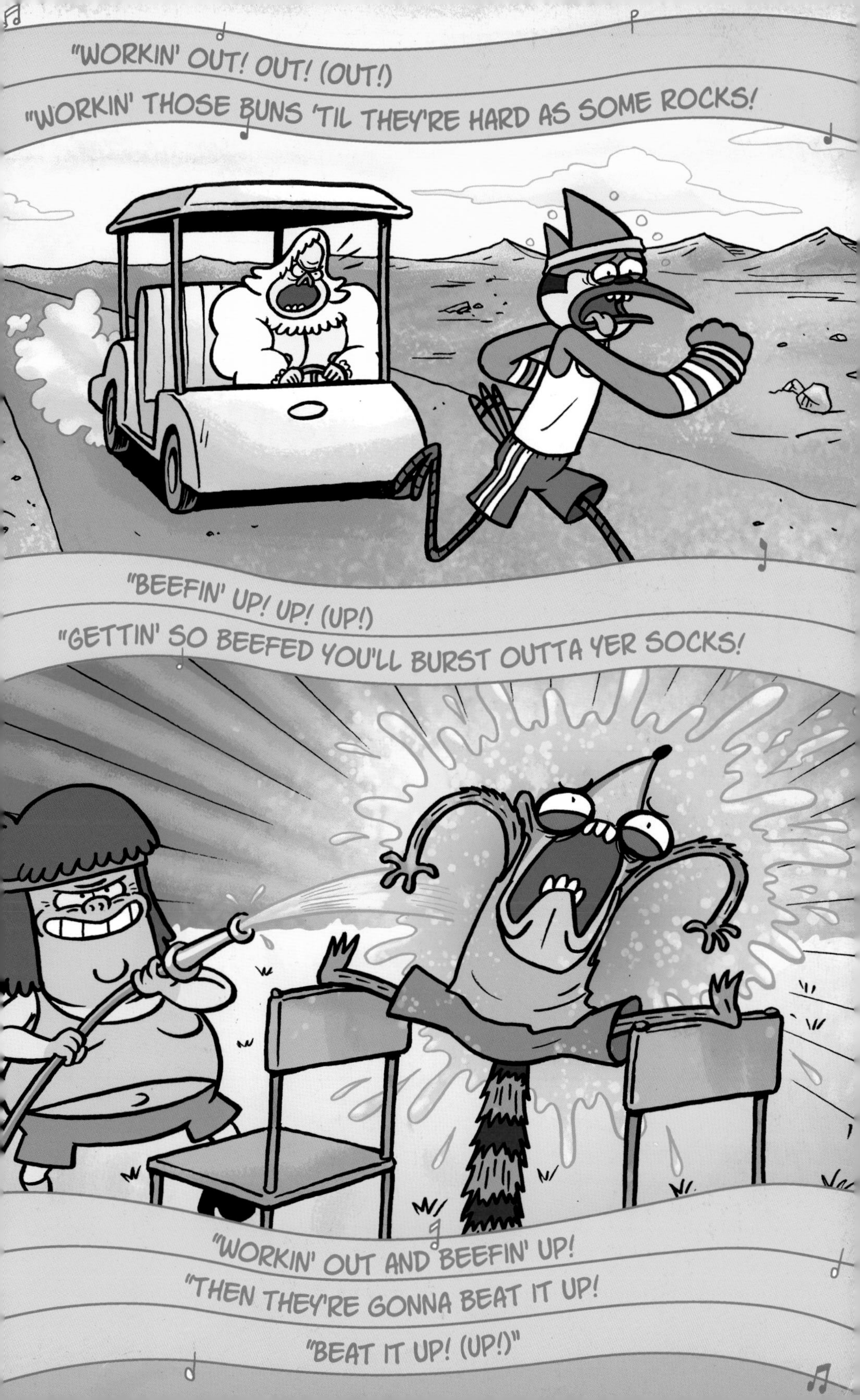
"WORKIN' OUT! OUT! (OUT!)
"WORKIN' THOSE BUNS 'TIL THEY'RE HARD AS SOME ROCKS!
"BEEFIN' UP! UP! (UP!)
"GETTIN' SO BEEFED YOU'LL BURST OUTTA YER SOCKS!
"WORKIN' OUT AND BEEFIN' UP!
"THEN THEY'RE GONNA BEAT IT UP!
"BEAT IT UP! (UP!)"

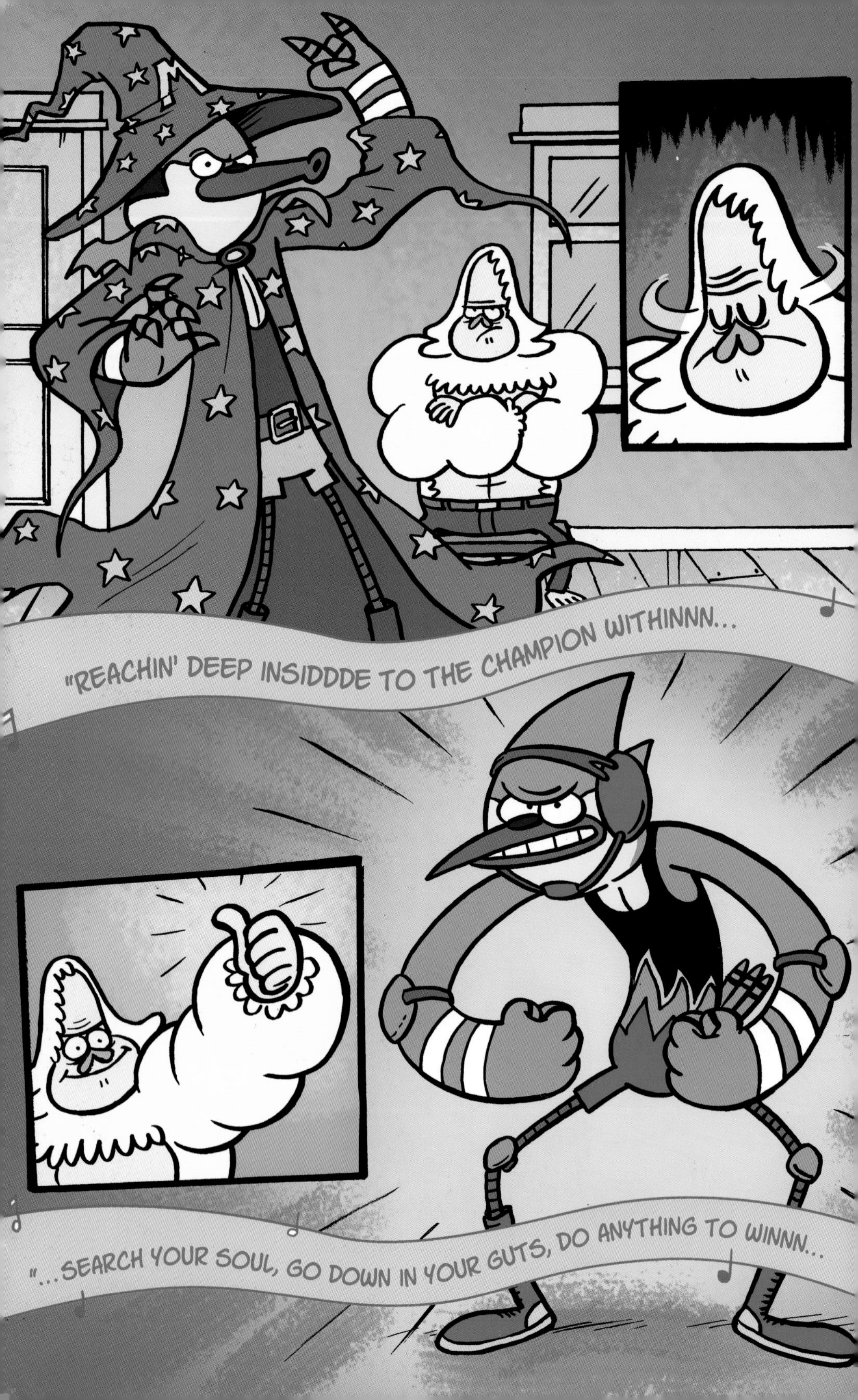
"REACHIN' DEEP INSIDDDE TO THE CHAMPION WITHINNN...
"...SEARCH YOUR SOUL, GO DOWN IN YOUR GUTS, DO ANYTHING TO WINNN...

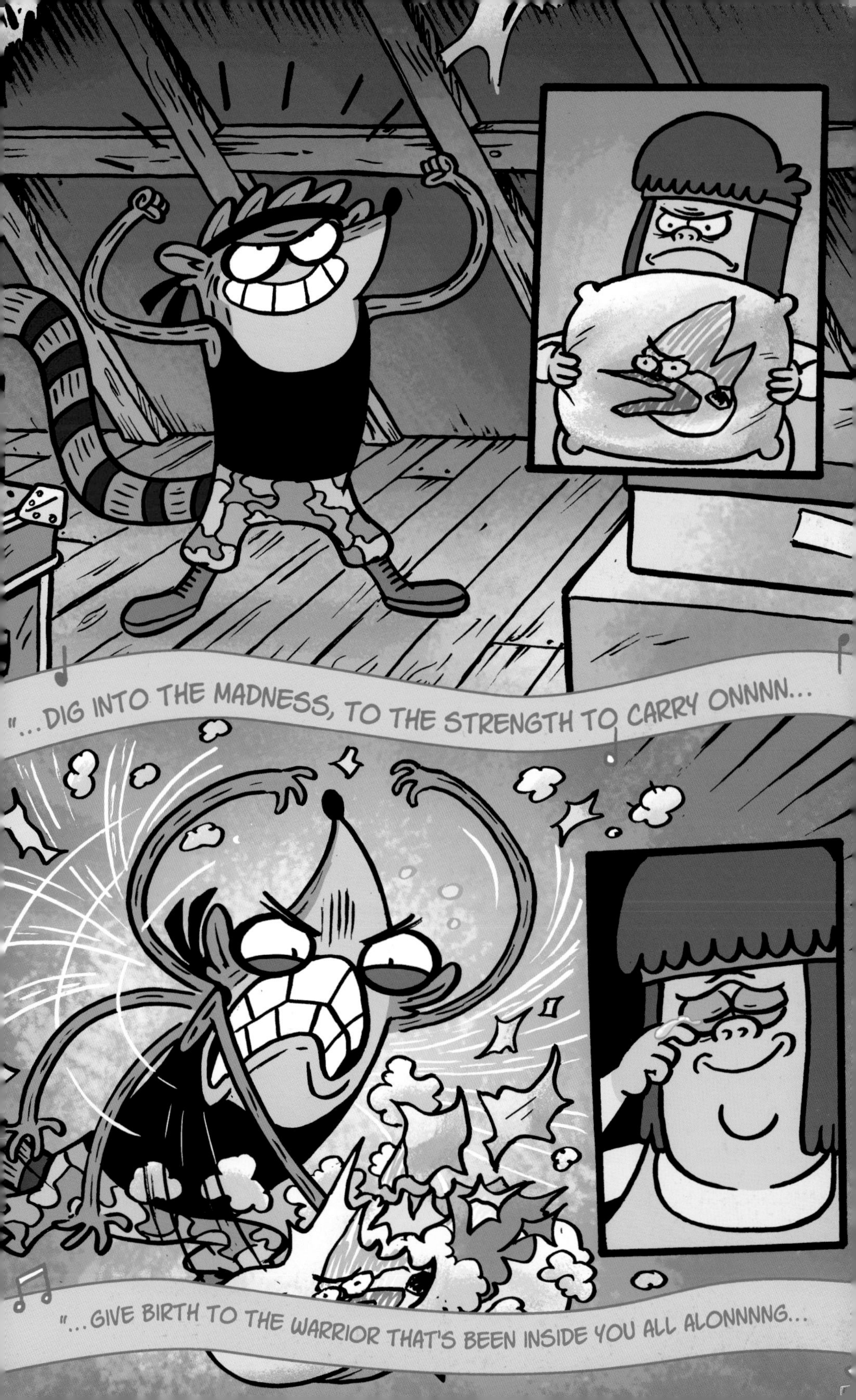
"...DIG INTO THE MADNESS, TO THE STRENGTH TO CARRY ONNNN...
"...GIVE BIRTH TO THE WARRIOR THAT'S BEEN INSIDE YOU ALL ALONNNNG...

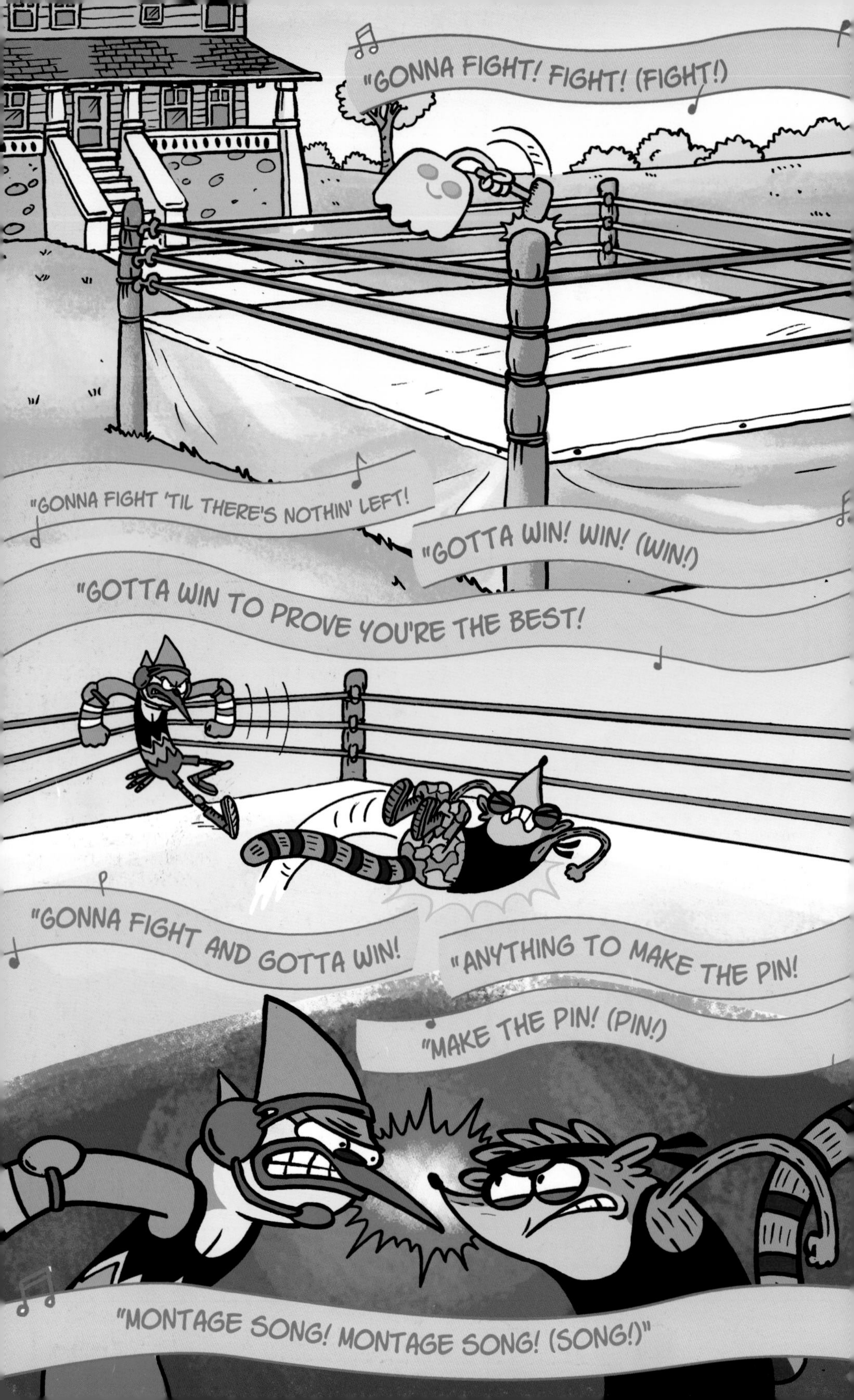
"GONNA FIGHT! FIGHT! (FIGHT!)
"GONNA FIGHT 'TIL THERE'S NOTHIN' LEFT!
"GOTTA WIN! WIN! (WIN!)
"GOTTA WIN TO PROVE YOU'RE THE BEST!
"GONNA FIGHT AND GOTTA WIN!
"ANYTHING TO MAKE THE PIN!
"MAKE THE PIN! (PIN!)
"MONTAGE SONG! MONTAGE SONG! (SONG!)"

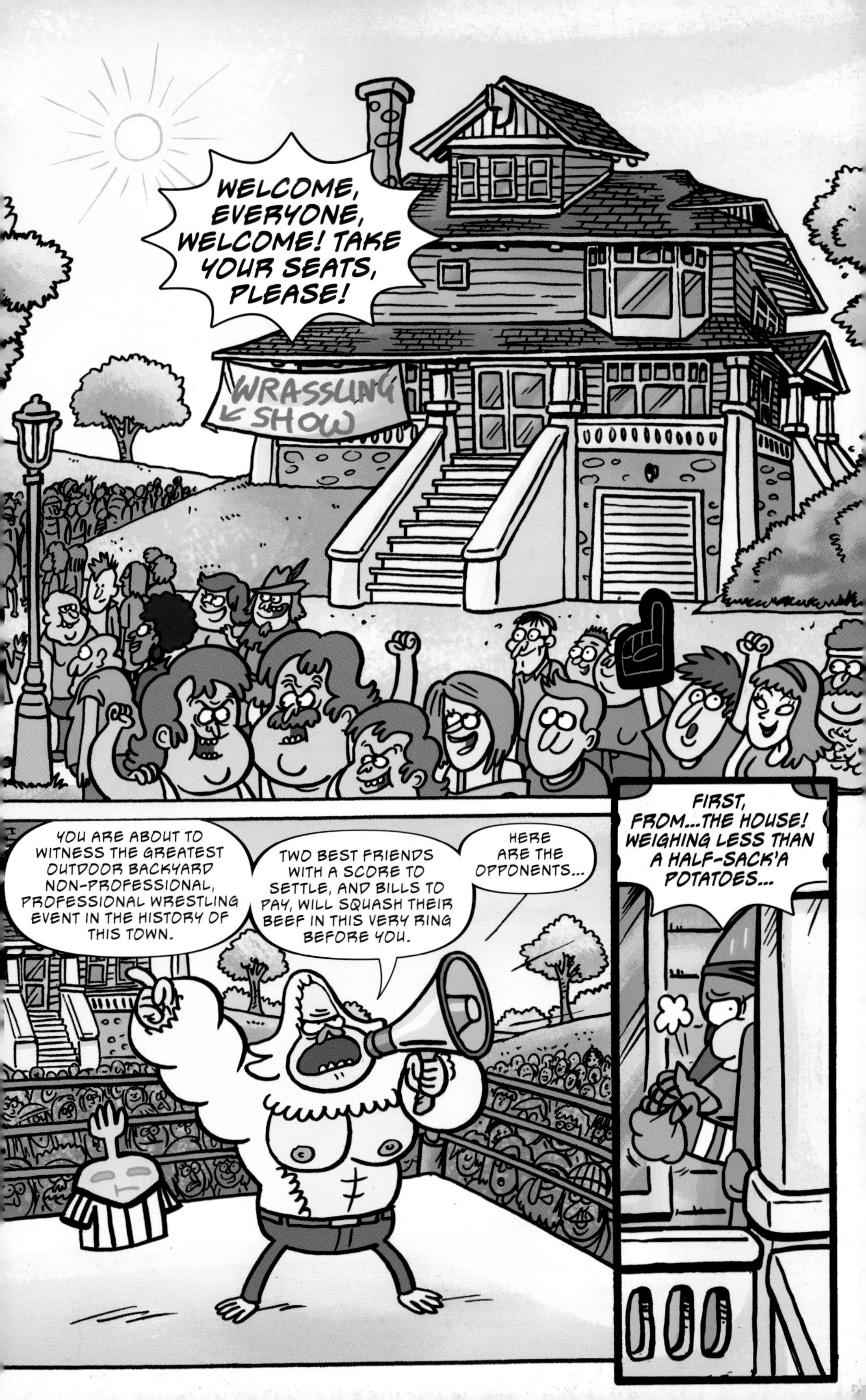
WELCOME, EVERYONE, WELCOME! TAKE YOUR SEATS, PLEASE!
WRASSLING SHOW
YOU ARE ABOUT TO WITNESS THE GREATEST OUTDOOR BACKYARD NON-PROFESSIONAL, PROFESSIONAL WRESTLING EVENT IN THE HISTORY OF THIS TOWN.
TWO BEST FRIENDS WITH A SCORE TO SETTLE, AND BILLS TO PAY, WILL SQUASH THEIR BEEF IN THIS VERY RING BEFORE YOU.
HERE ARE THE OPPONENTS...
FIRST, FROM...THE HOUSE! WEIGHING LESS THAN A HALF-SACK'A POTATOES...

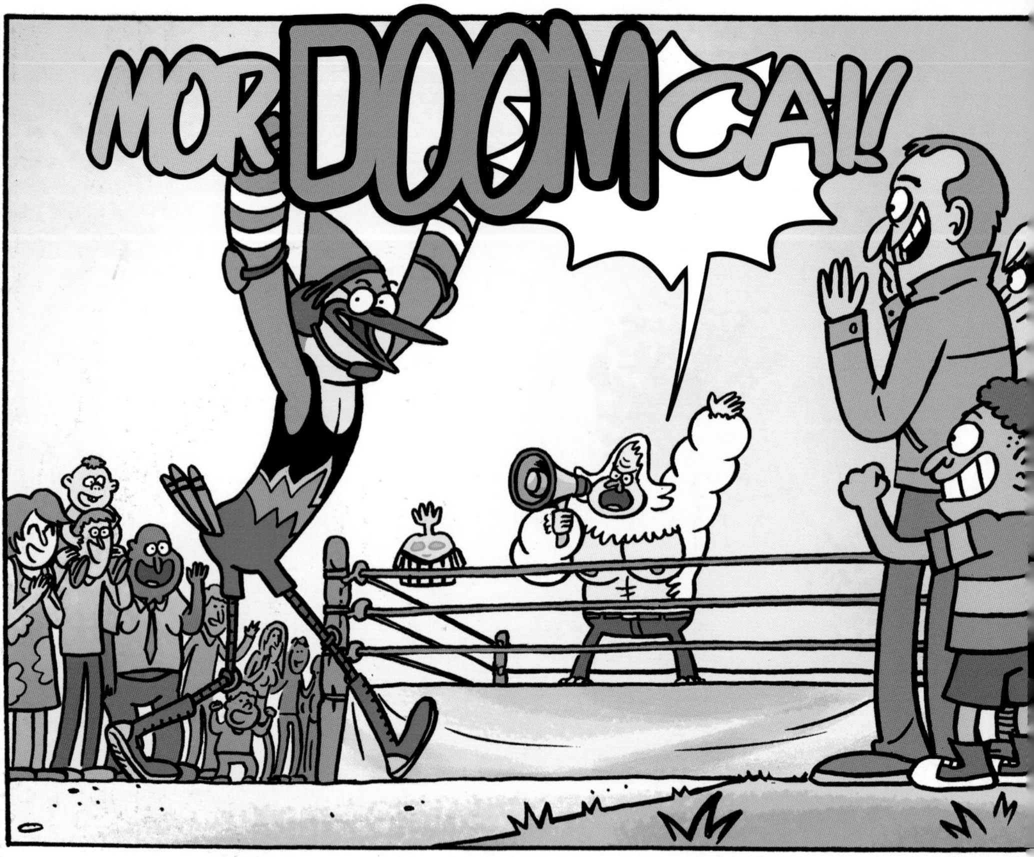
MORDOOMCAI!

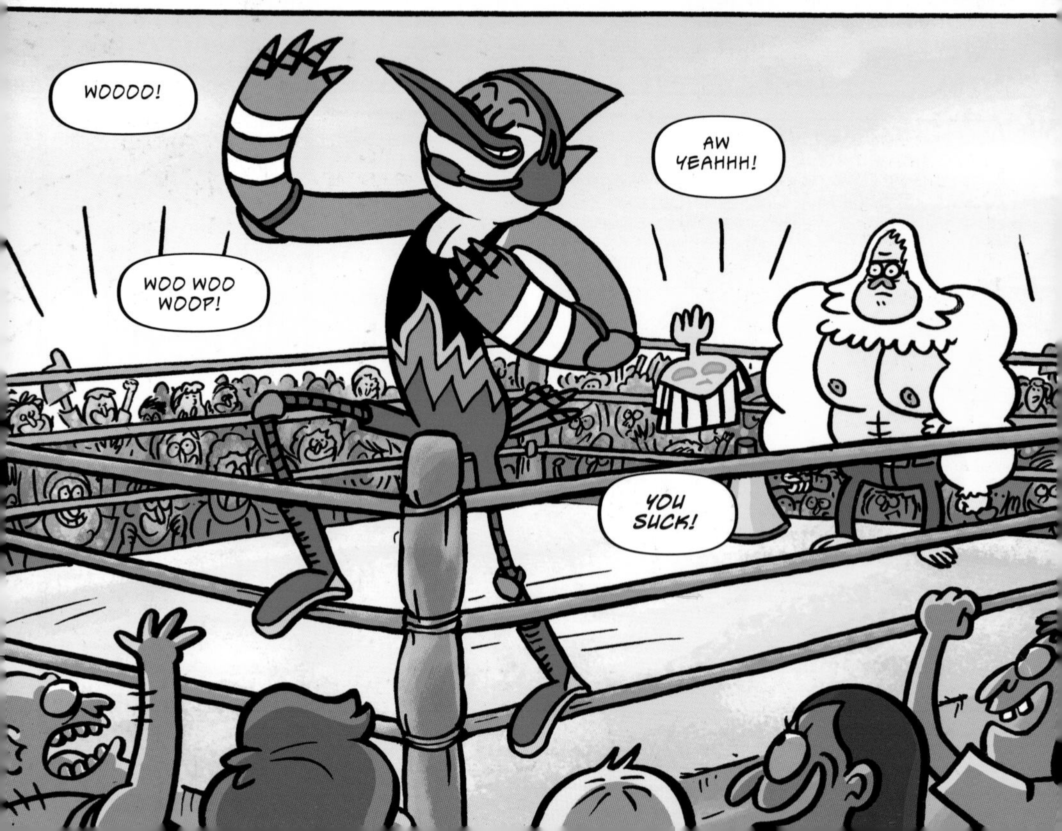
WOOOO!
AW YEAHHH!
WOO WOO WOOP!
YOU SUCK!

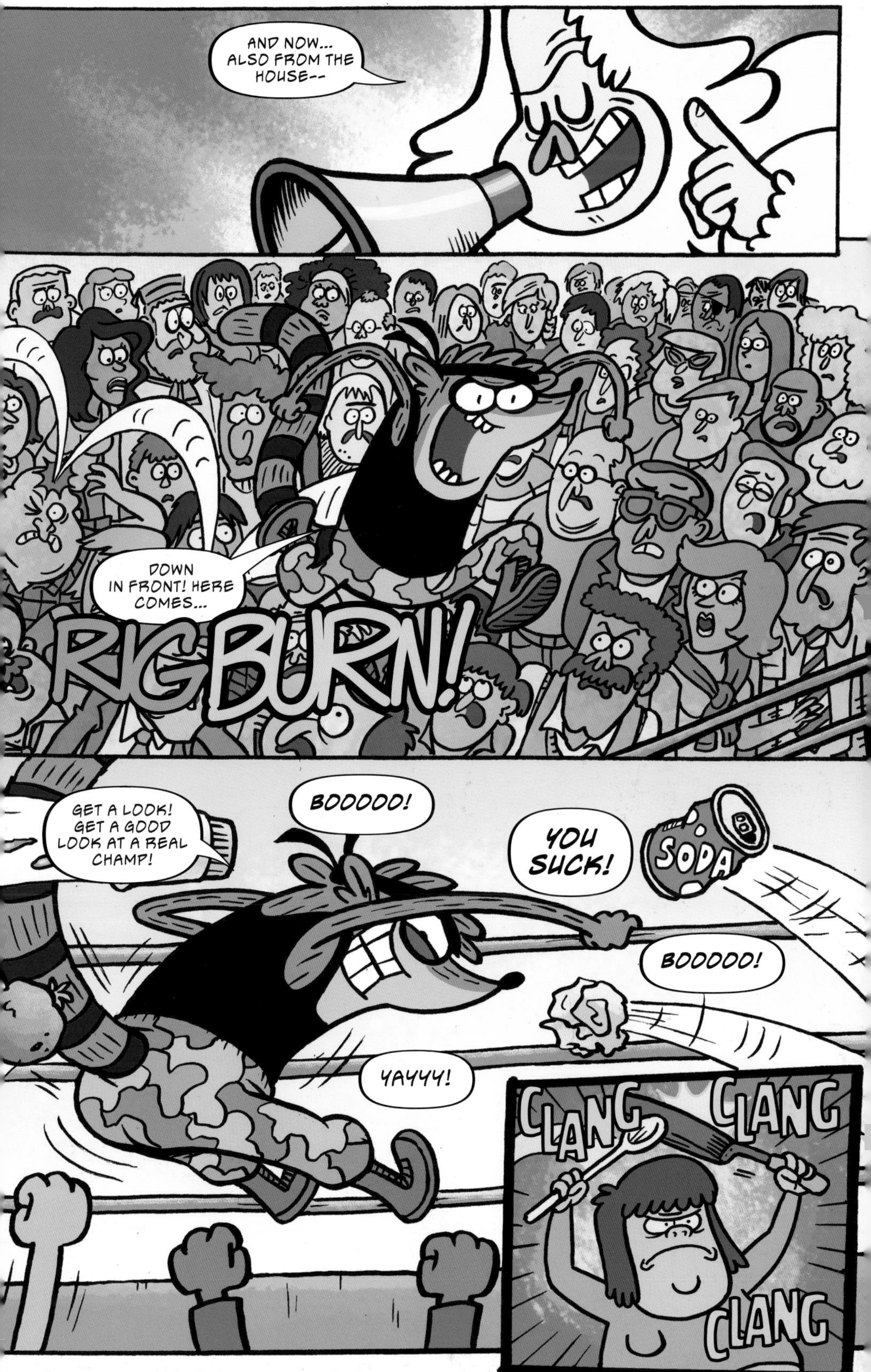
AND NOW... ALSO FROM THE HOUSE--
DOWN IN FRONT! HERE COMES...
RIGBURN!
GET A LOOK! GET A GOOD LOOK AT A REAL CHAMP!
BOOOOO!
YOU SUCK!
SODA
BOOOOO!
YAYYY!
CLANG
CLANG
CLANG

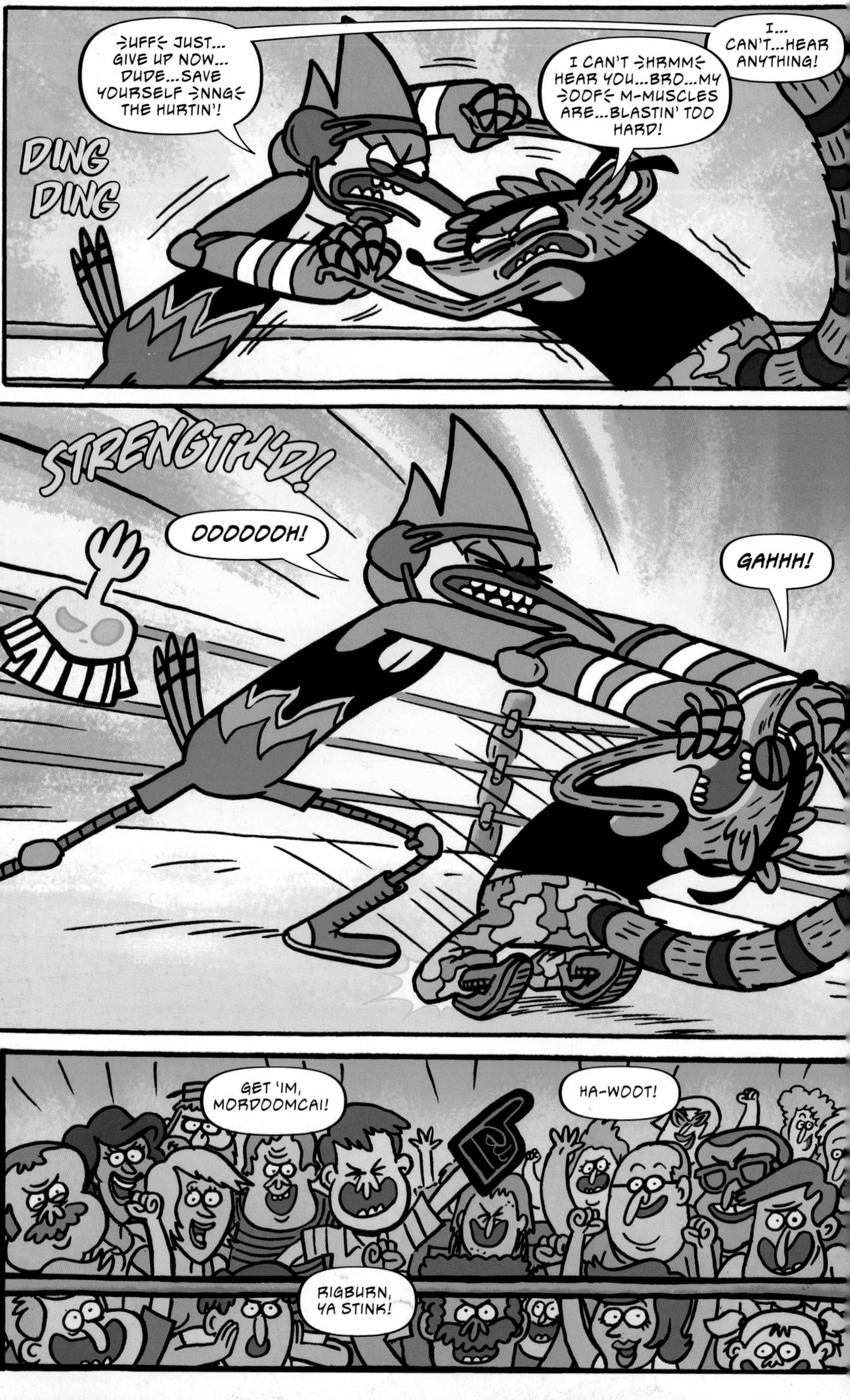

>UFF< JUST... GIVE UP NOW... DUDE...SAVE YOURSELF >NNG< THE HURTIN'!
I CAN'T >HRMM< HEAR YOU...BRO...MY >OOF< M-MUSCLES ARE...BLASTIN' TOO HARD!
I... CAN'T...HEAR ANYTHING!
DING DING
STRENGTH'D!
OOOOOOH!
GAHHH!
GET 'IM, MORDOOMCAI!
HA-WOOT!
RIGBURN, YA STINK!

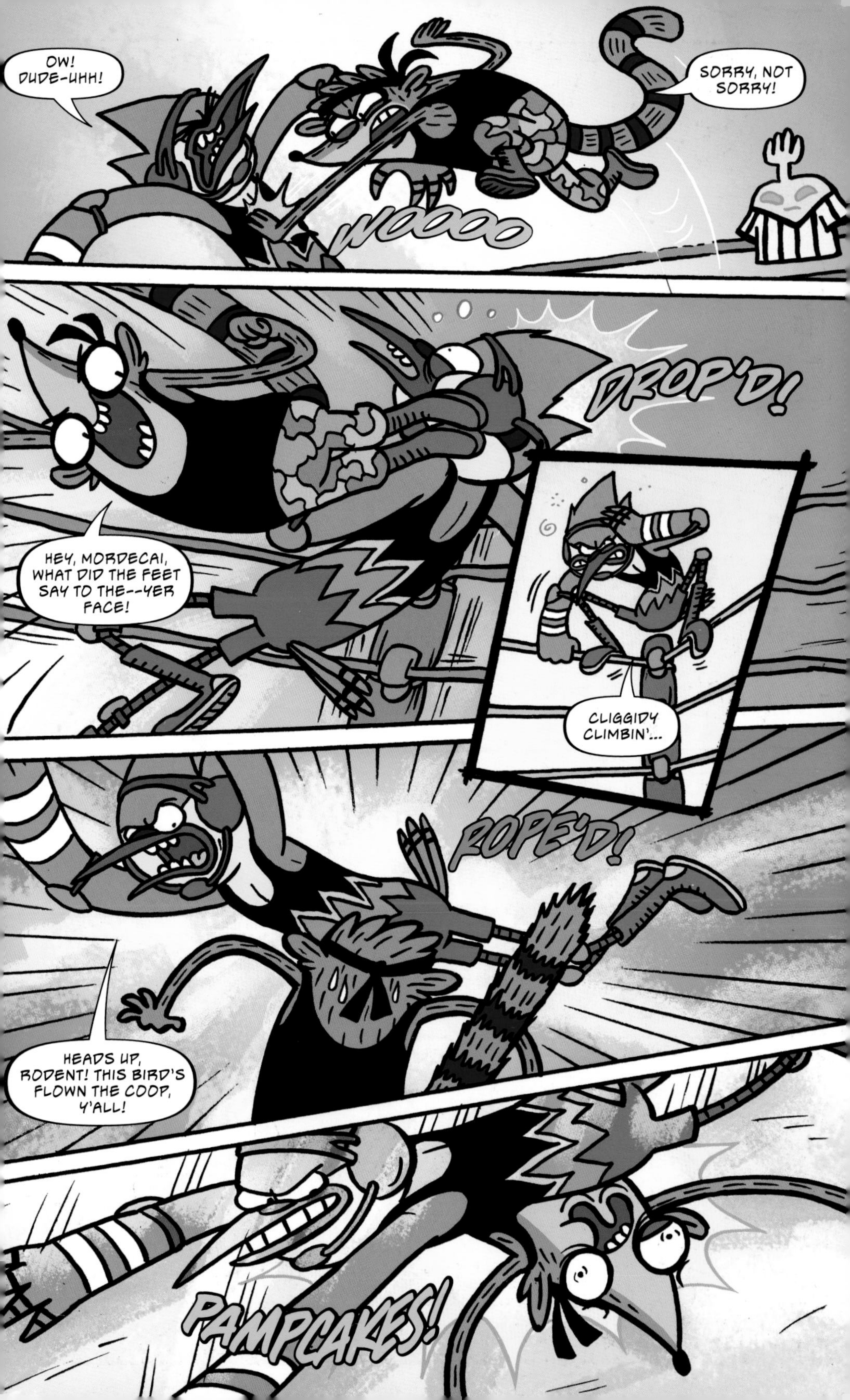
OW! DUDE-UHH!
SORRY, NOT SORRY!
WOOOO
DROP'D!
HEY, MORDECAI, WHAT DID THE FEET SAY TO THE--YER FACE!
CLIGGIDY CLIMBIN'...
ROPE'D!
HEADS UP, RODENT! THIS BIRD'S FLOWN THE COOP, Y'ALL!
PAMPCAKES!

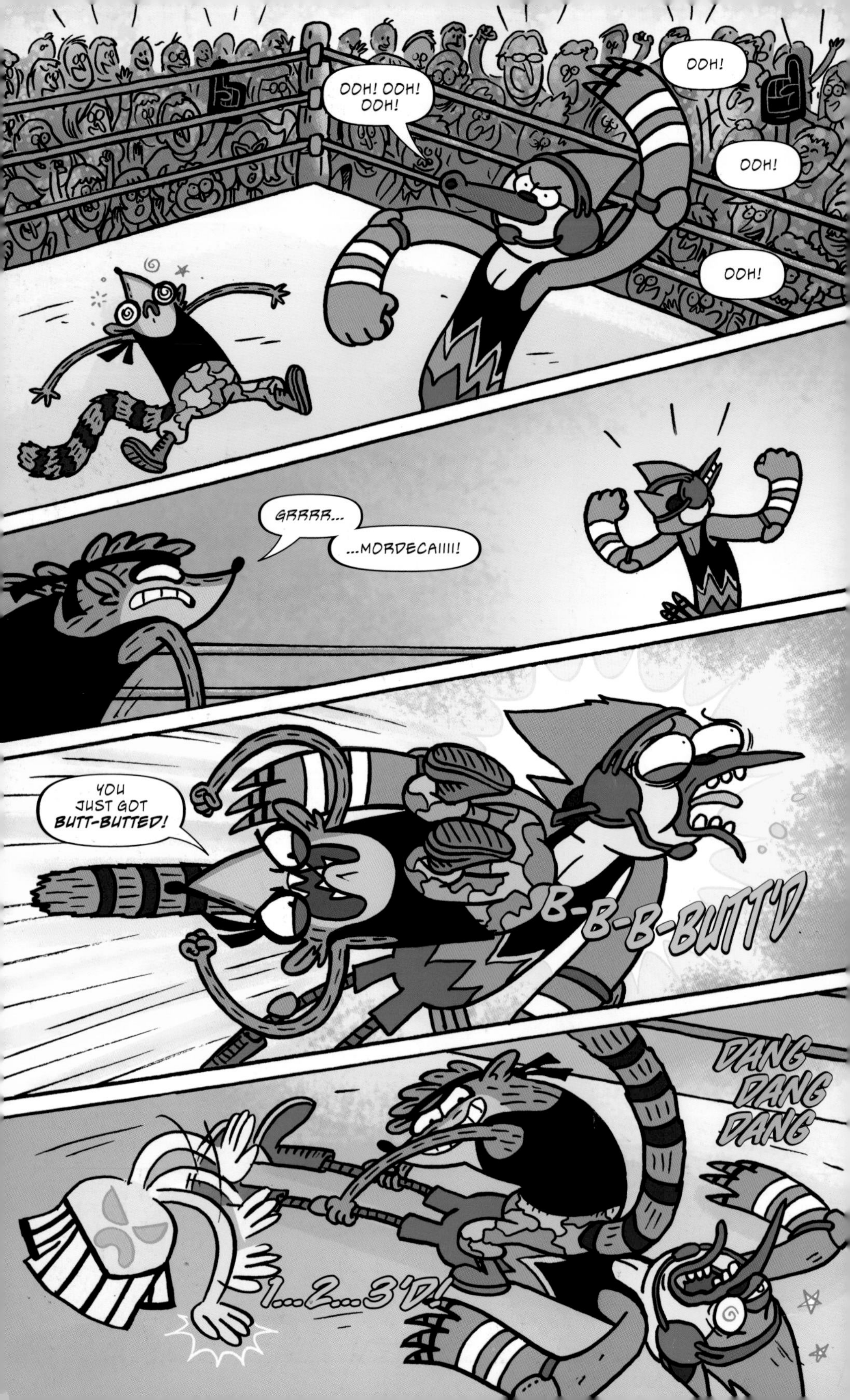
OOH! OOH! OOH!
OOH!
OOH!
OOH!
GRRRR...
...MORDECAIIII!
YOU JUST GOT BUTT-BUTTED!
B-B-B-BUTT'D
DANG DANG DANG
1...2...3'D!

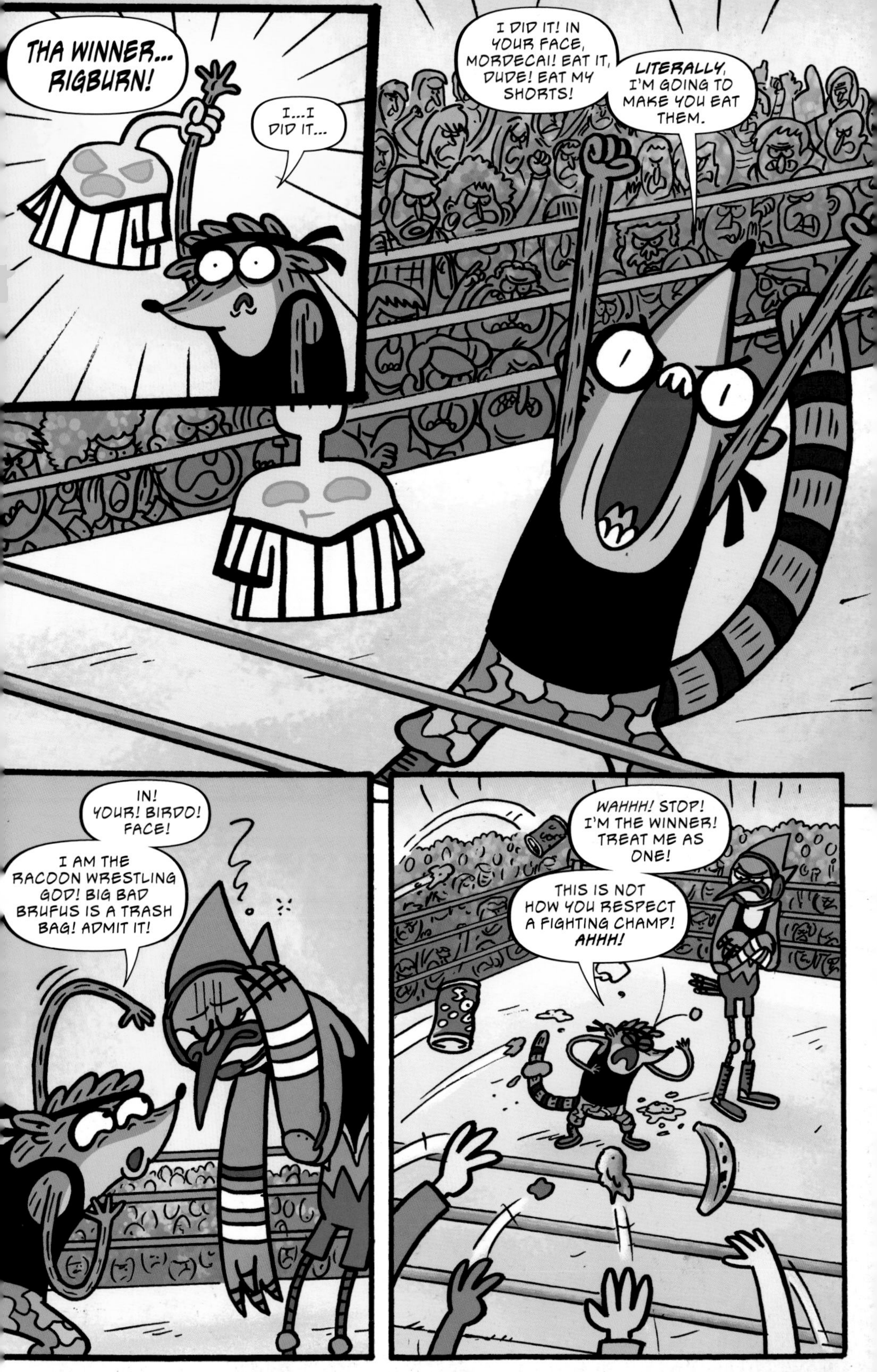
THA WINNER... RIGBURN!
I...I DID IT...
I DID IT! IN YOUR FACE, MORDECAI! EAT IT, DUDE! EAT MY SHORTS!
LITERALLY, I'M GOING TO MAKE YOU EAT THEM.
IN! YOUR! BIRDO! FACE!
I AM THE RACOON WRESTLING GOD! BIG BAD BRUFUS IS A TRASH BAG! ADMIT IT!
WAHHH! STOP! I'M THE WINNER! TREAT ME AS ONE!
THIS IS NOT HOW YOU RESPECT A FIGHTING CHAMP! AHHH!

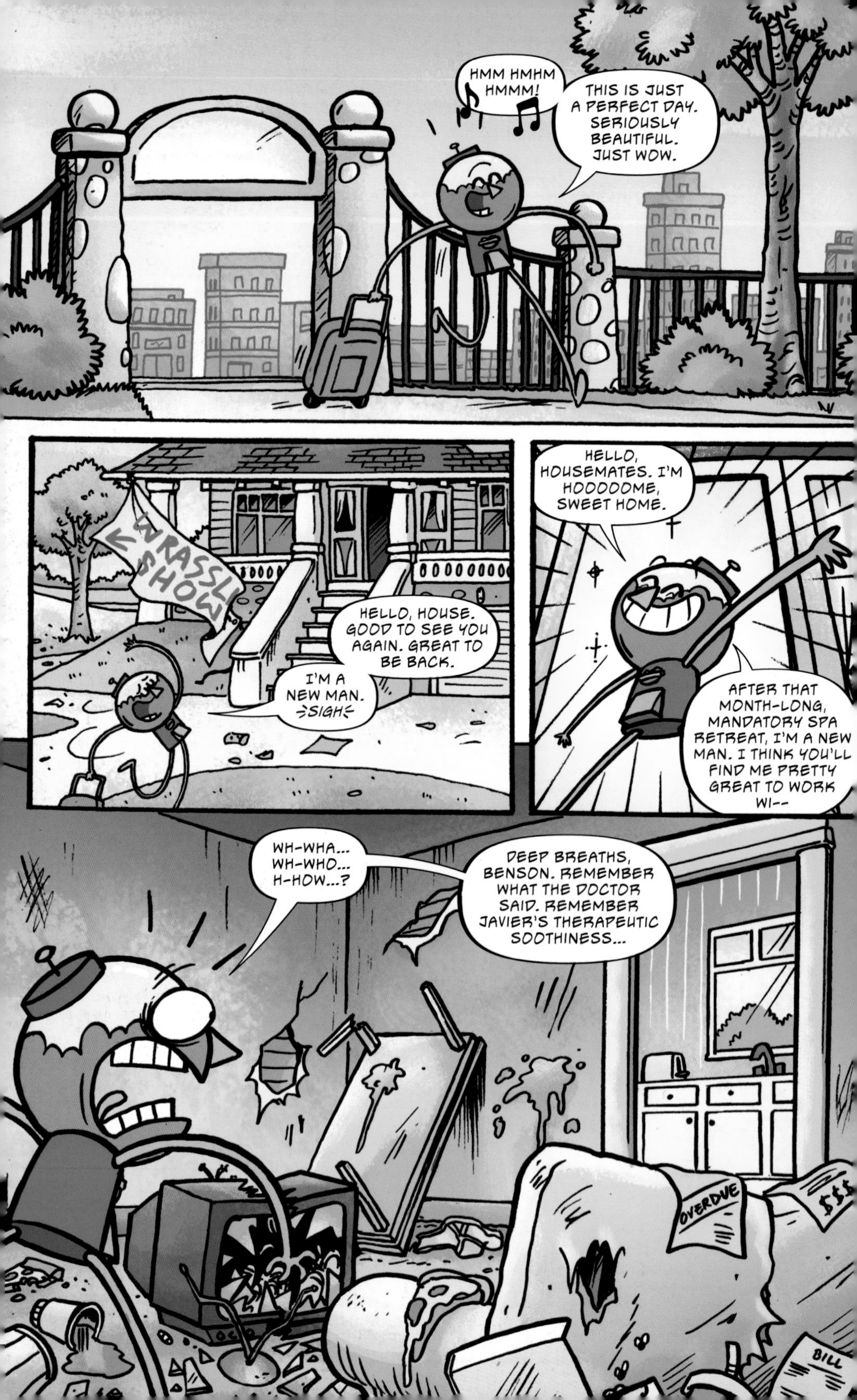
HMM HMHM HMMM!
THIS IS JUST A PERFECT DAY. SERIOUSLY BEAUTIFUL. JUST WOW.
WRASSLIN SHOW
HELLO, HOUSE. GOOD TO SEE YOU AGAIN. GREAT TO BE BACK.
I'M A NEW MAN. SIGH
HELLO, HOUSEMATES. I'M HOOOOOME, SWEET HOME.
AFTER THAT MONTH-LONG, MANDATORY SPA RETREAT, I'M A NEW MAN. I THINK YOU'LL FIND ME PRETTY GREAT TO WORK WI--
WH-WHA... WH-WHO... H-HOW...?
DEEP BREATHS, BENSON. REMEMBER WHAT THE DOCTOR SAID. REMEMBER JAVIER'S THERAPEUTIC SOOTHINESS...
OVERDUE
BILL

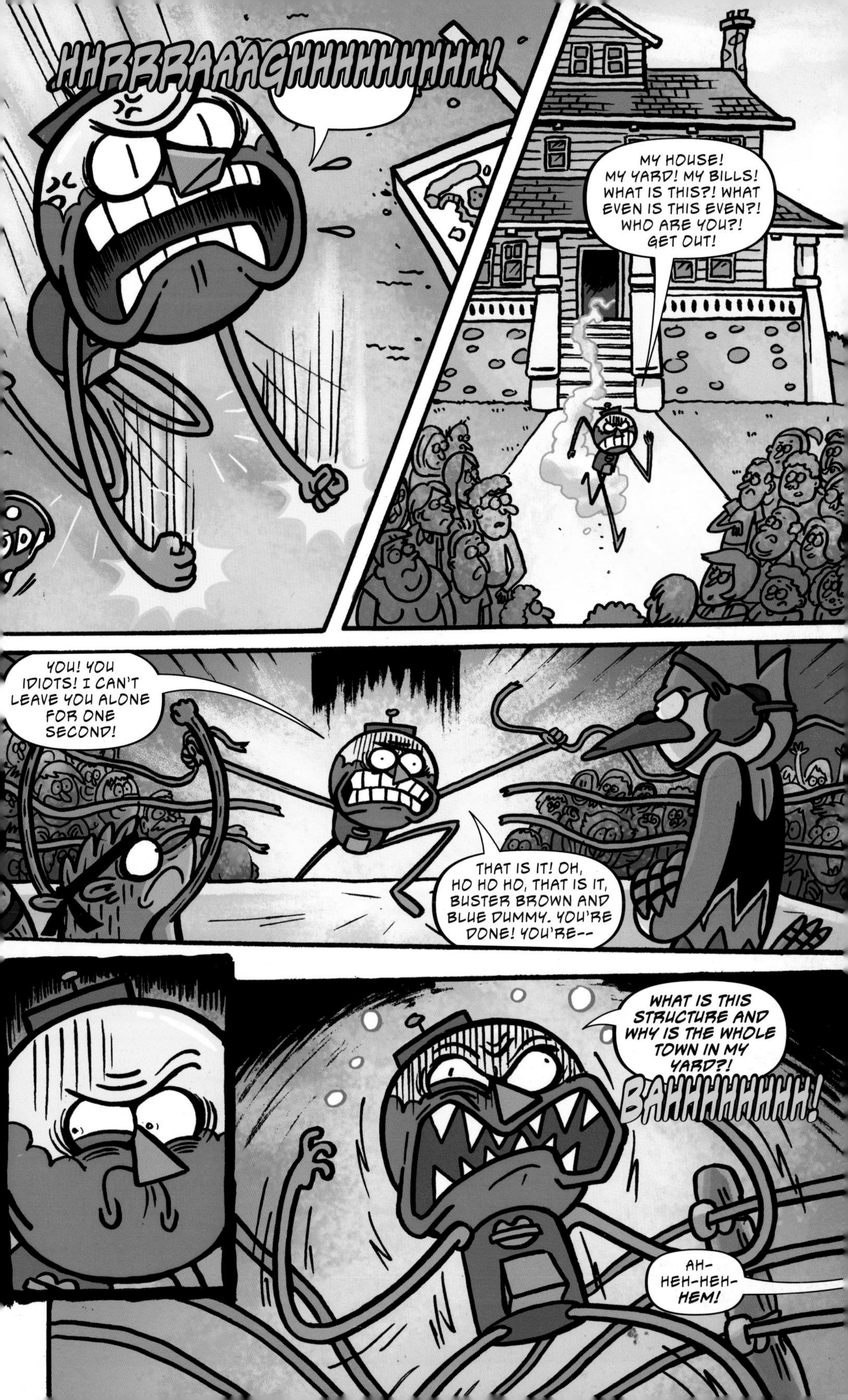
HHRRRAAAGHHHHHHHHH!
MY HOUSE! MY YARD! MY BILLS! WHAT IS THIS?! WHAT EVEN IS THIS EVEN?! WHO ARE YOU?! GET OUT!
YOU! YOU IDIOTS! I CAN'T LEAVE YOU ALONE FOR ONE SECOND!
THAT IS IT! OH, HO HO HO, THAT IS IT, BUSTER BROWN AND BLUE DUMMY. YOU'RE DONE! YOU'RE--
WHAT IS THIS STRUCTURE AND WHY IS THE WHOLE TOWN IN MY YARD?!
BAHHHHHHHH!
AH-HEH-HEH-HEM!

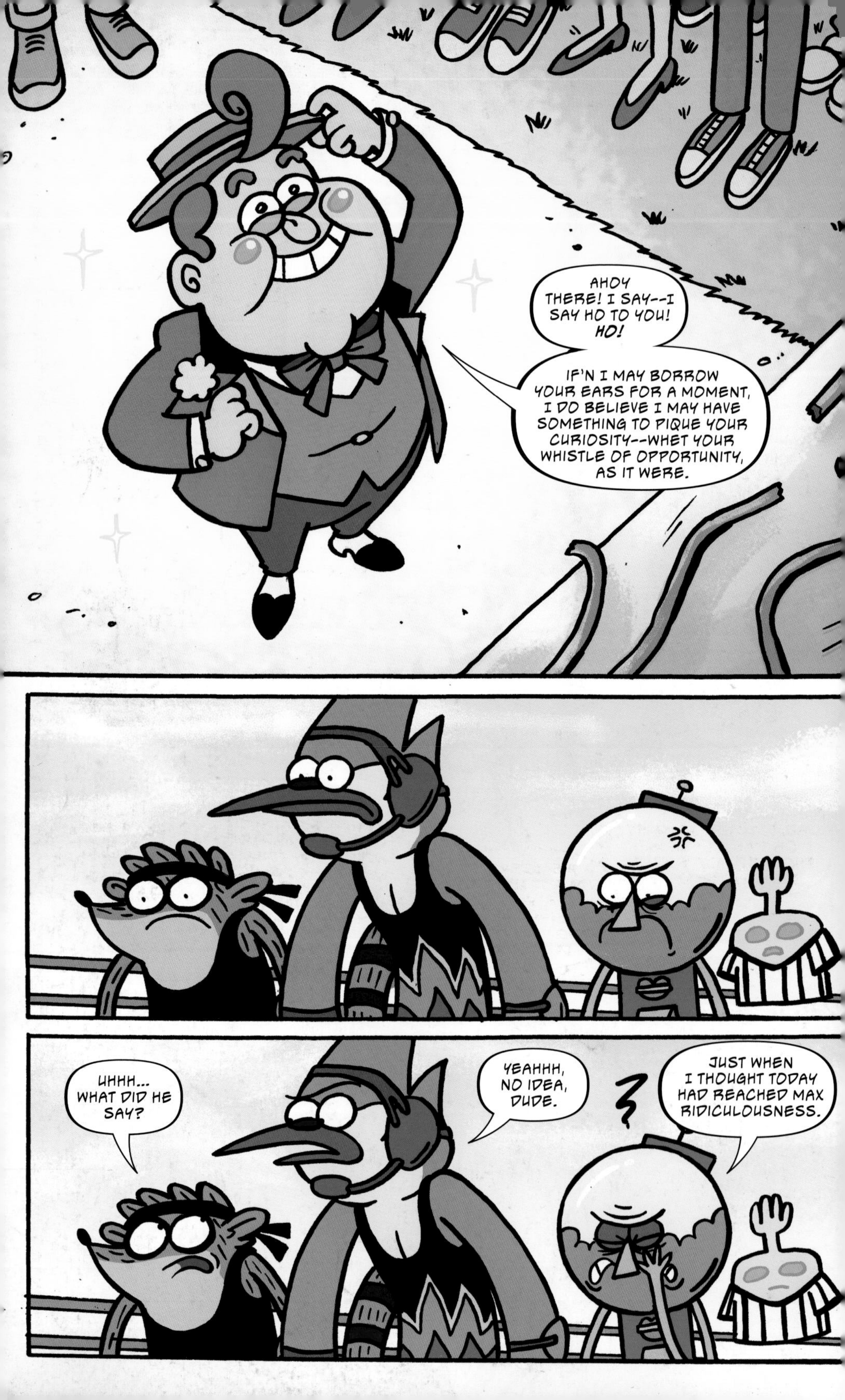
AHOY THERE! I SAY--I SAY HO TO YOU! HO!
IF'N I MAY BORROW YOUR EARS FOR A MOMENT, I DO BELIEVE I MAY HAVE SOMETHING TO PIQUE YOUR CURIOSITY--WHET YOUR WHISTLE OF OPPORTUNITY, AS IT WERE.
UHHH... WHAT DID HE SAY?
YEAHHH, NO IDEA, DUDE.
JUST WHEN I THOUGHT TODAY HAD REACHED MAX RIDICULOUSNESS.

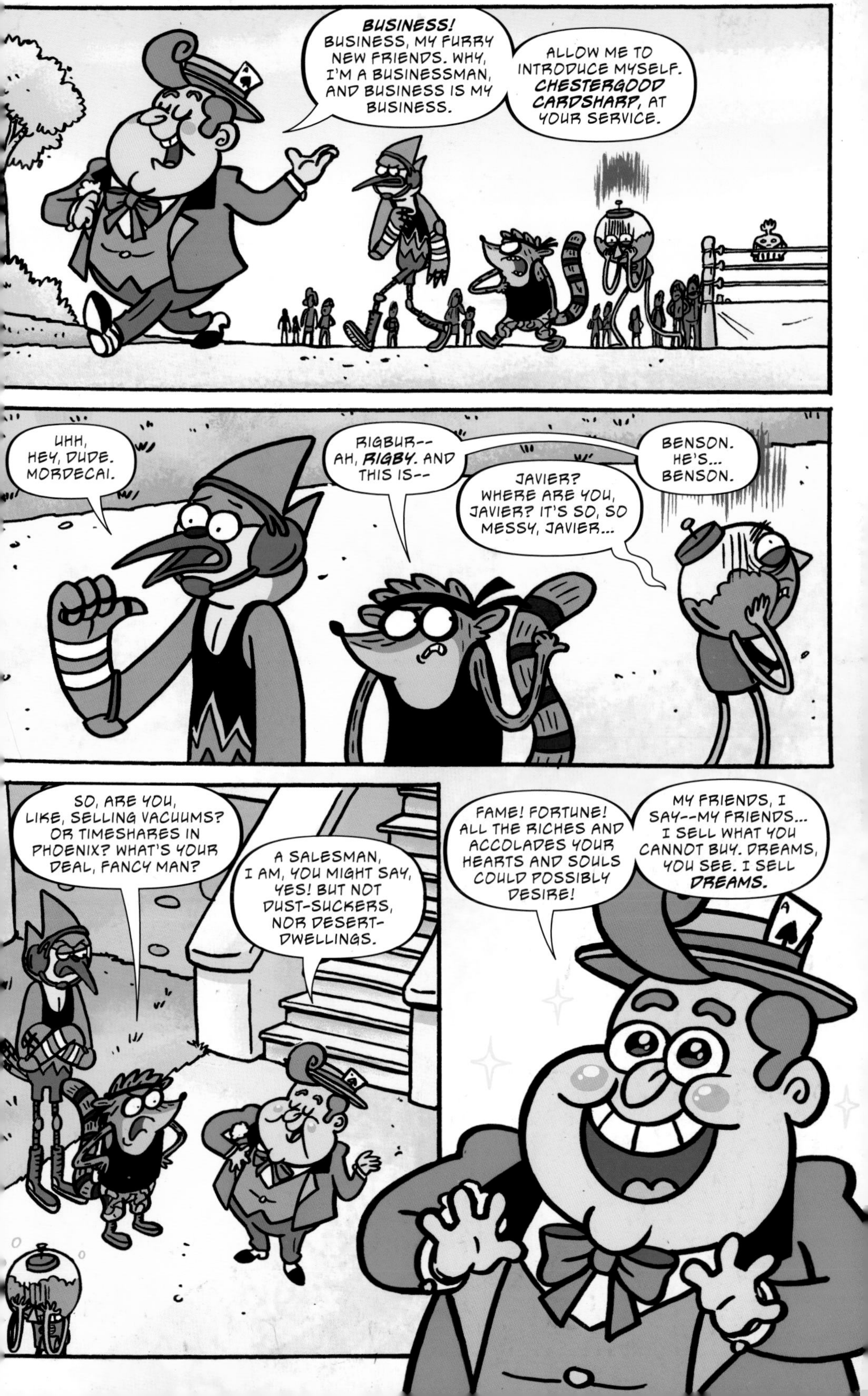

BUSINESS! BUSINESS, MY FURRY NEW FRIENDS. WHY, I'M A BUSINESSMAN, AND BUSINESS IS MY BUSINESS.
ALLOW ME TO INTRODUCE MYSELF. CHESTERGOOD CARDSHARP, AT YOUR SERVICE.
UHH, HEY, DUDE. MORDECAI.
RIGBUR-- AH, RIGBY. AND THIS IS--
BENSON. HE'S... BENSON.
JAVIER? WHERE ARE YOU, JAVIER? IT'S SO, SO MESSY, JAVIER...
SO, ARE YOU, LIKE, SELLING VACUUMS? OR TIMESHARES IN PHOENIX? WHAT'S YOUR DEAL, FANCY MAN?
A SALESMAN, I AM, YOU MIGHT SAY, YES! BUT NOT DUST-SUCKERS, NOR DESERT-DWELLINGS.
FAME! FORTUNE! ALL THE RICHES AND ACCOLADES YOUR HEARTS AND SOULS COULD POSSIBLY DESIRE!
MY FRIENDS, I SAY--MY FRIENDS... I SELL WHAT YOU CANNOT BUY. DREAMS, YOU SEE. I SELL DREAMS.

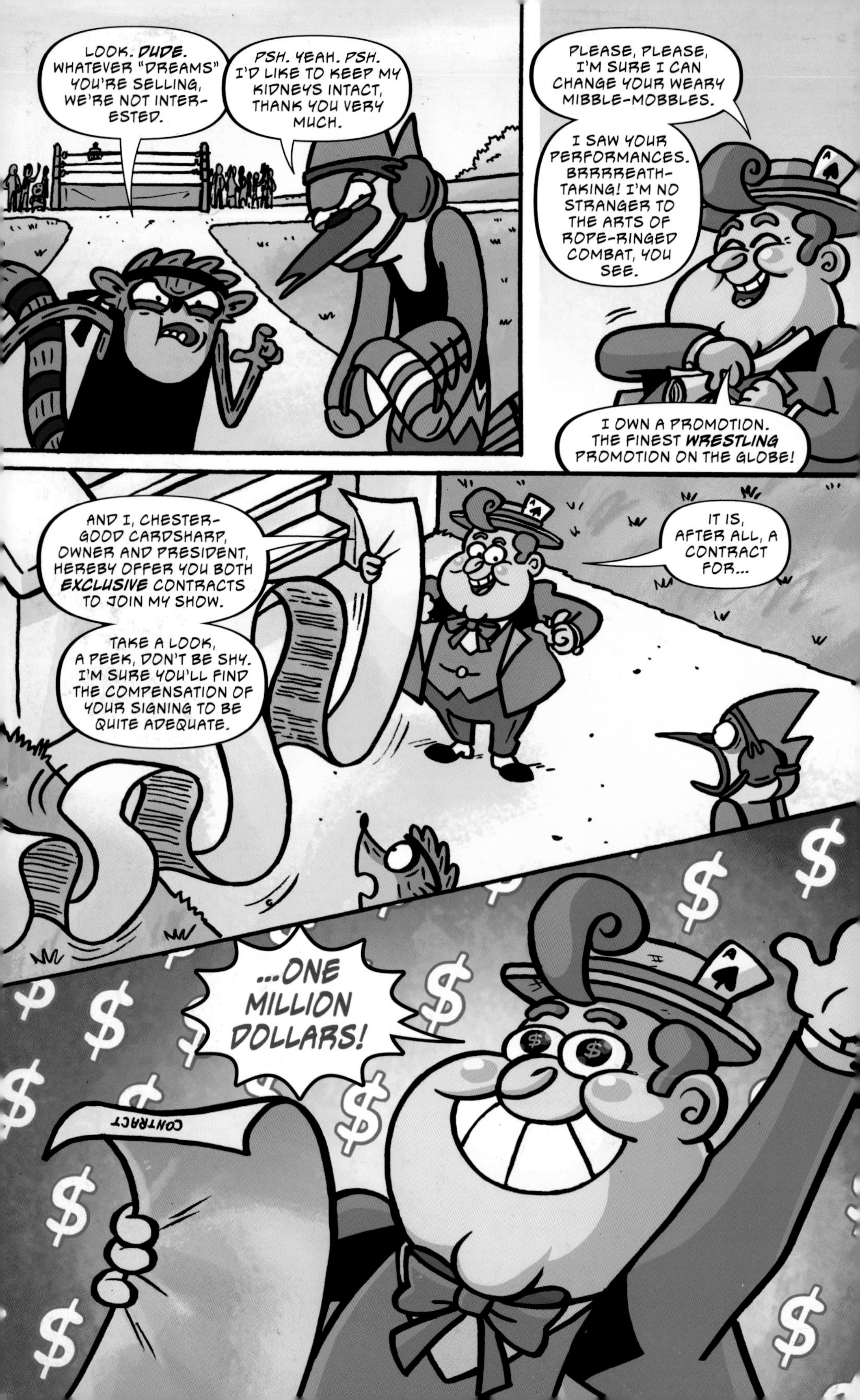
LOOK. DUDE. WHATEVER "DREAMS" YOU'RE SELLING, WE'RE NOT INTER-ESTED.
PSH. YEAH. PSH. I'D LIKE TO KEEP MY KIDNEYS INTACT, THANK YOU VERY MUCH.
PLEASE, PLEASE, I'M SURE I CAN CHANGE YOUR WEARY MIBBLE-MOBBLES.
I SAW YOUR PERFORMANCES. BRRRREATH-TAKING! I'M NO STRANGER TO THE ARTS OF ROPE-RINGED COMBAT, YOU SEE.
I OWN A PROMOTION. THE FINEST WRESTLING PROMOTION ON THE GLOBE!
AND I, CHESTER-GOOD CARDSHARP, OWNER AND PRESIDENT, HEREBY OFFER YOU BOTH EXCLUSIVE CONTRACTS TO JOIN MY SHOW.
TAKE A LOOK, A PEEK, DON'T BE SHY. I'M SURE YOU'LL FIND THE COMPENSATION OF YOUR SIGNING TO BE QUITE ADEQUATE.
IT IS, AFTER ALL, A CONTRACT FOR...
...ONE MILLION DOLLARS!
CONTRACT

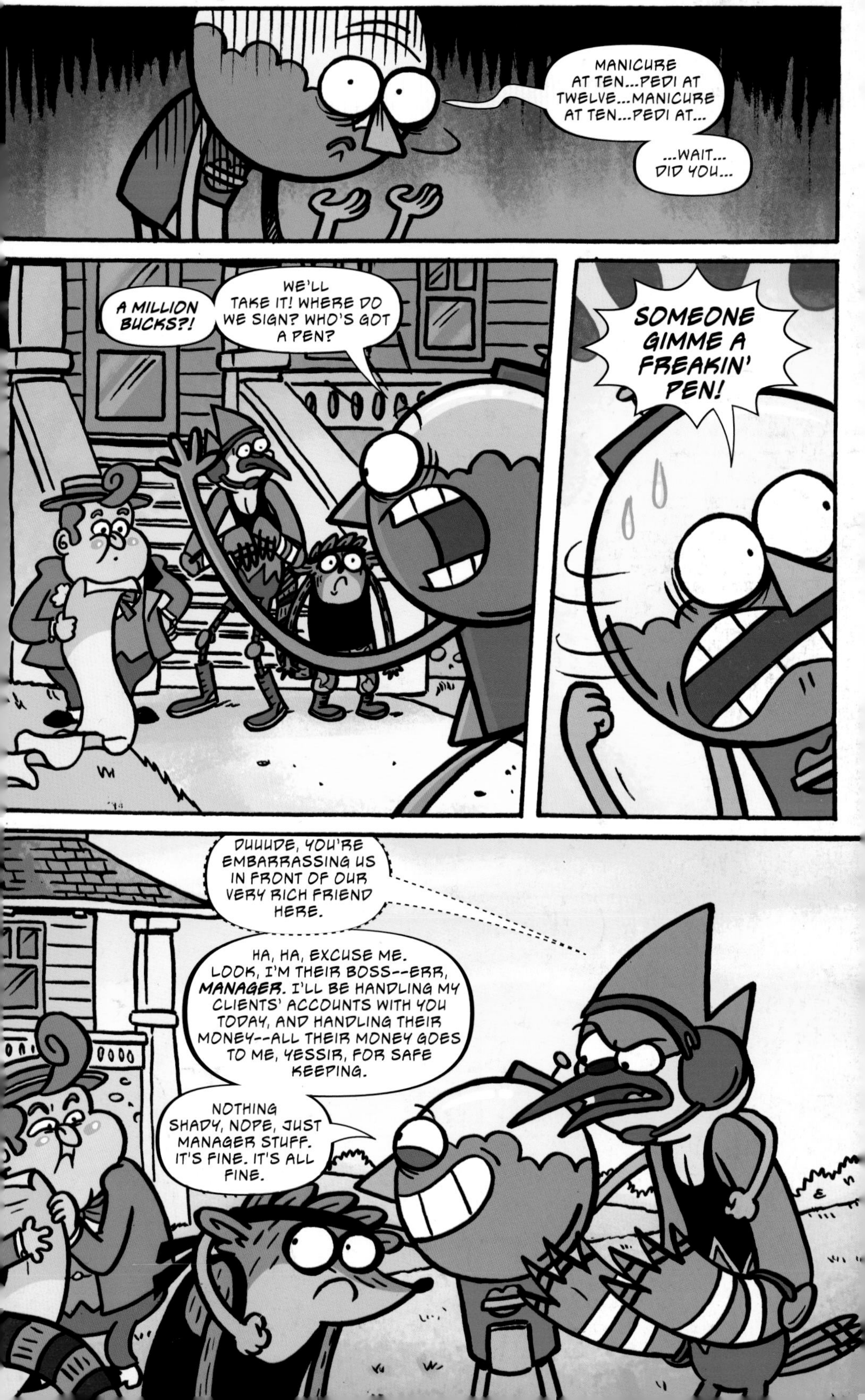
MANICURE AT TEN...PEDI AT TWELVE...MANICURE AT TEN...PEDI AT...
...WAIT... DID YOU...
A MILLION BUCKS?!
WE'LL TAKE IT! WHERE DO WE SIGN? WHO'S GOT A PEN?
SOMEONE GIMME A FREAKIN' PEN!
DUUUDE, YOU'RE EMBARRASSING US IN FRONT OF OUR VERY RICH FRIEND HERE.
HA, HA, EXCUSE ME. LOOK, I'M THEIR BOSS--ERR, MANAGER. I'LL BE HANDLING MY CLIENTS' ACCOUNTS WITH YOU TODAY, AND HANDLING THEIR MONEY--ALL THEIR MONEY GOES TO ME, YESSIR, FOR SAFE KEEPING.
NOTHING SHADY, NOPE, JUST MANAGER STUFF. IT'S FINE. IT'S ALL FINE.

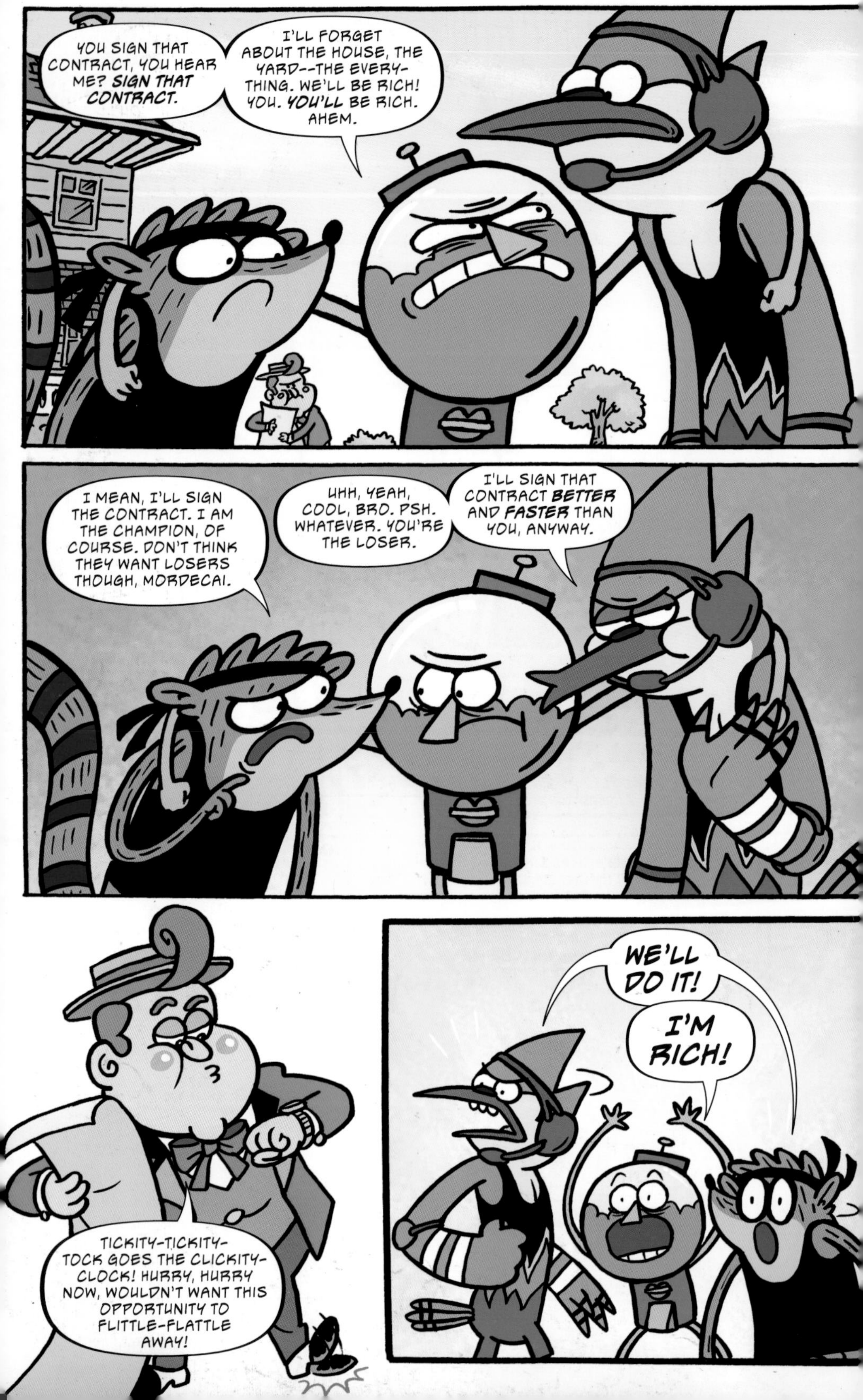
YOU SIGN THAT CONTRACT, YOU HEAR ME? SIGN THAT CONTRACT.
I'LL FORGET ABOUT THE HOUSE, THE YARD--THE EVERY-THING. WE'LL BE RICH! YOU. YOU'LL BE RICH. AHEM.
I MEAN, I'LL SIGN THE CONTRACT. I AM THE CHAMPION, OF COURSE. DON'T THINK THEY WANT LOSERS THOUGH, MORDECAI.
UHH, YEAH, COOL, BRO. PSH. WHATEVER. YOU'RE THE LOSER.
I'LL SIGN THAT CONTRACT BETTER AND FASTER THAN YOU, ANYWAY.
TICKITY-TICKITY-TOCK GOES THE CLICKITY-CLOCK! HURRY, HURRY NOW, WOULDN'T WANT THIS OPPORTUNITY TO FLITTLE-FLATTLE AWAY!
WE'LL DO IT!
I'M RICH!

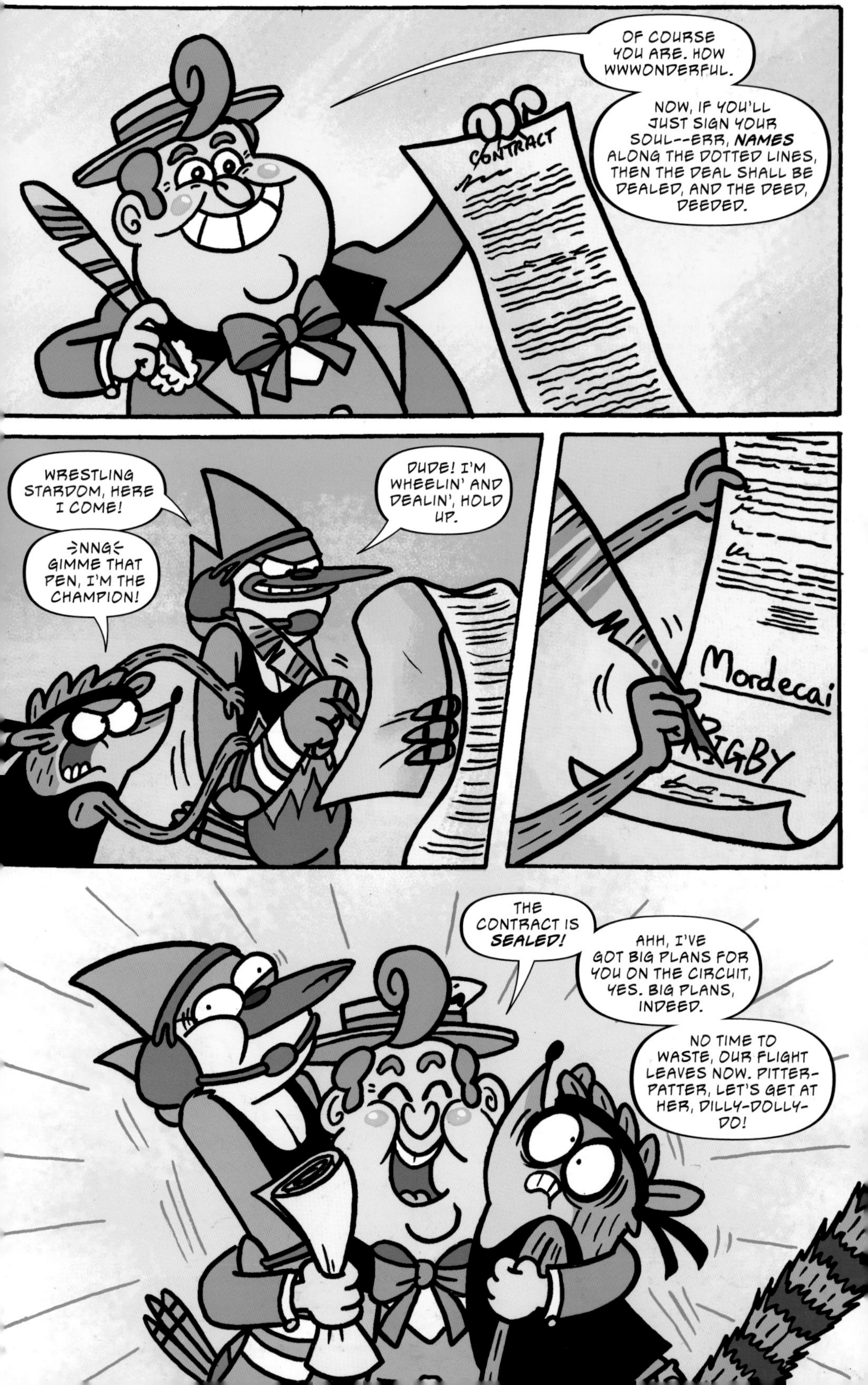
OF COURSE YOU ARE. HOW WWWONDERFUL.
NOW, IF YOU'LL JUST SIGN YOUR SOUL--ERR, ***NAMES*** ALONG THE DOTTED LINES, THEN THE DEAL SHALL BE DEALED, AND THE DEED, DEEDED.
CONTRACT
WRESTLING STARDOM, HERE I COME!
DUDE! I'M WHEELIN' AND DEALIN', HOLD UP.
NNG GIMME THAT PEN, I'M THE CHAMPION!
Mordecai
RIGBY
THE CONTRACT IS ***SEALED!***
AHH, I'VE GOT BIG PLANS FOR YOU ON THE CIRCUIT, YES. BIG PLANS, INDEED.
NO TIME TO WASTE, OUR FLIGHT LEAVES NOW. PITTER-PATTER, LET'S GET AT HER, DILLY-DOLLY-DO!

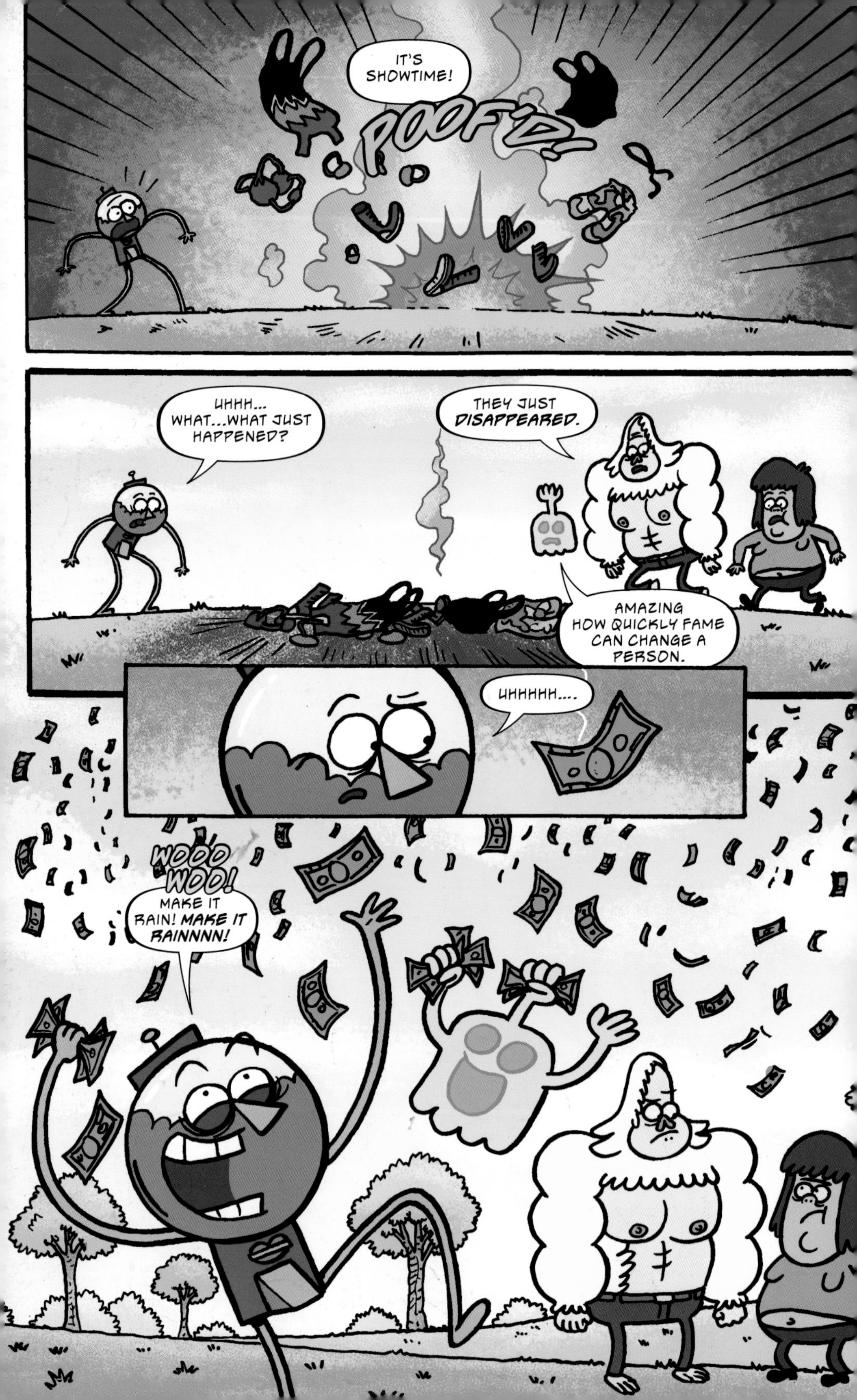
IT'S SHOWTIME!
POOF'D!
UHHH... WHAT...WHAT JUST HAPPENED?
THEY JUST DISAPPEARED.
AMAZING HOW QUICKLY FAME CAN CHANGE A PERSON.
UHHHHH....
WOOO WOO!
MAKE IT RAIN! MAKE IT RAINNNN!

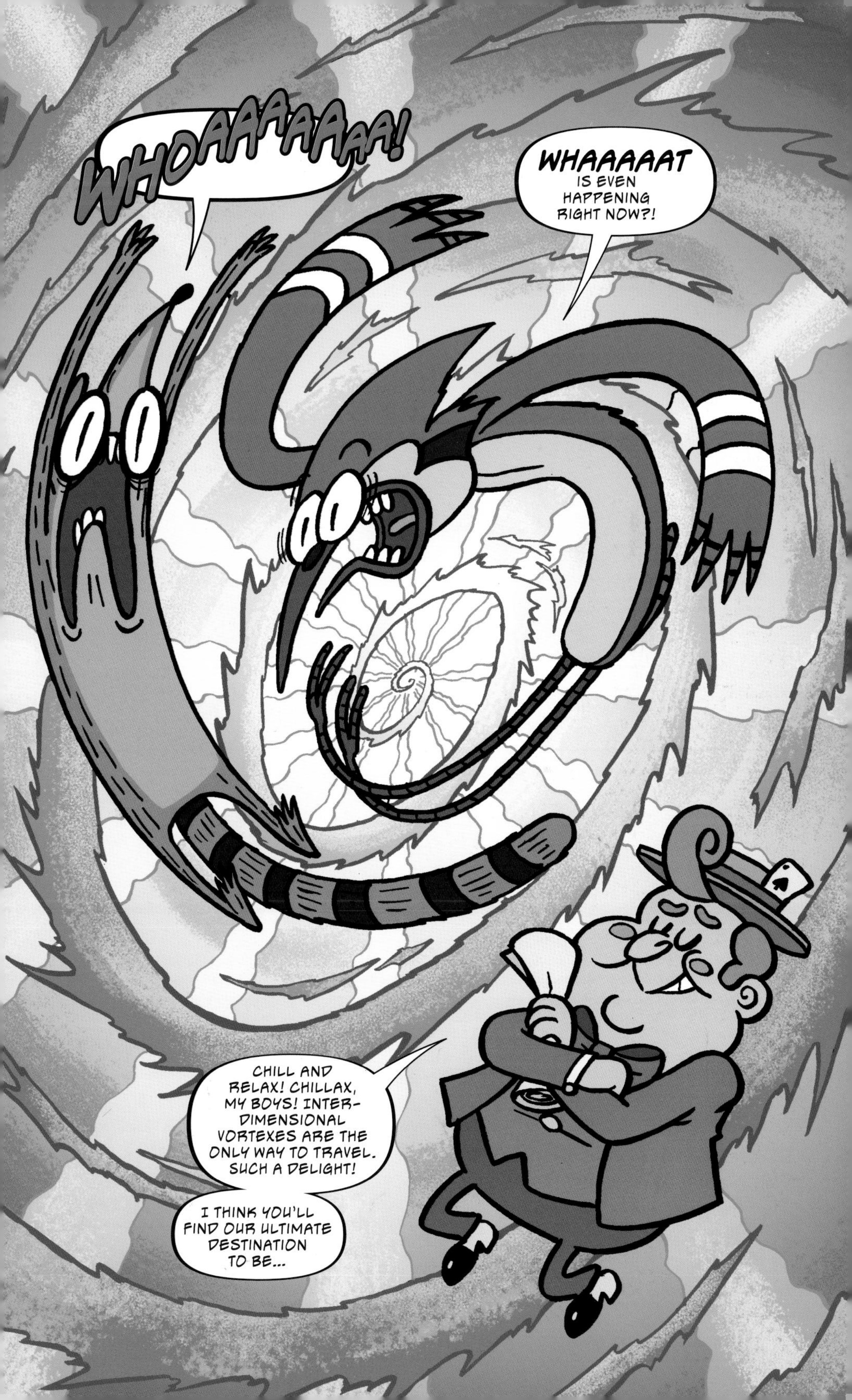
WHOAAAAAAAA!
WHAAAAAT IS EVEN HAPPENING RIGHT NOW?!
CHILL AND RELAX! CHILLAX, MY BOYS! INTER-DIMENSIONAL VORTEXES ARE THE ONLY WAY TO TRAVEL. SUCH A DELIGHT!
I THINK YOU'LL FIND OUR ULTIMATE DESTINATION TO BE...

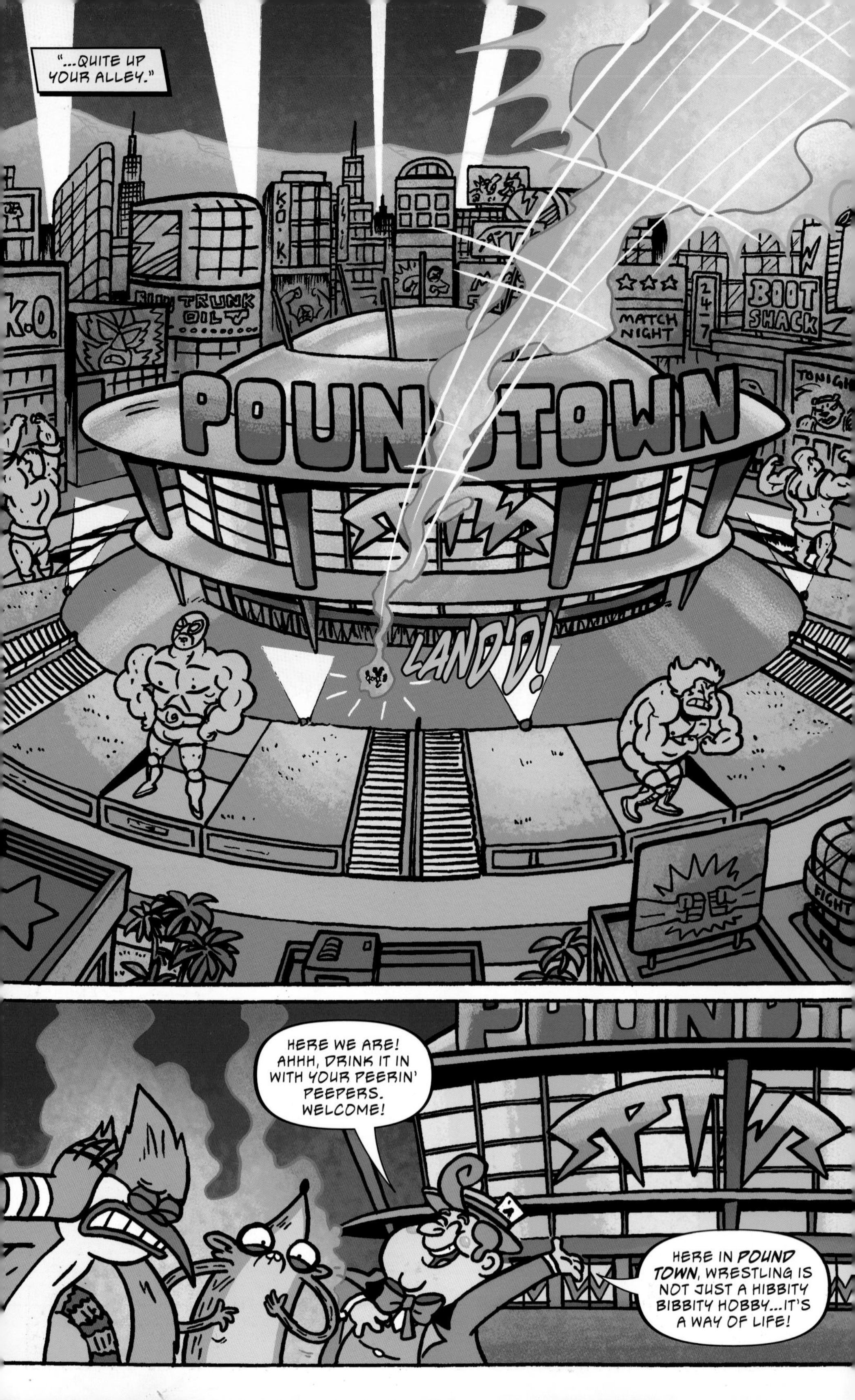
"...QUITE UP YOUR ALLEY."
K.O.
TRUNK OIL
MATCH NIGHT
BOOT SHACK
LAND'D!
HERE WE ARE! AHHH, DRINK IT IN WITH YOUR PEERIN' PEEPERS. WELCOME!
HERE IN *POUND TOWN*, WRESTLING IS NOT JUST A HIBBITY BIBBITY HOBBY...IT'S A WAY OF LIFE!

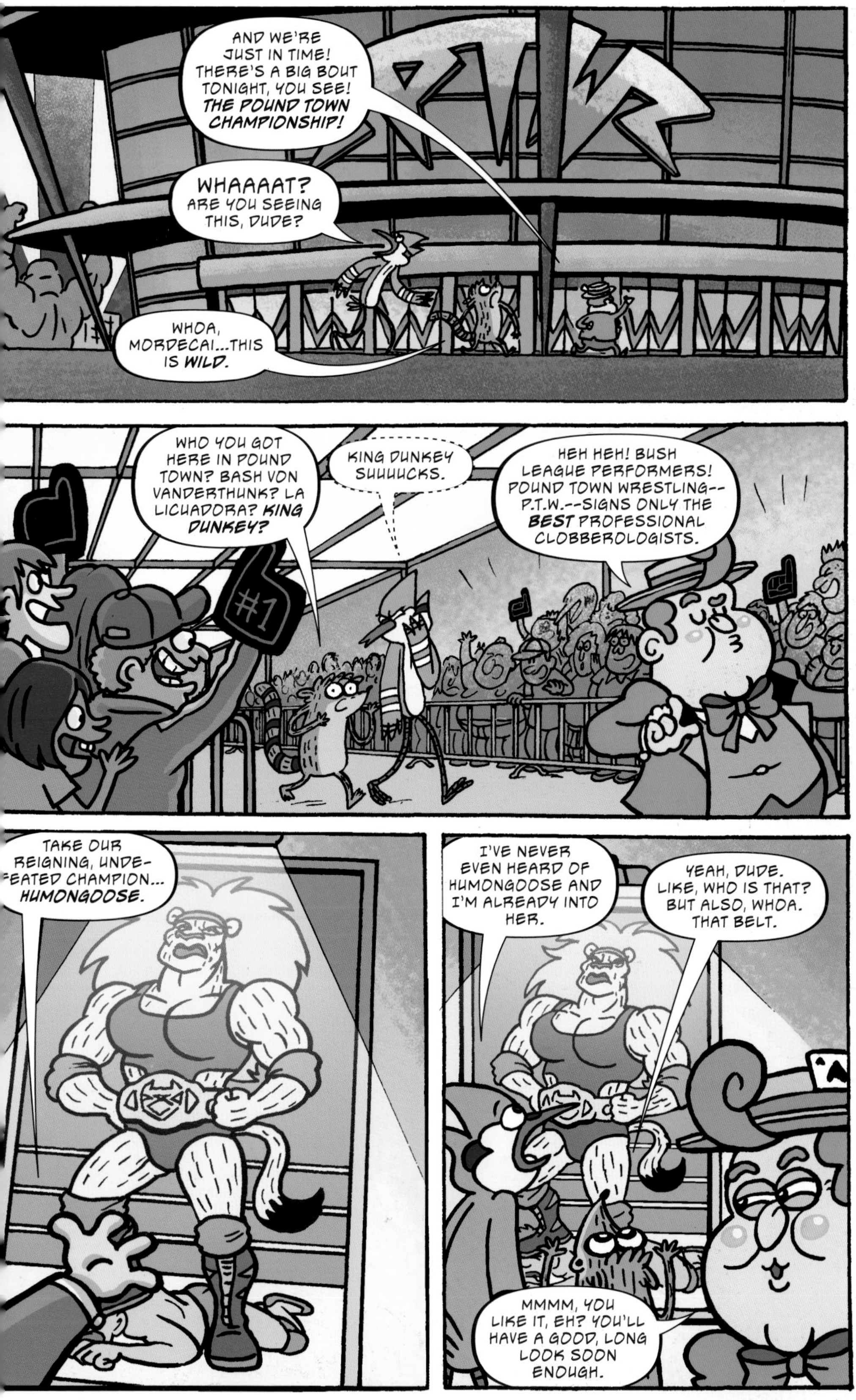
AND WE'RE JUST IN TIME! THERE'S A BIG BOUT TONIGHT, YOU SEE! THE POUND TOWN CHAMPIONSHIP!
WHAAAAT? ARE YOU SEEING THIS, DUDE?
WHOA, MORDECAI...THIS IS WILD.
WHO YOU GOT HERE IN POUND TOWN? BASH VON VANDERTHUNK? LA LICUADORA? KING DUNKEY?
KING DUNKEY SUUUUCKS.
HEH HEH! BUSH LEAGUE PERFORMERS! POUND TOWN WRESTLING--P.T.W.--SIGNS ONLY THE BEST PROFESSIONAL CLOBBEROLOGISTS.
#1
TAKE OUR REIGNING, UNDEFEATED CHAMPION... HUMONGOOSE.
I'VE NEVER EVEN HEARD OF HUMONGOOSE AND I'M ALREADY INTO HER.
YEAH, DUDE. LIKE, WHO IS THAT? BUT ALSO, WHOA. THAT BELT.
MMMM, YOU LIKE IT, EH? YOU'LL HAVE A GOOD, LONG LOOK SOON ENOUGH.

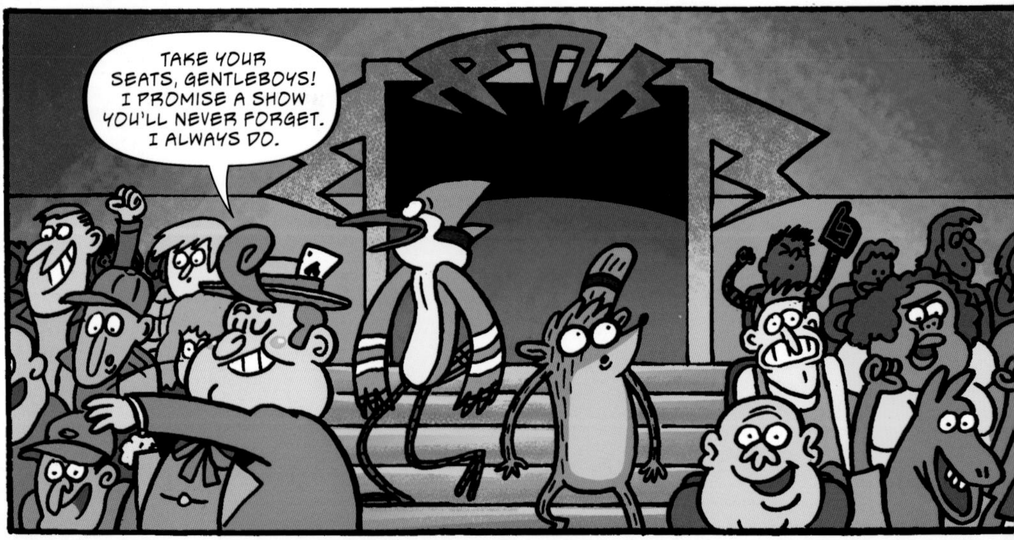
TAKE YOUR SEATS, GENTLEBOYS! I PROMISE A SHOW YOU'LL NEVER FORGET. I ALWAYS DO.

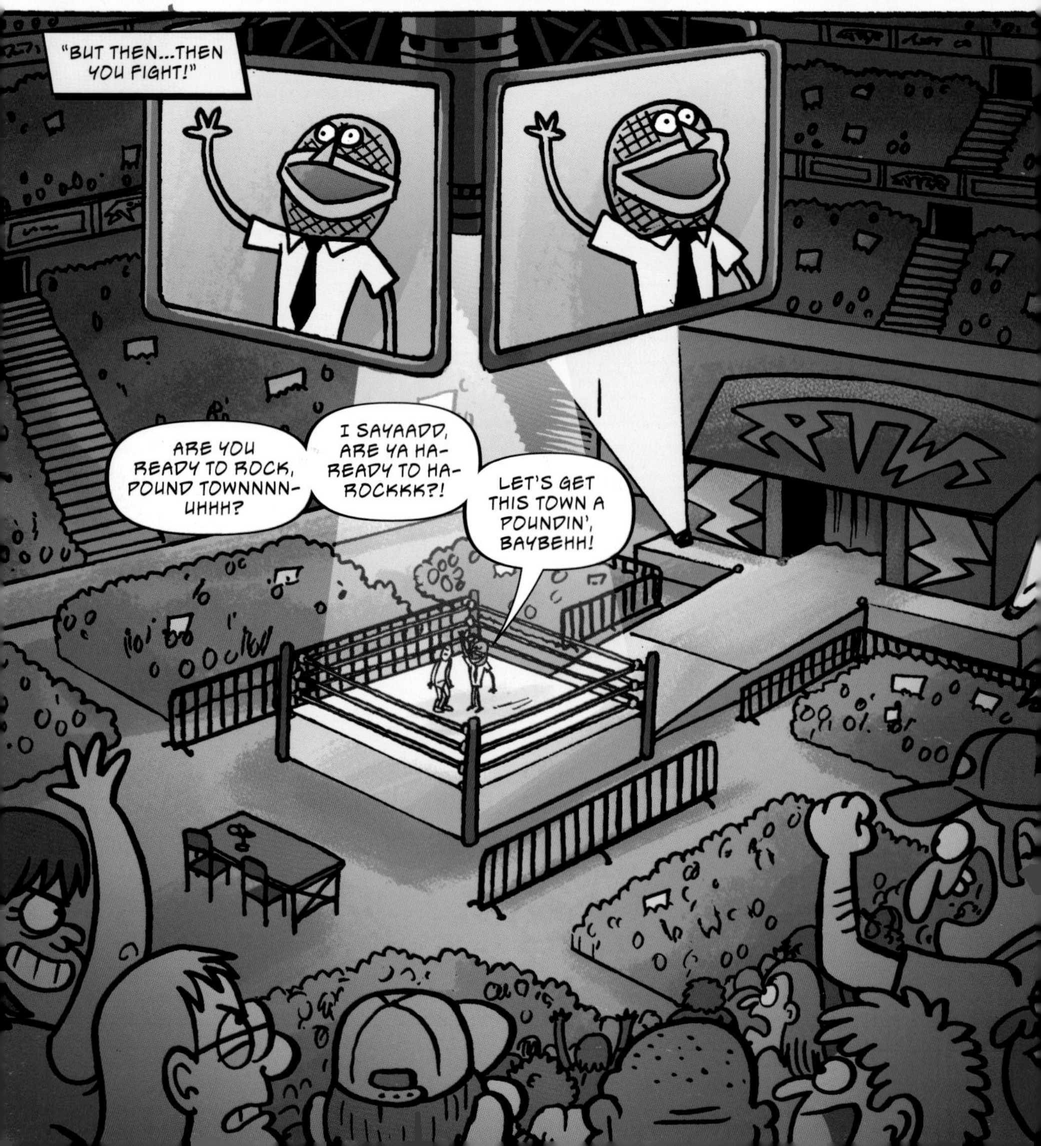
"BUT THEN...THEN YOU FIGHT!"
ARE YOU READY TO ROCK, POUND TOWNNNN-UHHH?
I SAYAADD, ARE YA HA-READY TO HA-ROCKKK?!
LET'S GET THIS TOWN A POUNDIN', BAYBEHH!

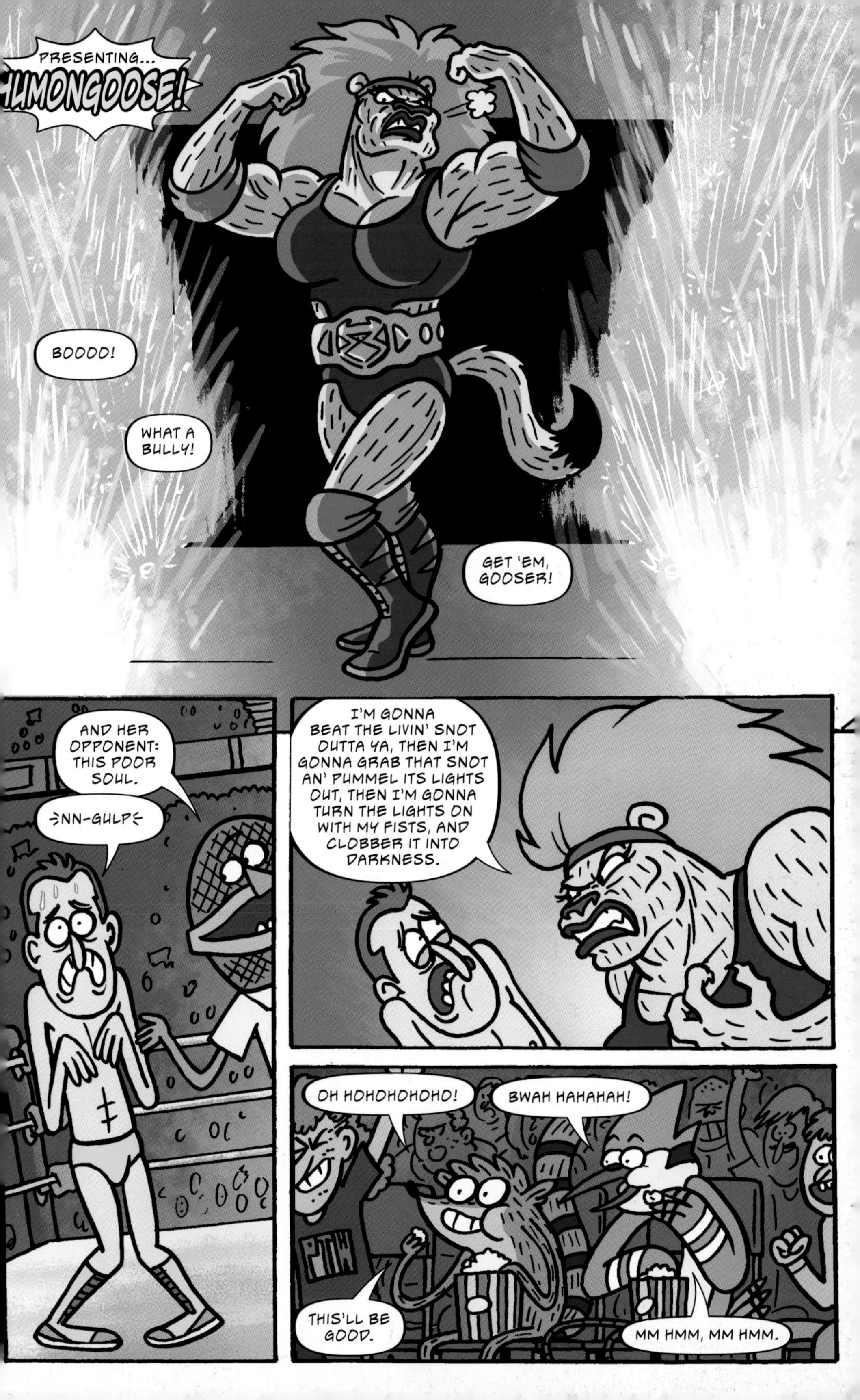
PRESENTING...
HUMONGOOSE!
BOOOO!
WHAT A BULLY!
GET 'EM, GOOSER!
AND HER OPPONENT: THIS POOR SOUL.
NN-GULP
I'M GONNA BEAT THE LIVIN' SNOT OUTTA YA, THEN I'M GONNA GRAB THAT SNOT AN' PUMMEL ITS LIGHTS OUT, THEN I'M GONNA TURN THE LIGHTS ON WITH MY FISTS, AND CLOBBER IT INTO DARKNESS.
OH HOHOHOHOHO!
BWAH HAHAHAH!
THIS'LL BE GOOD.
MM HMM, MM HMM.

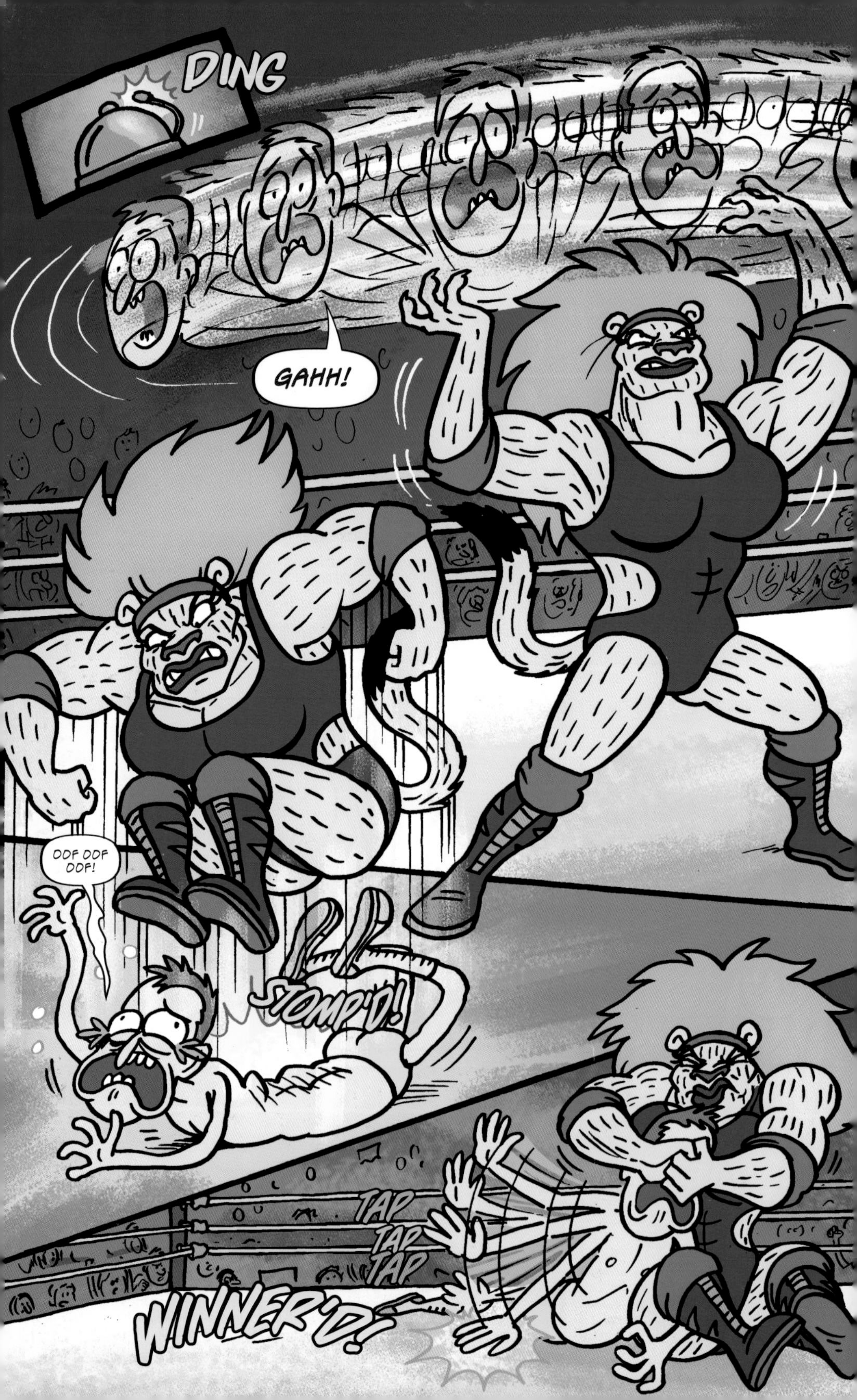
DING
GAHH!
OOF OOF OOF!
STOMP'D!
TAP
TAP
TAP
WINNER'D!

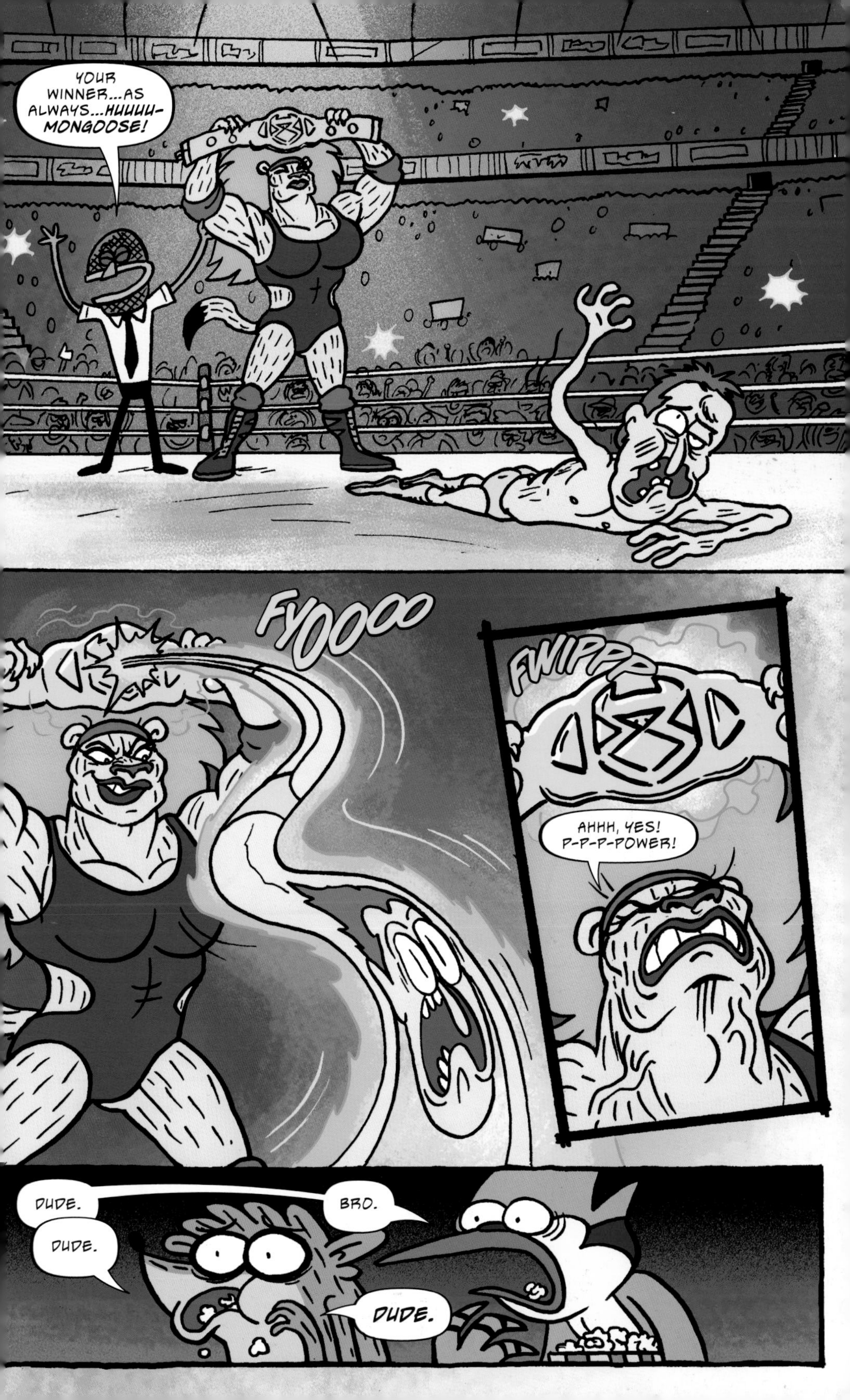

YOUR WINNER...AS ALWAYS...HUUUU-MONGOOSE!
FYOOOO
FWIPPP
AHHH, YES! P-P-P-POWER!
DUDE.
BRO.
DUDE.
DUDE.

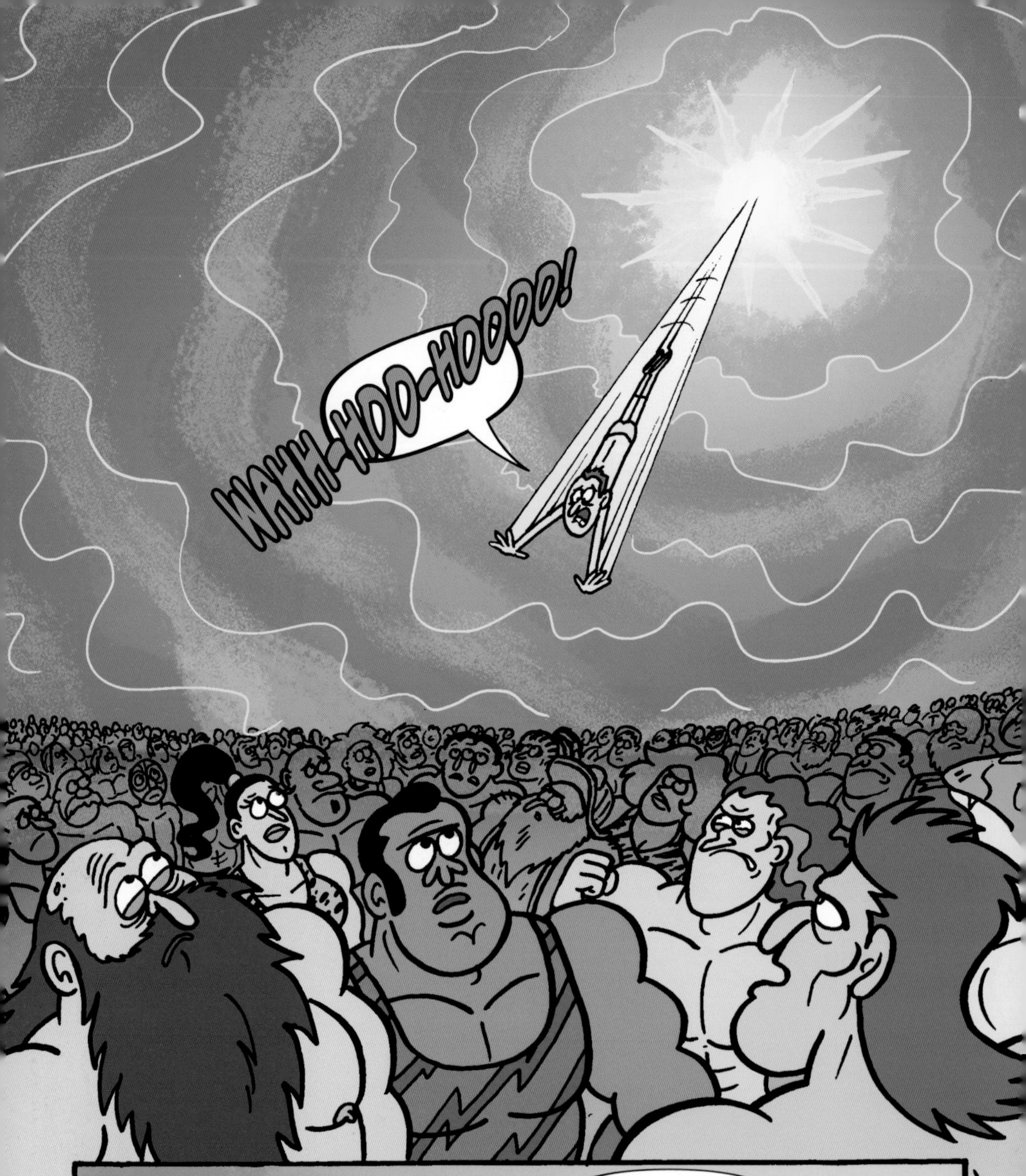
WAHH-HOO-HOOOO!

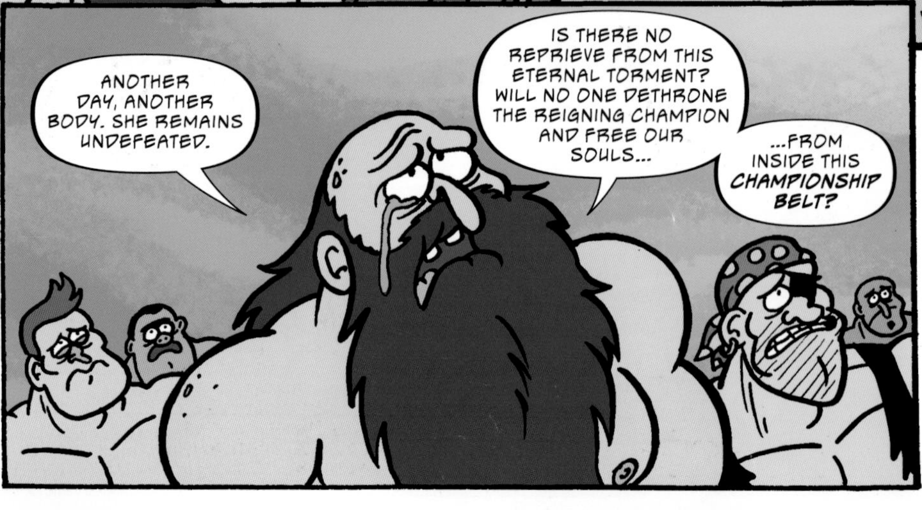
ANOTHER DAY, ANOTHER BODY. SHE REMAINS UNDEFEATED.
IS THERE NO REPRIEVE FROM THIS ETERNAL TORMENT? WILL NO ONE DETHRONE THE REIGNING CHAMPION AND FREE OUR SOULS...
...FROM INSIDE THIS *CHAMPIONSHIP BELT?*

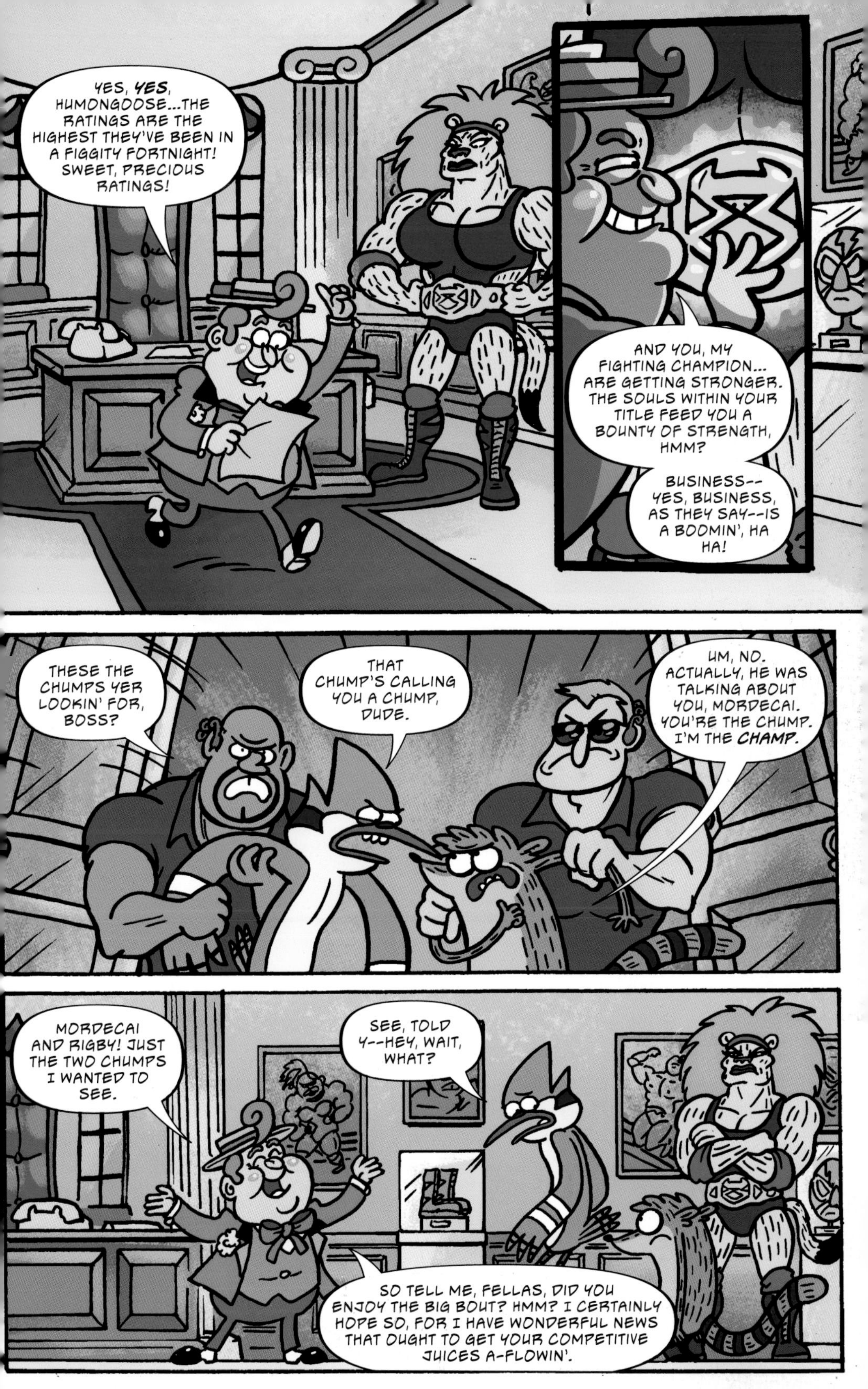
YES, *YES*, HUMONGOOSE...THE RATINGS ARE THE HIGHEST THEY'VE BEEN IN A FIGGITY FORTNIGHT! SWEET, PRECIOUS RATINGS!
AND YOU, MY FIGHTING CHAMPION... ARE GETTING STRONGER. THE SOULS WITHIN YOUR TITLE FEED YOU A BOUNTY OF STRENGTH, HMM?
BUSINESS--YES, BUSINESS, AS THEY SAY--IS A BOOMIN', HA HA!
THESE THE CHUMPS YER LOOKIN' FOR, BOSS?
THAT CHUMP'S CALLING YOU A CHUMP, DUDE.
UM, NO. ACTUALLY, HE WAS TALKING ABOUT YOU, MORDECAI. YOU'RE THE CHUMP. I'M THE *CHAMP*.
MORDECAI AND RIGBY! JUST THE TWO CHUMPS I WANTED TO SEE.
SEE, TOLD Y--HEY, WAIT, WHAT?
SO TELL ME, FELLAS, DID YOU ENJOY THE BIG BOUT? HMM? I CERTAINLY HOPE SO, FOR I HAVE WONDERFUL NEWS THAT OUGHT TO GET YOUR COMPETITIVE JUICES A-FLOWIN'.

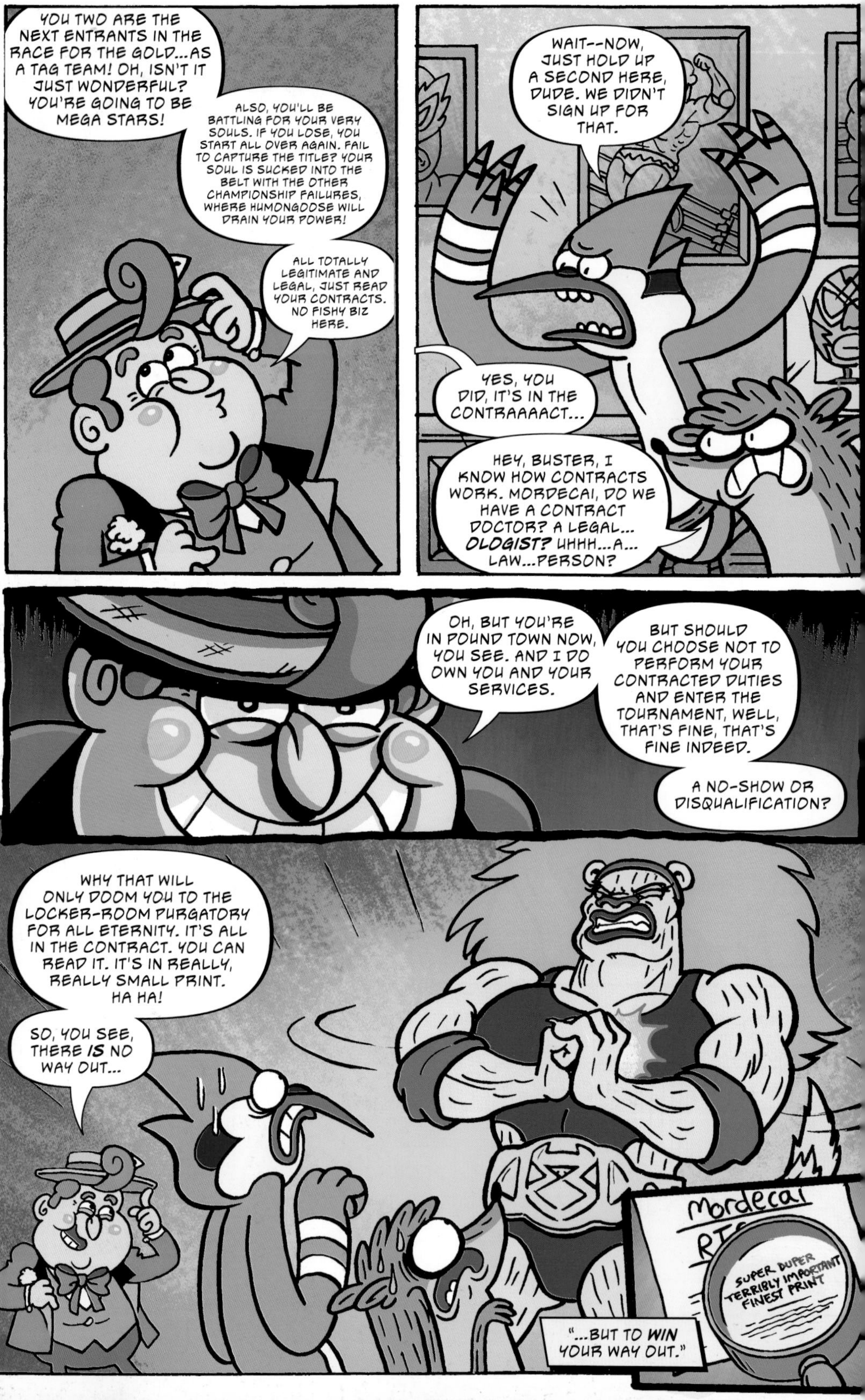
YOU TWO ARE THE NEXT ENTRANTS IN THE RACE FOR THE GOLD...AS A TAG TEAM! OH, ISN'T IT JUST WONDERFUL? YOU'RE GOING TO BE MEGA STARS!
ALSO, YOU'LL BE BATTLING FOR YOUR VERY SOULS. IF YOU LOSE, YOU START ALL OVER AGAIN. FAIL TO CAPTURE THE TITLE? YOUR SOUL IS SUCKED INTO THE BELT WITH THE OTHER CHAMPIONSHIP FAILURES, WHERE HUMONGOOSE WILL DRAIN YOUR POWER!
ALL TOTALLY LEGITIMATE AND LEGAL, JUST READ YOUR CONTRACTS. NO FISHY BIZ HERE.
WAIT--NOW, JUST HOLD UP A SECOND HERE, DUDE. WE DIDN'T SIGN UP FOR THAT.
YES, YOU DID, IT'S IN THE CONTRAAAACT...
HEY, BUSTER, I KNOW HOW CONTRACTS WORK. MORDECAI, DO WE HAVE A CONTRACT DOCTOR? A LEGAL... ***OLOGIST?*** UHHH...A... LAW...PERSON?
OH, BUT YOU'RE IN POUND TOWN NOW, YOU SEE. AND I DO OWN YOU AND YOUR SERVICES.
BUT SHOULD YOU CHOOSE NOT TO PERFORM YOUR CONTRACTED DUTIES AND ENTER THE TOURNAMENT, WELL, THAT'S FINE, THAT'S FINE INDEED.
A NO-SHOW OR DISQUALIFICATION?
WHY THAT WILL ONLY DOOM YOU TO THE LOCKER-ROOM PURGATORY FOR ALL ETERNITY. IT'S ALL IN THE CONTRACT. YOU CAN READ IT. IT'S IN REALLY, REALLY SMALL PRINT. HA HA!
SO, YOU SEE, THERE ***IS*** NO WAY OUT...
"...BUT TO ***WIN*** YOUR WAY OUT."
Mordecai
SUPER DUPER TERRIBLY IMPORTANT FINEST PRINT

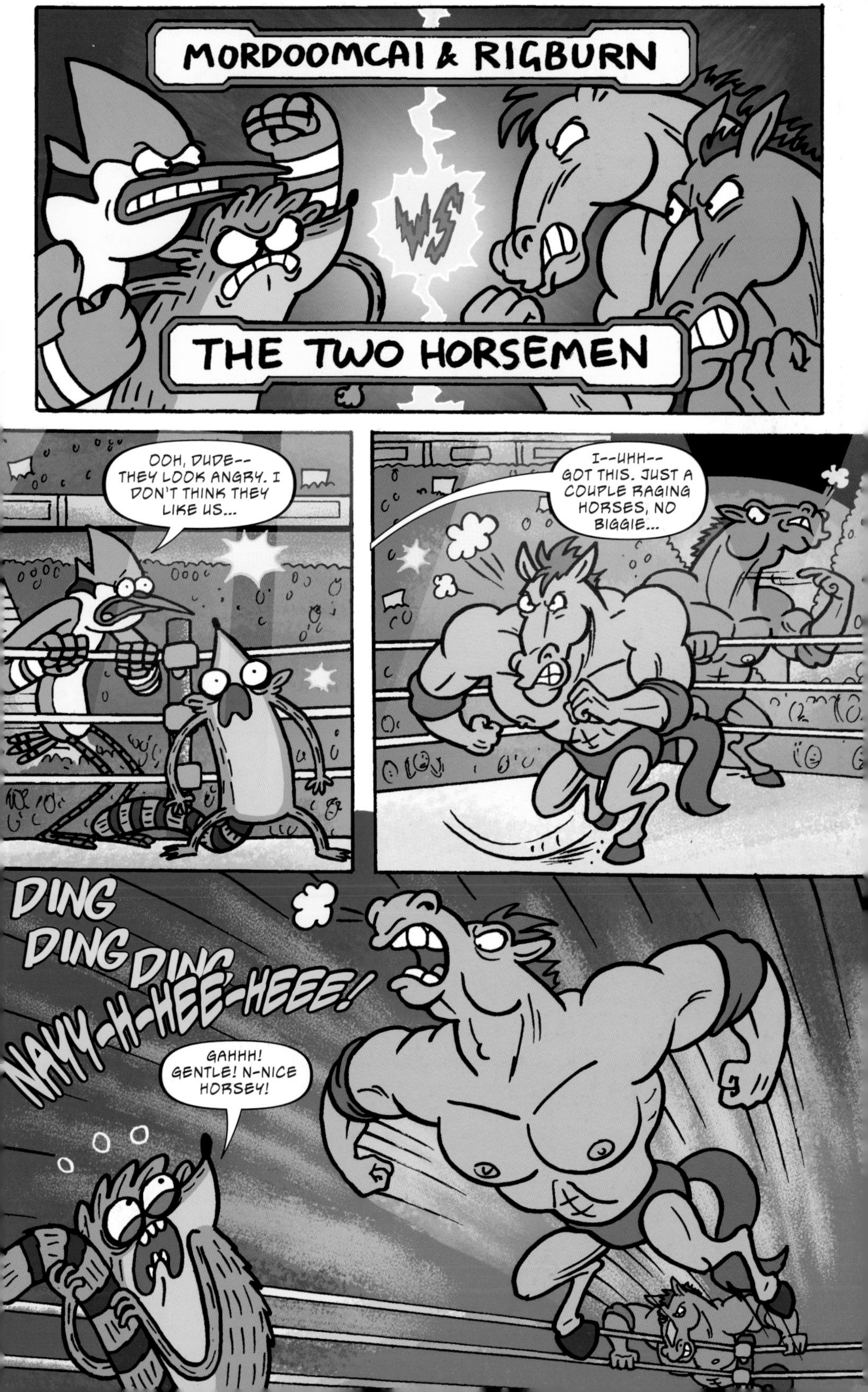
MORDOOMCAI & RIGBURN
VS
THE TWO HORSEMEN
OOH, DUDE-- THEY LOOK ANGRY. I DON'T THINK THEY LIKE US...
I--UHH-- GOT THIS. JUST A COUPLE RAGING HORSES, NO BIGGIE...
DING DING DING
NAYY-H-HEE-HEEE!
GAHHH! GENTLE! N-NICE HORSEY!

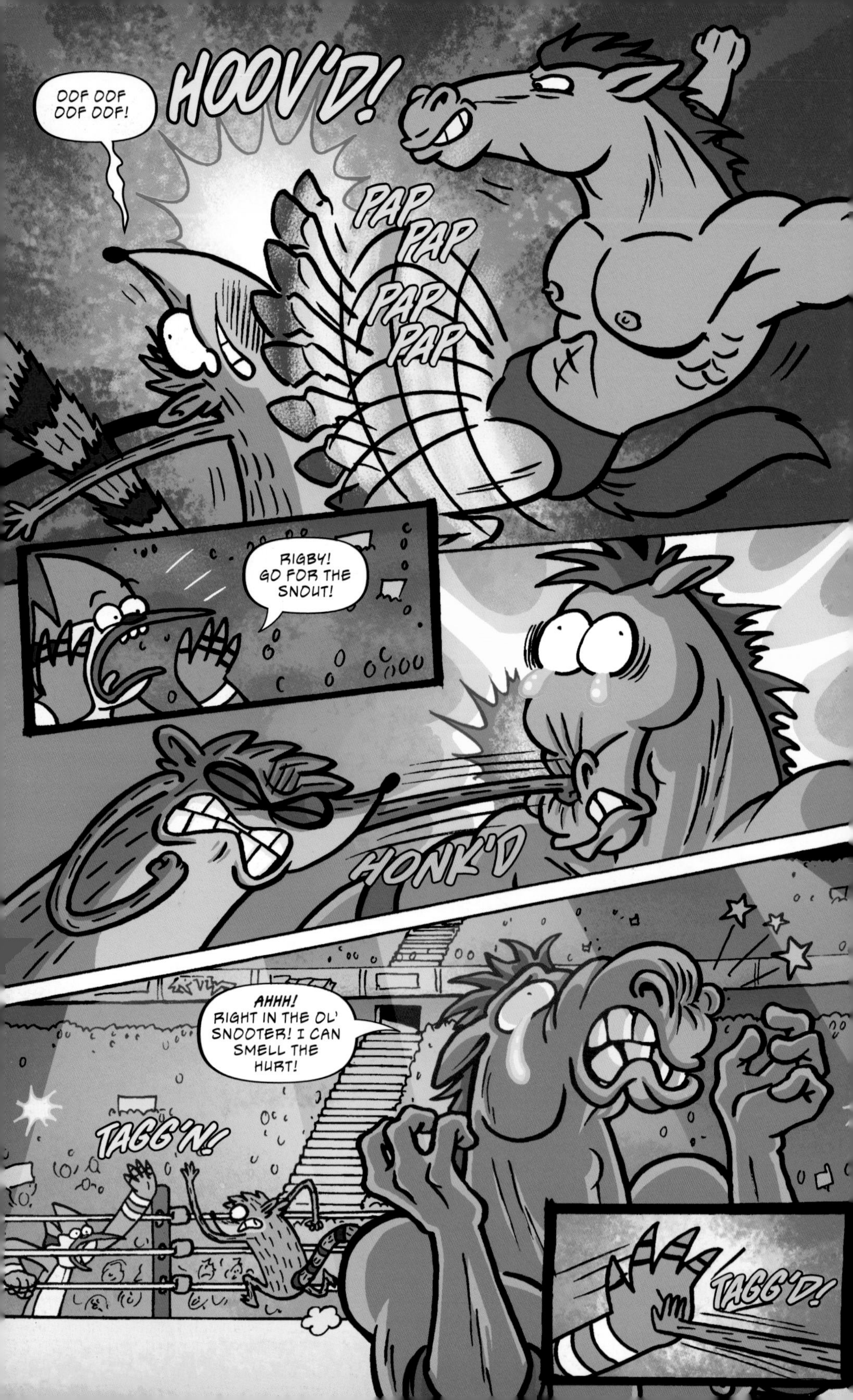
OOF OOF OOF OOF!
HOOV'D!
PAP PAP PAP PAP
RIGBY! GO FOR THE SNOUT!
HONK'D
AHHH! RIGHT IN THE OL' SNOOTER! I CAN SMELL THE HURT!
TAGG'N!
TAGG'D!

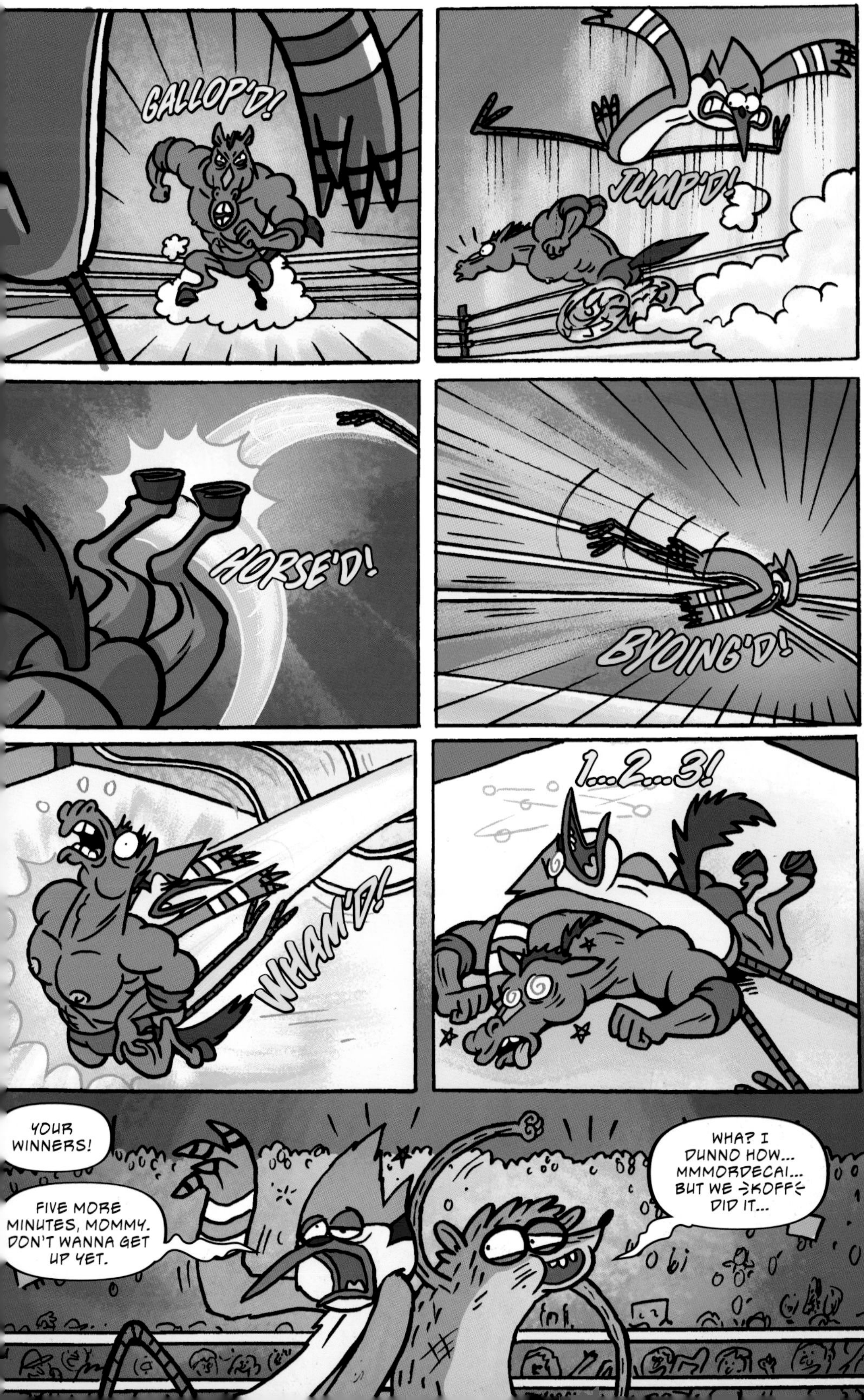
GALLOP'D!
JUMP'D!
HORSE'D!
BYOING'D!
WHAM'D!
1...2...3!
YOUR WINNERS!
FIVE MORE MINUTES, MOMMY. DON'T WANNA GET UP YET.
WHA? I DUNNO HOW... MMMORDECAI... BUT WE *KOFF* DID IT...

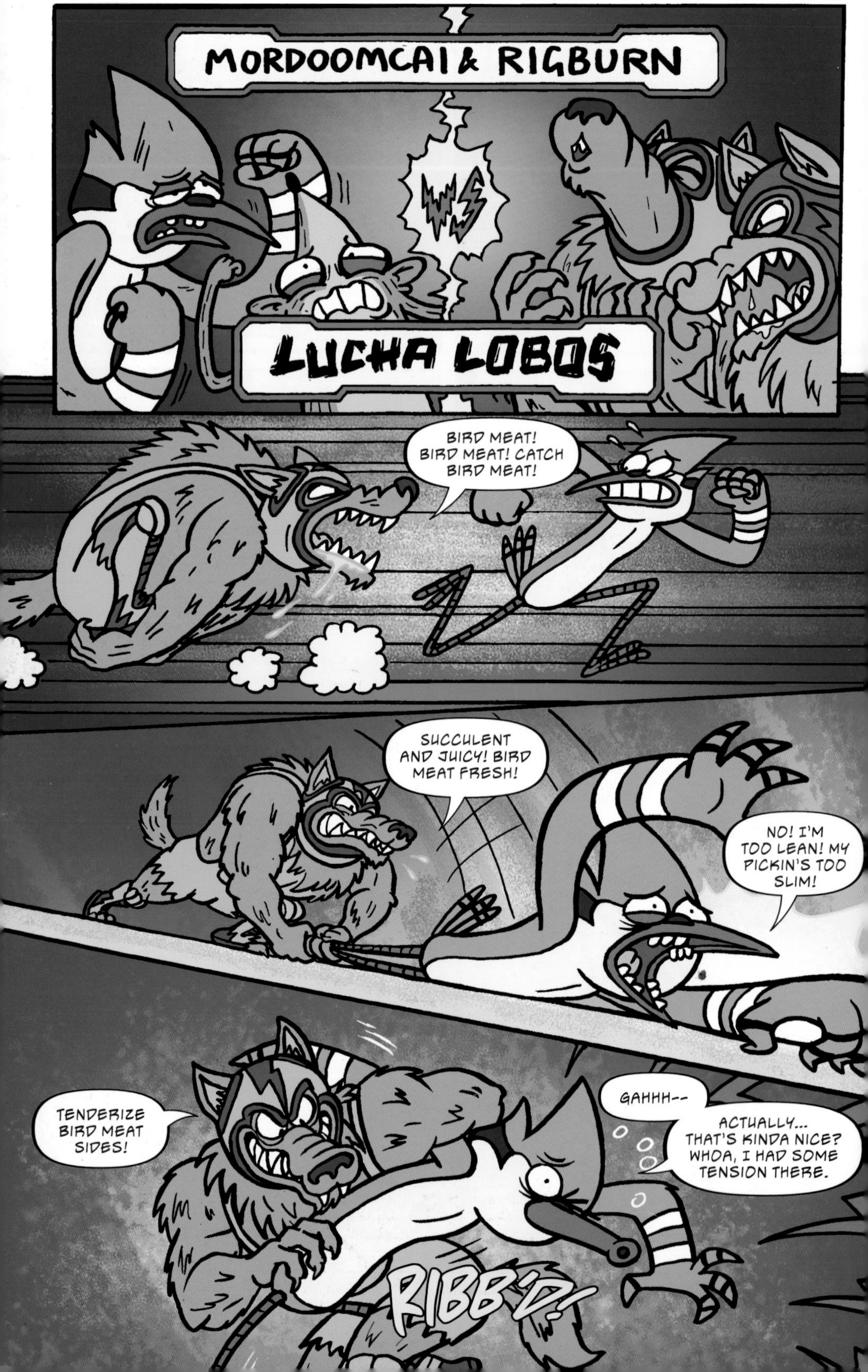
MORDOOMCAI & RIGBURN
VS
LUCHA LOBOS
BIRD MEAT! BIRD MEAT! CATCH BIRD MEAT!
SUCCULENT AND JUICY! BIRD MEAT FRESH!
NO! I'M TOO LEAN! MY PICKIN'S TOO SLIM!
TENDERIZE BIRD MEAT SIDES!
GAHHH--
ACTUALLY... THAT'S KINDA NICE? WHOA, I HAD SOME TENSION THERE.
RIBB'D!

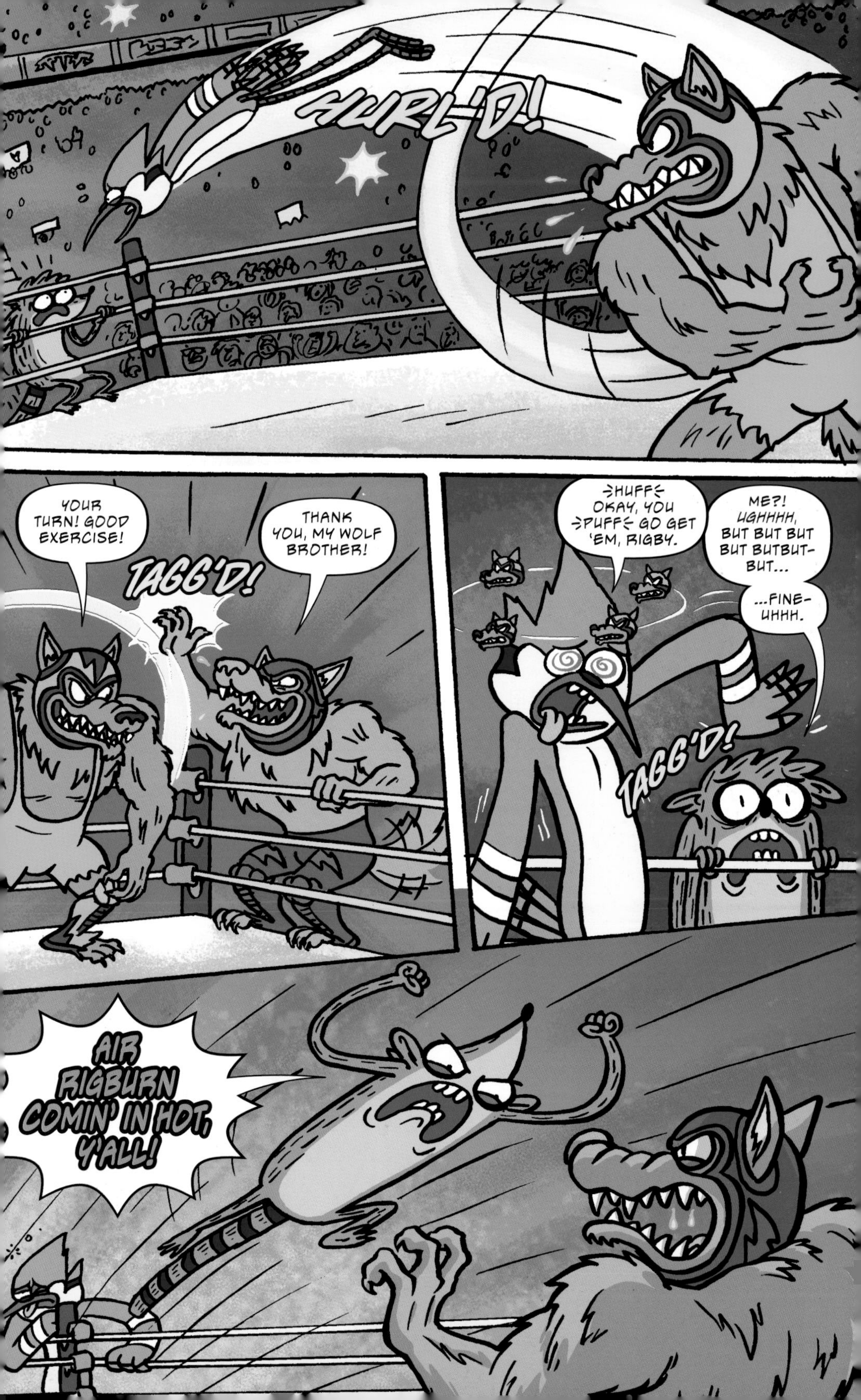
HURL'D!
YOUR TURN! GOOD EXERCISE!
TAGG'D!
THANK YOU, MY WOLF BROTHER!
⋺HUFF⋲ OKAY, YOU ⋺PUFF⋲ GO GET 'EM, RIGBY.
ME?! UGHHHH, BUT BUT BUT BUT BUTBUT-BUT...
...FINE-UHHH.
TAGG'D!
AIR RIGBURN COMIN' IN HOT, Y'ALL!

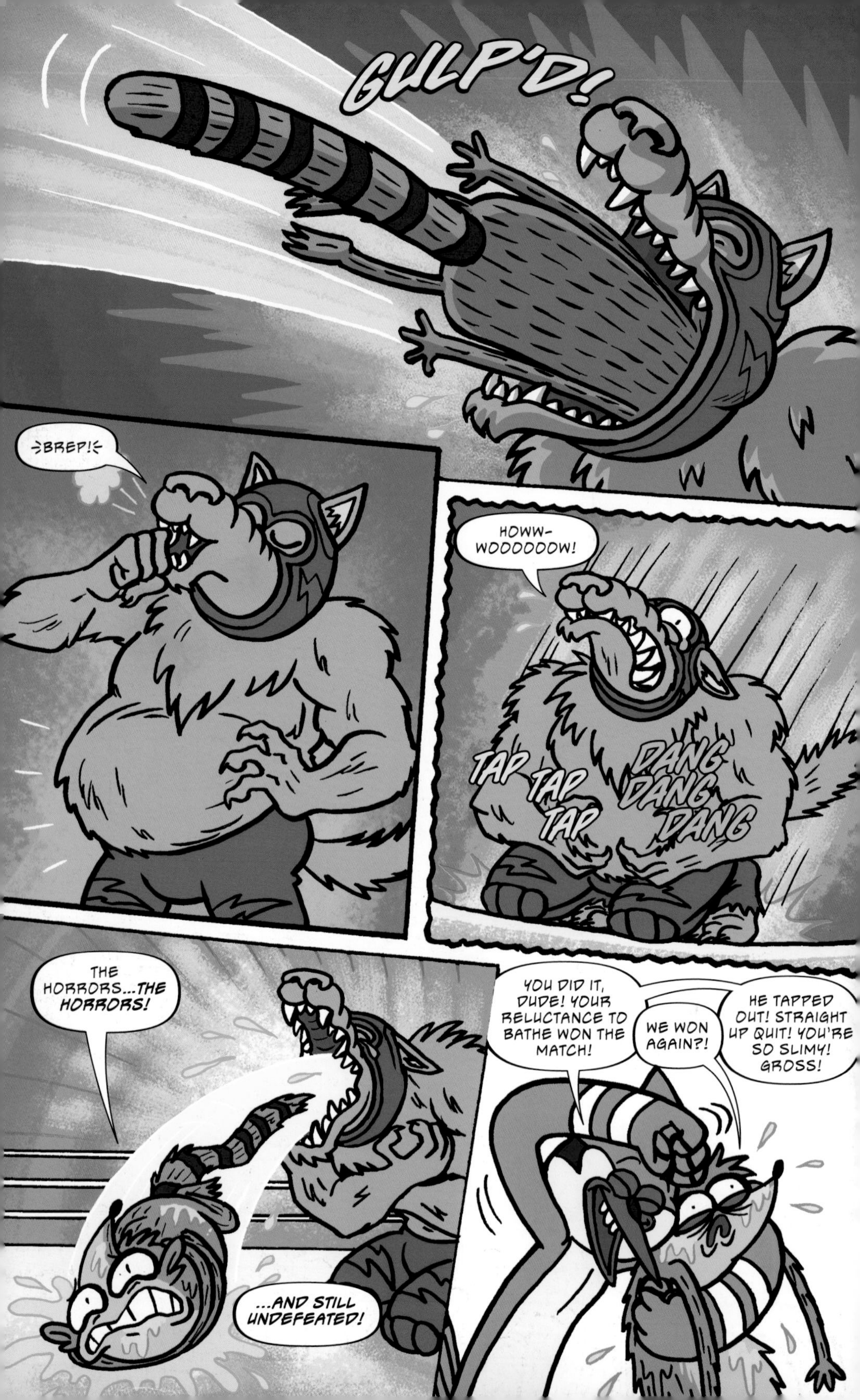
GULP'D!
BREP!
HOWW-WOOOOOOW!
TAP TAP TAP
DANG DANG DANG
THE HORRORS...THE HORRORS!
...AND STILL UNDEFEATED!
YOU DID IT, DUDE! YOUR RELUCTANCE TO BATHE WON THE MATCH!
WE WON AGAIN?!
HE TAPPED OUT! STRAIGHT UP QUIT! YOU'RE SO SLIMY! GROSS!

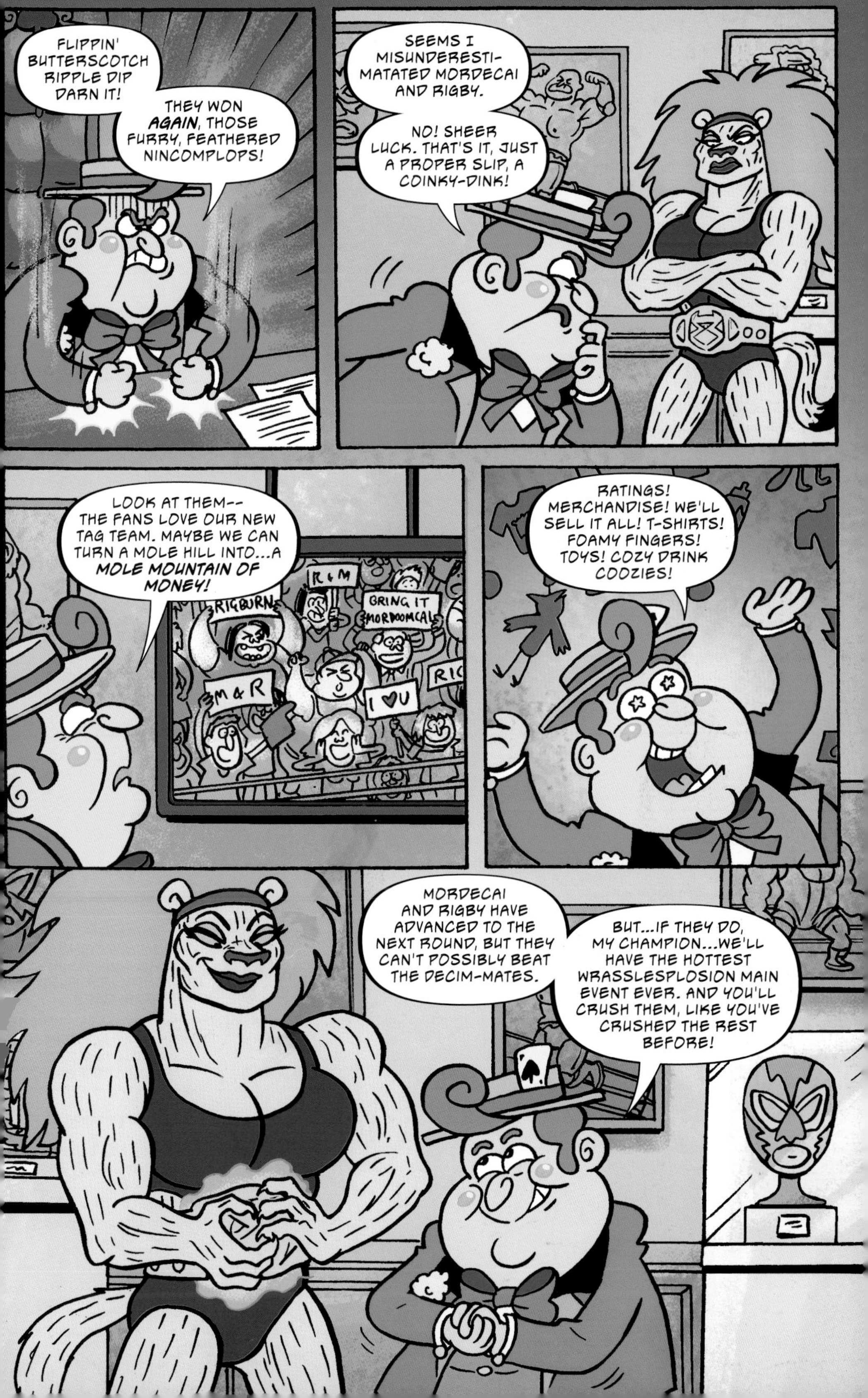

FLIPPIN' BUTTERSCOTCH RIPPLE DIP DARN IT!
THEY WON AGAIN, THOSE FURRY, FEATHERED NINCOMPLOPS!
SEEMS I MISUNDERESTI-MATATED MORDECAI AND RIGBY.
NO! SHEER LUCK. THAT'S IT, JUST A PROPER SLIP, A COINKY-DINK!
LOOK AT THEM-- THE FANS LOVE OUR NEW TAG TEAM. MAYBE WE CAN TURN A MOLE HILL INTO...A MOLE MOUNTAIN OF MONEY!
R+M
RIGBURN
BRING IT MORDOOMCAI
M&R
I ♥ U
RATINGS! MERCHANDISE! WE'LL SELL IT ALL! T-SHIRTS! FOAMY FINGERS! TOYS! COZY DRINK COOZIES!
MORDECAI AND RIGBY HAVE ADVANCED TO THE NEXT ROUND, BUT THEY CAN'T POSSIBLY BEAT THE DECIM-MATES.
BUT...IF THEY DO, MY CHAMPION...WE'LL HAVE THE HOTTEST WRASSLESPLOSION MAIN EVENT EVER. AND YOU'LL CRUSH THEM, LIKE YOU'VE CRUSHED THE REST BEFORE!

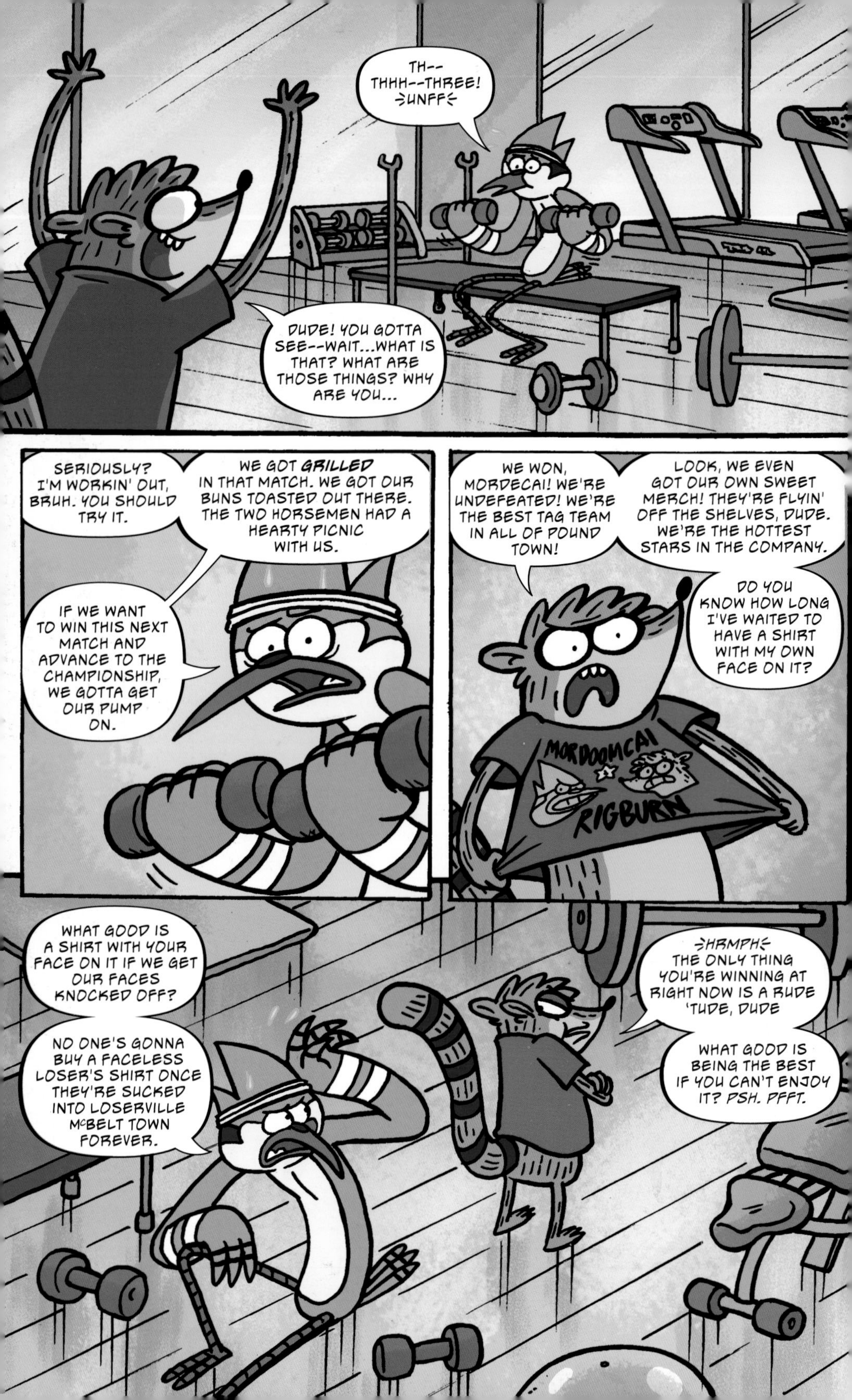
TH-- THHH--THREE! ≒UNFF≒
DUDE! YOU GOTTA SEE--WAIT...WHAT IS THAT? WHAT ARE THOSE THINGS? WHY ARE YOU...
SERIOUSLY? I'M WORKIN' OUT, BRUH. YOU SHOULD TRY IT.
WE GOT GRILLED IN THAT MATCH. WE GOT OUR BUNS TOASTED OUT THERE. THE TWO HORSEMEN HAD A HEARTY PICNIC WITH US.
IF WE WANT TO WIN THIS NEXT MATCH AND ADVANCE TO THE CHAMPIONSHIP, WE GOTTA GET OUR PUMP ON.
WE WON, MORDECAI! WE'RE UNDEFEATED! WE'RE THE BEST TAG TEAM IN ALL OF POUND TOWN!
LOOK, WE EVEN GOT OUR OWN SWEET MERCH! THEY'RE FLYIN' OFF THE SHELVES, DUDE. WE'RE THE HOTTEST STARS IN THE COMPANY.
DO YOU KNOW HOW LONG I'VE WAITED TO HAVE A SHIRT WITH MY OWN FACE ON IT?
MORDOOMCAI
RIGBURN
WHAT GOOD IS A SHIRT WITH YOUR FACE ON IT IF WE GET OUR FACES KNOCKED OFF?
NO ONE'S GONNA BUY A FACELESS LOSER'S SHIRT ONCE THEY'RE SUCKED INTO LOSERVILLE McBELT TOWN FOREVER.
≒HRMPH≒ THE ONLY THING YOU'RE WINNING AT RIGHT NOW IS A RUDE 'TUDE, DUDE
WHAT GOOD IS BEING THE BEST IF YOU CAN'T ENJOY IT? PSH. PFFT.

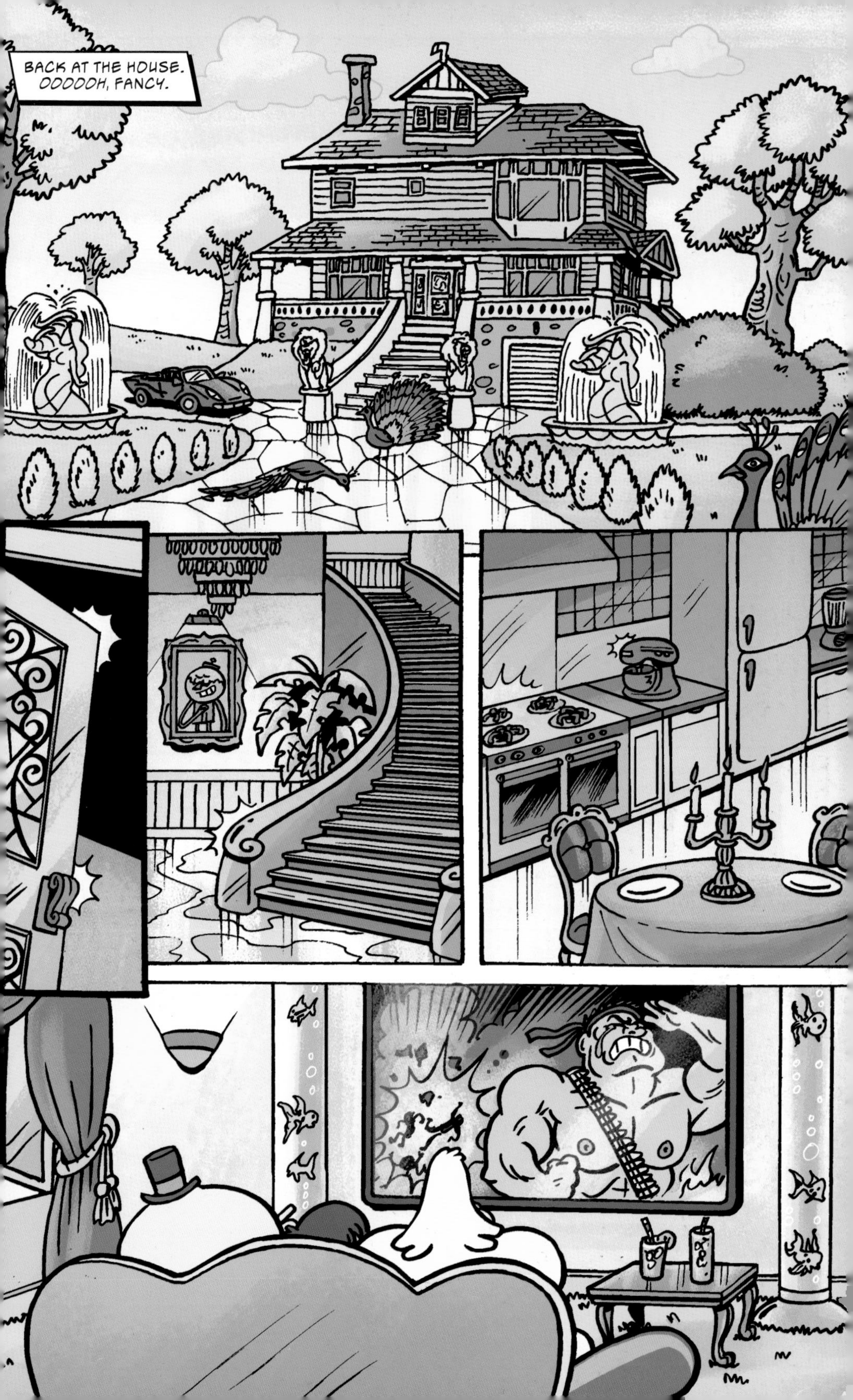
BACK AT THE HOUSE.
OOOOOH, FANCY.

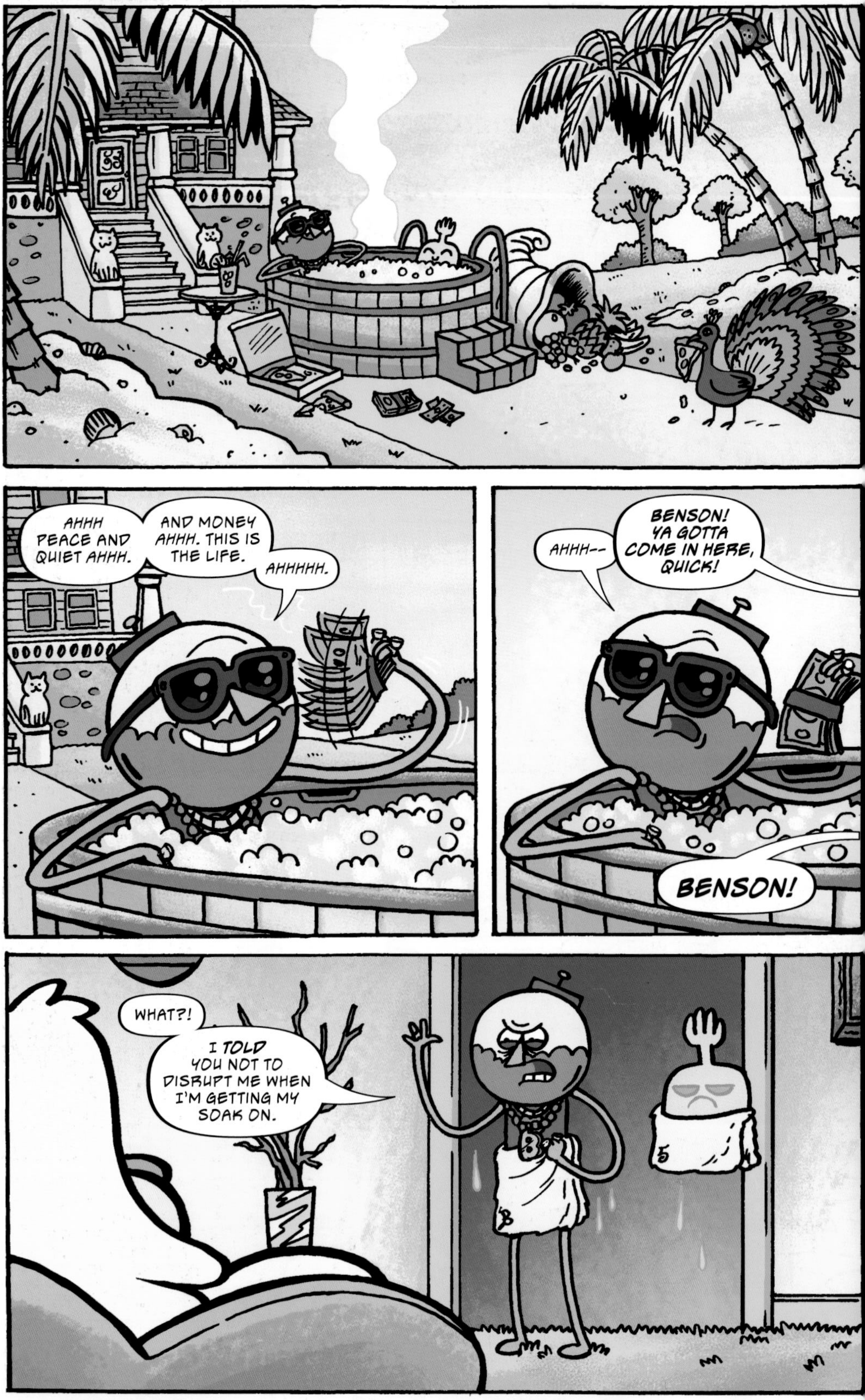

AHHH PEACE AND QUIET AHHH.
AND MONEY AHHH. THIS IS THE LIFE.
AHHHHH.
AHHH--
BENSON! YA GOTTA COME IN HERE, QUICK!
BENSON!
WHAT?!
I TOLD YOU NOT TO DISRUPT ME WHEN I'M GETTING MY SOAK ON.

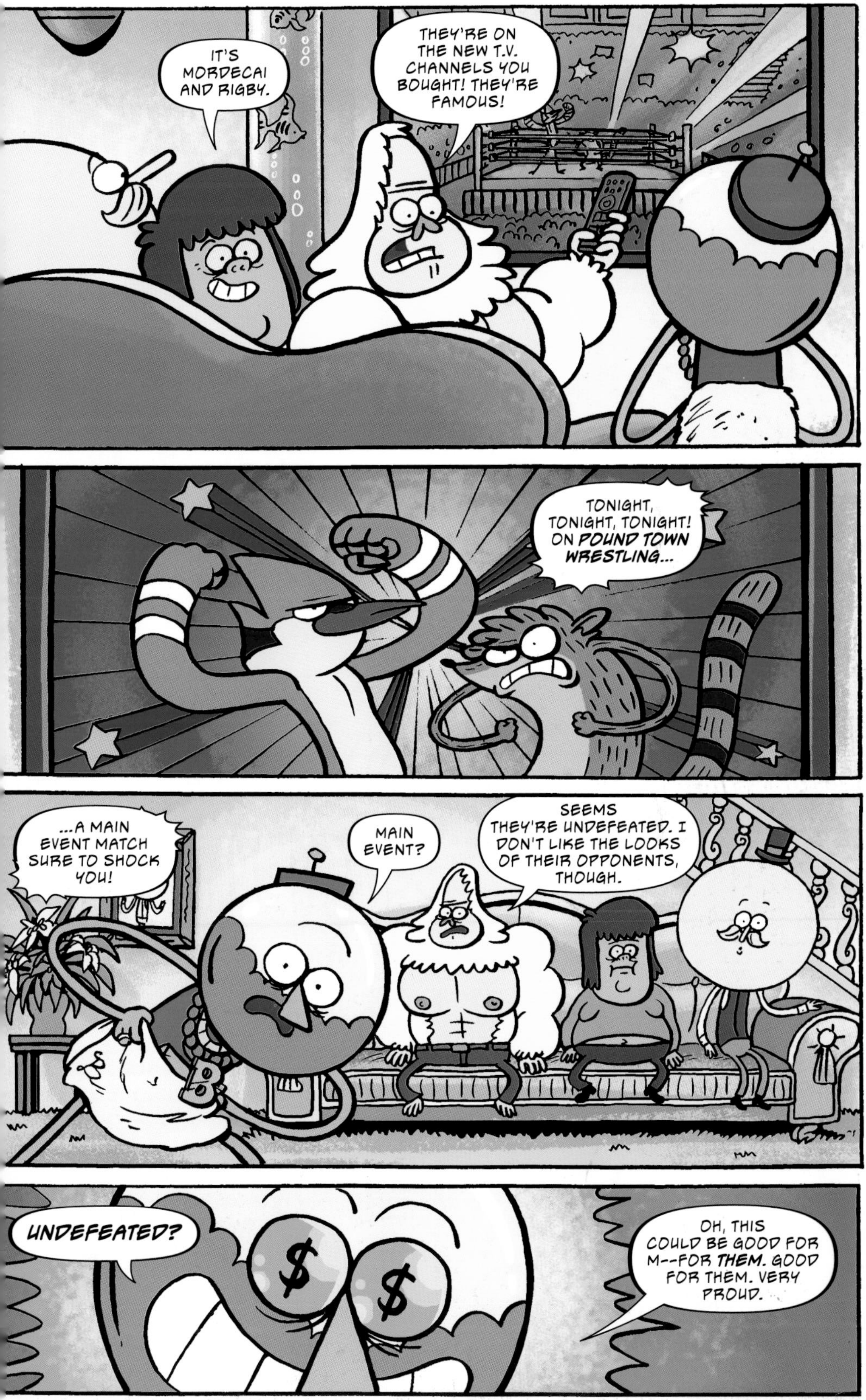
IT'S MORDECAI AND RIGBY.
THEY'RE ON THE NEW T.V. CHANNELS YOU BOUGHT! THEY'RE FAMOUS!
TONIGHT, TONIGHT, TONIGHT! ON POUND TOWN WRESTLING...
...A MAIN EVENT MATCH SURE TO SHOCK YOU!
MAIN EVENT?
SEEMS THEY'RE UNDEFEATED. I DON'T LIKE THE LOOKS OF THEIR OPPONENTS, THOUGH.
UNDEFEATED?
OH, THIS COULD BE GOOD FOR M--FOR THEM. GOOD FOR THEM. VERY PROUD.

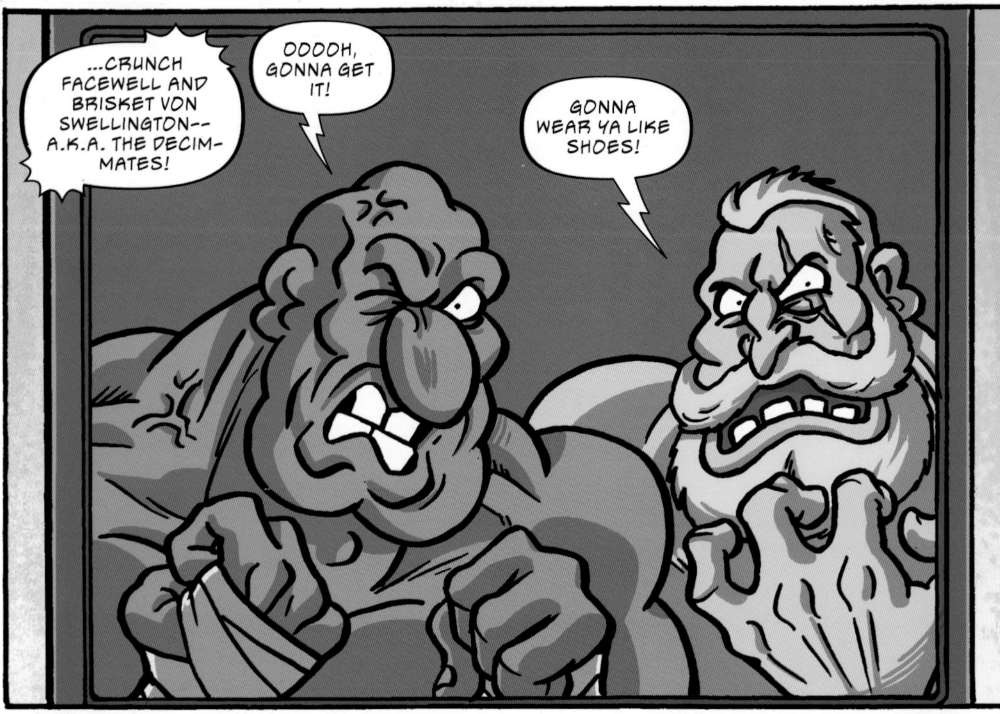
...CRUNCH FACEWELL AND BRISKET VON SWELLINGTON-- A.K.A. THE DECIMATES!
OOOOH, GONNA GET IT!
GONNA WEAR YA LIKE SHOES!

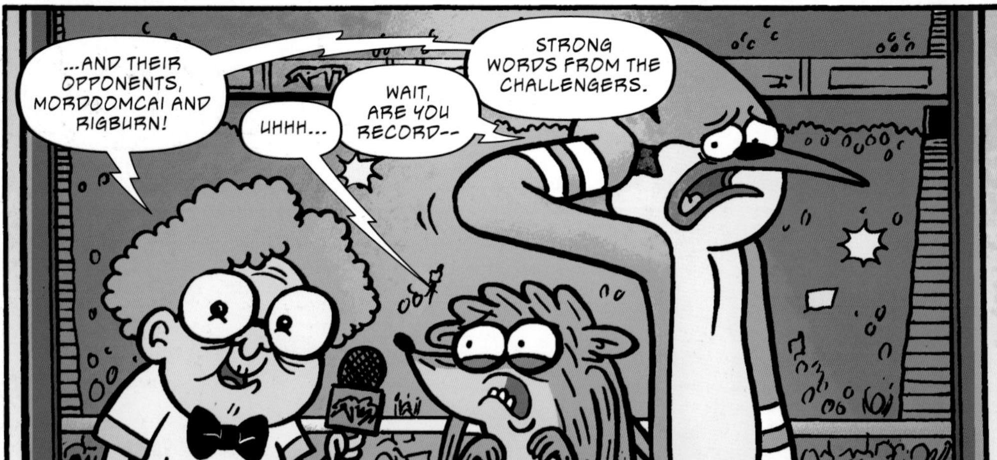
...AND THEIR OPPONENTS, MORDOOMCAI AND RIGBURN!
STRONG WORDS FROM THE CHALLENGERS.
UHHH...
WAIT, ARE YOU RECORD--

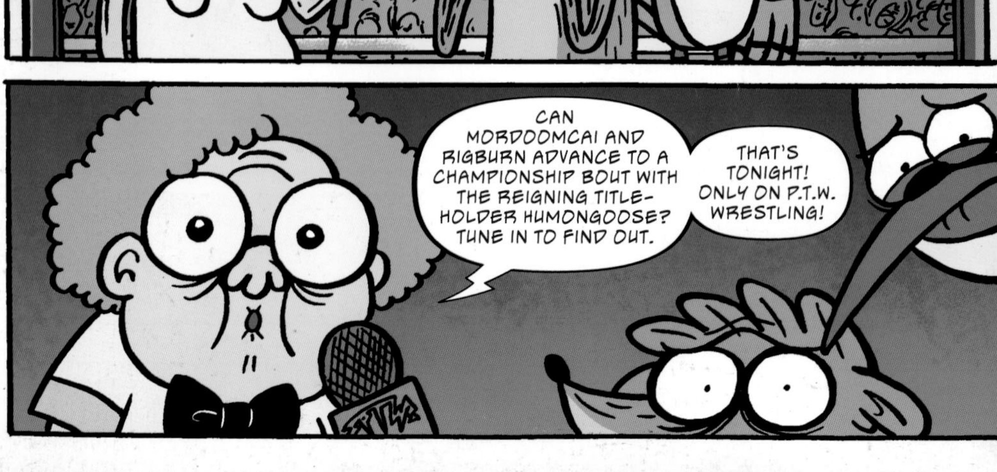
CAN MORDOOMCAI AND RIGBURN ADVANCE TO A CHAMPIONSHIP BOUT WITH THE REIGNING TITLE-HOLDER HUMONGOOSE? TUNE IN TO FIND OUT.
THAT'S TONIGHT! ONLY ON P.T.W. WRESTLING!

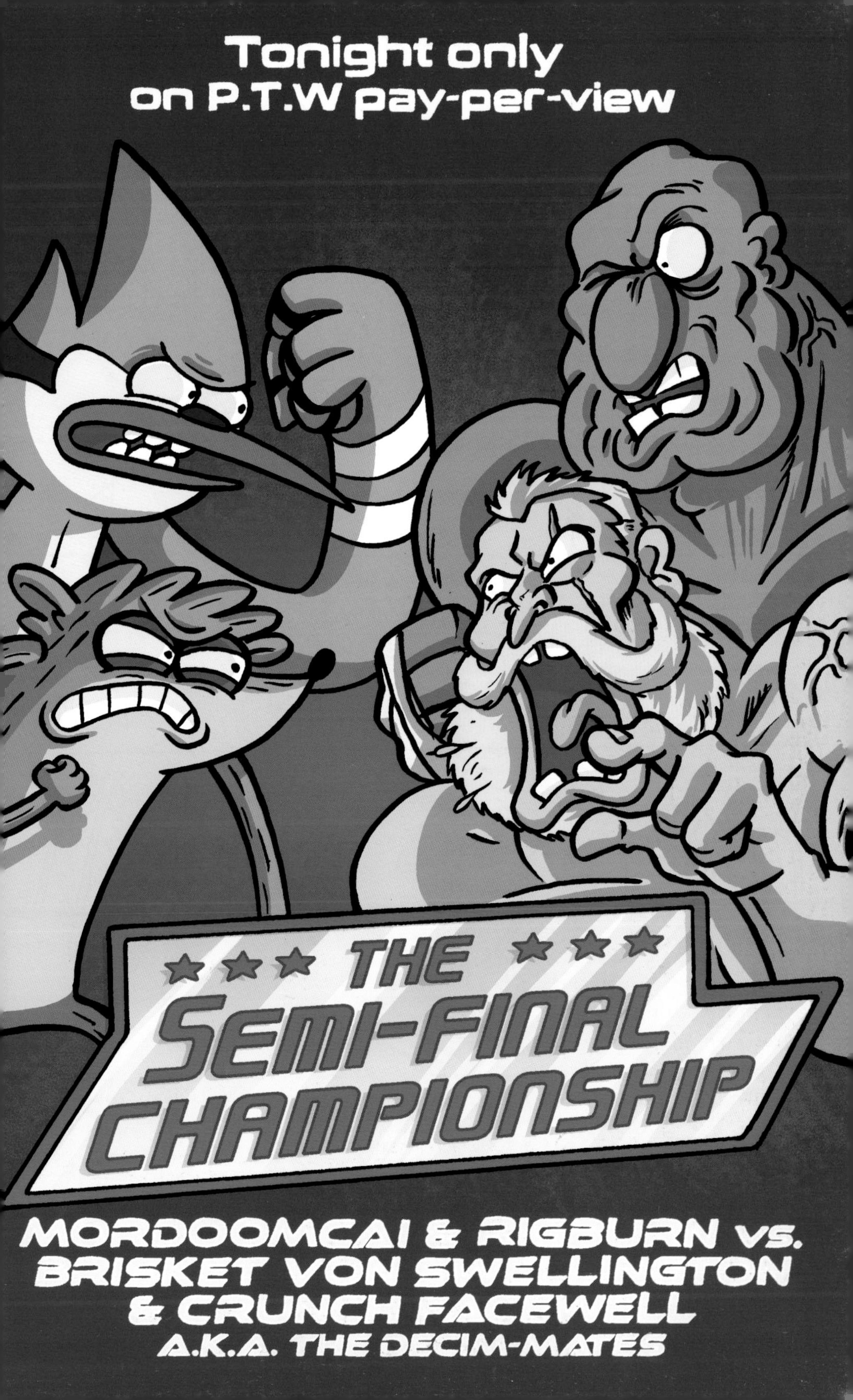
Tonight only
on P.T.W pay-per-view
THE
SEMI-FINAL
CHAMPIONSHIP
MORDOOMCAI & RIGBURN vs.
BRISKET VON SWELLINGTON
& CRUNCH FACEWELL
A.K.A. THE DECIM-MATES

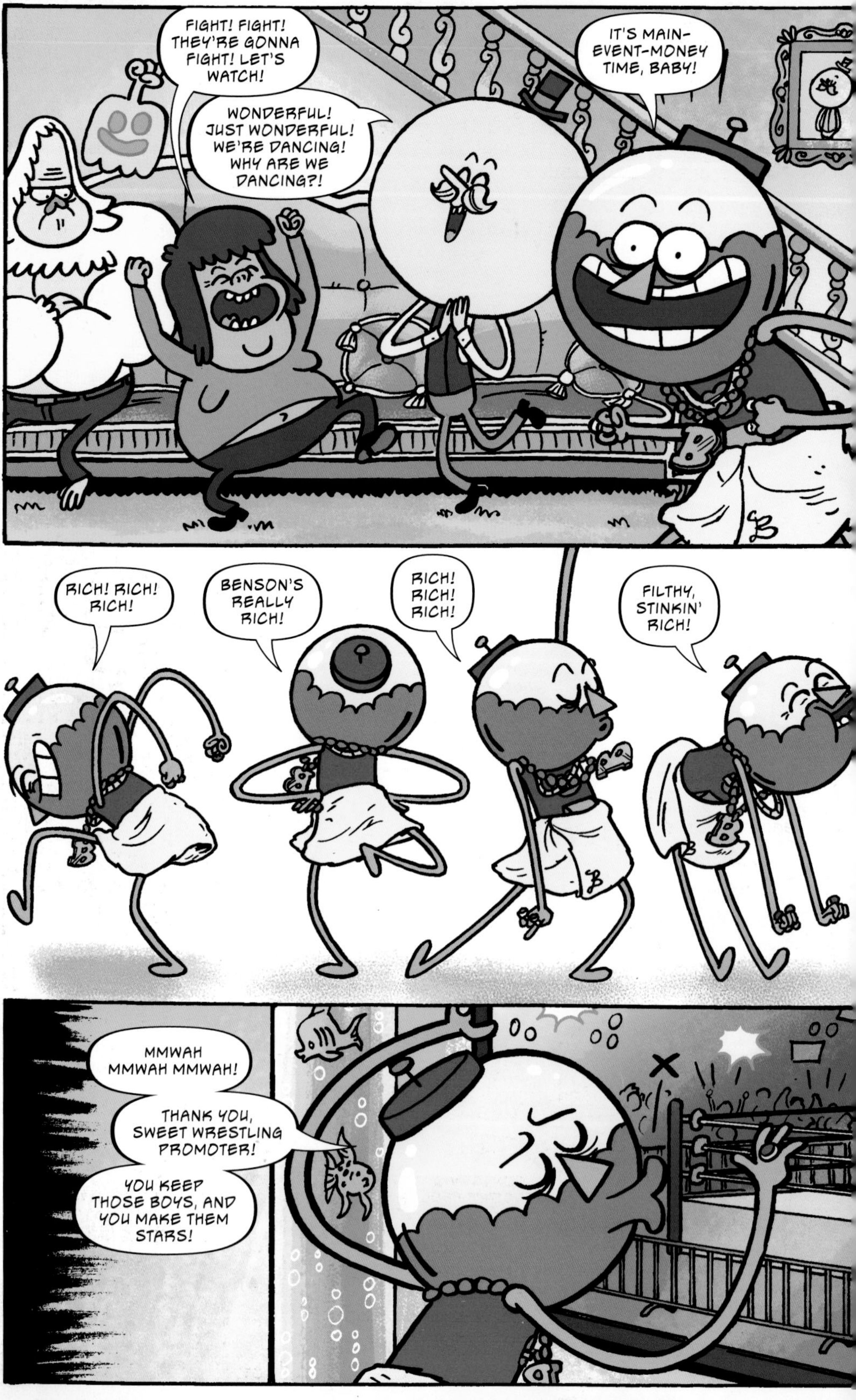
FIGHT! FIGHT! THEY'RE GONNA FIGHT! LET'S WATCH!
WONDERFUL! JUST WONDERFUL! WE'RE DANCING! WHY ARE WE DANCING?!
IT'S MAIN-EVENT-MONEY TIME, BABY!
RICH! RICH! RICH!
BENSON'S REALLY RICH!
RICH! RICH! RICH!
FILTHY, STINKIN' RICH!
MMWAH MMWAH MMWAH!
THANK YOU, SWEET WRESTLING PROMOTER!
YOU KEEP THOSE BOYS, AND YOU MAKE THEM STARS!

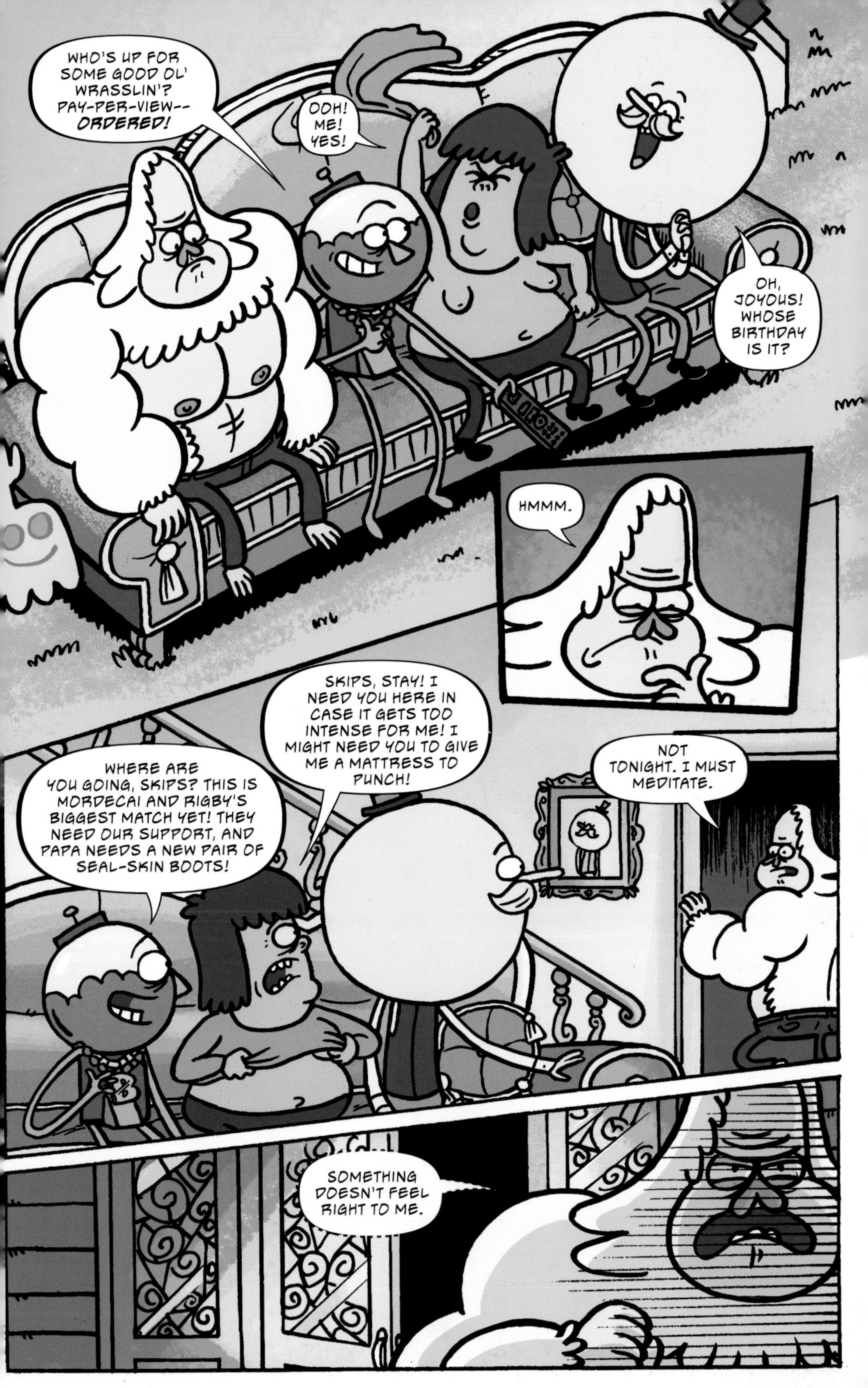
WHO'S UP FOR SOME GOOD OL' WRASSLIN'? PAY-PER-VIEW--ORDERED!
OOH! ME! YES!
OH, JOYOUS! WHOSE BIRTHDAY IS IT?
HMMM.
WHERE ARE YOU GOING, SKIPS? THIS IS MORDECAI AND RIGBY'S BIGGEST MATCH YET! THEY NEED OUR SUPPORT, AND PAPA NEEDS A NEW PAIR OF SEAL-SKIN BOOTS!
SKIPS, STAY! I NEED YOU HERE IN CASE IT GETS TOO INTENSE FOR ME! I MIGHT NEED YOU TO GIVE ME A MATTRESS TO PUNCH!
NOT TONIGHT. I MUST MEDITATE.
SOMETHING DOESN'T FEEL RIGHT TO ME.

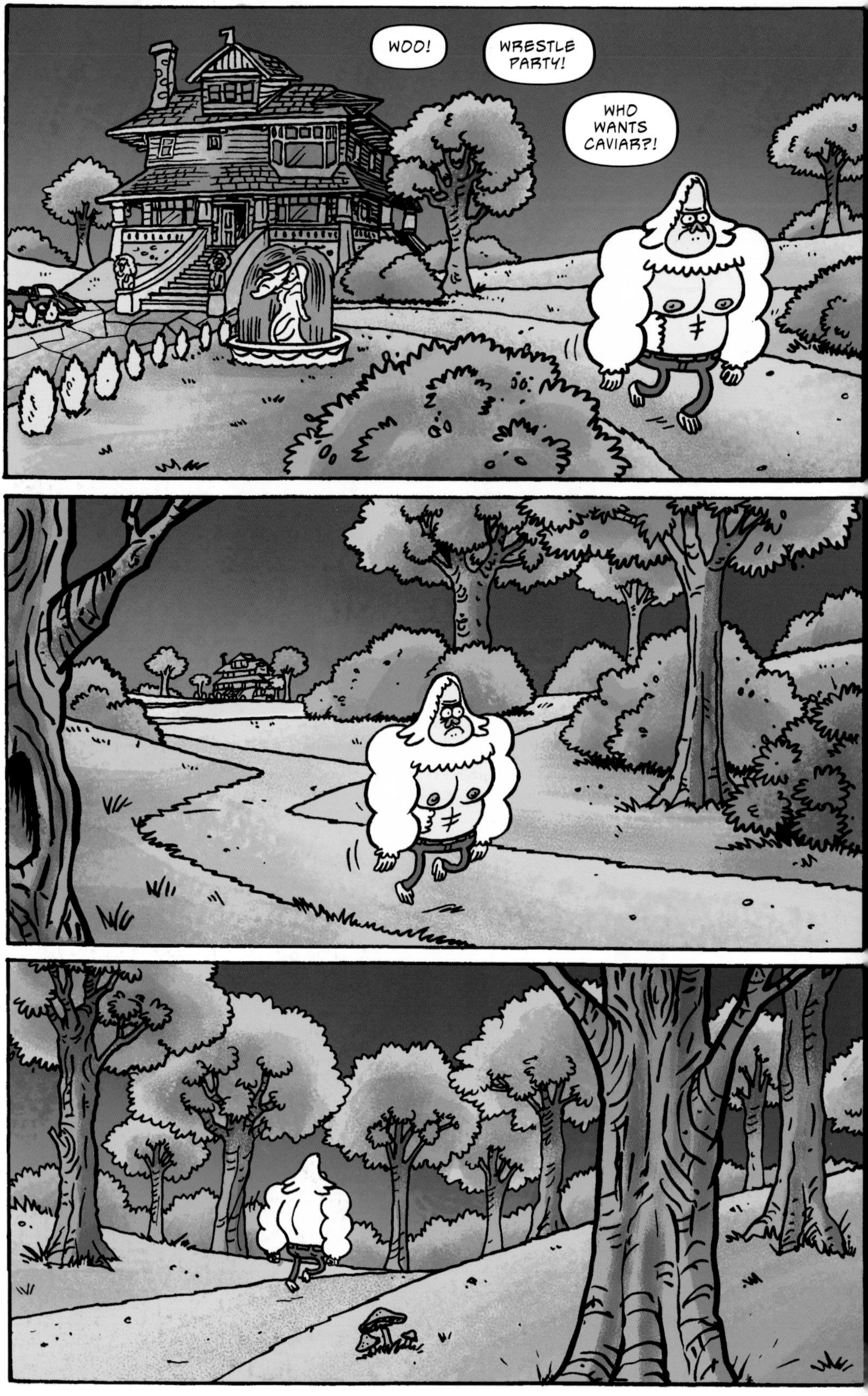
WOO!
WRESTLE PARTY!
WHO WANTS CAVIAR?!

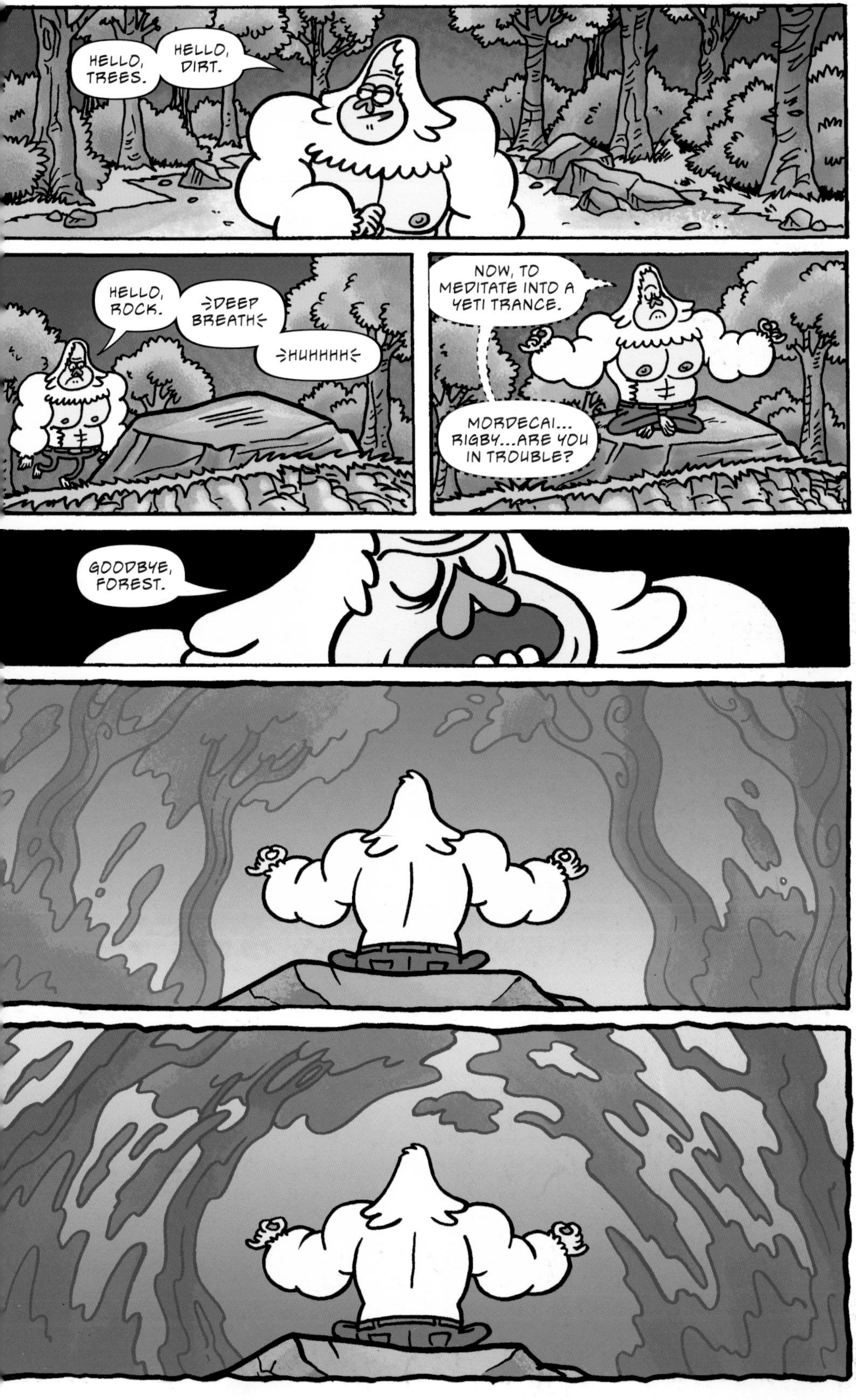
HELLO, TREES.
HELLO, DIRT.
HELLO, ROCK.
DEEP BREATH
HUHHHH
NOW, TO MEDITATE INTO A YETI TRANCE.
MORDECAI... RIGBY...ARE YOU IN TROUBLE?
GOODBYE, FOREST.

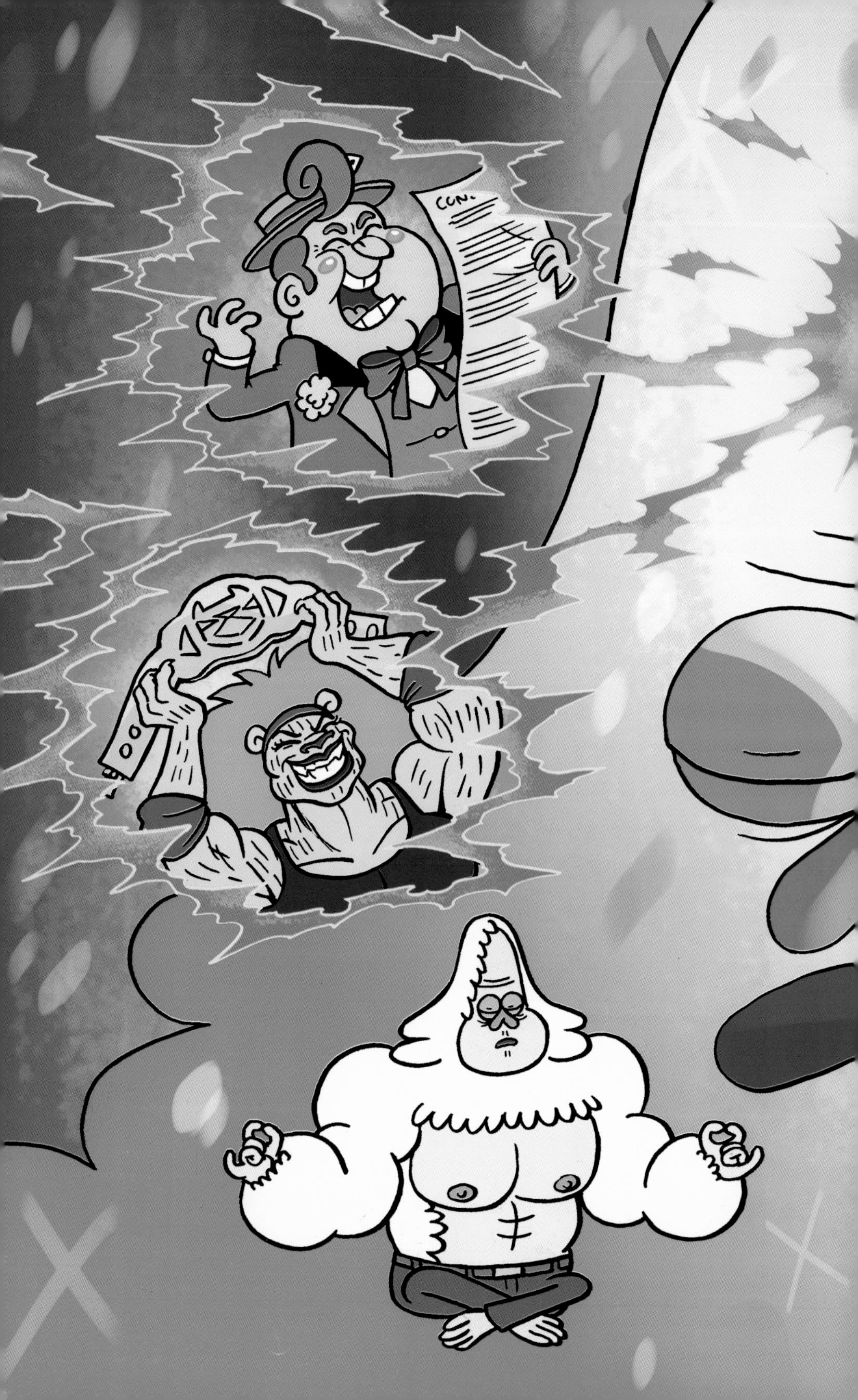

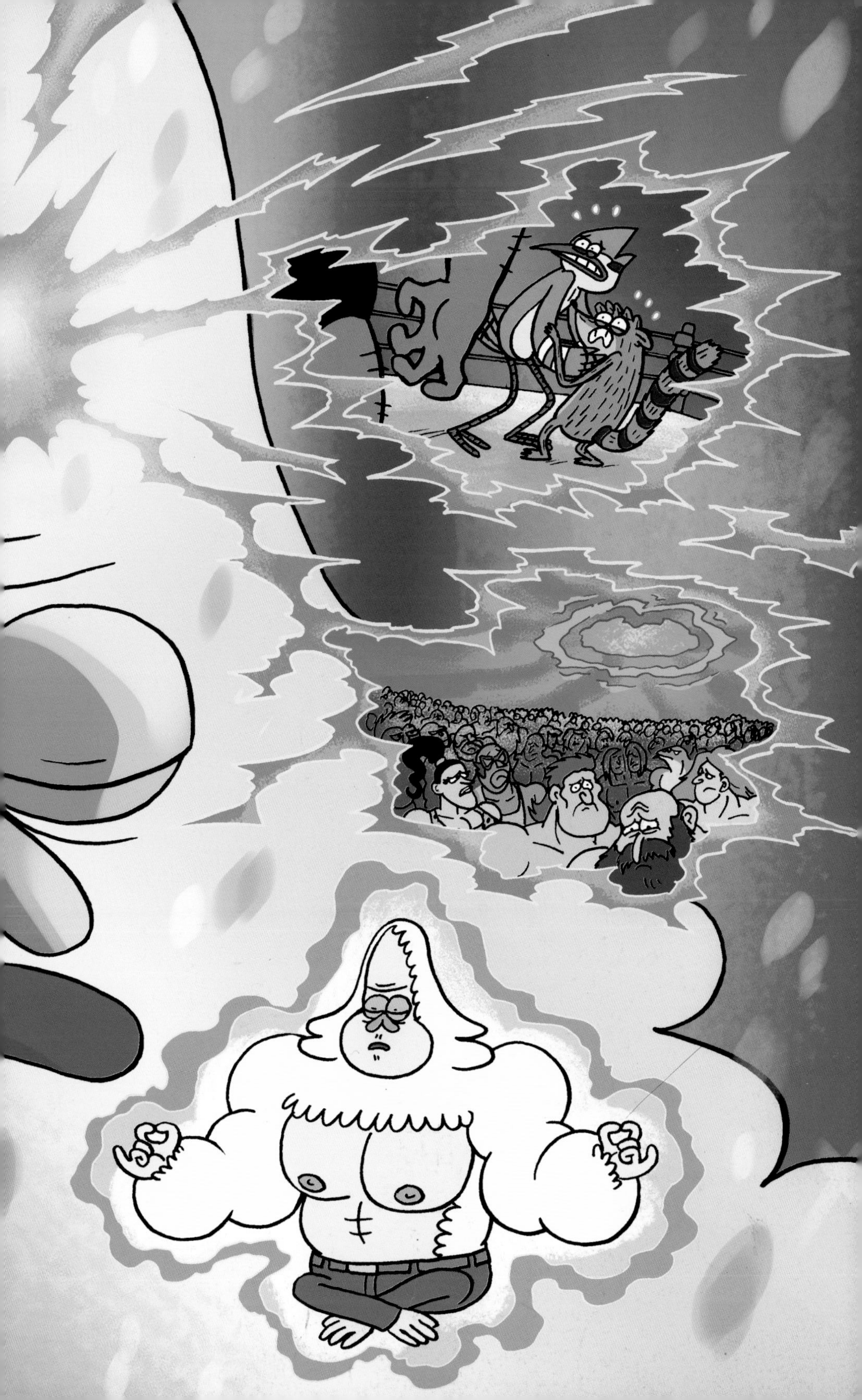

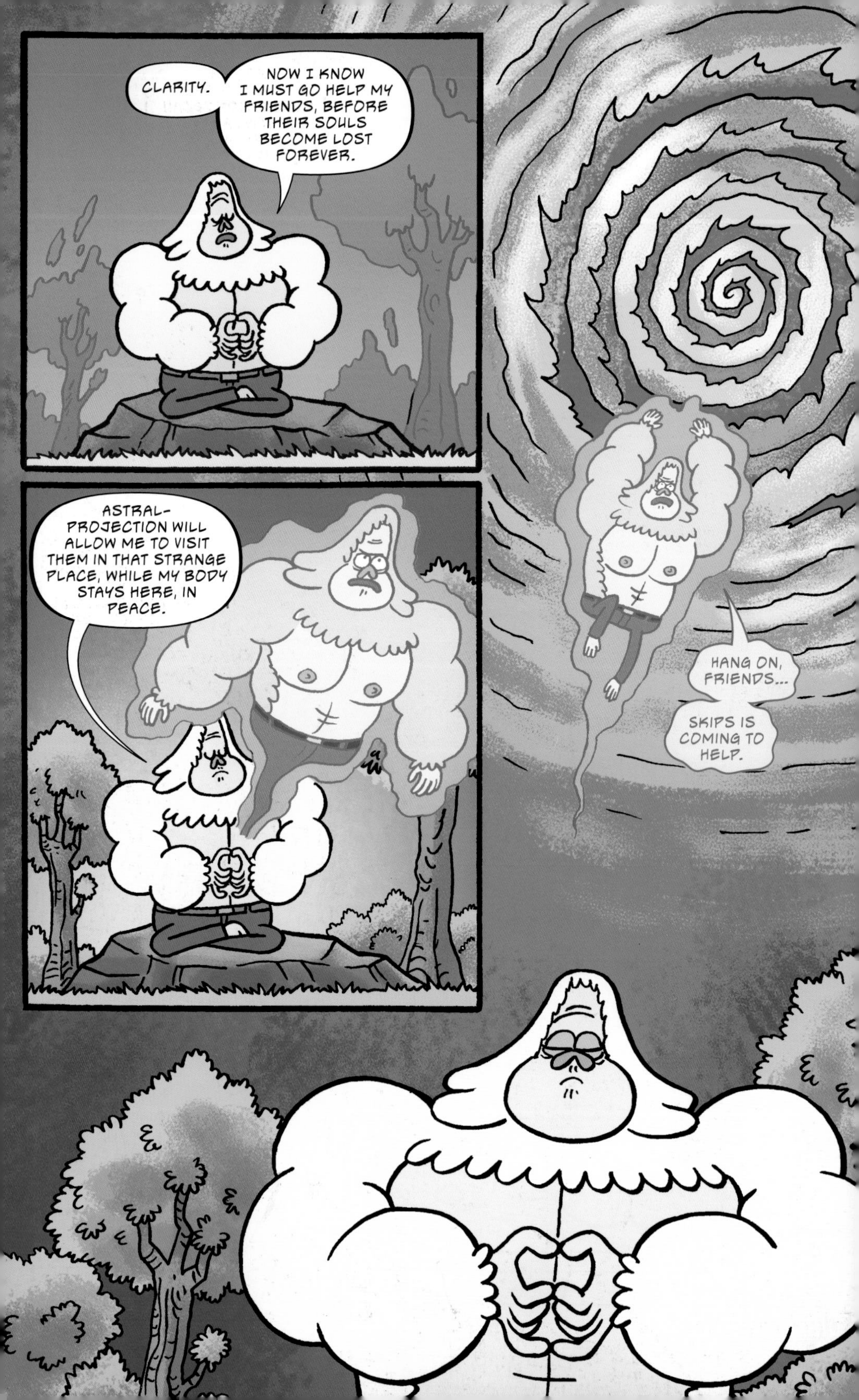
CLARITY.
NOW I KNOW I MUST GO HELP MY FRIENDS, BEFORE THEIR SOULS BECOME LOST FOREVER.
ASTRAL-PROJECTION WILL ALLOW ME TO VISIT THEM IN THAT STRANGE PLACE, WHILE MY BODY STAYS HERE, IN PEACE.
HANG ON, FRIENDS...
SKIPS IS COMING TO HELP.

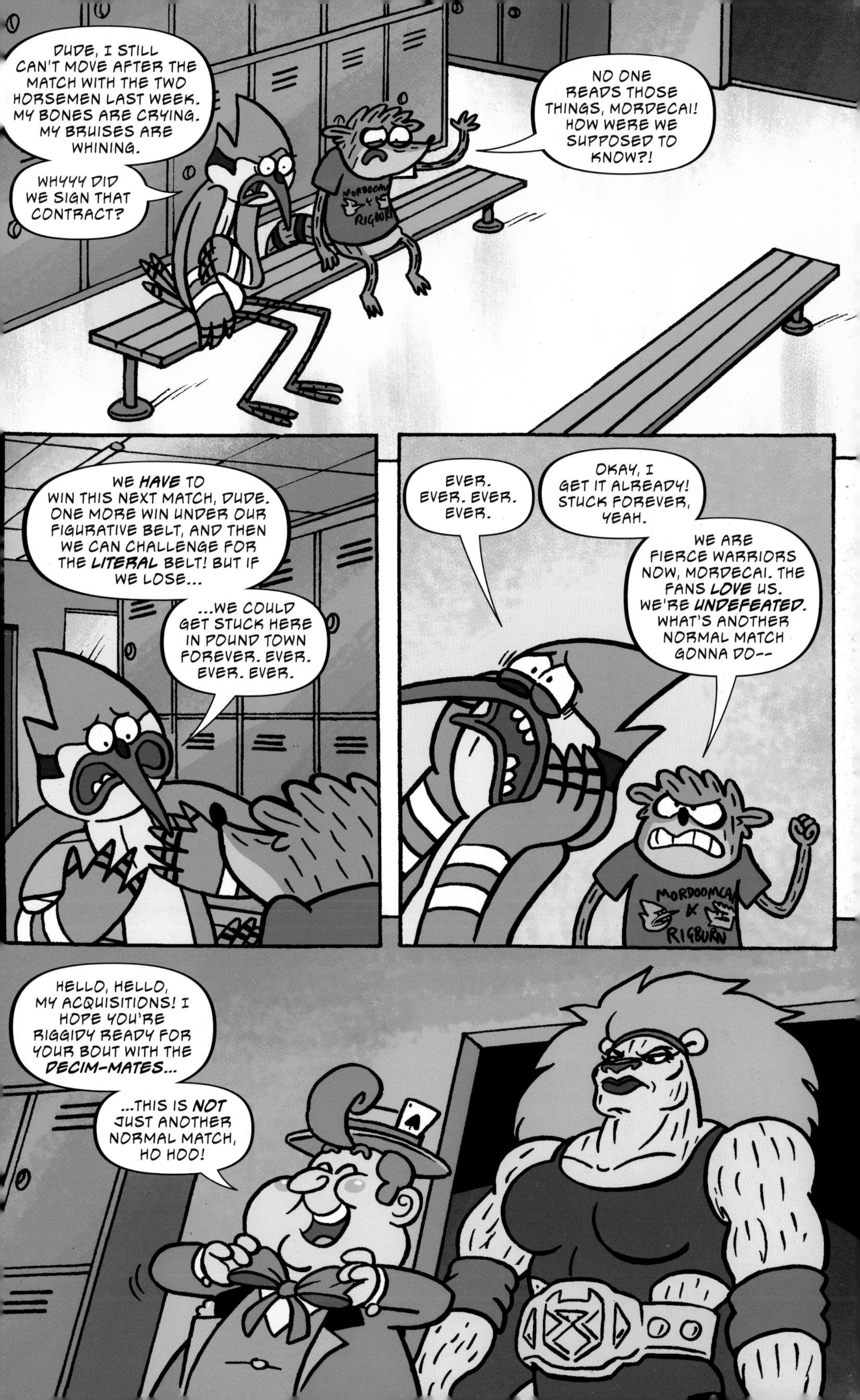
DUDE, I STILL CAN'T MOVE AFTER THE MATCH WITH THE TWO HORSEMEN LAST WEEK. MY BONES ARE CRYING. MY BRUISES ARE WHINING.
WHYYY DID WE SIGN THAT CONTRACT?
NO ONE READS THOSE THINGS, MORDECAI! HOW WERE WE SUPPOSED TO KNOW?!
MORDOOMCAI + RIGBURN
WE HAVE TO WIN THIS NEXT MATCH, DUDE. ONE MORE WIN UNDER OUR FIGURATIVE BELT, AND THEN WE CAN CHALLENGE FOR THE LITERAL BELT! BUT IF WE LOSE...
...WE COULD GET STUCK HERE IN POUND TOWN FOREVER. EVER. EVER. EVER.
EVER. EVER. EVER. EVER.
OKAY, I GET IT ALREADY! STUCK FOREVER, YEAH.
WE ARE FIERCE WARRIORS NOW, MORDECAI. THE FANS LOVE US. WE'RE UNDEFEATED. WHAT'S ANOTHER NORMAL MATCH GONNA DO--
MORDOOMCAI & RIGBURN
HELLO, HELLO, MY ACQUISITIONS! I HOPE YOU'RE BIGGIDY READY FOR YOUR BOUT WITH THE DECIM-MATES...
...THIS IS NOT JUST ANOTHER NORMAL MATCH, HO HOO!

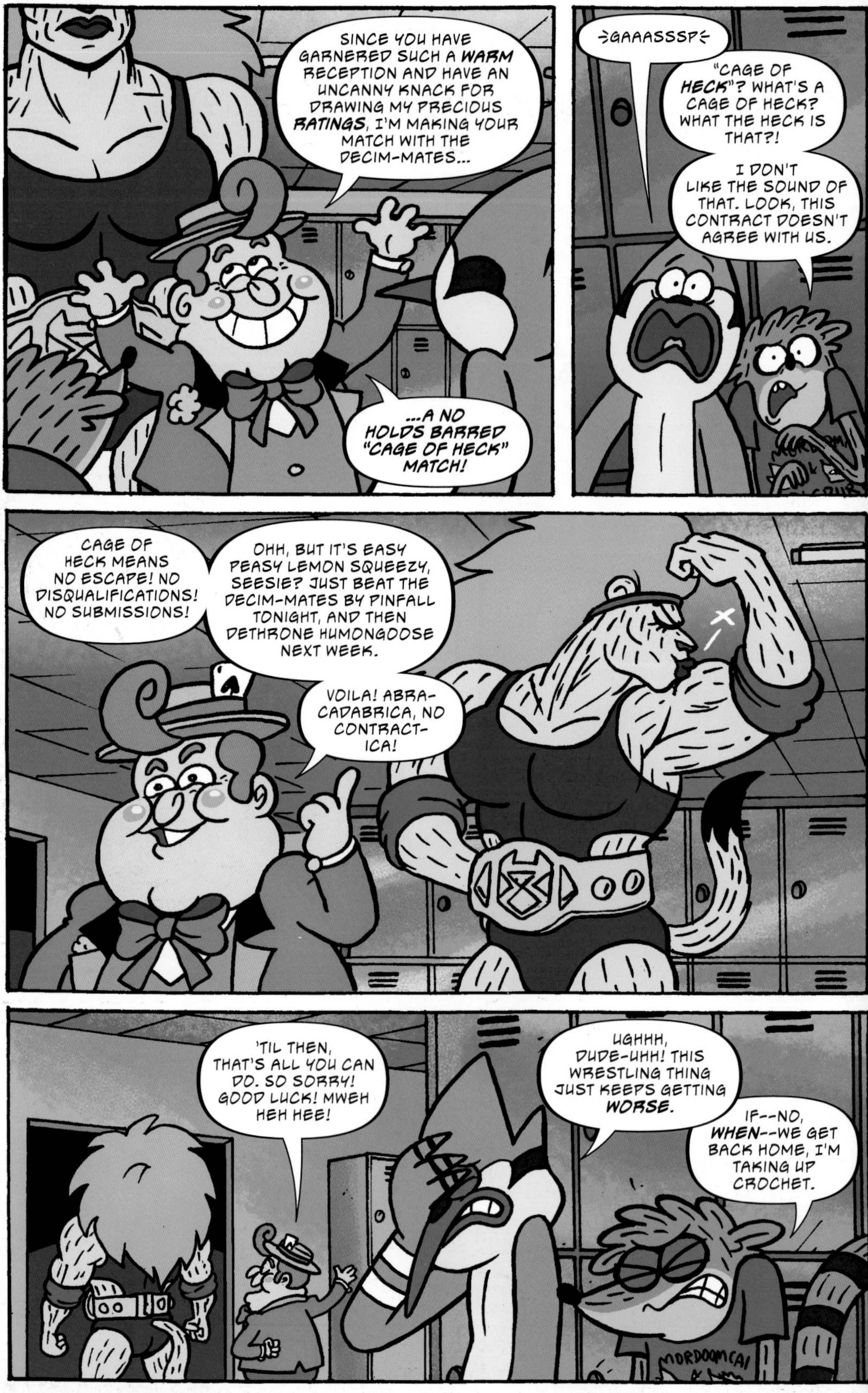
SINCE YOU HAVE GARNERED SUCH A WARM RECEPTION AND HAVE AN UNCANNY KNACK FOR DRAWING MY PRECIOUS RATINGS, I'M MAKING YOUR MATCH WITH THE DECIM-MATES...
...A NO HOLDS BARRED "CAGE OF HECK" MATCH!
GAAAASSSP
"CAGE OF HECK"? WHAT'S A CAGE OF HECK? WHAT THE HECK IS THAT?!
I DON'T LIKE THE SOUND OF THAT. LOOK, THIS CONTRACT DOESN'T AGREE WITH US.
CAGE OF HECK MEANS NO ESCAPE! NO DISQUALIFICATIONS! NO SUBMISSIONS!
OHH, BUT IT'S EASY PEASY LEMON SQUEEZY, SEESIE? JUST BEAT THE DECIM-MATES BY PINFALL TONIGHT, AND THEN DETHRONE HUMONGOOSE NEXT WEEK.
VOILA! ABRA-CADABRICA, NO CONTRACT-ICA!
'TIL THEN, THAT'S ALL YOU CAN DO. SO SORRY! GOOD LUCK! MWEH HEH HEE!
UGHHH, DUDE-UHH! THIS WRESTLING THING JUST KEEPS GETTING WORSE.
IF--NO, WHEN--WE GET BACK HOME, I'M TAKING UP CROCHET.
MORDOOMCAI

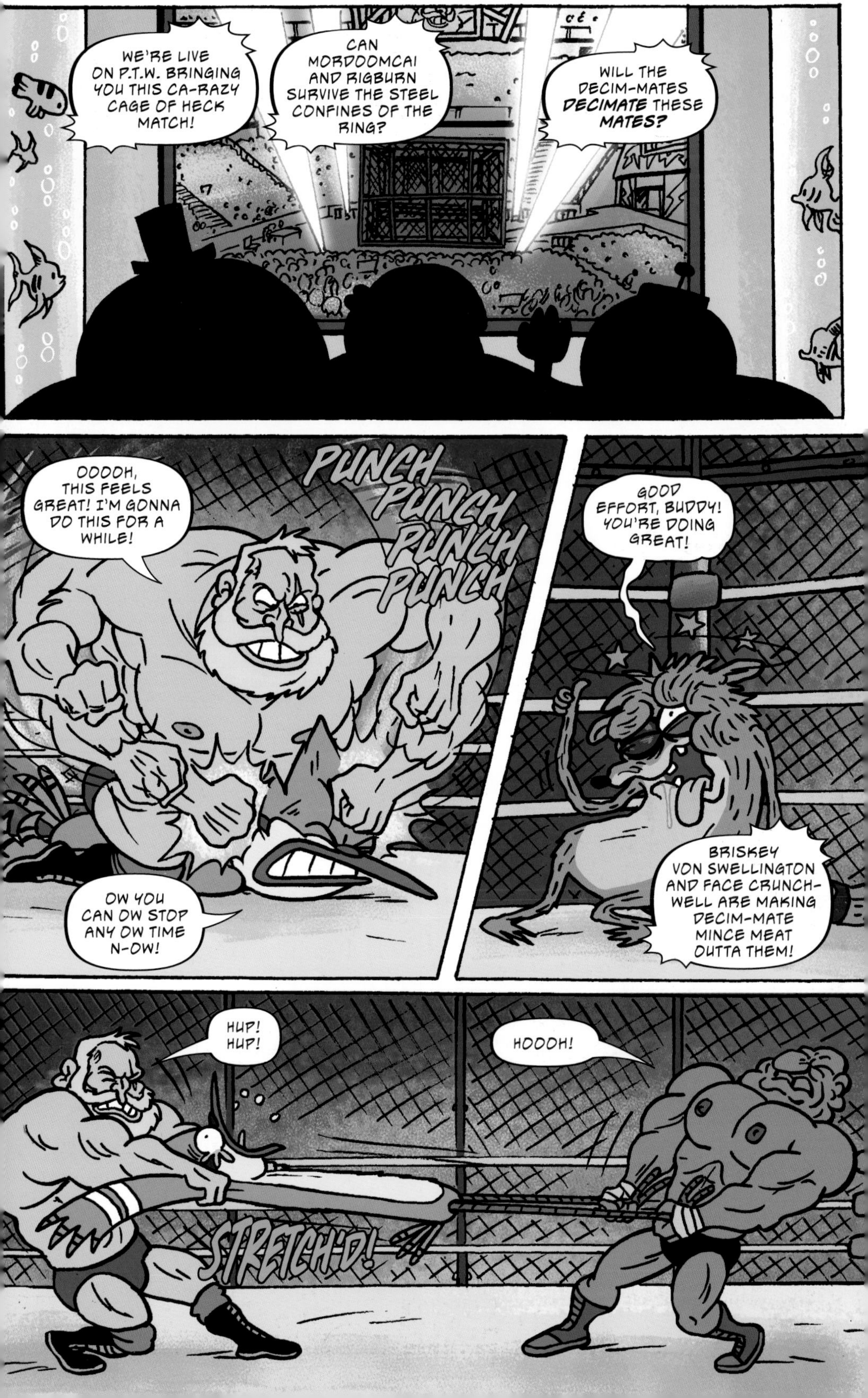
WE'RE LIVE ON P.T.W. BRINGING YOU THIS CA-RAZY CAGE OF HECK MATCH!
CAN MORDOOMCAI AND RIGBURN SURVIVE THE STEEL CONFINES OF THE RING?
WILL THE DECIM-MATES *DECIMATE* THESE *MATES?*
OOOOH, THIS FEELS GREAT! I'M GONNA DO THIS FOR A WHILE!
PUNCH PUNCH PUNCH PUNCH
OW YOU CAN OW STOP ANY OW TIME N-OW!
GOOD EFFORT, BUDDY! YOU'RE DOING GREAT!
BRISKEY VON SWELLINGTON AND FACE CRUNCH-WELL ARE MAKING DECIM-MATE MINCE MEAT OUTTA THEM!
HUP! HUP!
HOOOH!
STRETCH'D!

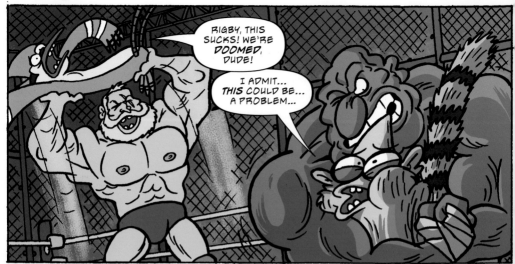

RIGBY, THIS SUCKS! WE'RE *DOOMED,* DUDE!

I ADMIT... *THIS* COULD BE... A PROBLEM...

NICE POUNDIN', MATE!

GOOD HURTIN', MATE!

WAIT, THAT'S IT...WE NEED TO BE A BETTER *TEAM.*

OOH, WORK *TOGETHER* TO OVERCOME ADVERSITY? *LAME.*

NO, RIGBY. THINK ABOUT IT. THE DECIM-MATES ARE A KICK-BUTT TEAM. MAYBE WE JUST NEED TO GET ON THE SAME BRAIN-TRAIN THEN *WE'LL* BE THE BUTT-KICKERS.

MORDECAI, YOU'VE SAID SOME *CRAZY* THINGS IN YOUR TIME...BUT I'M ALSO CONCUSSED AND SEEING TWO OF YOU.

FRIEND'D!

OOOH TEAM WORRRK!

OOOH OOOH OOOH!

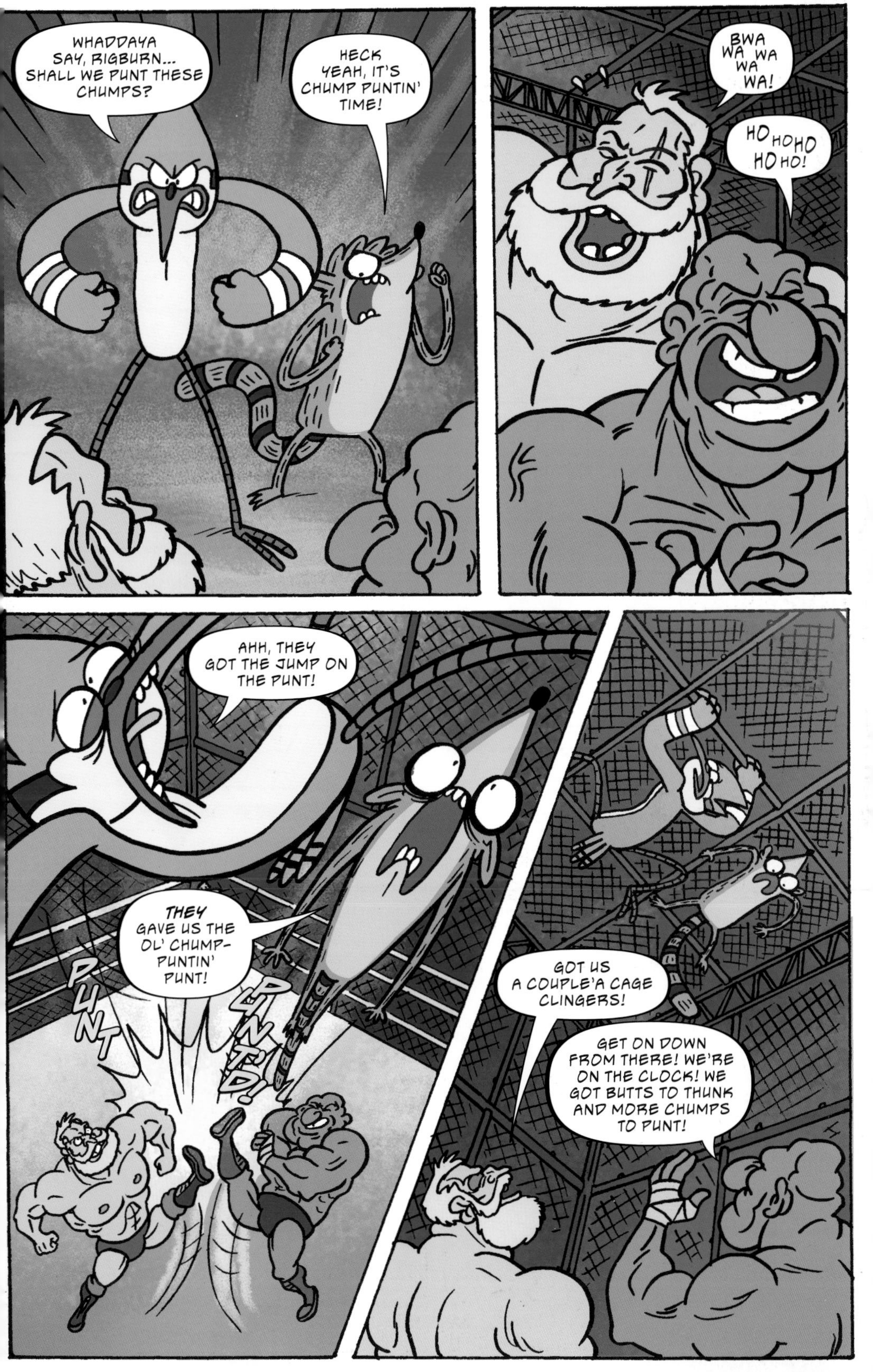
WHADDAYA SAY, RIGBURN... SHALL WE PUNT THESE CHUMPS?
HECK YEAH, IT'S CHUMP PUNTIN' TIME!
BWA WA WA WA WA!
HO HO HO HO HO!
AHH, THEY GOT THE JUMP ON THE PUNT!
THEY GAVE US THE OL' CHUMP-PUNTIN' PUNT!
PUNT
PUNT'D!
GOT US A COUPLE'A CAGE CLINGERS!
GET ON DOWN FROM THERE! WE'RE ON THE CLOCK! WE GOT BUTTS TO THUNK AND MORE CHUMPS TO PUNT!

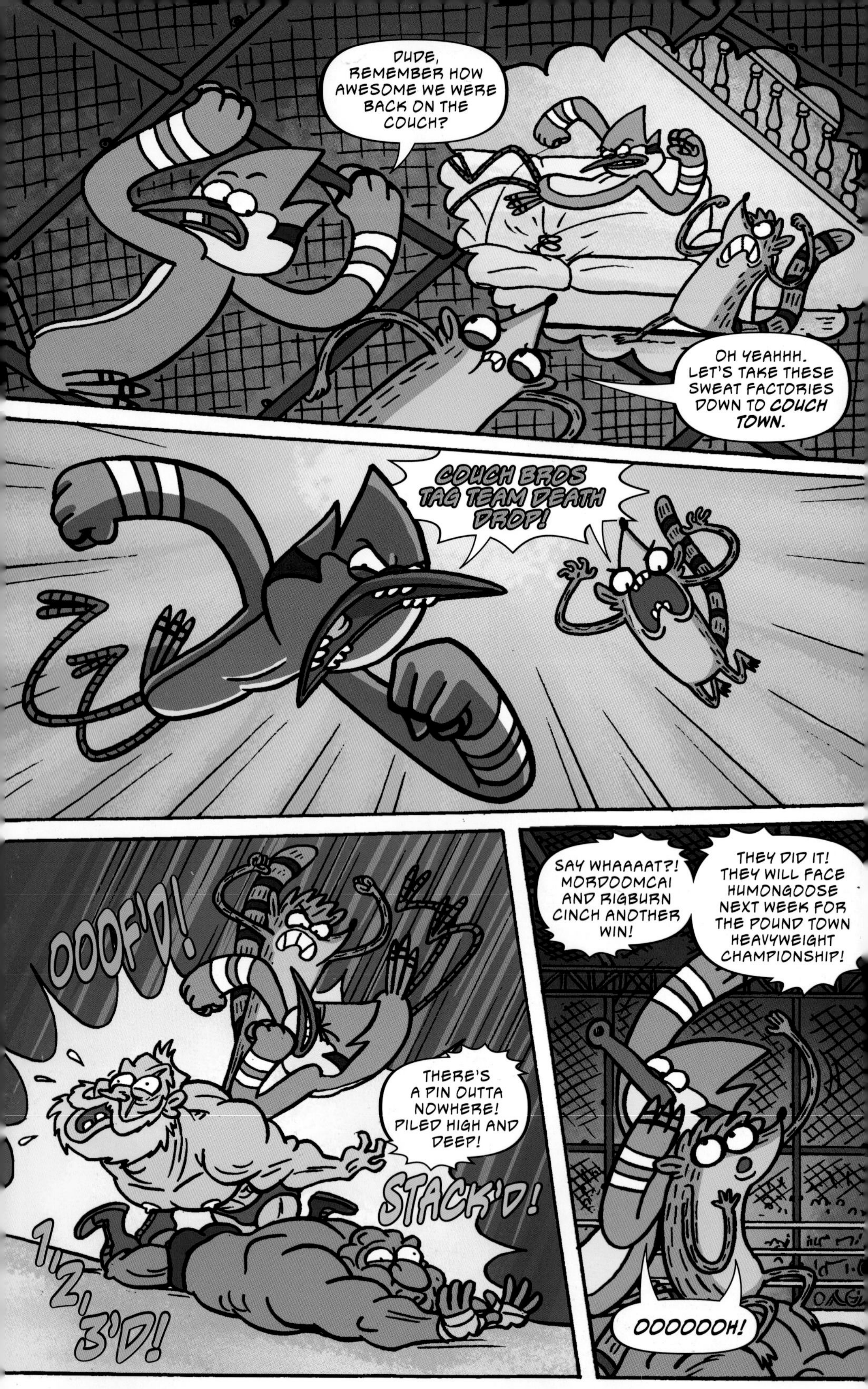
DUDE, REMEMBER HOW AWESOME WE WERE BACK ON THE COUCH?
OH YEAHHH. LET'S TAKE THESE SWEAT FACTORIES DOWN TO COUCH TOWN.
COUCH BROS TAG TEAM DEATH DROP!
OOOF'D!
THERE'S A PIN OUTTA NOWHERE! PILED HIGH AND DEEP!
STACK'D!
1, 2, 3'D!
SAY WHAAAAT?! MORDOOMCAI AND RIGBURN CINCH ANOTHER WIN!
THEY DID IT! THEY WILL FACE HUMONGOOSE NEXT WEEK FOR THE POUND TOWN HEAVYWEIGHT CHAMPIONSHIP!
OOOOOOH!

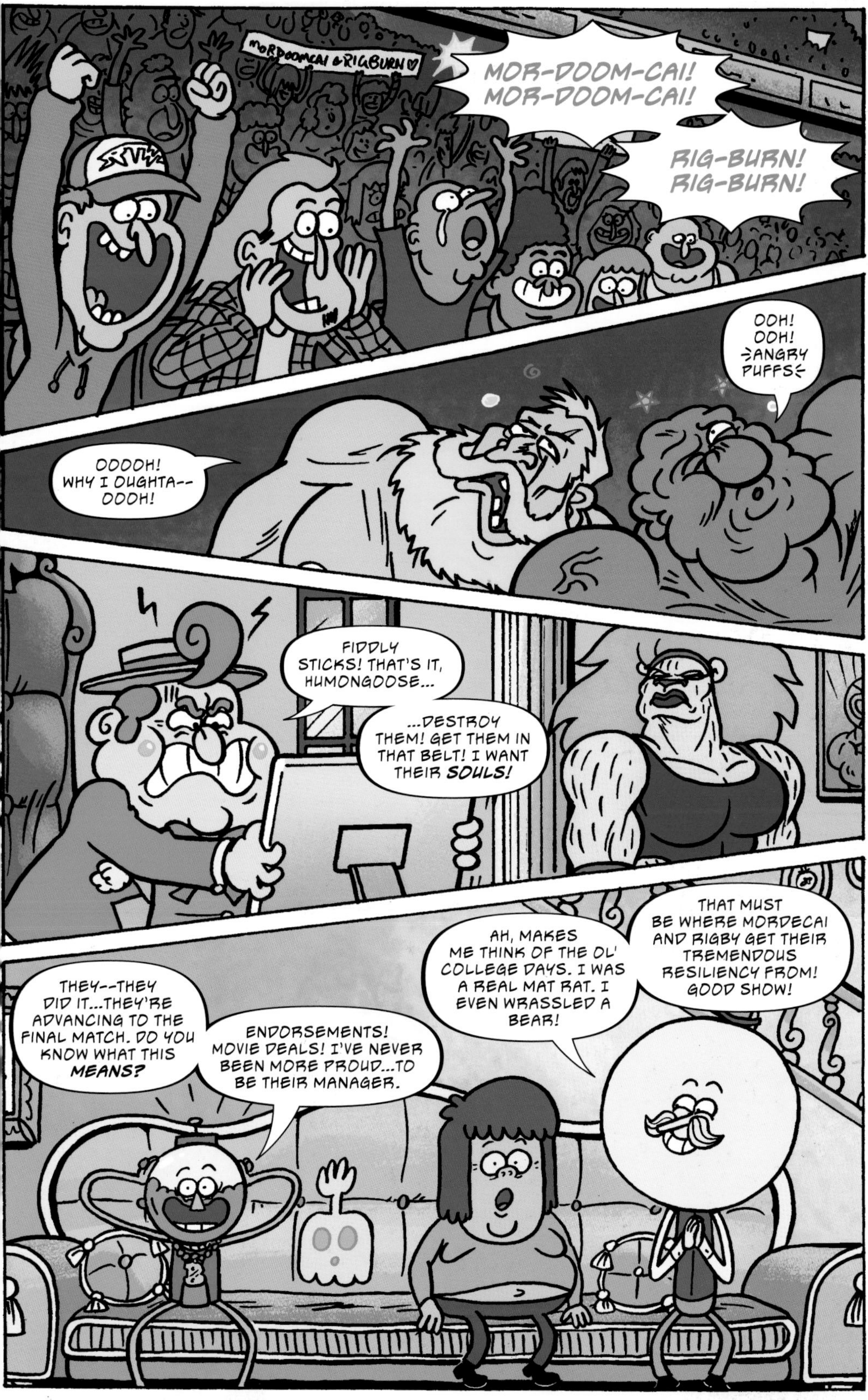
MORDOOMCAI & RIGBURN ♥
MOR-DOOM-CAI! MOR-DOOM-CAI!
RIG-BURN! RIG-BURN!
OOH! OOH! ⪢ANGRY PUFFS⪡
OOOOH! WHY I OUGHTA-- OOOH!
FIDDLY STICKS! THAT'S IT, HUMONGOOSE...
...DESTROY THEM! GET THEM IN THAT BELT! I WANT THEIR SOULS!
THEY--THEY DID IT...THEY'RE ADVANCING TO THE FINAL MATCH. DO YOU KNOW WHAT THIS MEANS?
ENDORSEMENTS! MOVIE DEALS! I'VE NEVER BEEN MORE PROUD...TO BE THEIR MANAGER.
AH, MAKES ME THINK OF THE OL' COLLEGE DAYS. I WAS A REAL MAT RAT. I EVEN WRASSLED A BEAR!
THAT MUST BE WHERE MORDECAI AND RIGBY GET THEIR TREMENDOUS RESILIENCY FROM! GOOD SHOW!

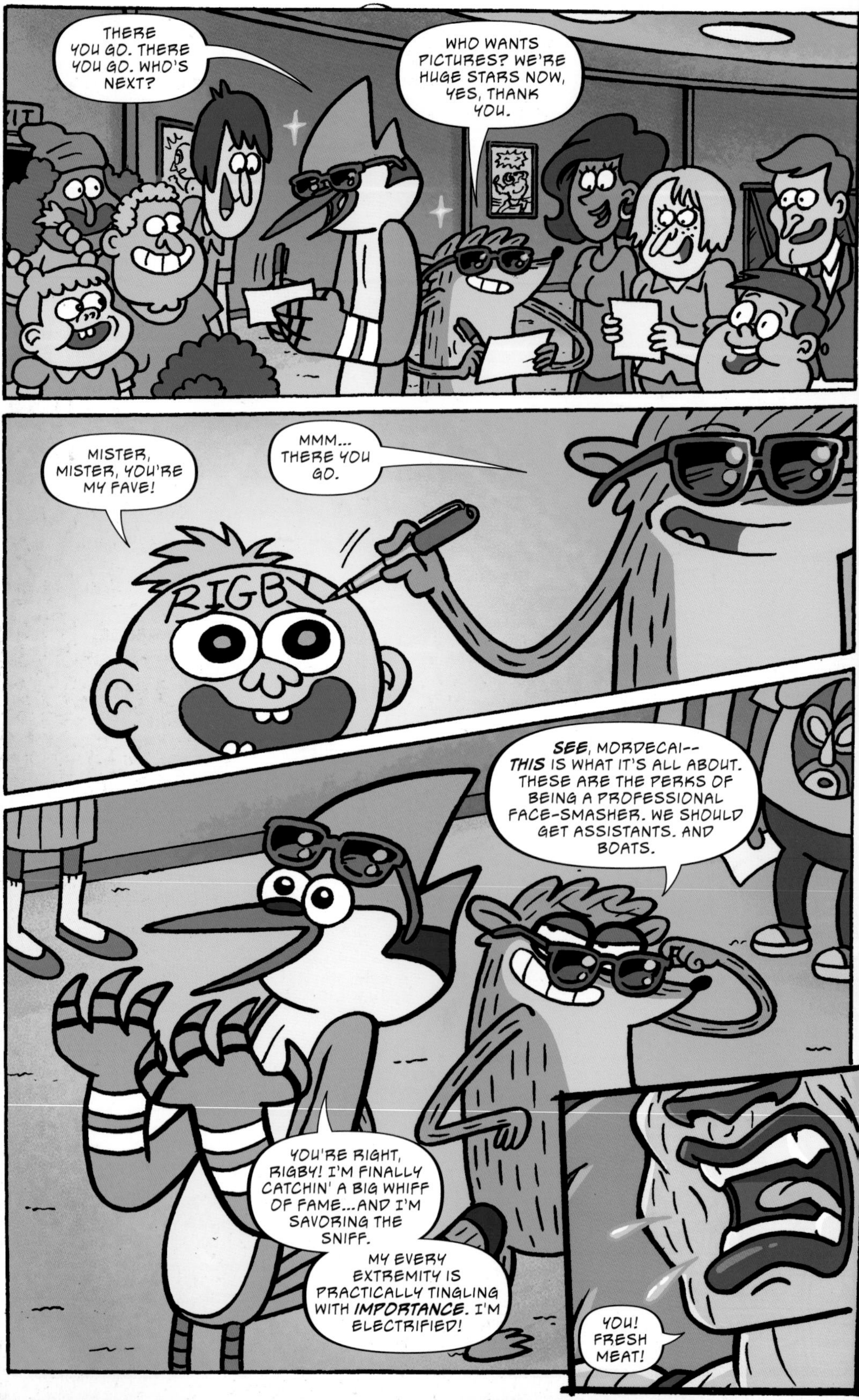
THERE YOU GO. THERE YOU GO. WHO'S NEXT?
WHO WANTS PICTURES? WE'RE HUGE STARS NOW, YES, THANK YOU.
MISTER, MISTER, YOU'RE MY FAVE!
MMM... THERE YOU GO.
RIGB
SEE, MORDECAI-- **THIS** IS WHAT IT'S ALL ABOUT. THESE ARE THE PERKS OF BEING A PROFESSIONAL FACE-SMASHER. WE SHOULD GET ASSISTANTS. AND BOATS.
YOU'RE RIGHT, RIGBY! I'M FINALLY CATCHIN' A BIG WHIFF OF FAME...AND I'M SAVORING THE SNIFF.
MY EVERY EXTREMITY IS PRACTICALLY TINGLING WITH **IMPORTANCE**. I'M ELECTRIFIED!
YOU! FRESH MEAT!

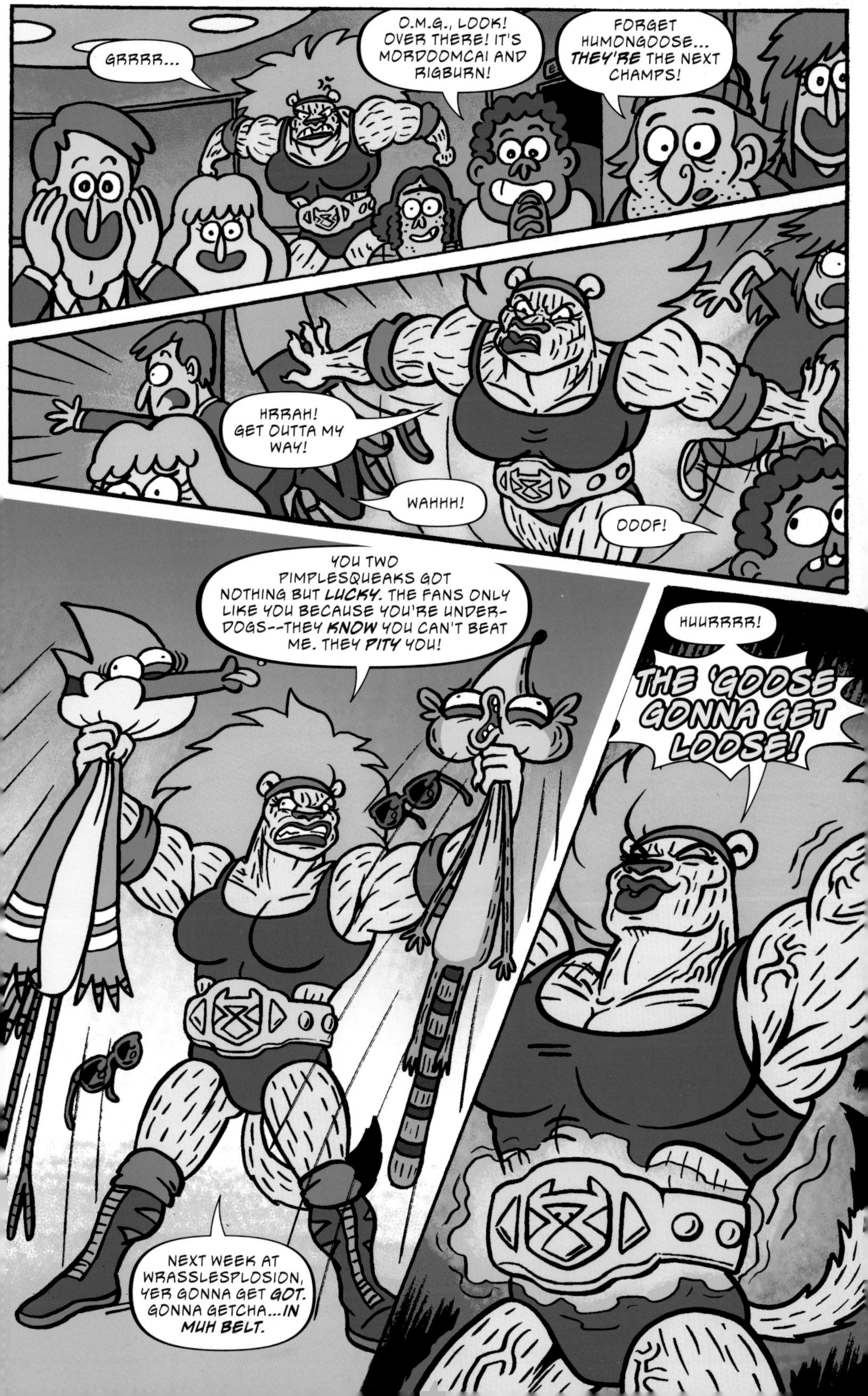
GRRRR...
O.M.G., LOOK! OVER THERE! IT'S MORDOOMCAI AND RIGBURN!
FORGET HUMONGOOSE... THEY'RE THE NEXT CHAMPS!
HRRAH! GET OUTTA MY WAY!
WAHHH!
OOOF!
YOU TWO PIMPLESQUEAKS GOT NOTHING BUT LUCKY. THE FANS ONLY LIKE YOU BECAUSE YOU'RE UNDER-DOGS--THEY KNOW YOU CAN'T BEAT ME. THEY PITY YOU!
NEXT WEEK AT WRASSLESPLOSION, YER GONNA GET GOT. GONNA GETCHA...IN MUH BELT.
HUURRRR!
THE 'GOOSE GONNA GET LOOSE!

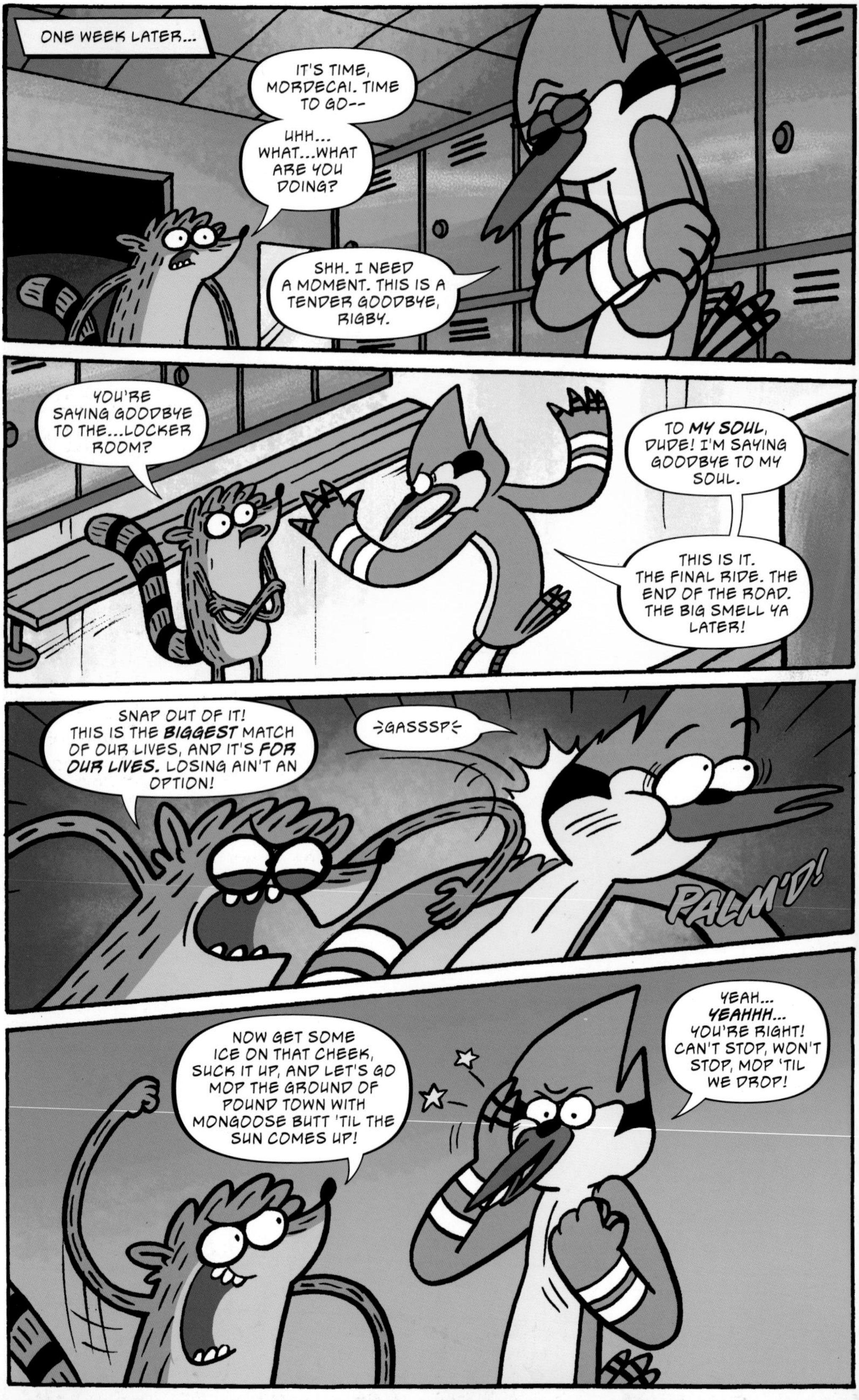
ONE WEEK LATER...
IT'S TIME, MORDECAI. TIME TO GO--
UHH... WHAT...WHAT ARE YOU DOING?
SHH. I NEED A MOMENT. THIS IS A TENDER GOODBYE, RIGBY.
YOU'RE SAYING GOODBYE TO THE...LOCKER ROOM?
TO MY SOUL, DUDE! I'M SAYING GOODBYE TO MY SOUL.
THIS IS IT. THE FINAL RIDE. THE END OF THE ROAD. THE BIG SMELL YA LATER!
SNAP OUT OF IT! THIS IS THE BIGGEST MATCH OF OUR LIVES, AND IT'S FOR OUR LIVES. LOSING AIN'T AN OPTION!
GASSSP
PALM'D!
NOW GET SOME ICE ON THAT CHEEK, SUCK IT UP, AND LET'S GO MOP THE GROUND OF POUND TOWN WITH MONGOOSE BUTT 'TIL THE SUN COMES UP!
YEAH... YEAHHH... YOU'RE RIGHT! CAN'T STOP, WON'T STOP, MOP 'TIL WE DROP!

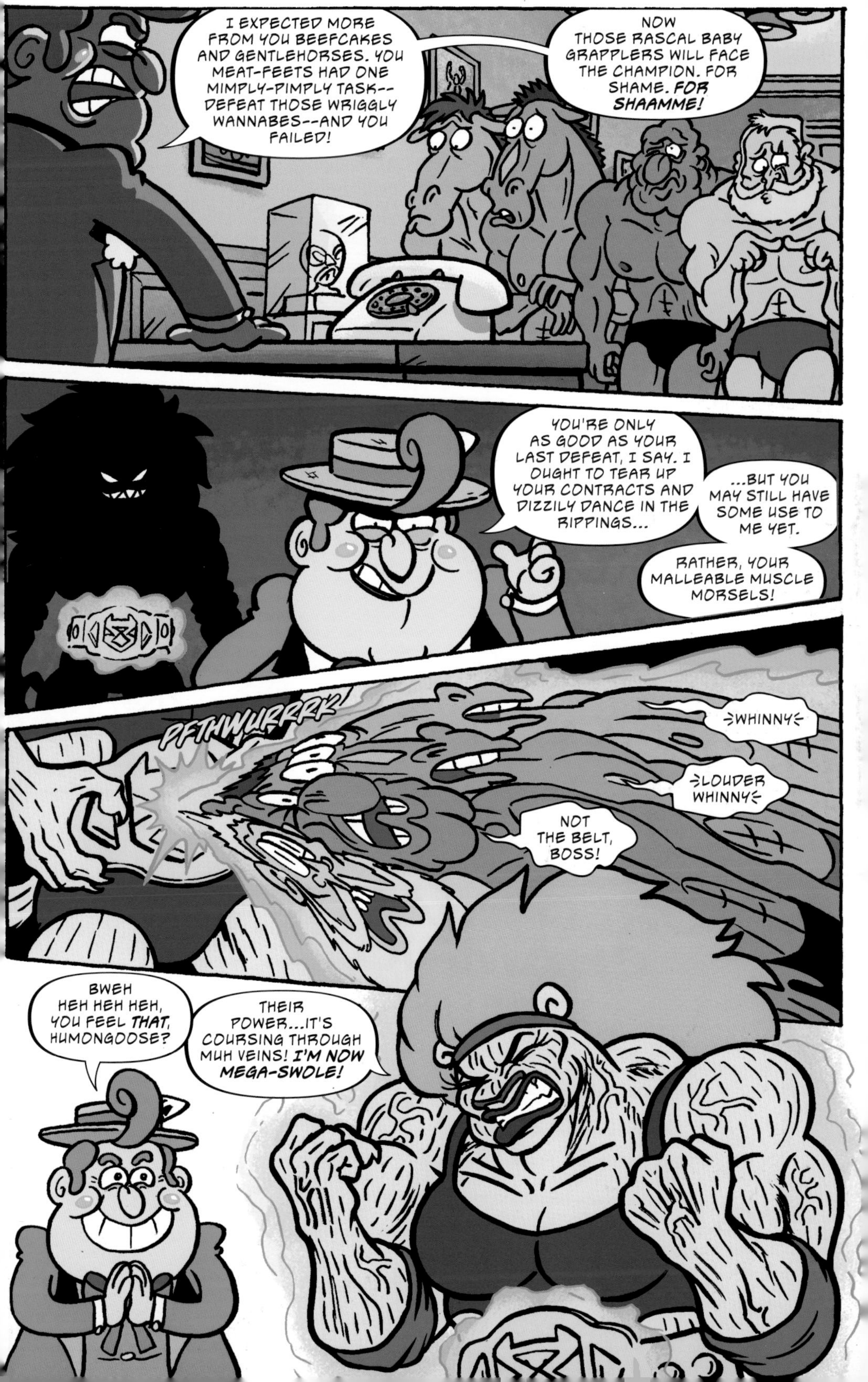
I EXPECTED MORE FROM YOU BEEFCAKES AND GENTLEHORSES. YOU MEAT-FEETS HAD ONE MIMPLY-PIMPLY TASK--DEFEAT THOSE WRIGGLY WANNABES--AND YOU FAILED!
NOW THOSE RASCAL BABY GRAPPLERS WILL FACE THE CHAMPION. FOR SHAME. *FOR SHAAMME!*
YOU'RE ONLY AS GOOD AS YOUR LAST DEFEAT, I SAY. I OUGHT TO TEAR UP YOUR CONTRACTS AND DIZZILY DANCE IN THE RIPPINGS...
...BUT YOU MAY STILL HAVE SOME USE TO ME YET.
RATHER, YOUR MALLEABLE MUSCLE MORSELS!
PFTHWURRRRK
WHINNY
LOUDER WHINNY
NOT THE BELT, BOSS!
BWEH HEH HEH HEH, YOU FEEL *THAT*, HUMONGOOSE?
THEIR POWER...IT'S COURSING THROUGH MUH VEINS! *I'M NOW MEGA-SWOLE!*

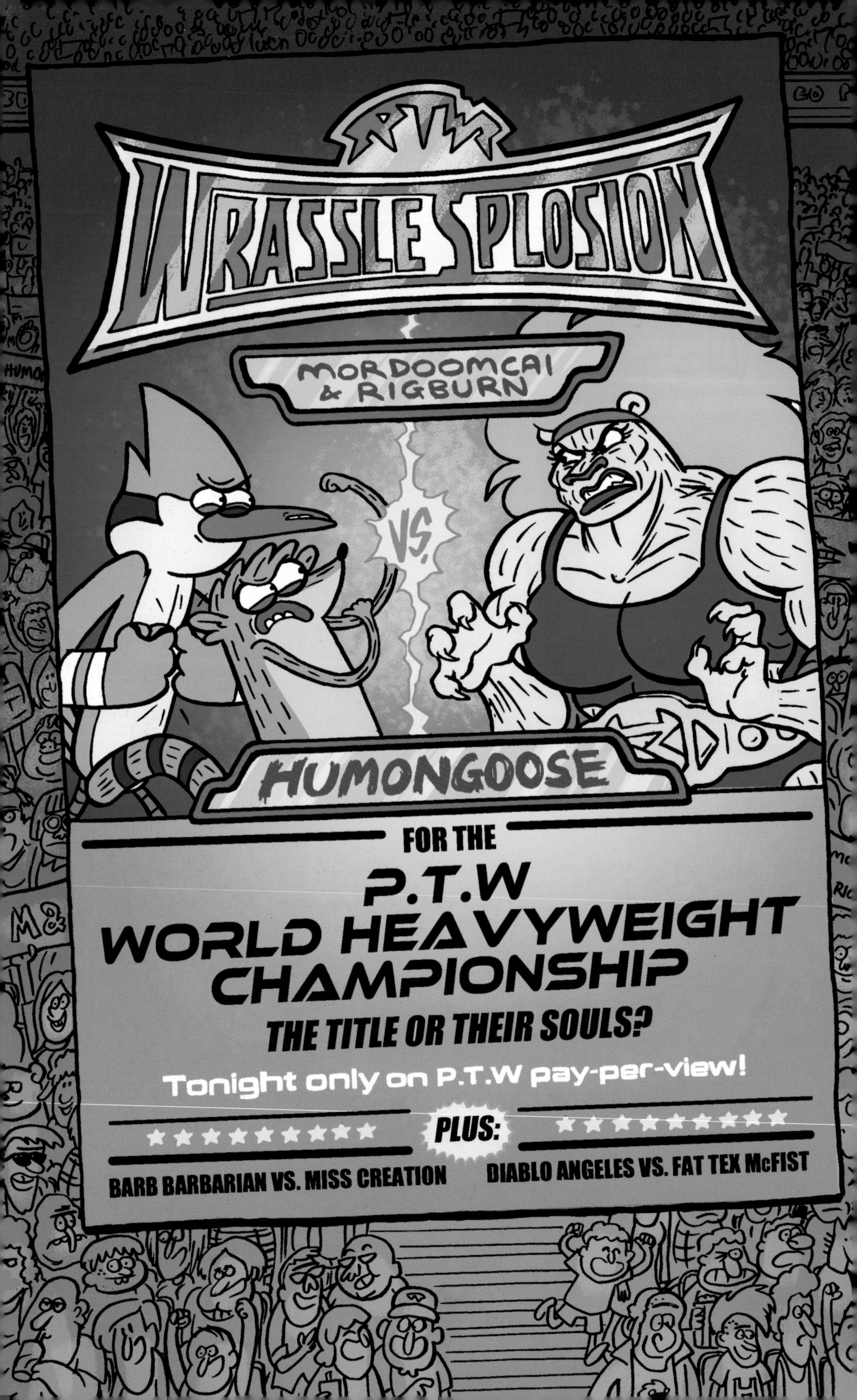
PTW
WRASSLESPLOSION
MORDOOMCAI & RIGBURN
VS.
HUMONGOOSE
FOR THE
P.T.W
WORLD HEAVYWEIGHT CHAMPIONSHIP
THE TITLE OR THEIR SOULS?
Tonight only on P.T.W pay-per-view!
PLUS:
BARB BARBARIAN VS. MISS CREATION
DIABLO ANGELES VS. FAT TEX McFIST

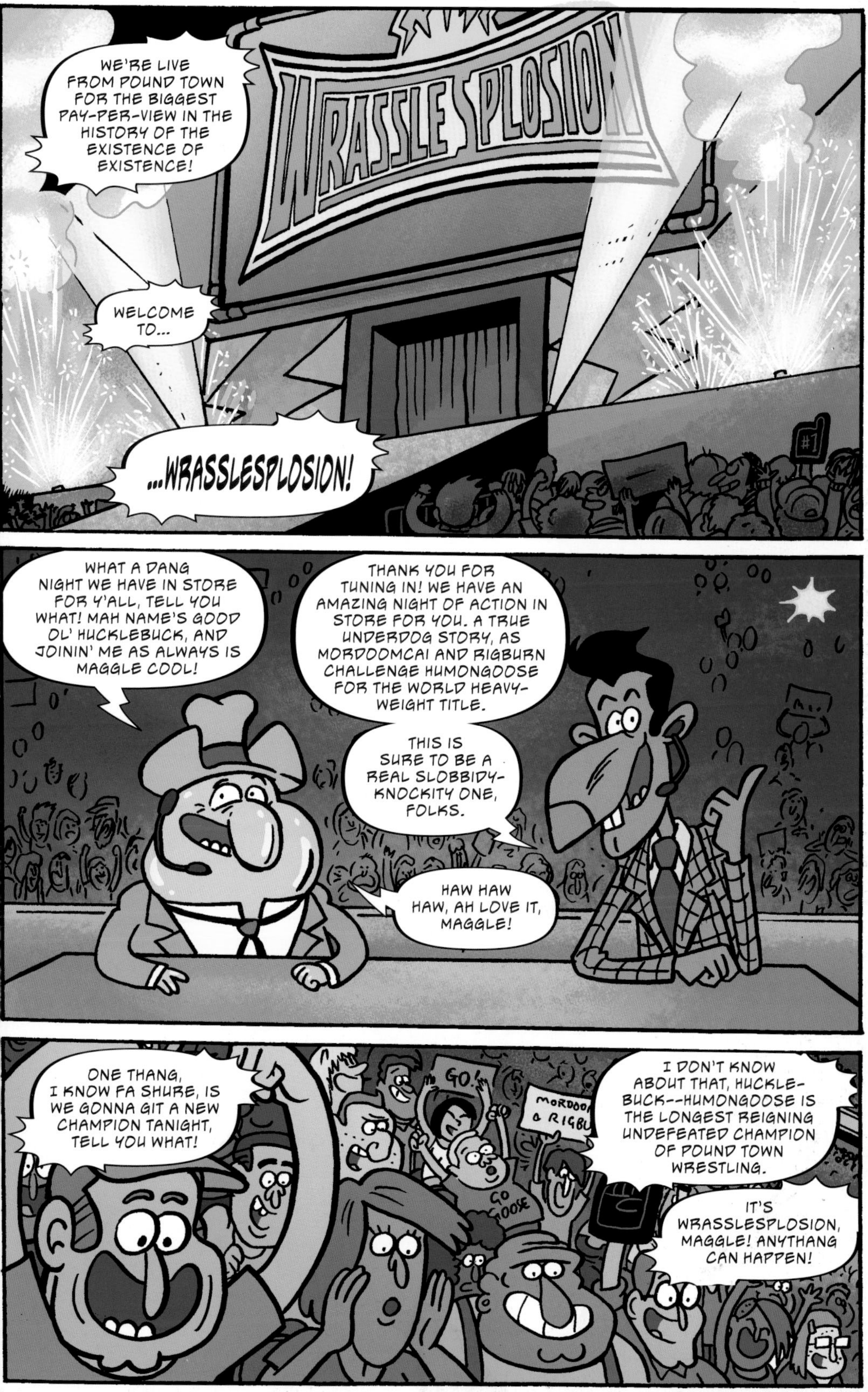
WE'RE LIVE FROM POUND TOWN FOR THE BIGGEST PAY-PER-VIEW IN THE HISTORY OF THE EXISTENCE OF EXISTENCE!
WRASSLESPLOSION
WELCOME TO...
...WRASSLESPLOSION!
#1
WHAT A DANG NIGHT WE HAVE IN STORE FOR Y'ALL, TELL YOU WHAT! MAH NAME'S GOOD OL' HUCKLEBUCK, AND JOININ' ME AS ALWAYS IS MAGGLE COOL!
THANK YOU FOR TUNING IN! WE HAVE AN AMAZING NIGHT OF ACTION IN STORE FOR YOU. A TRUE UNDERDOG STORY, AS MORDOOMCAI AND RIGBURN CHALLENGE HUMONGOOSE FOR THE WORLD HEAVY-WEIGHT TITLE.
THIS IS SURE TO BE A REAL SLOBBIDY-KNOCKITY ONE, FOLKS.
HAW HAW HAW, AH LOVE IT, MAGGLE!
ONE THANG, I KNOW FA SHURE, IS WE GONNA GIT A NEW CHAMPION TANIGHT, TELL YOU WHAT!
GO!
GO GOOSE
I DON'T KNOW ABOUT THAT, HUCKLE-BUCK--HUMONGOOSE IS THE LONGEST REIGNING UNDEFEATED CHAMPION OF POUND TOWN WRESTLING.
IT'S WRASSLESPLOSION, MAGGLE! ANYTHANG CAN HAPPEN!

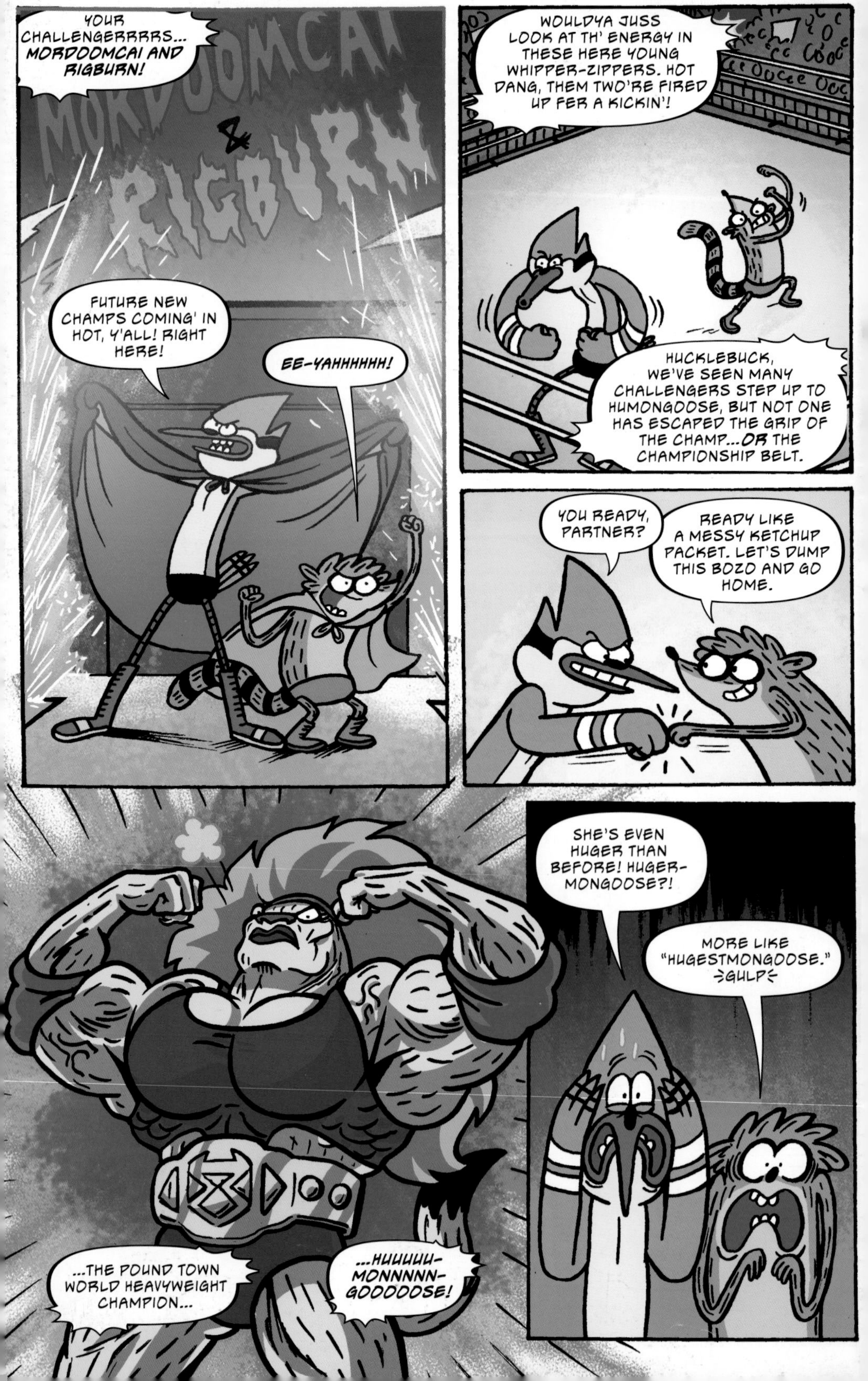
YOUR CHALLENGERRRRS... MORDOOMCAI AND RIGBURN!
MORDOOMCAI & RIGBURN
FUTURE NEW CHAMPS COMING' IN HOT, Y'ALL! RIGHT HERE!
EE-YAHHHHHH!
WOULDYA JUSS LOOK AT TH' ENERGY IN THESE HERE YOUNG WHIPPER-ZIPPERS. HOT DANG, THEM TWO'RE FIRED UP FER A KICKIN'!
HUCKLEBUCK, WE'VE SEEN MANY CHALLENGERS STEP UP TO HUMONGOOSE, BUT NOT ONE HAS ESCAPED THE GRIP OF THE CHAMP...OR THE CHAMPIONSHIP BELT.
YOU READY, PARTNER?
READY LIKE A MESSY KETCHUP PACKET. LET'S DUMP THIS BOZO AND GO HOME.
...THE POUND TOWN WORLD HEAVYWEIGHT CHAMPION...
...HUUUUU-MONNNNN-GOOOOOSE!
SHE'S EVEN HUGER THAN BEFORE! HUGER-MONGOOSE?!
MORE LIKE "HUGESTMONGOOSE." GULP

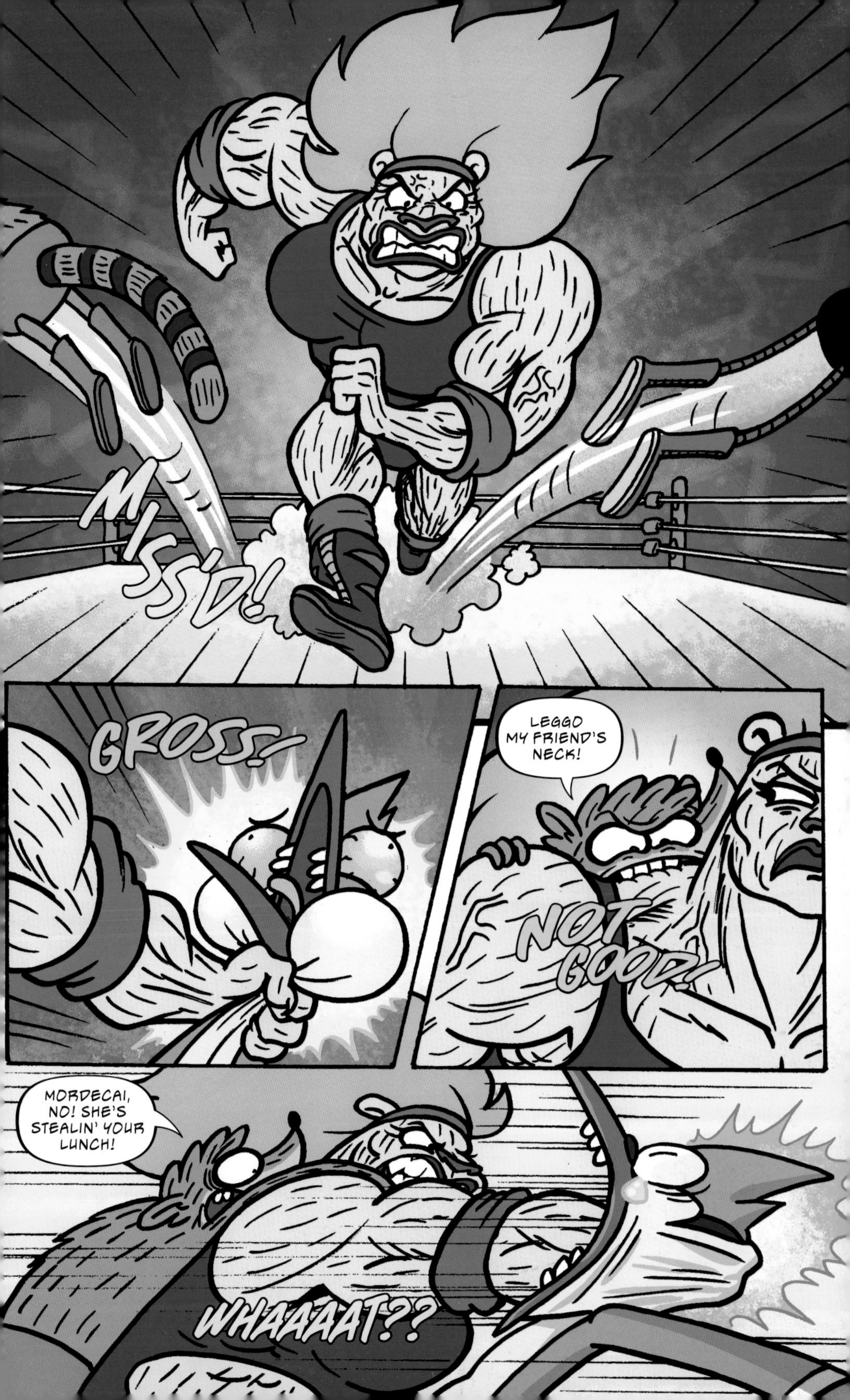
MISS'D!
GROSS!
LEGGO MY FRIEND'S NECK!
NOT GOOD!
MORDECAI, NO! SHE'S STEALIN' YOUR LUNCH!
WHAAAAT??

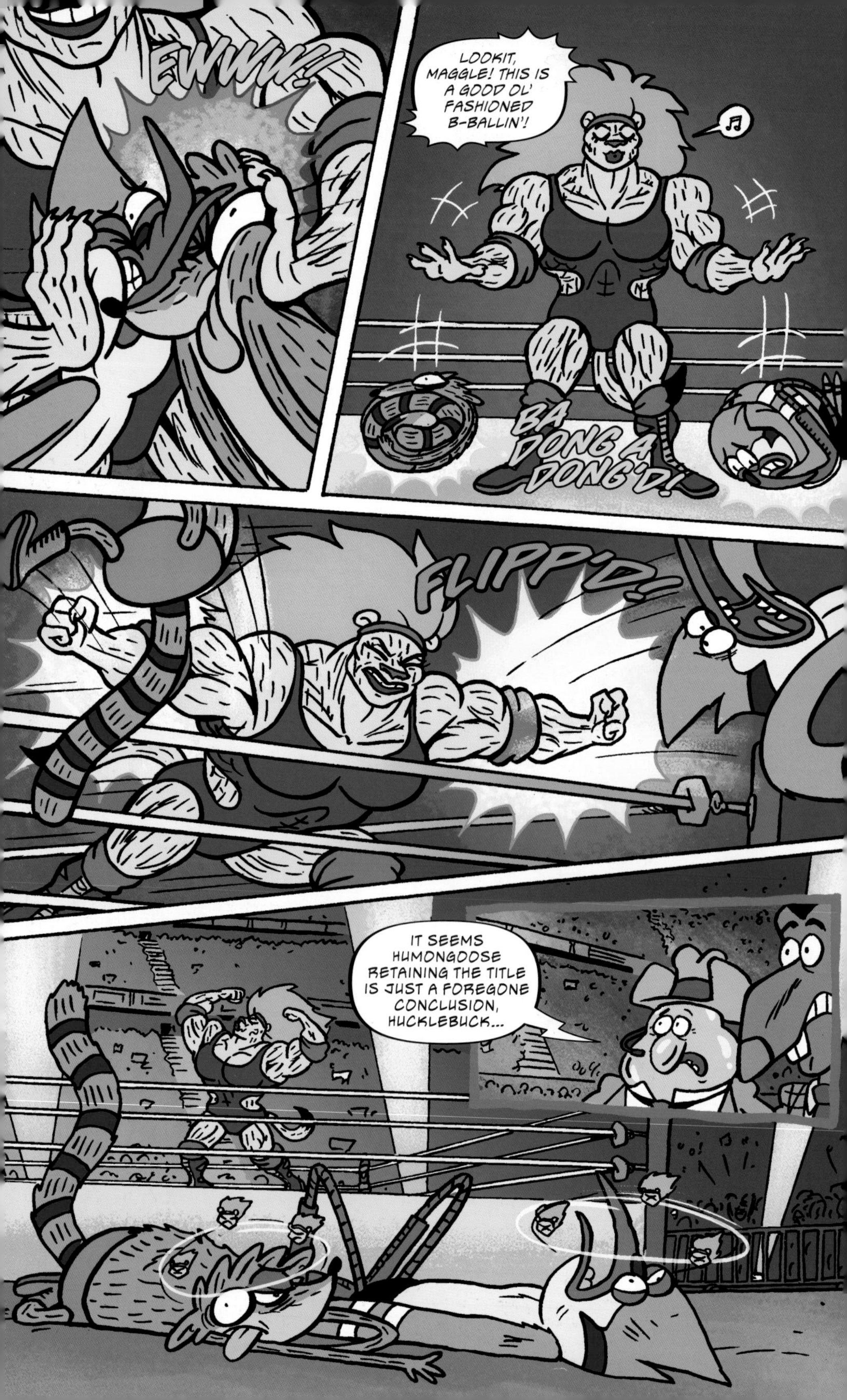
EWWW!!
LOOKIT, MAGGLE! THIS IS A GOOD OL' FASHIONED B-BALLIN'!
♫
BA DONG A DONG'D!
FLIPP'D!!
IT SEEMS HUMONGOOSE RETAINING THE TITLE IS JUST A FOREGONE CONCLUSION, HUCKLEBUCK...

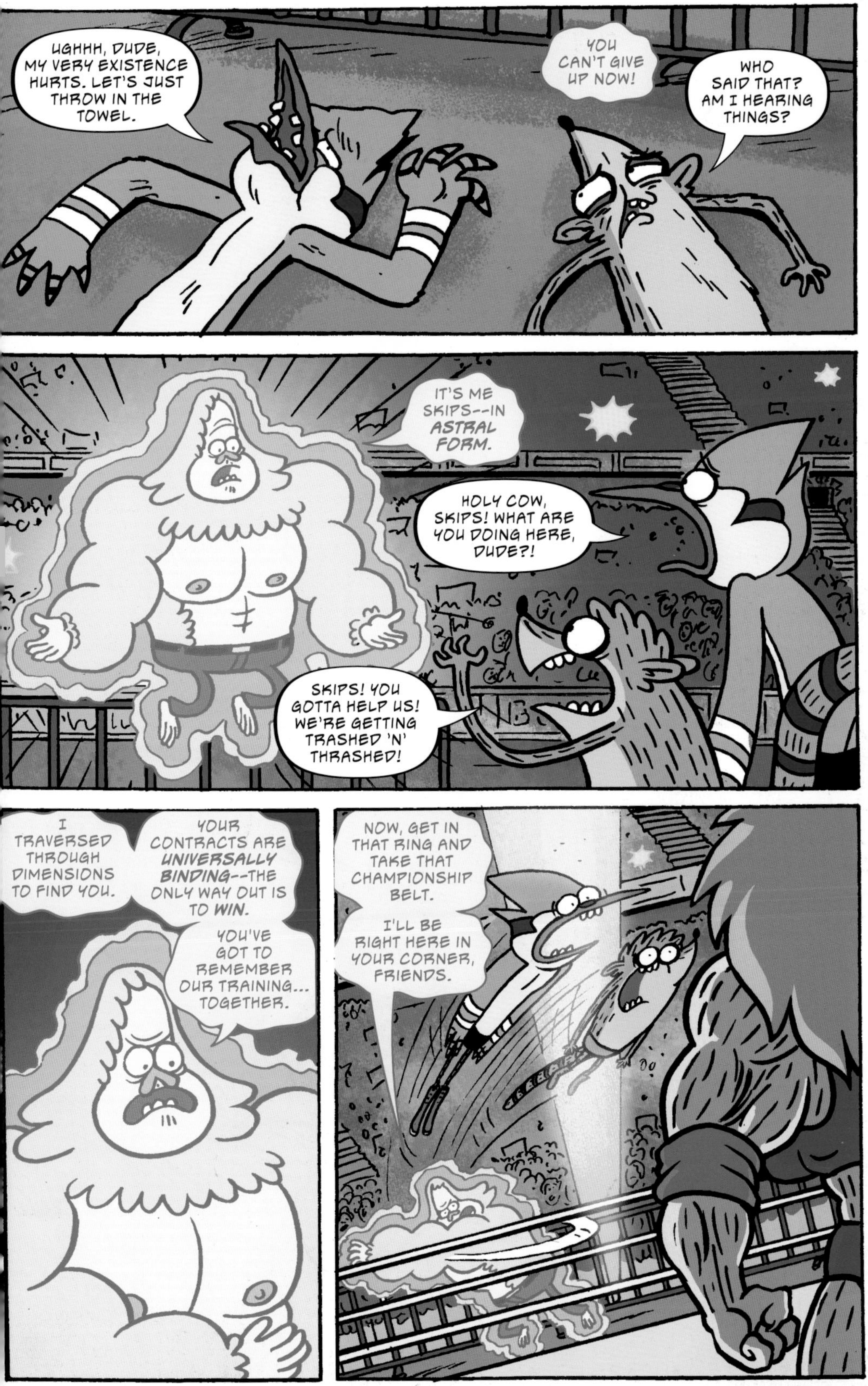
UGHHH, DUDE, MY VERY EXISTENCE HURTS. LET'S JUST THROW IN THE TOWEL.
YOU CAN'T GIVE UP NOW!
WHO SAID THAT? AM I HEARING THINGS?
IT'S ME SKIPS--IN *ASTRAL FORM.*
HOLY COW, SKIPS! WHAT ARE YOU DOING HERE, DUDE?!
SKIPS! YOU GOTTA HELP US! WE'RE GETTING TRASHED 'N' THRASHED!
I TRAVERSED THROUGH DIMENSIONS TO FIND YOU.
YOUR CONTRACTS ARE *UNIVERSALLY BINDING*--THE ONLY WAY OUT IS TO *WIN.*
YOU'VE GOT TO REMEMBER OUR TRAINING... TOGETHER.
NOW, GET IN THAT RING AND TAKE THAT CHAMPIONSHIP BELT.
I'LL BE RIGHT HERE IN YOUR CORNER, FRIENDS.

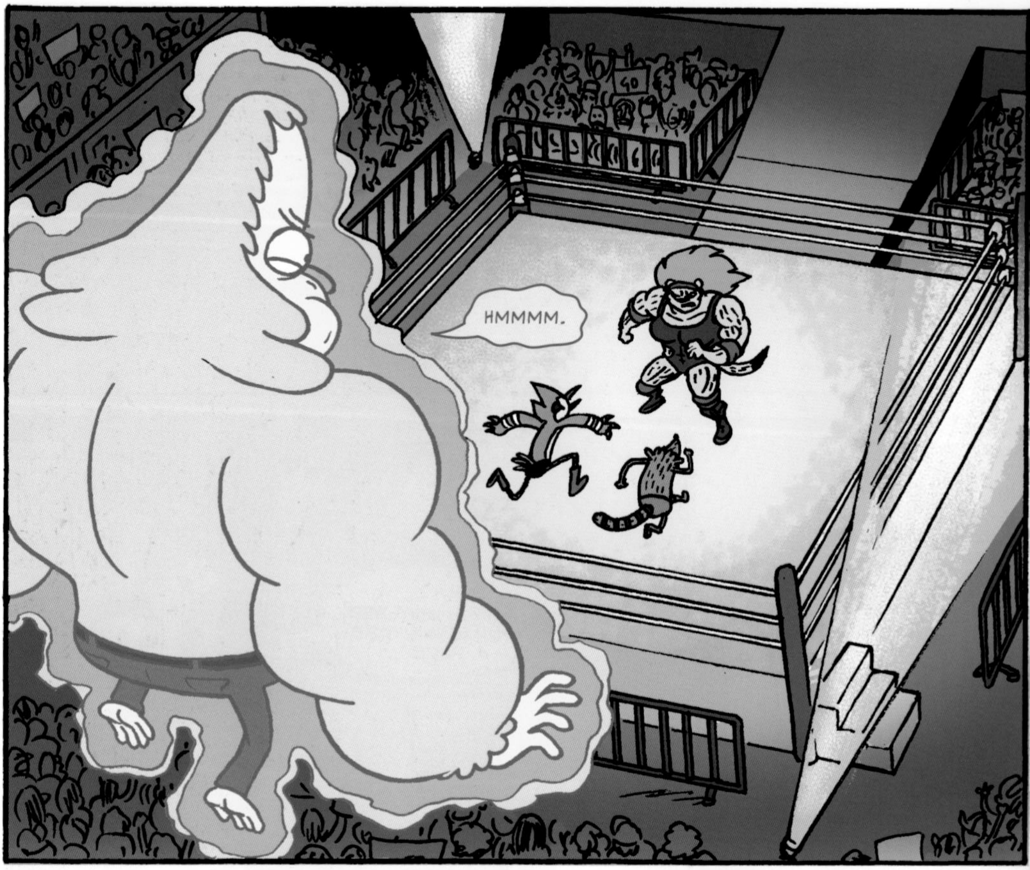
HMMMM.

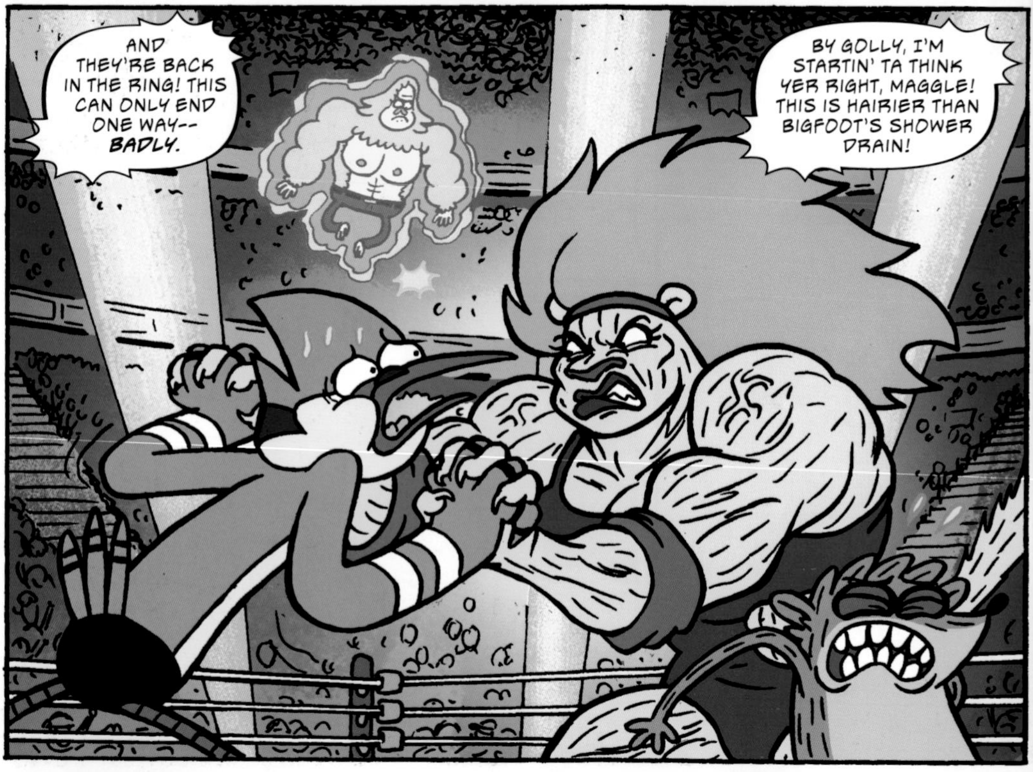
AND THEY'RE BACK IN THE RING! THIS CAN ONLY END ONE WAY-- BADLY.
BY GOLLY, I'M STARTIN' TA THINK YER RIGHT, MAGGLE! THIS IS HAIRIER THAN BIGFOOT'S SHOWER DRAIN!

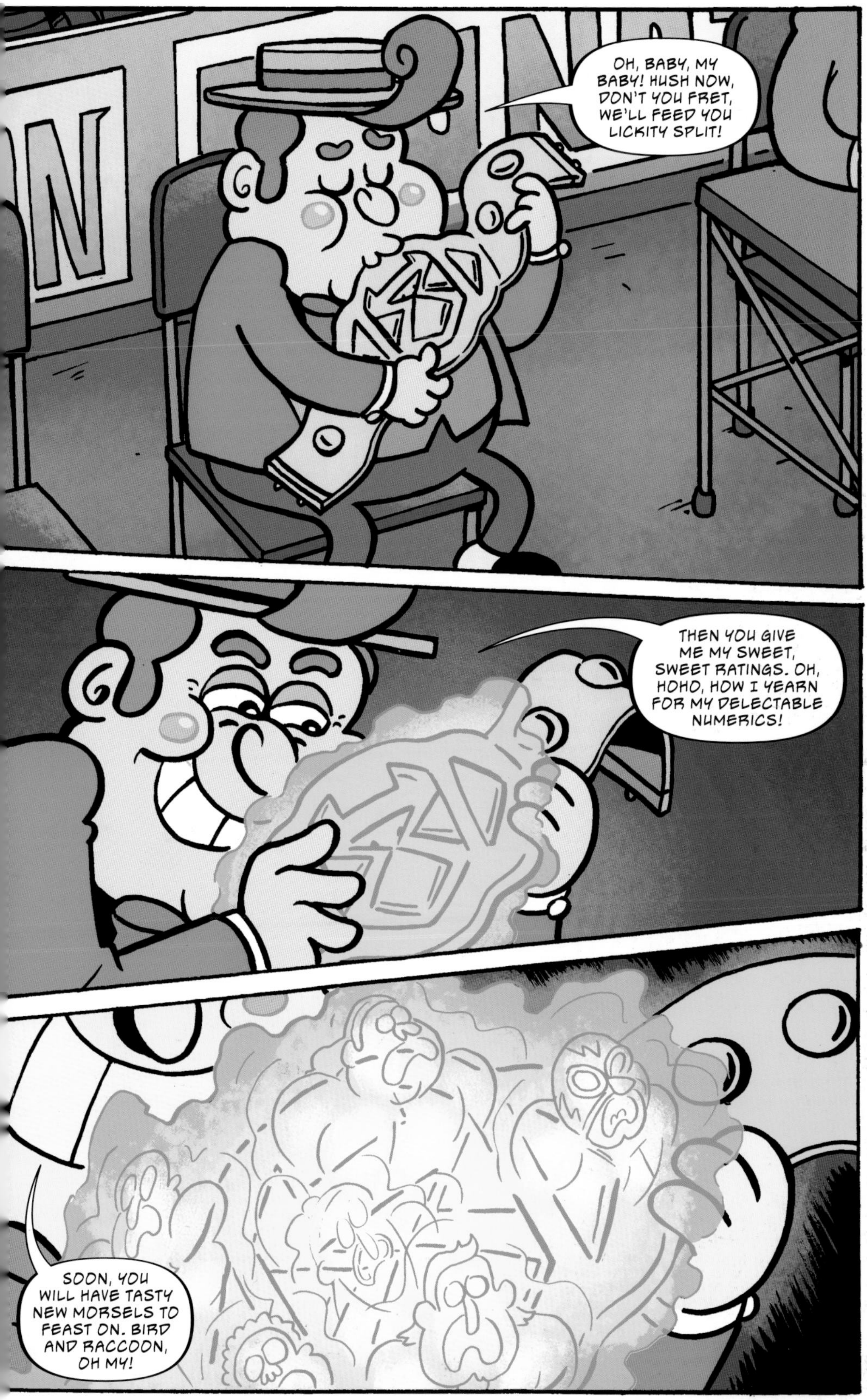
OH, BABY, MY BABY! HUSH NOW, DON'T YOU FRET, WE'LL FEED YOU LICKITY SPLIT!
THEN YOU GIVE ME MY SWEET, SWEET RATINGS. OH, HOHO, HOW I YEARN FOR MY DELECTABLE NUMERICS!
SOON, YOU WILL HAVE TASTY NEW MORSELS TO FEAST ON. BIRD AND RACCOON, OH MY!

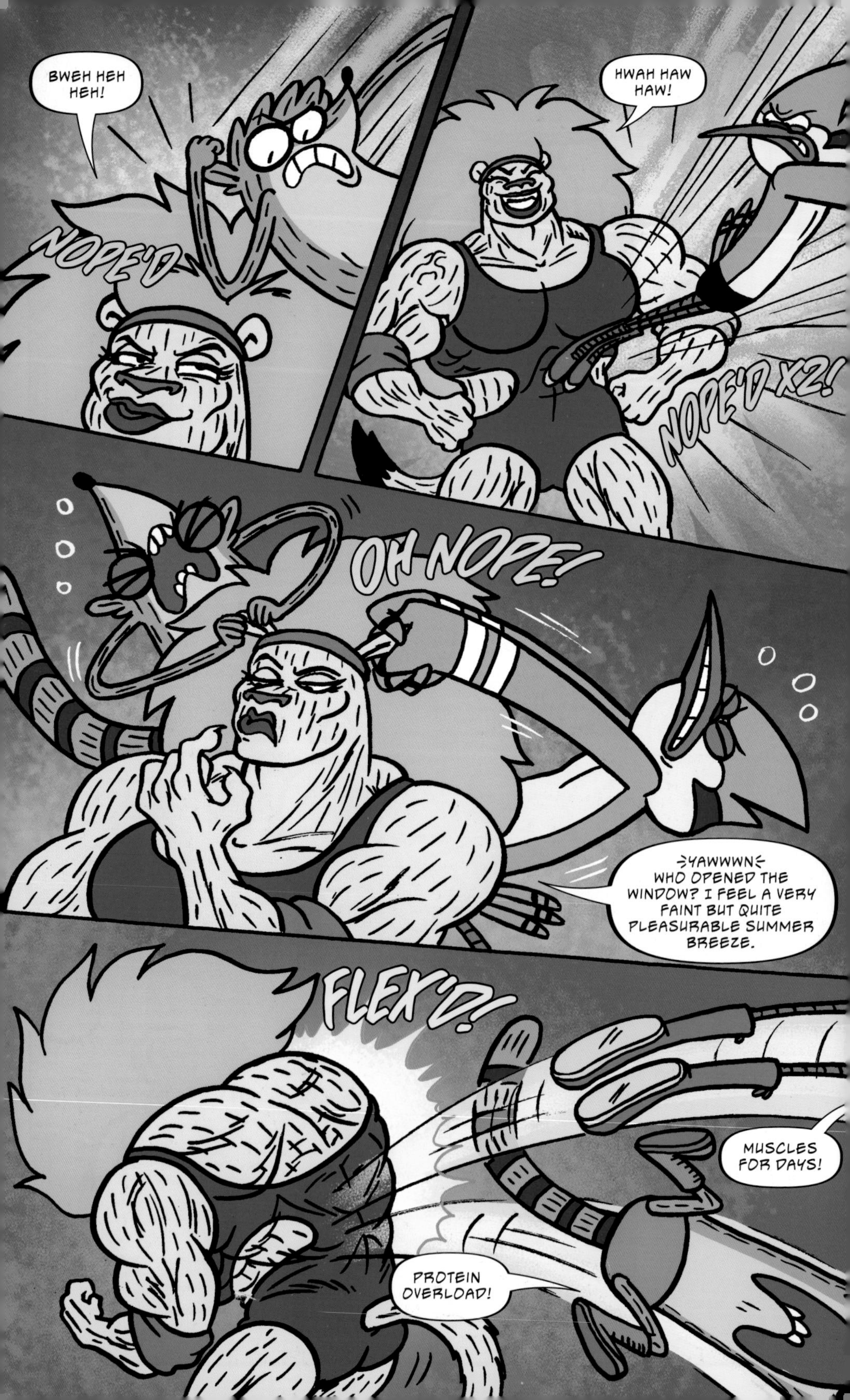
BWEH HEH HEH!
NOPE'D
HWAH HAW HAW!
NOPE'D X2!
OH NOPE!
≡YAWWWN≡ WHO OPENED THE WINDOW? I FEEL A VERY FAINT BUT QUITE PLEASURABLE SUMMER BREEZE.
FLEX'D!
MUSCLES FOR DAYS!
PROTEIN OVERLOAD!

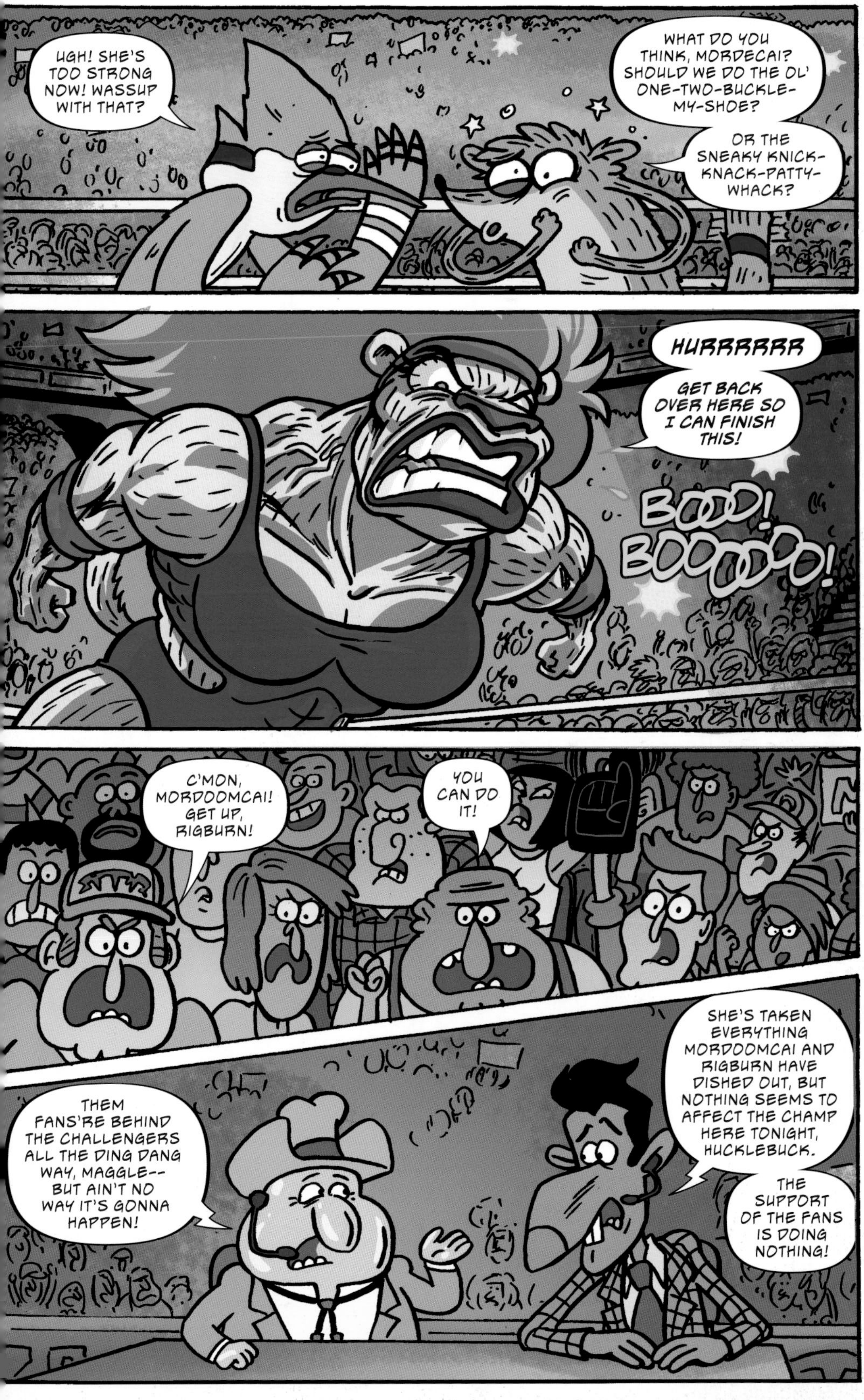
UGH! SHE'S TOO STRONG NOW! WASSUP WITH THAT?
WHAT DO YOU THINK, MORDECAI? SHOULD WE DO THE OL' ONE-TWO-BUCKLE-MY-SHOE?
OR THE SNEAKY KNICK-KNACK-PATTY-WHACK?
HURRRRRR
GET BACK OVER HERE SO I CAN FINISH THIS!
BOOO! BOOOOOO!
C'MON, MORDOOMCAI! GET UP, RIGBURN!
YOU CAN DO IT!
THEM FANS'RE BEHIND THE CHALLENGERS ALL THE DING DANG WAY, MAGGLE--BUT AIN'T NO WAY IT'S GONNA HAPPEN!
SHE'S TAKEN EVERYTHING MORDOOMCAI AND RIGBURN HAVE DISHED OUT, BUT NOTHING SEEMS TO AFFECT THE CHAMP HERE TONIGHT, HUCKLEBUCK.
THE SUPPORT OF THE FANS IS DOING NOTHING!

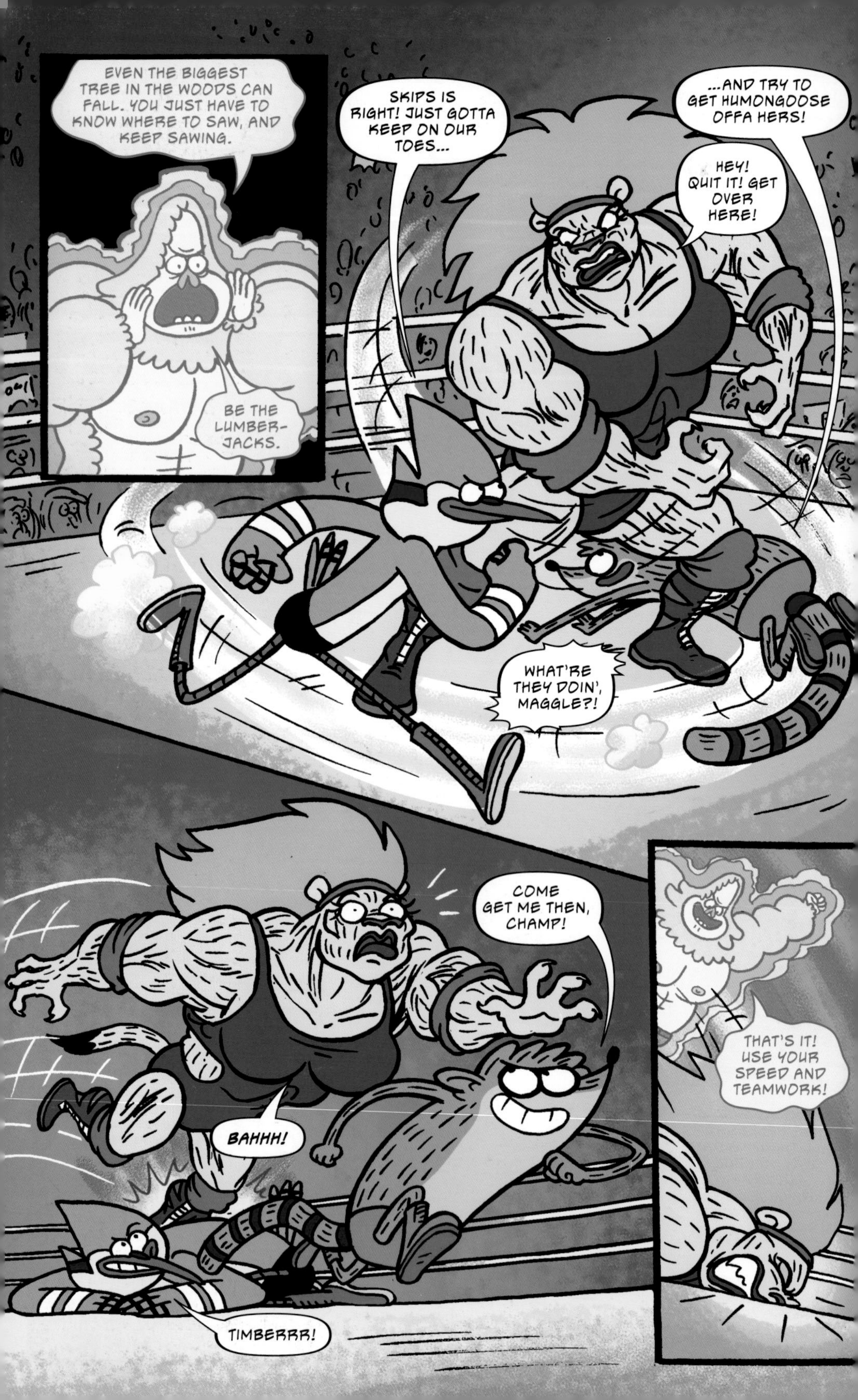
EVEN THE BIGGEST TREE IN THE WOODS CAN FALL. YOU JUST HAVE TO KNOW WHERE TO SAW, AND KEEP SAWING.
BE THE LUMBER-JACKS.
SKIPS IS RIGHT! JUST GOTTA KEEP ON OUR TOES...
...AND TRY TO GET HUMONGOOSE OFFA HERS!
HEY! QUIT IT! GET OVER HERE!
WHAT'RE THEY DOIN', MAGGLE?!
COME GET ME THEN, CHAMP!
BAHHH!
TIMBERRR!
THAT'S IT! USE YOUR SPEED AND TEAMWORK!

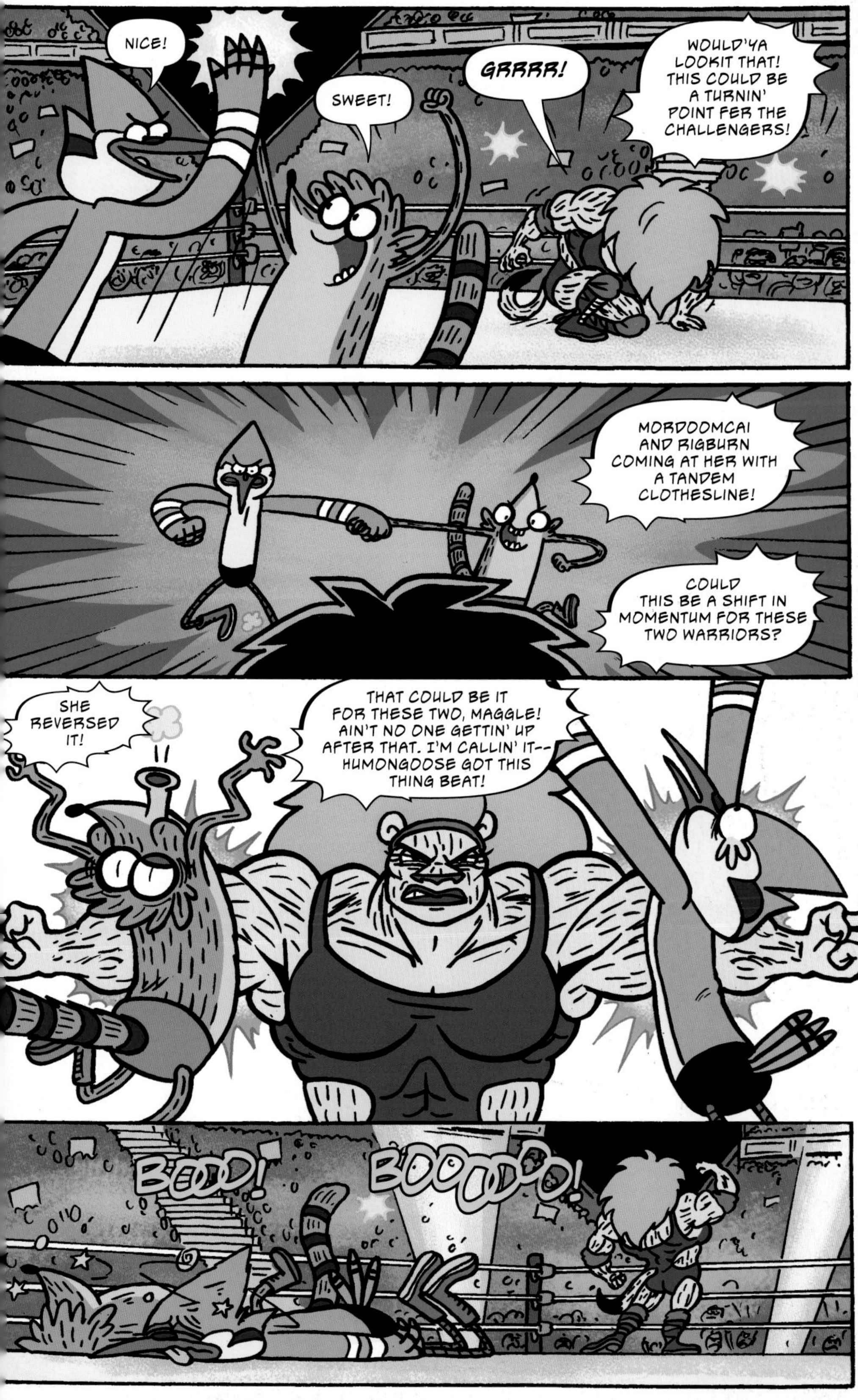
NICE!
SWEET!
GRRRR!
WOULD'YA LOOKIT THAT! THIS COULD BE A TURNIN' POINT FER THE CHALLENGERS!
MORDOOMCAI AND RIGBURN COMING AT HER WITH A TANDEM CLOTHESLINE!
COULD THIS BE A SHIFT IN MOMENTUM FOR THESE TWO WARRIORS?
SHE REVERSED IT!
THAT COULD BE IT FOR THESE TWO, MAGGLE! AIN'T NO ONE GETTIN' UP AFTER THAT. I'M CALLIN' IT-- HUMONGOOSE GOT THIS THING BEAT!
BOOO!
BOOOOOO!

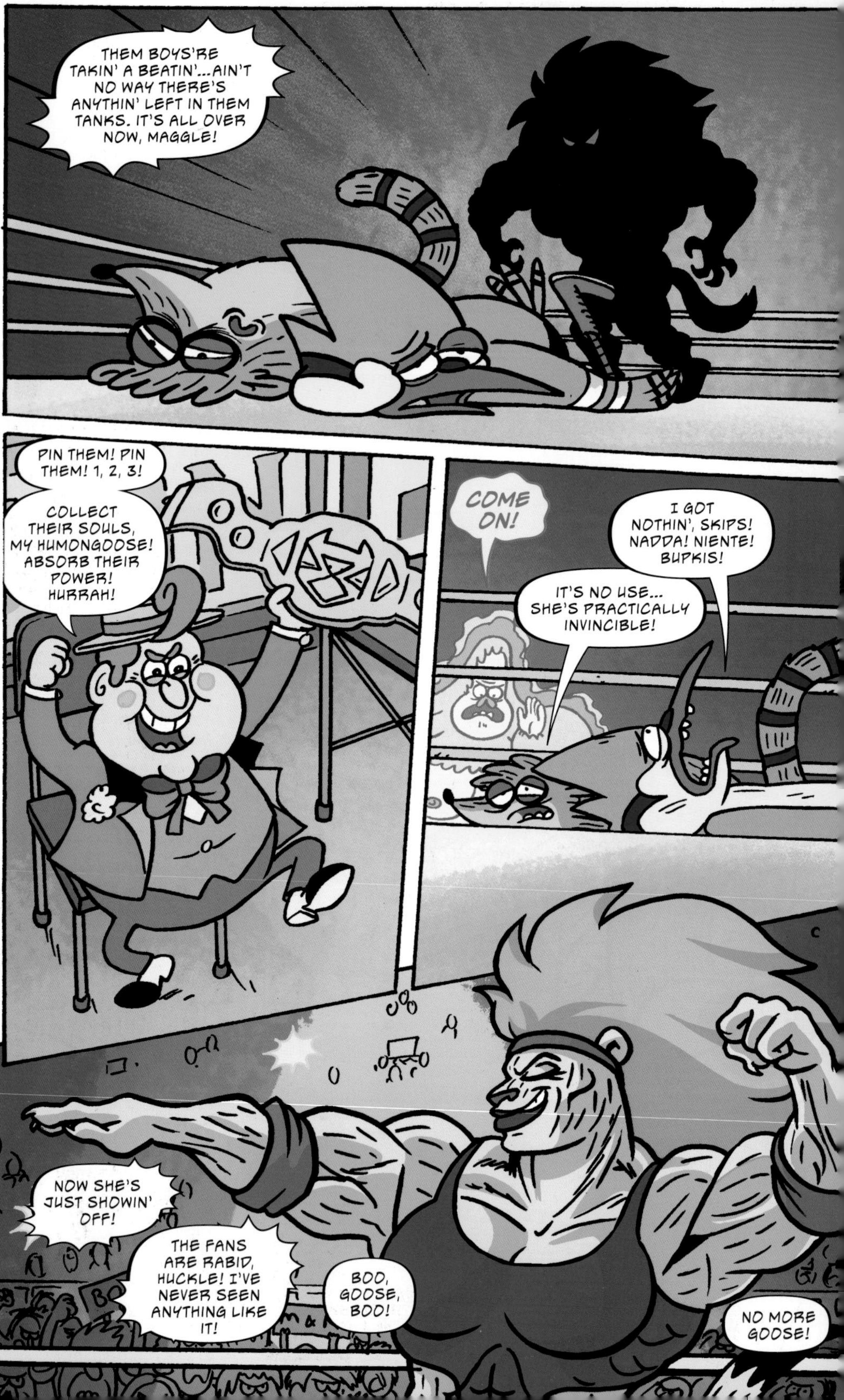
THEM BOYS'RE TAKIN' A BEATIN'...AIN'T NO WAY THERE'S ANYTHIN' LEFT IN THEM TANKS. IT'S ALL OVER NOW, MAGGLE!
PIN THEM! PIN THEM! 1, 2, 3!
COLLECT THEIR SOULS, MY HUMONGOOSE! ABSORB THEIR POWER! HURRAH!
COME ON!
I GOT NOTHIN', SKIPS! NADDA! NIENTE! BUPKIS!
IT'S NO USE... SHE'S PRACTICALLY INVINCIBLE!
NOW SHE'S JUST SHOWIN' OFF!
THE FANS ARE RABID, HUCKLE! I'VE NEVER SEEN ANYTHING LIKE IT!
BOO, GOOSE, BOO!
NO MORE GOOSE!

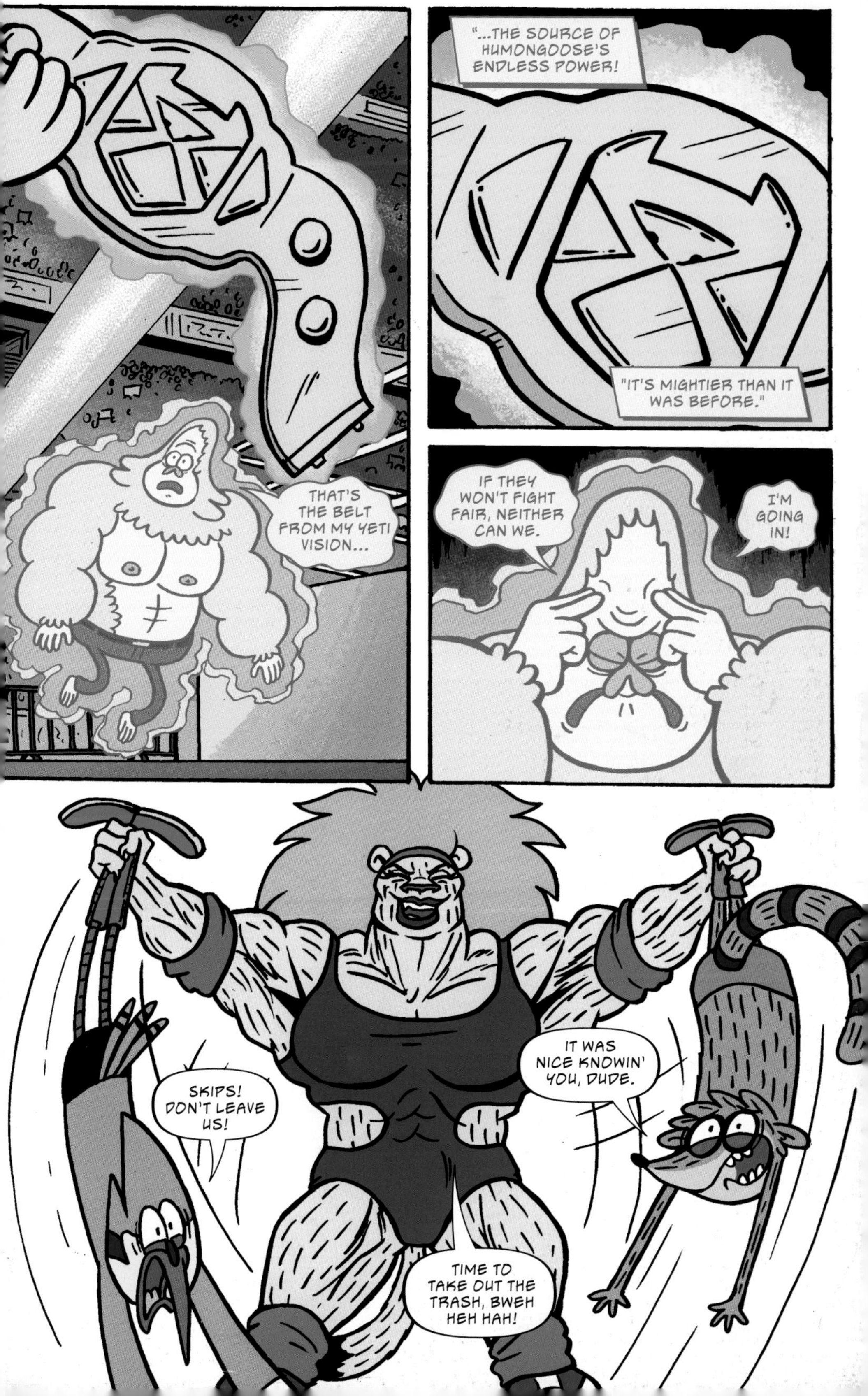
"...THE SOURCE OF HUMONGOOSE'S ENDLESS POWER!
"IT'S MIGHTIER THAN IT WAS BEFORE."
THAT'S THE BELT FROM MY YETI VISION...
IF THEY WON'T FIGHT FAIR, NEITHER CAN WE.
I'M GOING IN!
SKIPS! DON'T LEAVE US!
IT WAS NICE KNOWIN' YOU, DUDE.
TIME TO TAKE OUT THE TRASH, BWEH HEH HAH!

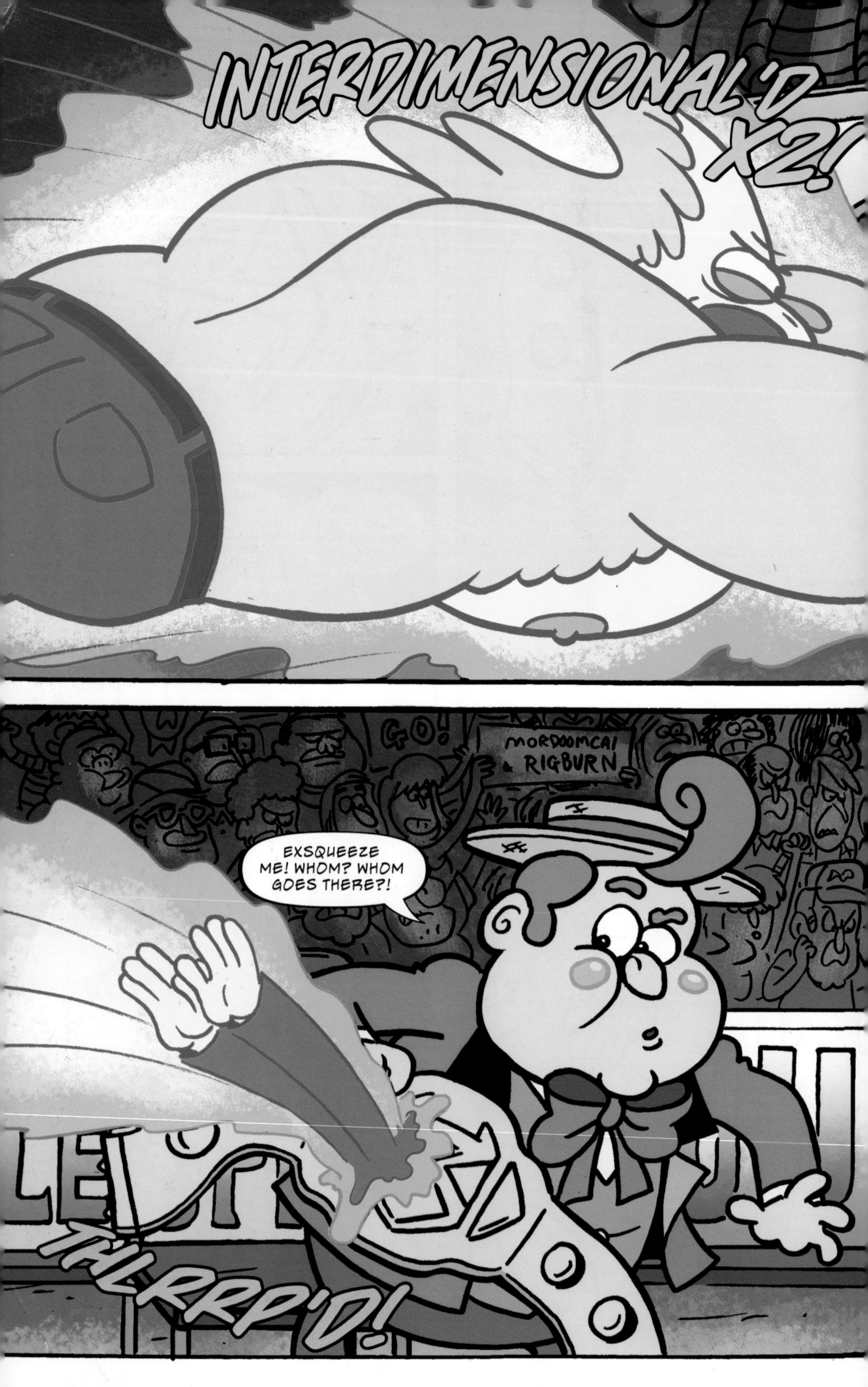
INTERDIMENSIONAL'D X2!
MORDOOMCAI & RIGBURN
GO!
EXSQUEEZE ME! WHOM? WHOM GOES THERE?!
THLRRP'D!

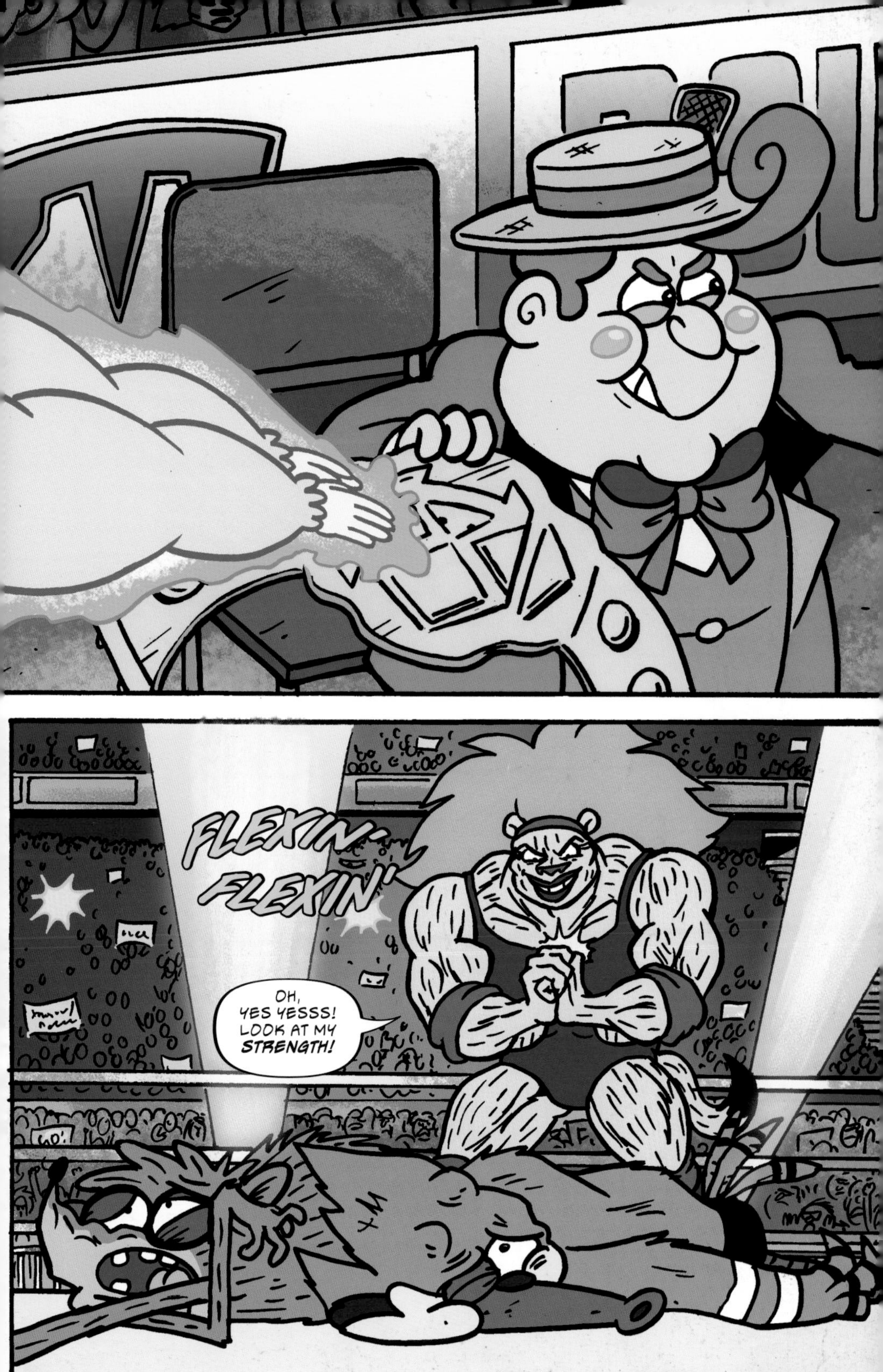
FLEXIN'
FLEXIN'
OH, YES YESSS! LOOK AT MY STRENGTH!

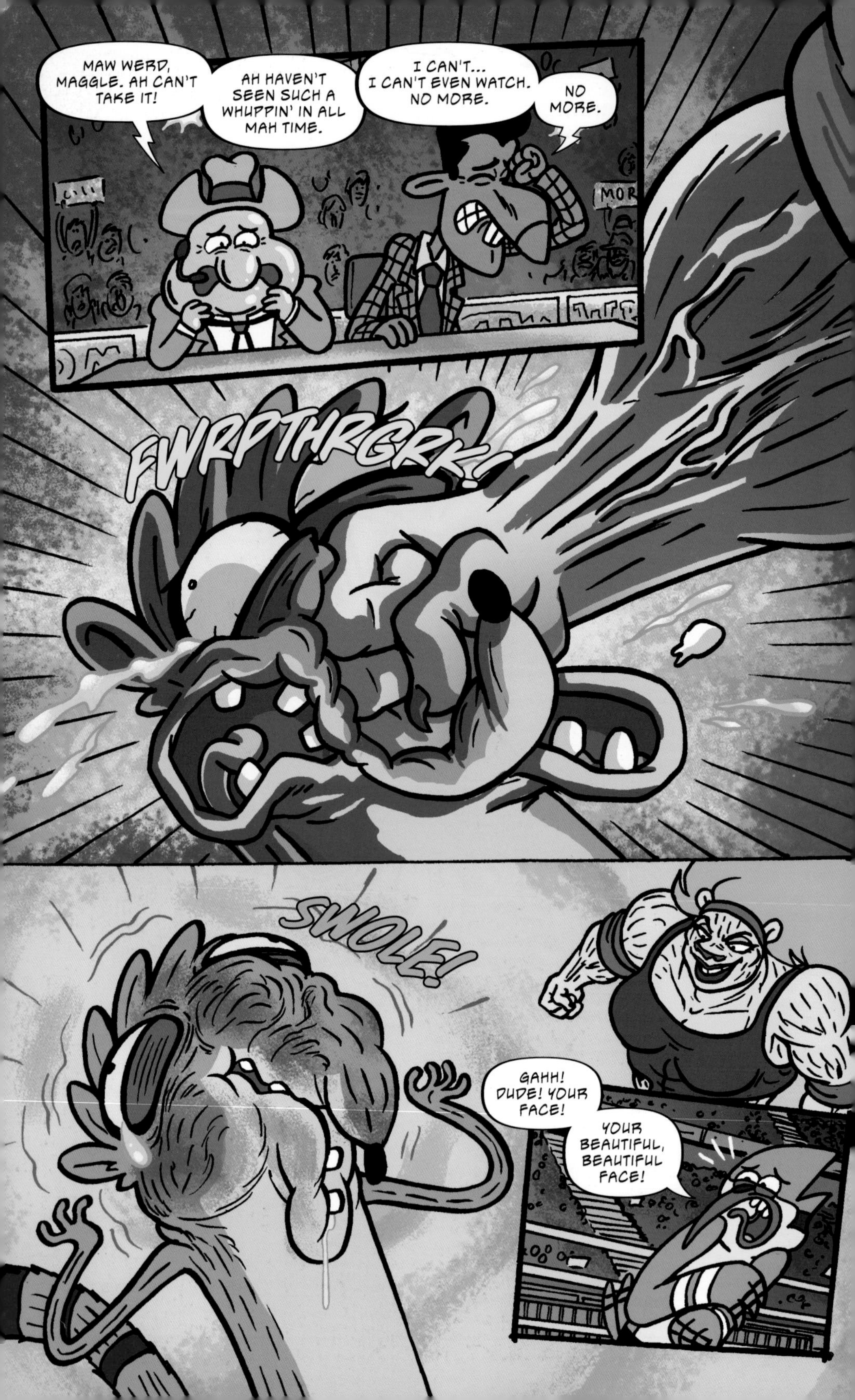
MAW WERD, MAGGLE. AH CAN'T TAKE IT!
AH HAVEN'T SEEN SUCH A WHUPPIN' IN ALL MAH TIME.
I CAN'T... I CAN'T EVEN WATCH. NO MORE.
NO MORE.
FWRPTHRGRK!
SWOLE!
GAHH! DUDE! YOUR FACE!
YOUR BEAUTIFUL, BEAUTIFUL FACE!

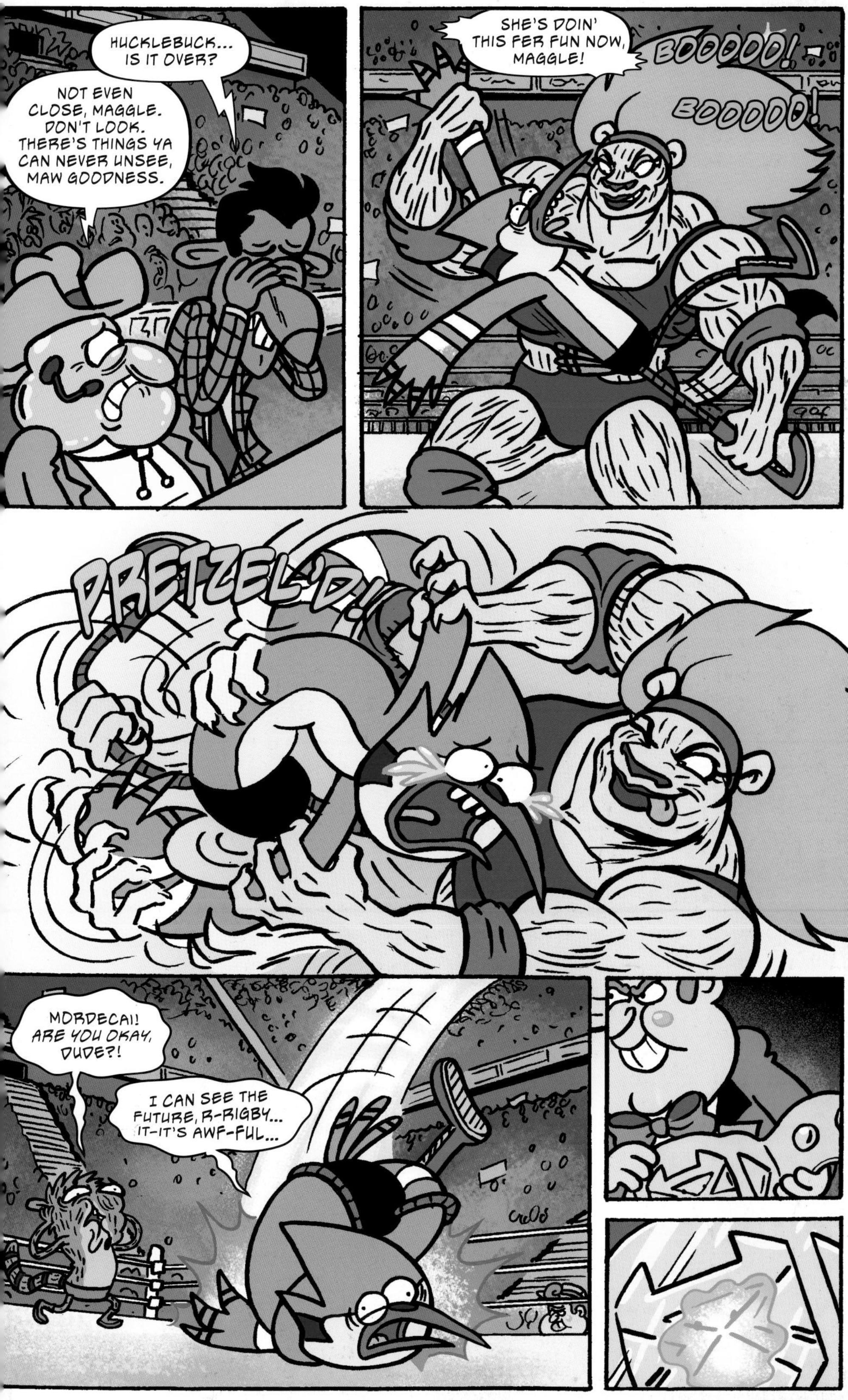
HUCKLEBUCK... IS IT OVER?
NOT EVEN CLOSE, MAGGLE. DON'T LOOK. THERE'S THINGS YA CAN NEVER UNSEE, MAW GOODNESS.
SHE'S DOIN' THIS FER FUN NOW, MAGGLE!
BOOOOO!
BOOOOO!
PRETZEL'D!
MORDECAI! ARE YOU OKAY, DUDE?!
I CAN SEE THE FUTURE, R-RIGBY... IT-IT'S AWF-FUL...

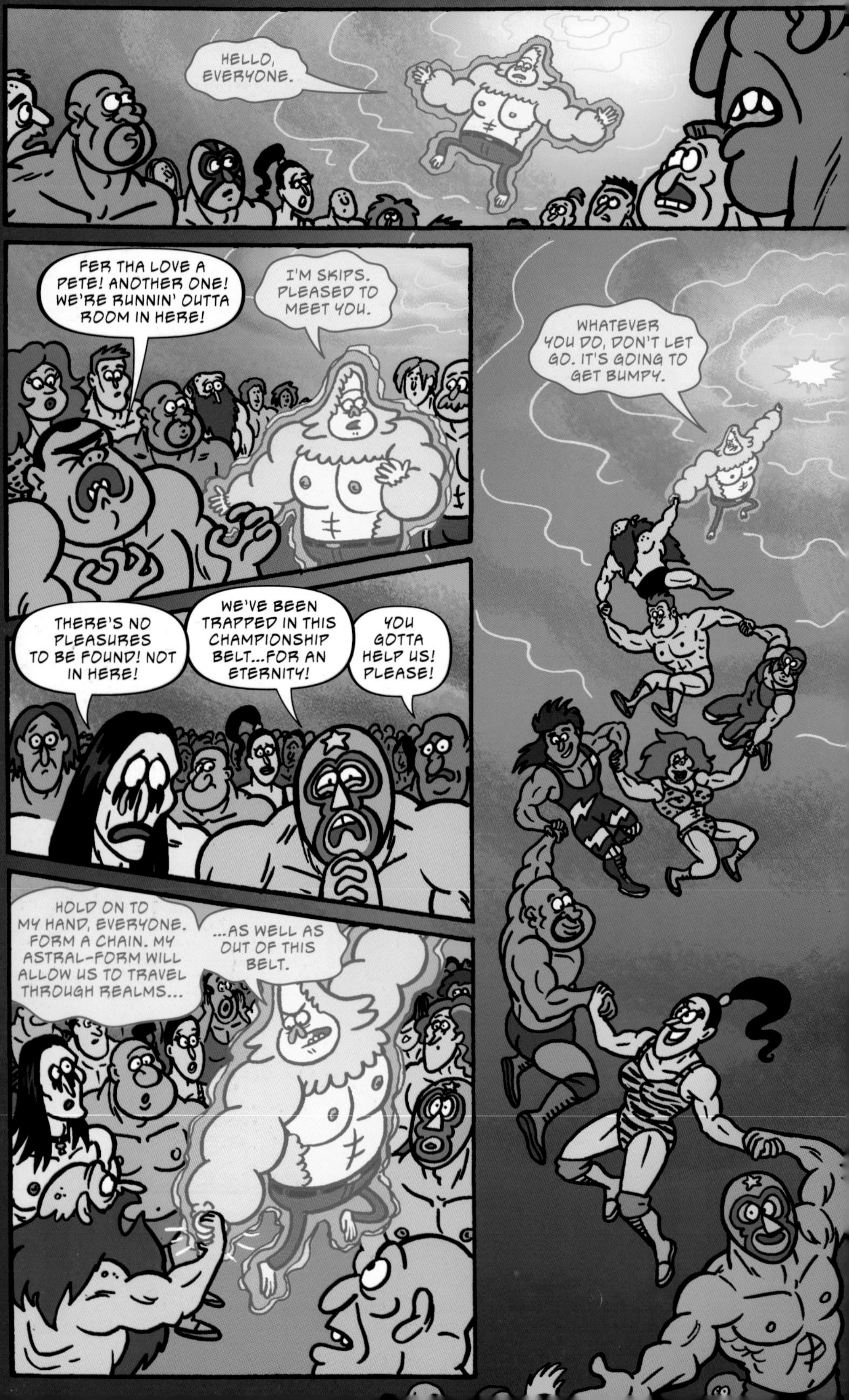
HELLO, EVERYONE.
FER THA LOVE A PETE! ANOTHER ONE! WE'RE RUNNIN' OUTTA ROOM IN HERE!
I'M SKIPS. PLEASED TO MEET YOU.
THERE'S NO PLEASURES TO BE FOUND! NOT IN HERE!
WE'VE BEEN TRAPPED IN THIS CHAMPIONSHIP BELT...FOR AN ETERNITY!
YOU GOTTA HELP US! PLEASE!
HOLD ON TO MY HAND, EVERYONE. FORM A CHAIN. MY ASTRAL-FORM WILL ALLOW US TO TRAVEL THROUGH REALMS...
...AS WELL AS OUT OF THIS BELT.
WHATEVER YOU DO, DON'T LET GO. IT'S GOING TO GET BUMPY.

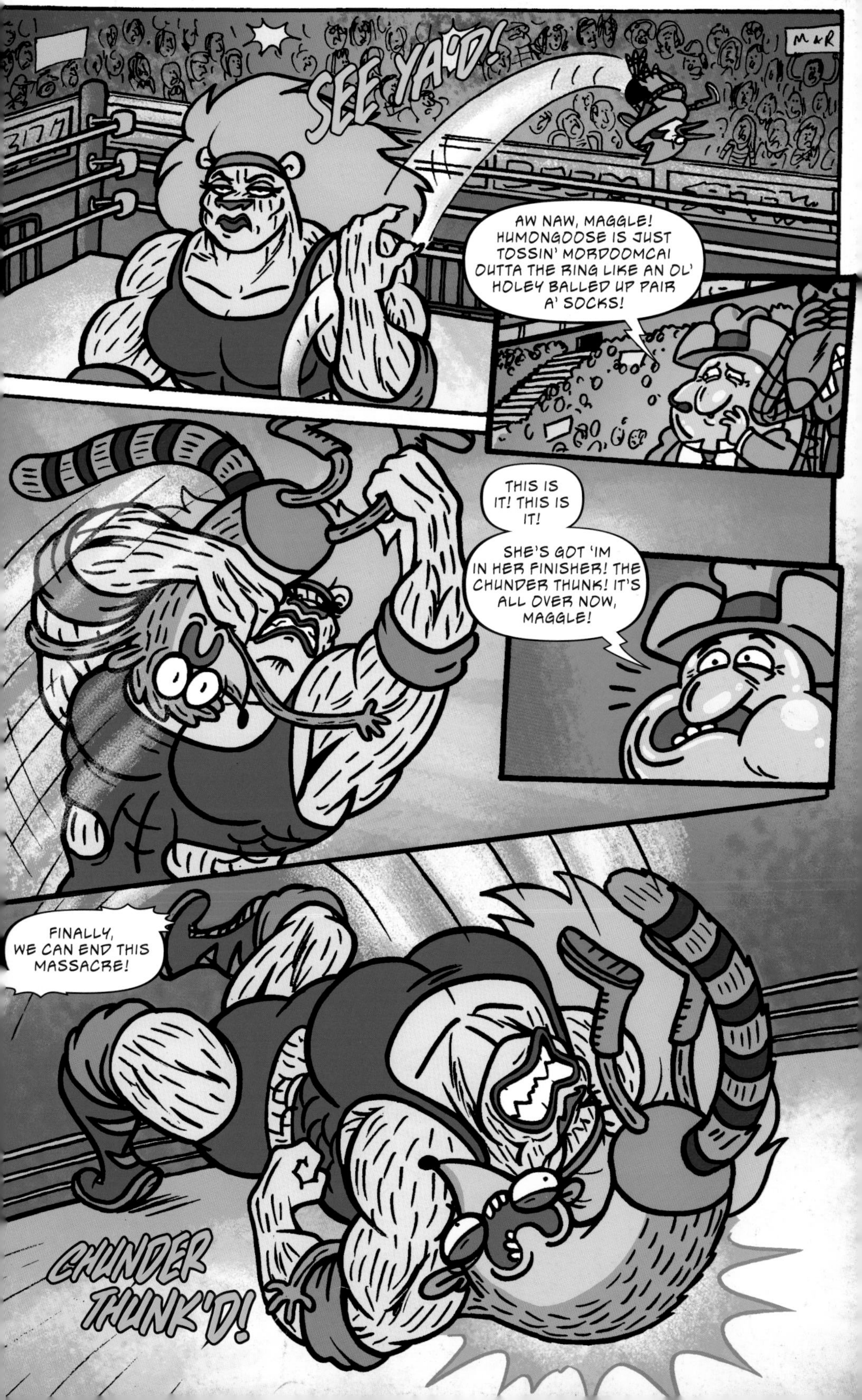
M&R
SEE YA'D!
AW NAW, MAGGLE! HUMONGOOSE IS JUST TOSSIN' MORDOOMCAI OUTTA THE RING LIKE AN OL' HOLEY BALLED UP PAIR A' SOCKS!
THIS IS IT! THIS IS IT!
SHE'S GOT 'IM IN HER FINISHER! THE CHUNDER THUNK! IT'S ALL OVER NOW, MAGGLE!
FINALLY, WE CAN END THIS MASSACRE!
CHUNDER THUNK'D!

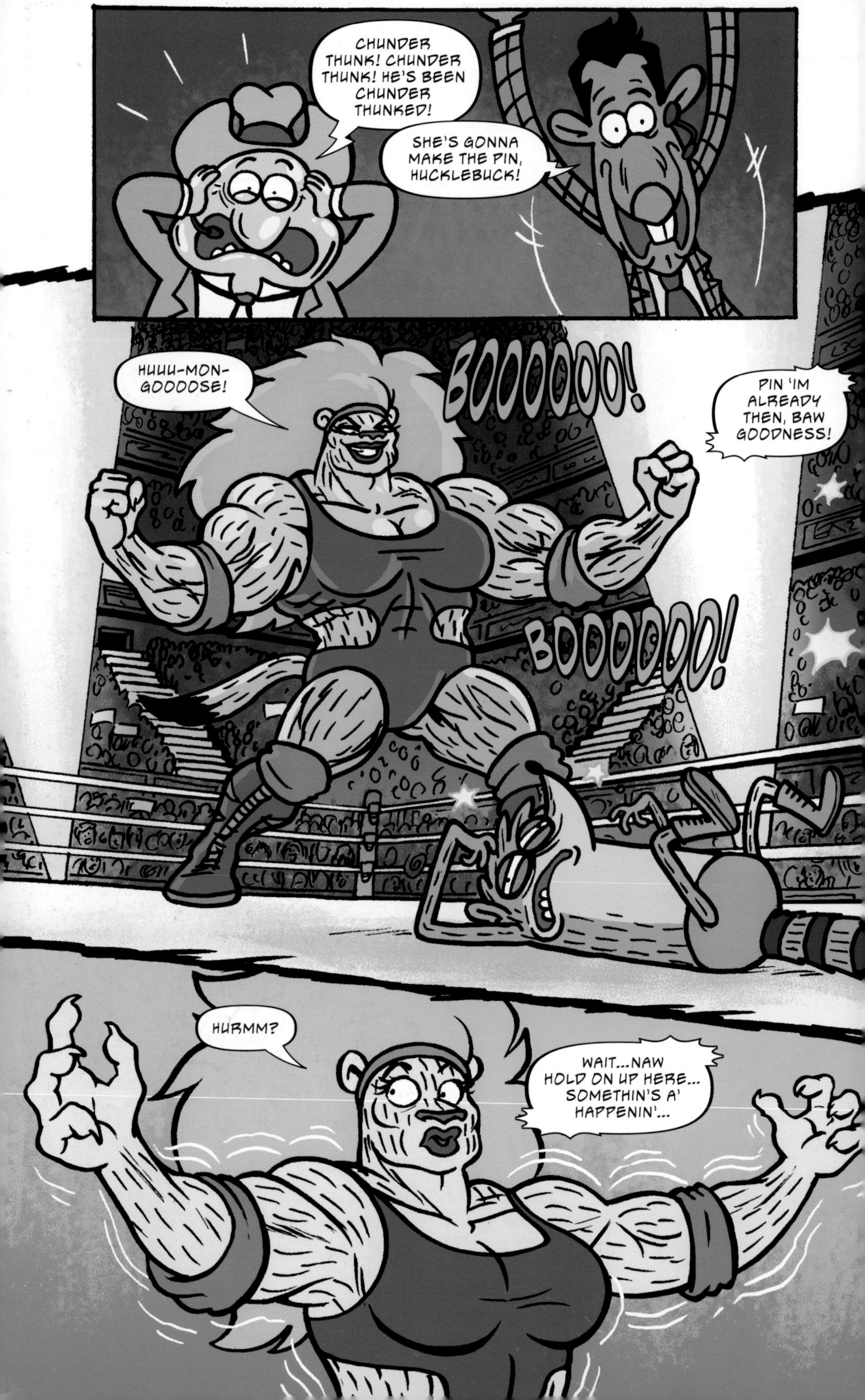
CHUNDER THUNK! CHUNDER THUNK! HE'S BEEN CHUNDER THUNKED!
SHE'S GONNA MAKE THE PIN, HUCKLEBUCK!
HUUU-MON-GOOOOSE!
BOOOOOO!
PIN 'IM ALREADY THEN, BAW GOODNESS!
BOOOOOO!
HURMM?
WAIT...NAW HOLD ON UP HERE... SOMETHIN'S A' HAPPENIN'...

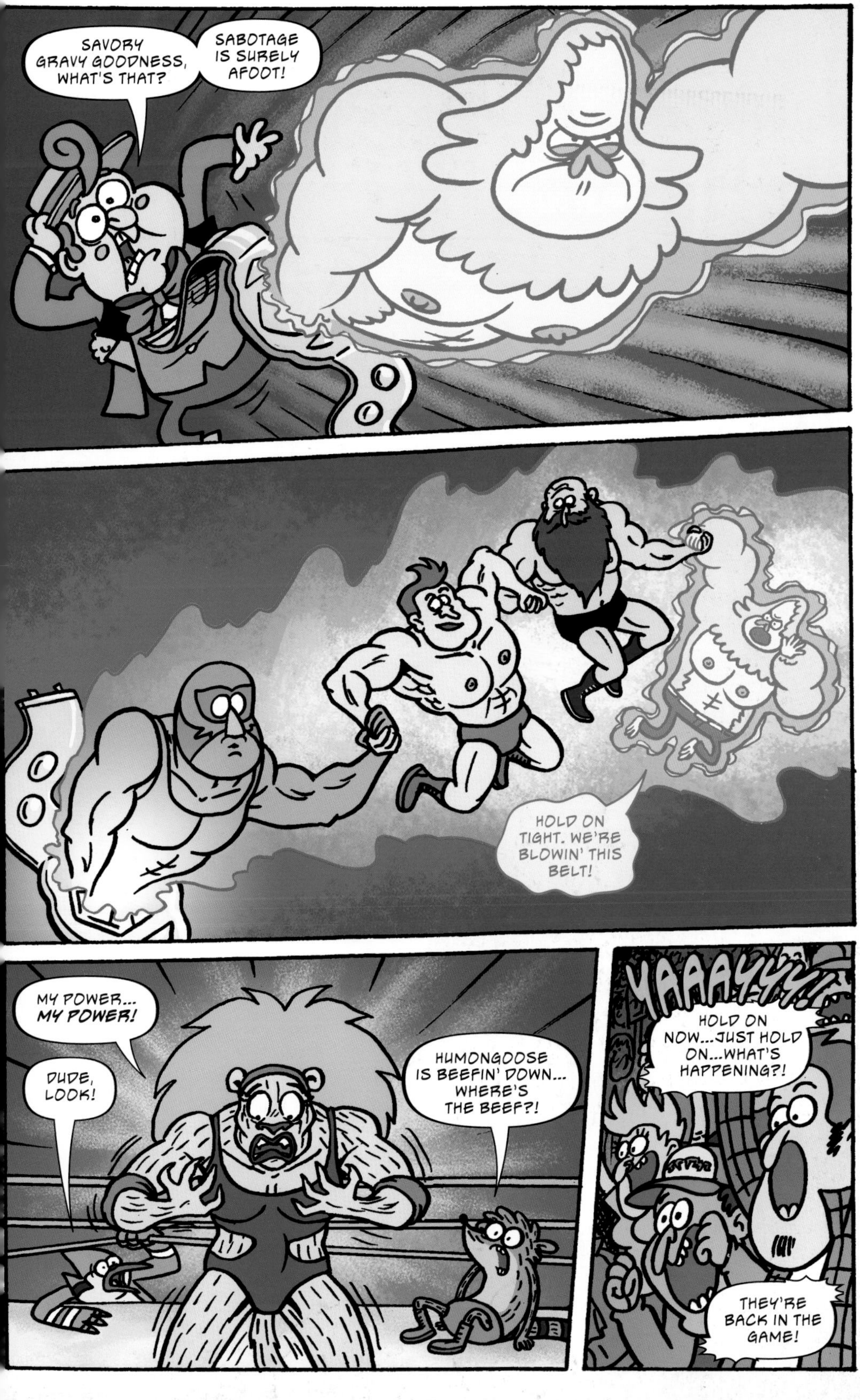
SAVORY GRAVY GOODNESS, WHAT'S THAT?
SABOTAGE IS SURELY AFOOT!
HOLD ON TIGHT. WE'RE BLOWIN' THIS BELT!
MY POWER... *MY POWER!*
DUDE, LOOK!
HUMONGOOSE IS BEEFIN' DOWN... WHERE'S THE BEEF?!
YAAAYYY!!
HOLD ON NOW...JUST HOLD ON...WHAT'S HAPPENING?!
THEY'RE BACK IN THE GAME!

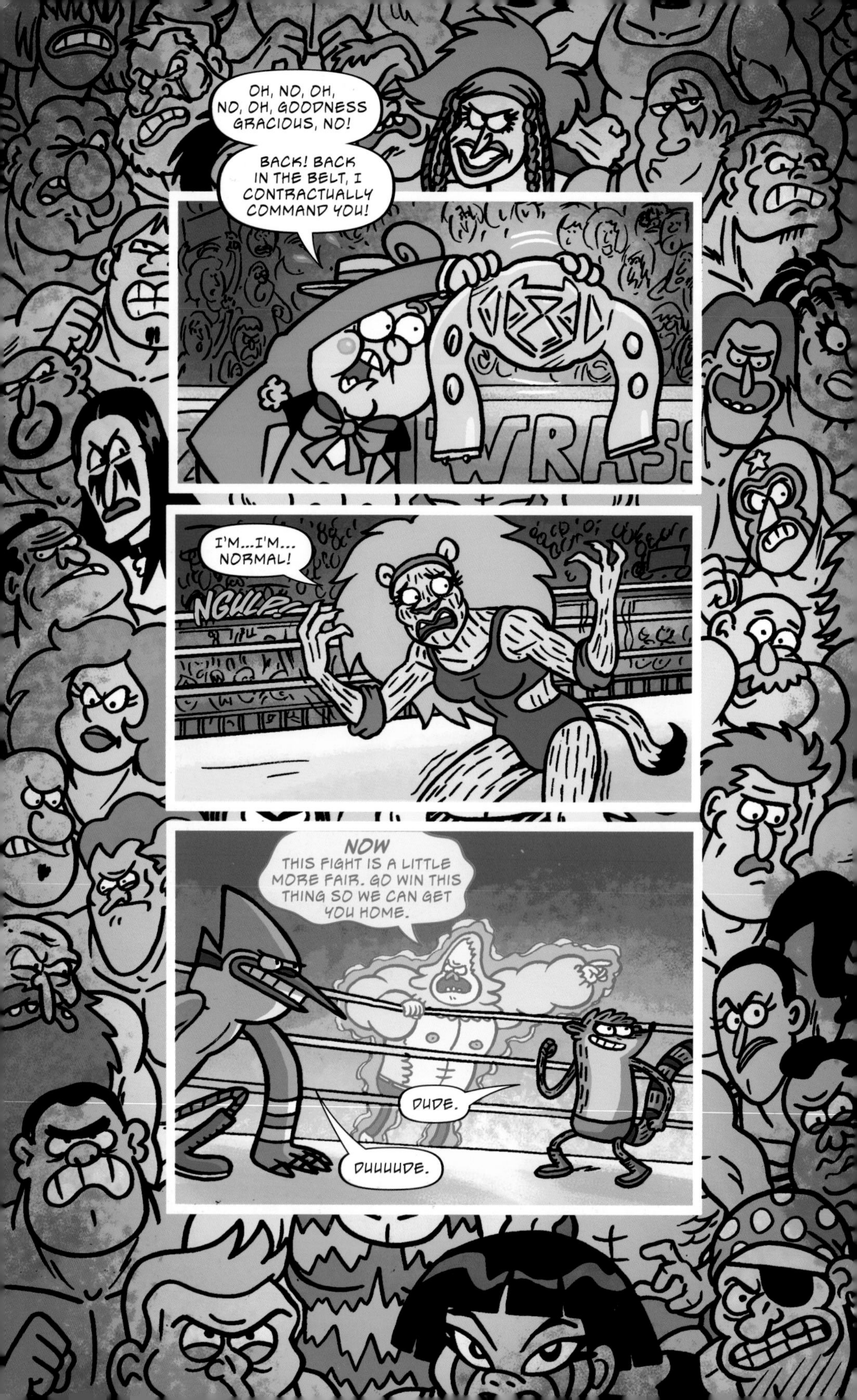
OH, NO, OH, NO, OH, GOODNESS GRACIOUS, NO!
BACK! BACK IN THE BELT, I CONTRACTUALLY COMMAND YOU!
WRAS
I'M...I'M... NORMAL!
NGULP
NOW THIS FIGHT IS A LITTLE MORE FAIR. GO WIN THIS THING SO WE CAN GET YOU HOME.
DUDE.
DUUUUDE.

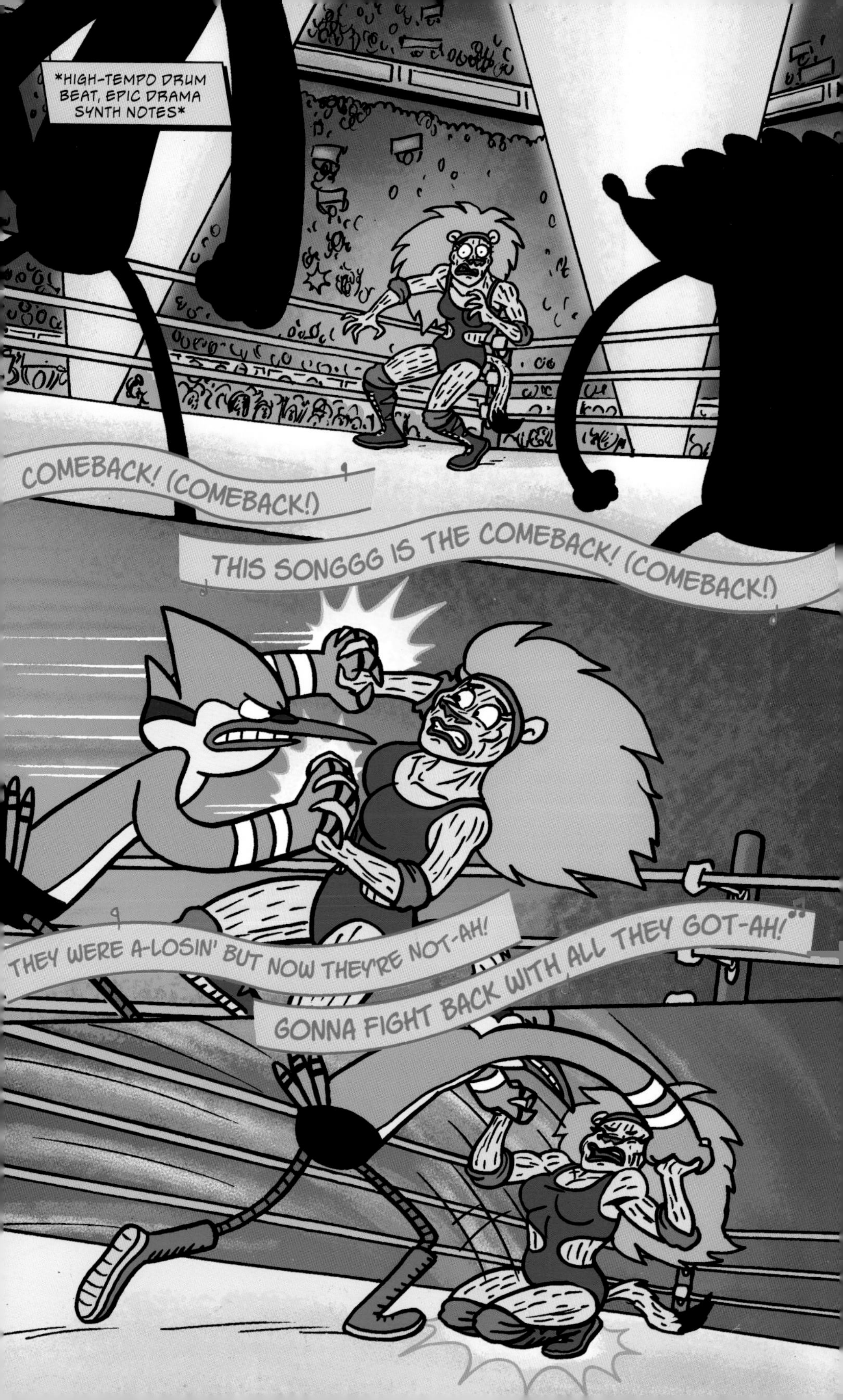

HIGH-TEMPO DRUM BEAT, EPIC DRAMA SYNTH NOTES
COMEBACK! (COMEBACK!)
THIS SONGGG IS THE COMEBACK! (COMEBACK!)
THEY WERE A-LOSIN' BUT NOW THEY'RE NOT-AH!
GONNA FIGHT BACK WITH ALL THEY GOT-AH!

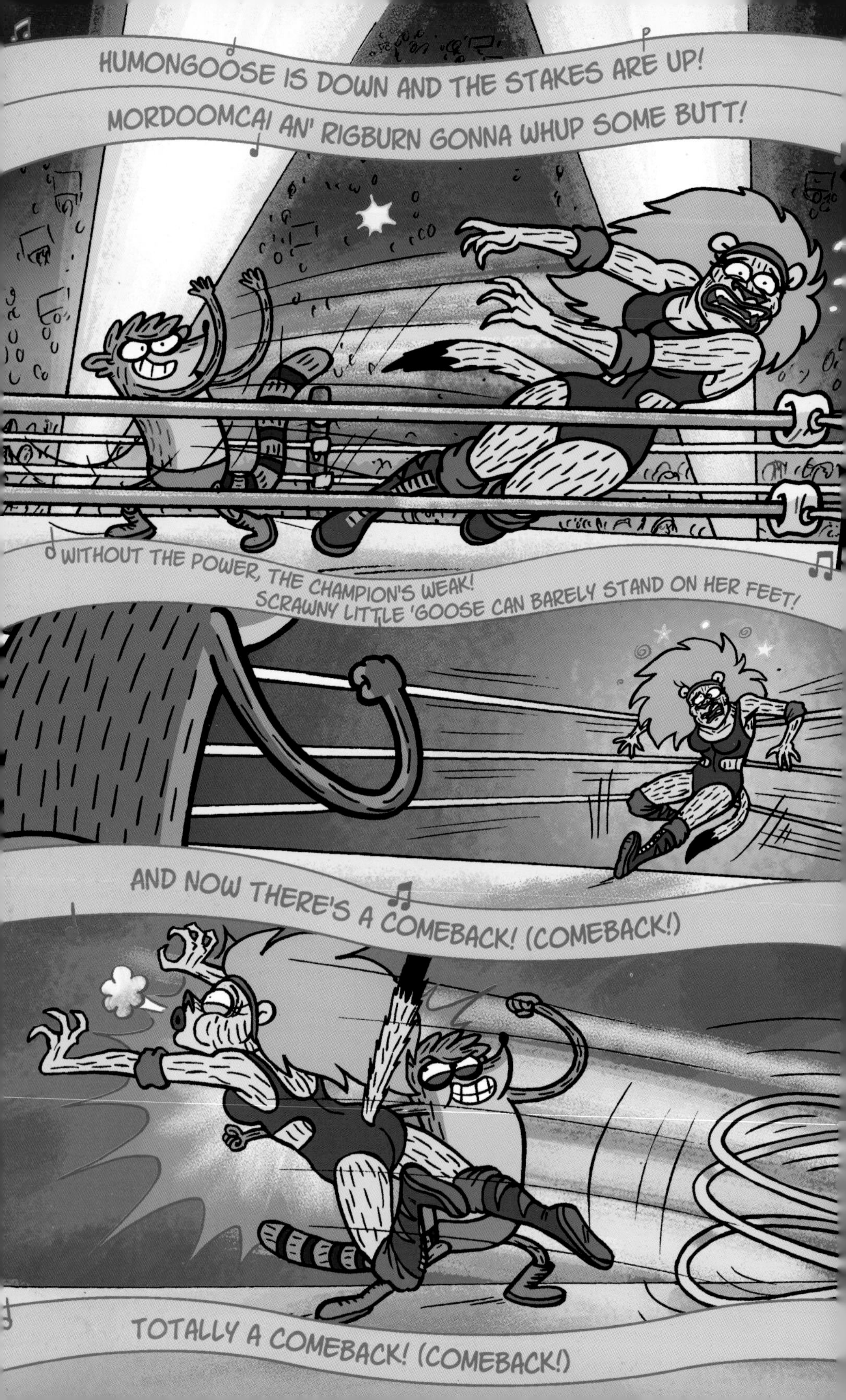
HUMONGOOSE IS DOWN AND THE STAKES ARE UP!
MORDOOMCAI AN' RIGBURN GONNA WHUP SOME BUTT!
WITHOUT THE POWER, THE CHAMPION'S WEAK!
SCRAWNY LITTLE 'GOOSE CAN BARELY STAND ON HER FEET!
AND NOW THERE'S A COMEBACK! (COMEBACK!)
TOTALLY A COMEBACK! (COMEBACK!)

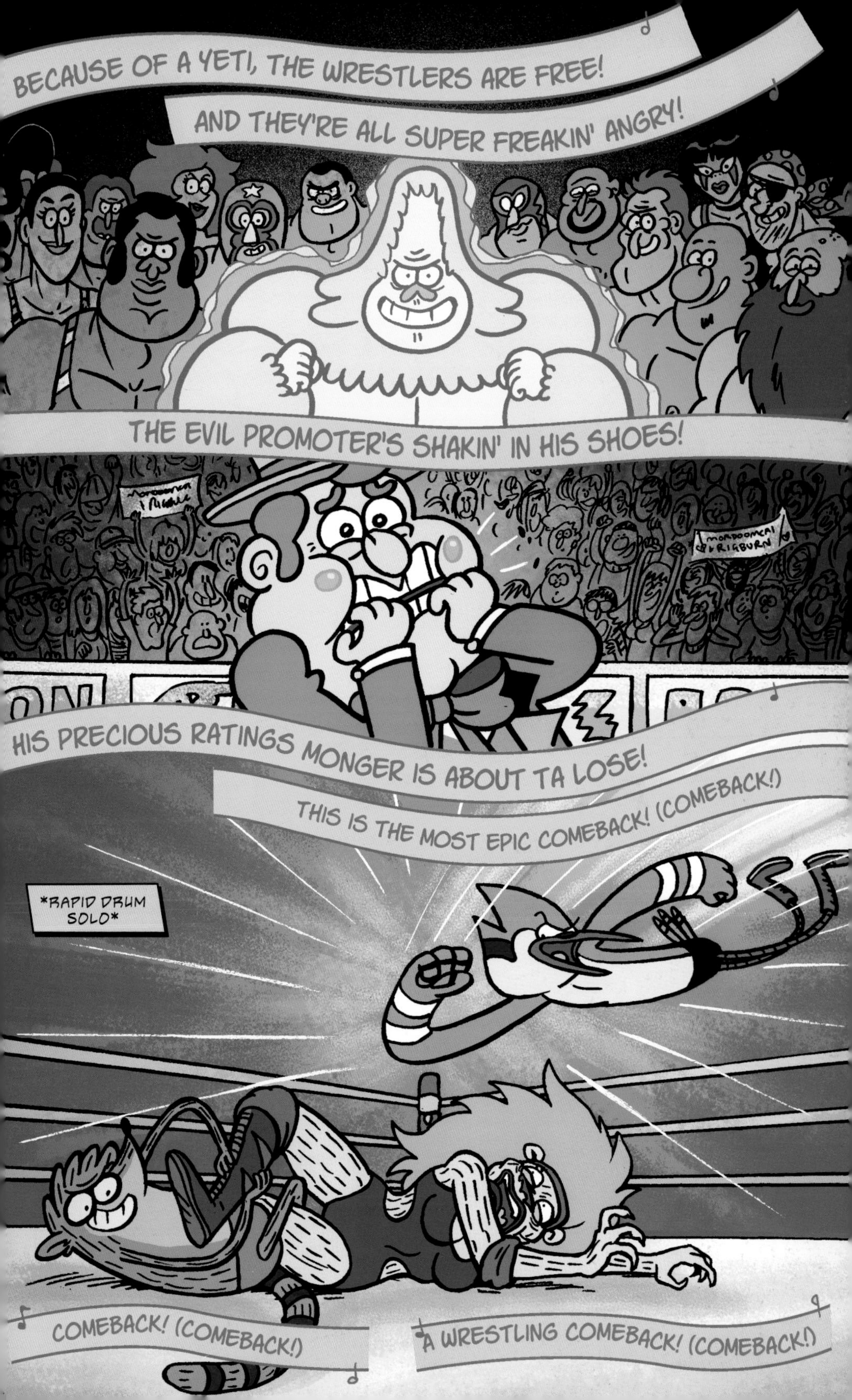
BECAUSE OF A YETI, THE WRESTLERS ARE FREE!
AND THEY'RE ALL SUPER FREAKIN' ANGRY!
THE EVIL PROMOTER'S SHAKIN' IN HIS SHOES!
HIS PRECIOUS RATINGS MONGER IS ABOUT TA LOSE!
THIS IS THE MOST EPIC COMEBACK! (COMEBACK!)
RAPID DRUM SOLO
COMEBACK! (COMEBACK!)
A WRESTLING COMEBACK! (COMEBACK!)

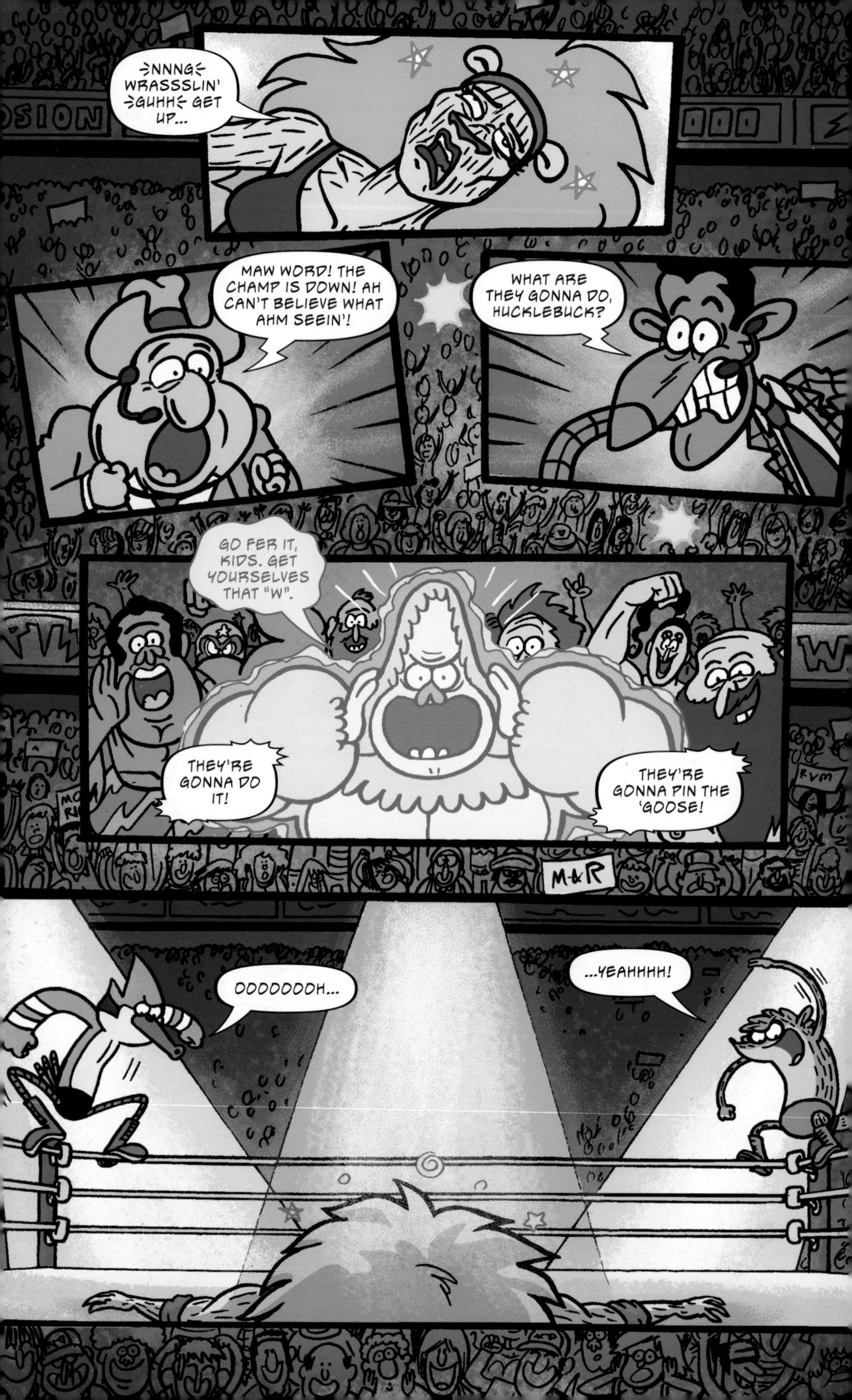

NNNG WRASSSLIN' GUHH GET UP...
MAW WORD! THE CHAMP IS DOWN! AH CAN'T BELIEVE WHAT AHM SEEIN'!
WHAT ARE THEY GONNA DO, HUCKLEBUCK?
GO FER IT, KIDS. GET YOURSELVES THAT "W".
THEY'RE GONNA DO IT!
THEY'RE GONNA PIN THE 'GOOSE!
M&R
OOOOOOOH...
...YEAHHHH!

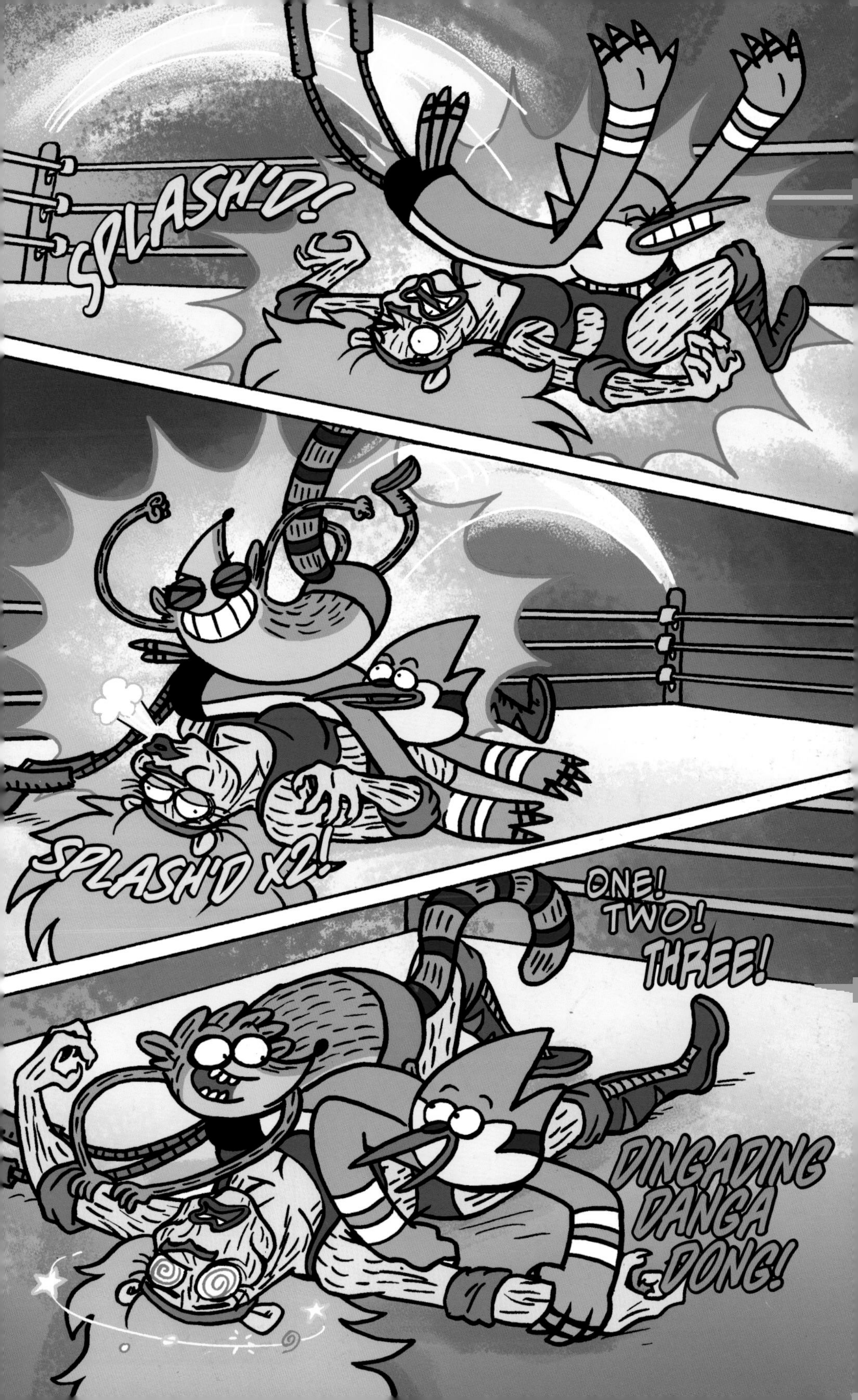
SPLASH'D!
SPLASH'D X2!
ONE!
TWO!
THREE!
DINGADING
DANGA
DONG!

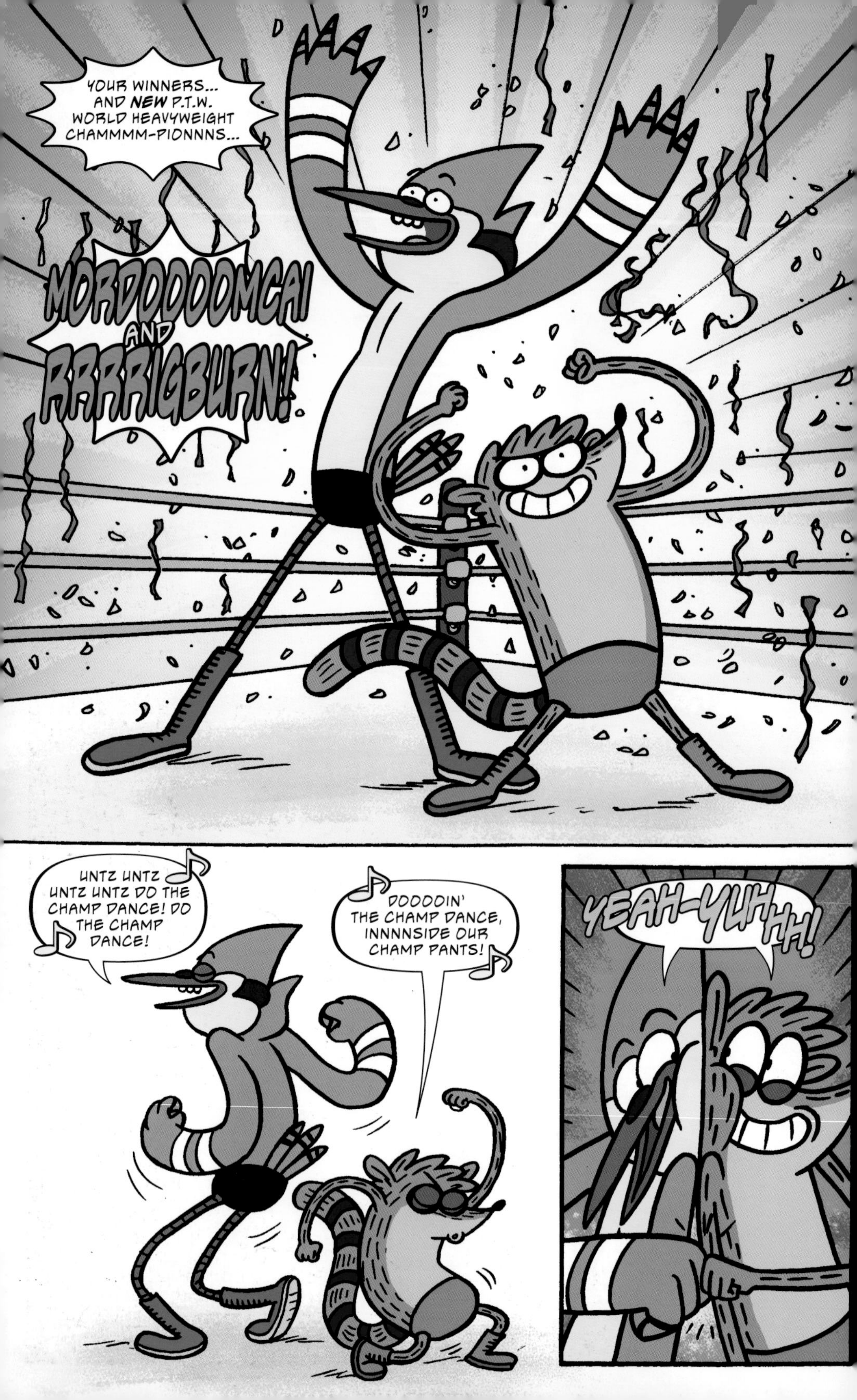
YOUR WINNERS... AND NEW P.T.W. WORLD HEAVYWEIGHT CHAMMMM-PIONNNS...
MORDOOOOOMCAI AND RRRRIGBURN!
UNTZ UNTZ UNTZ UNTZ DO THE CHAMP DANCE! DO THE CHAMP DANCE!
DOOOOIN' THE CHAMP DANCE, INNNNSIDE OUR CHAMP PANTS!
YEAH-YUHHH!

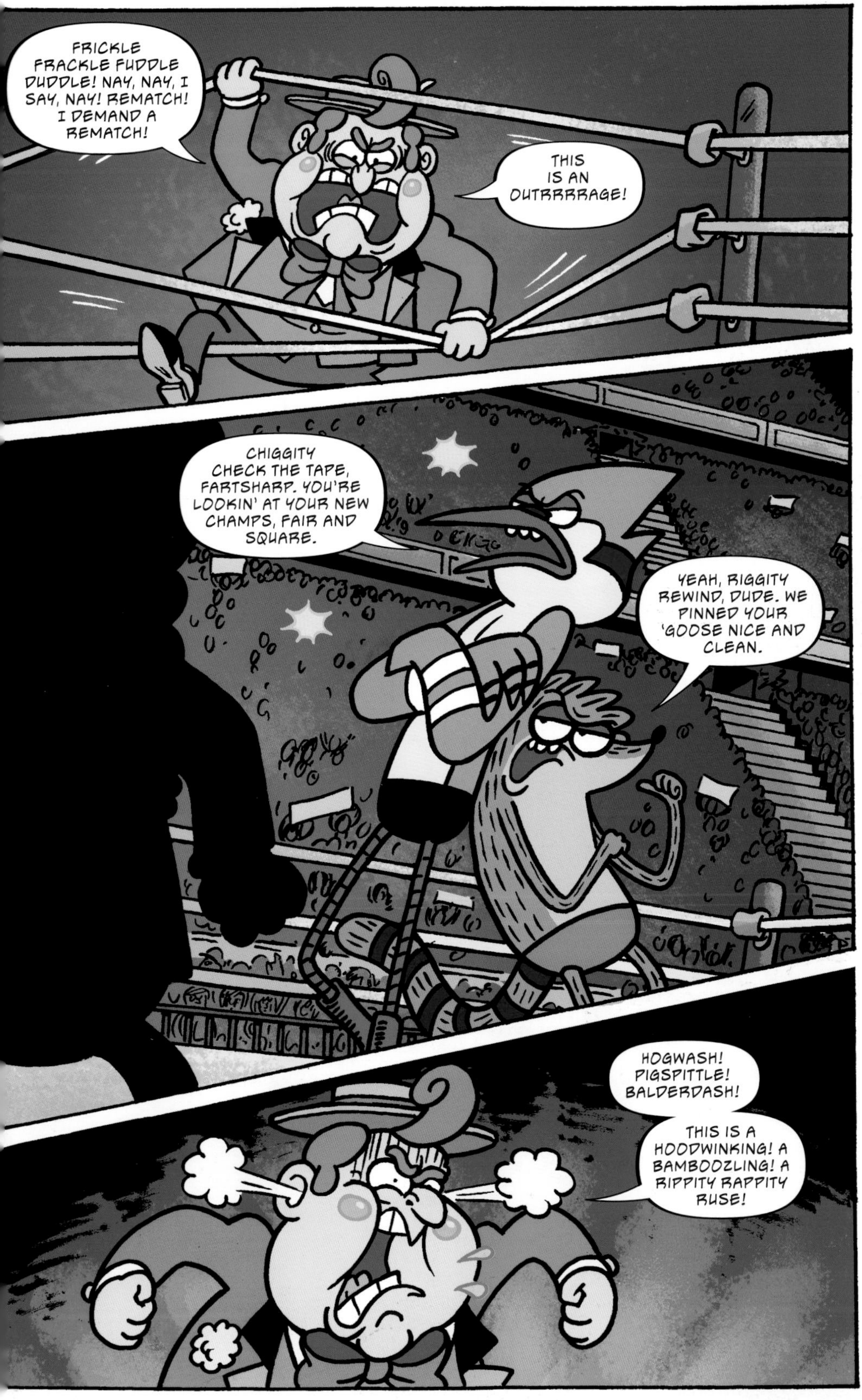
FRICKLE FRACKLE FUDDLE DUDDLE! NAY, NAY, I SAY, NAY! REMATCH! I DEMAND A REMATCH!
THIS IS AN OUTRRRRAGE!
CHIGGITY CHECK THE TAPE, FARTSHARP. YOU'RE LOOKIN' AT YOUR NEW CHAMPS, FAIR AND SQUARE.
YEAH, RIGGITY REWIND, DUDE. WE PINNED YOUR 'GOOSE NICE AND CLEAN.
HOGWASH! PIGSPITTLE! BALDERDASH!
THIS IS A HOODWINKING! A BAMBOOZLING! A RIPPITY RAPPITY RUSE!

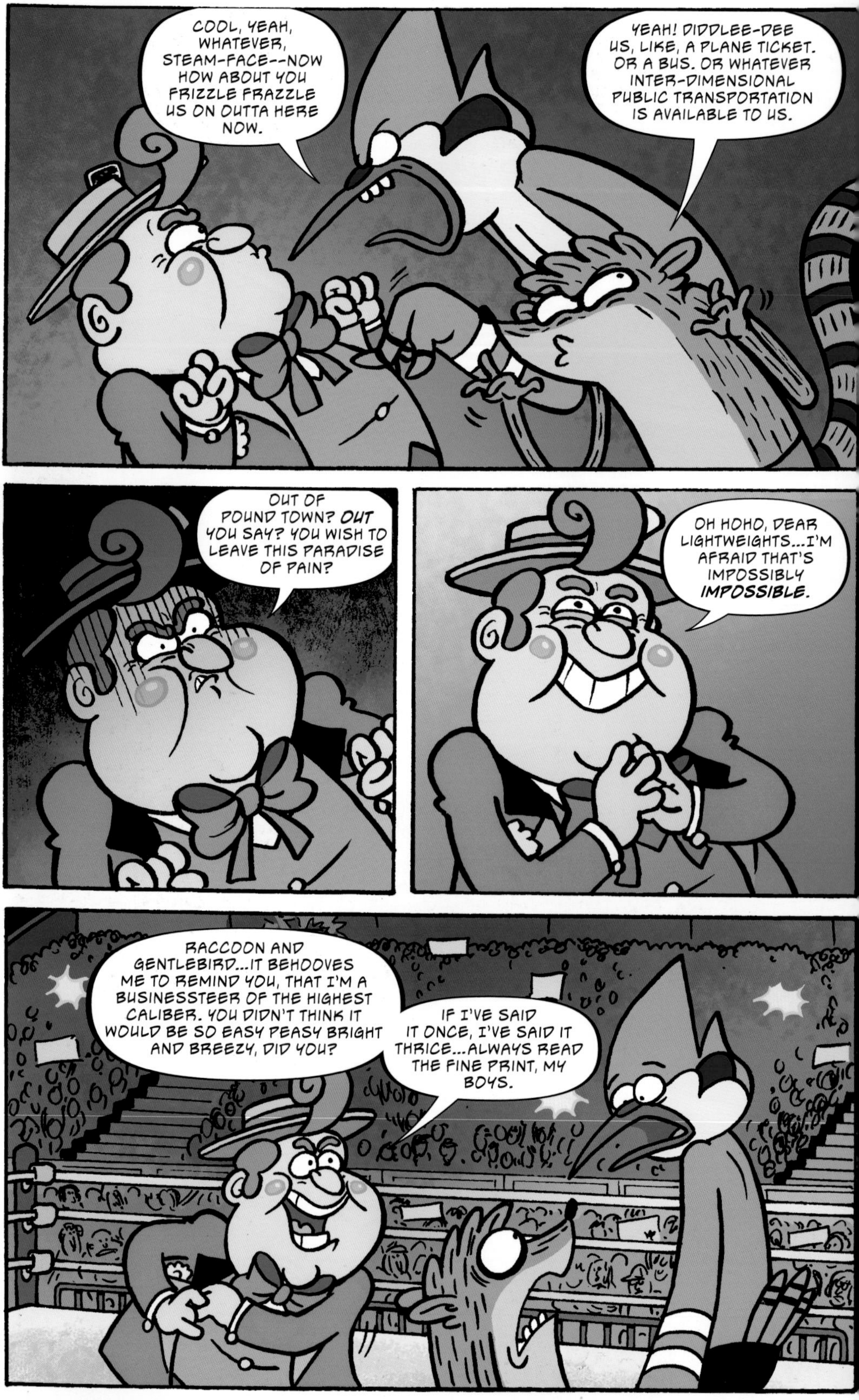
COOL, YEAH, WHATEVER, STEAM-FACE--NOW HOW ABOUT YOU FRIZZLE FRAZZLE US ON OUTTA HERE NOW.
YEAH! DIDDLEE-DEE US, LIKE, A PLANE TICKET. OR A BUS. OR WHATEVER INTER-DIMENSIONAL PUBLIC TRANSPORTATION IS AVAILABLE TO US.
OUT OF POUND TOWN? *OUT* YOU SAY? YOU WISH TO LEAVE THIS PARADISE OF PAIN?
OH HOHO, DEAR LIGHTWEIGHTS...I'M AFRAID THAT'S IMPOSSIBLY ***IMPOSSIBLE.***
RACCOON AND GENTLEBIRD...IT BEHOOVES ME TO REMIND YOU, THAT I'M A BUSINESSTEER OF THE HIGHEST CALIBER. YOU DIDN'T THINK IT WOULD BE SO EASY PEASY BRIGHT AND BREEZY, DID YOU?
IF I'VE SAID IT ONCE, I'VE SAID IT THRICE...ALWAYS READ THE FINE PRINT, MY BOYS.

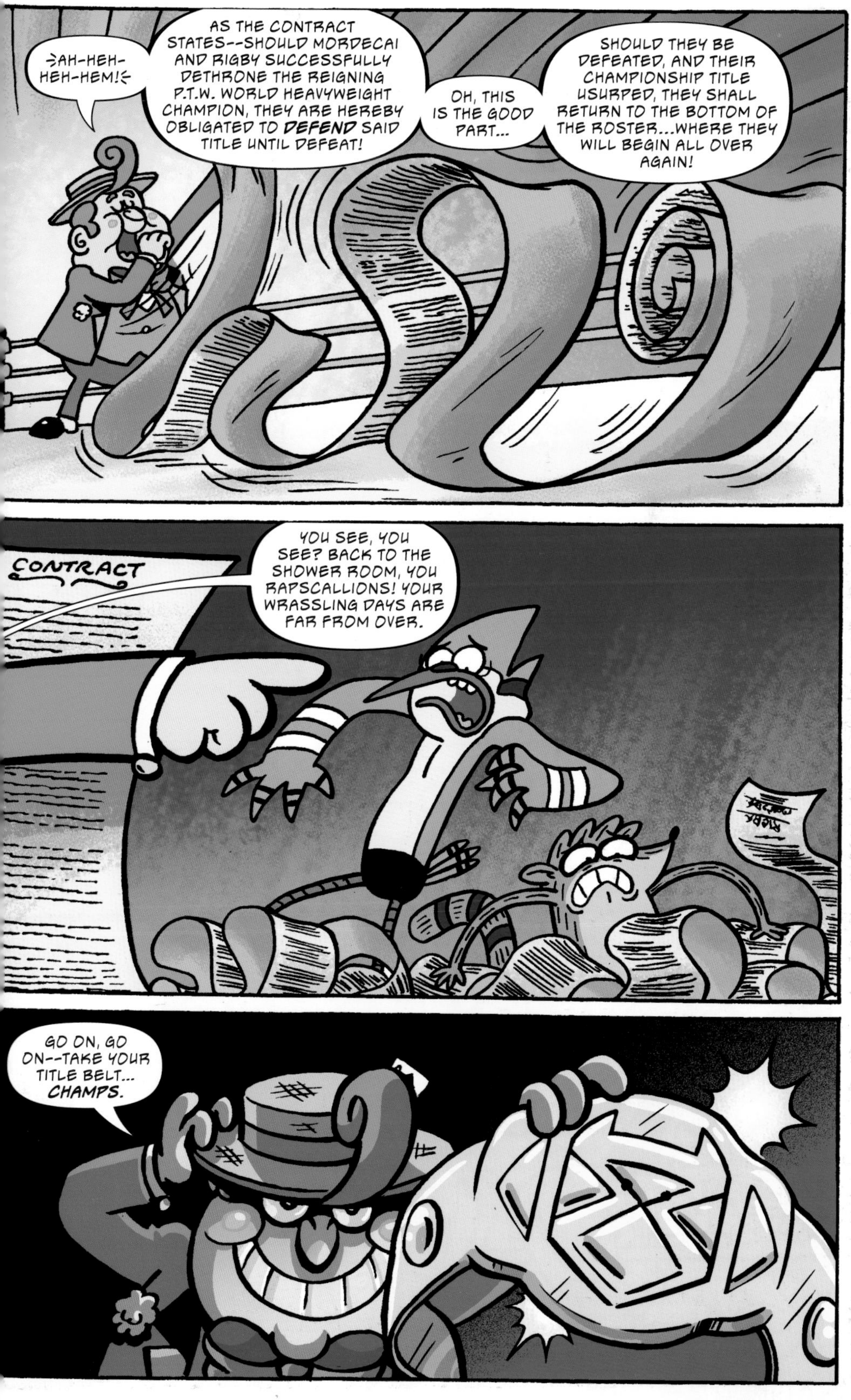

≥AH-HEH-HEH-HEM!≤
AS THE CONTRACT STATES--SHOULD MORDECAI AND RIGBY SUCCESSFULLY DETHRONE THE REIGNING P.T.W. WORLD HEAVYWEIGHT CHAMPION, THEY ARE HEREBY OBLIGATED TO ***DEFEND*** SAID TITLE UNTIL DEFEAT!
OH, THIS IS THE GOOD PART...
SHOULD THEY BE DEFEATED, AND THEIR CHAMPIONSHIP TITLE USURPED, THEY SHALL RETURN TO THE BOTTOM OF THE ROSTER...WHERE THEY WILL BEGIN ALL OVER AGAIN!
CONTRACT
YOU SEE, YOU SEE? BACK TO THE SHOWER ROOM, YOU RAPSCALLIONS! YOUR WRASSLING DAYS ARE FAR FROM OVER.
GO ON, GO ON--TAKE YOUR TITLE BELT... ***CHAMPS.***

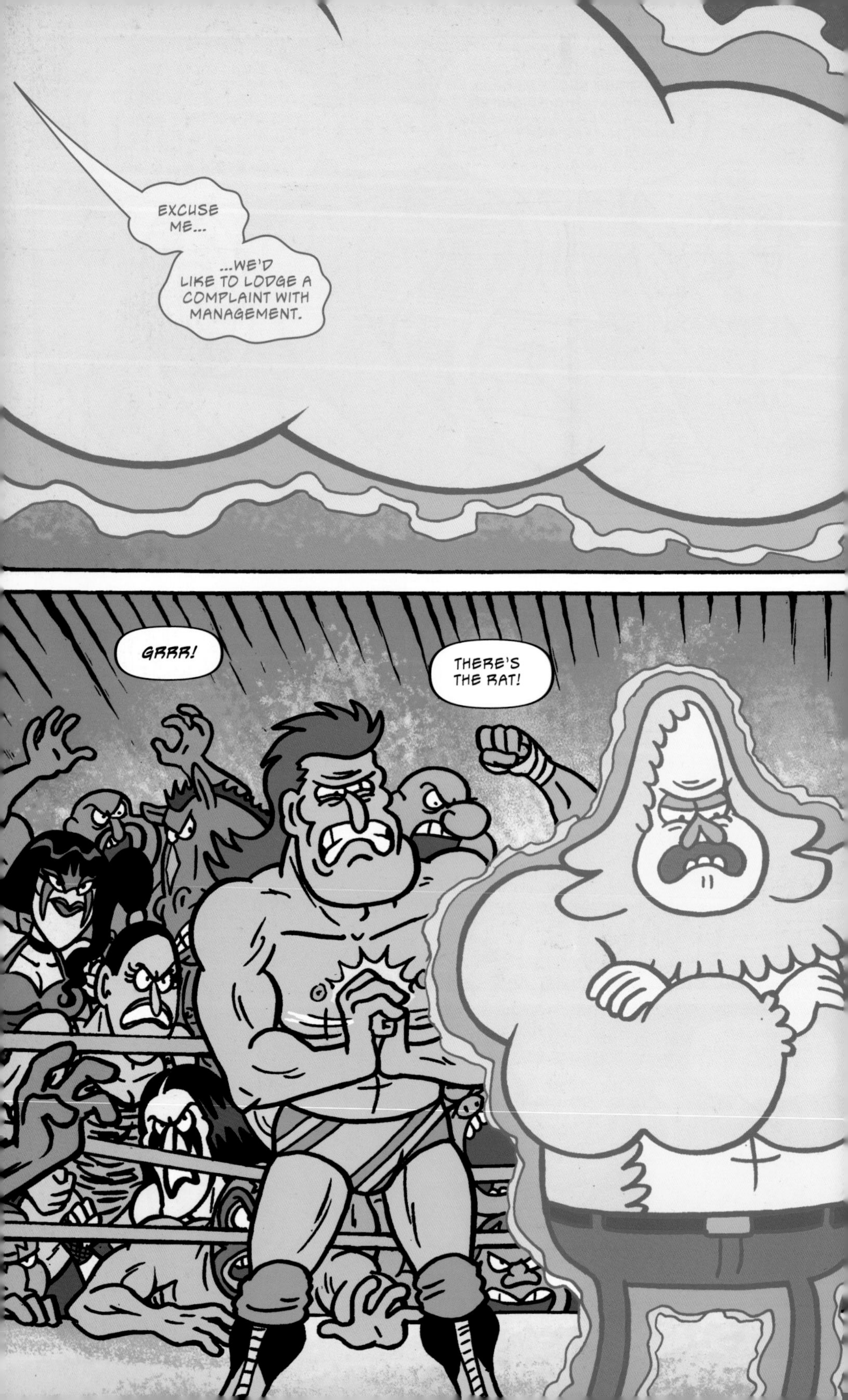
EXCUSE ME...
...WE'D LIKE TO LODGE A COMPLAINT WITH MANAGEMENT.
GRRR!
THERE'S THE RAT!

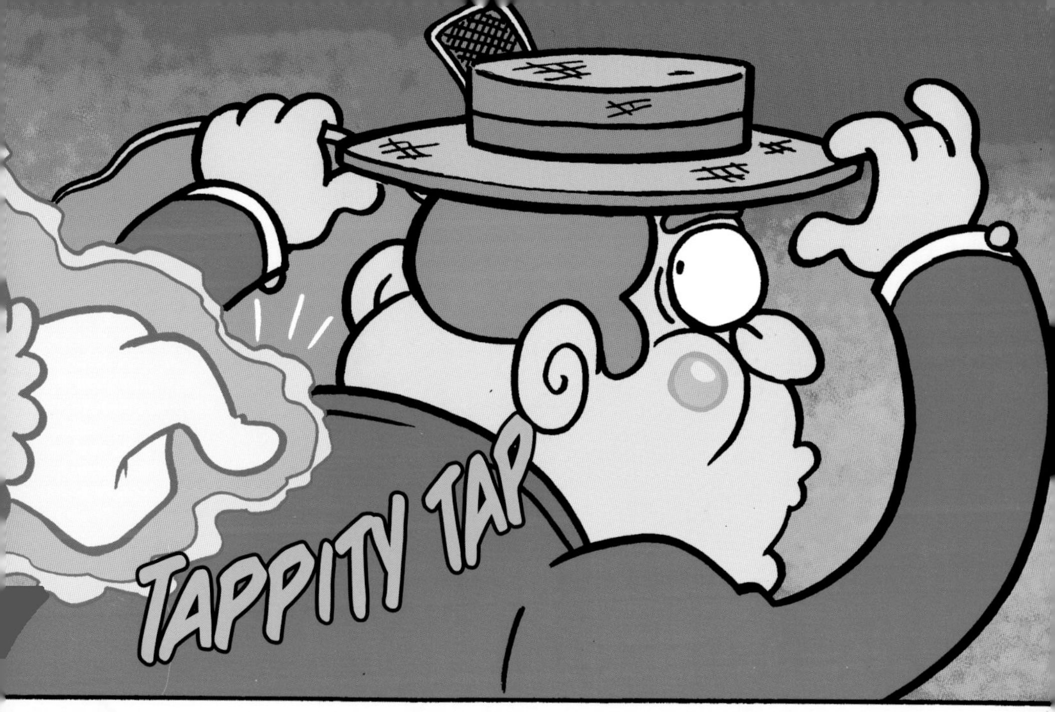
TAPPITY TAP

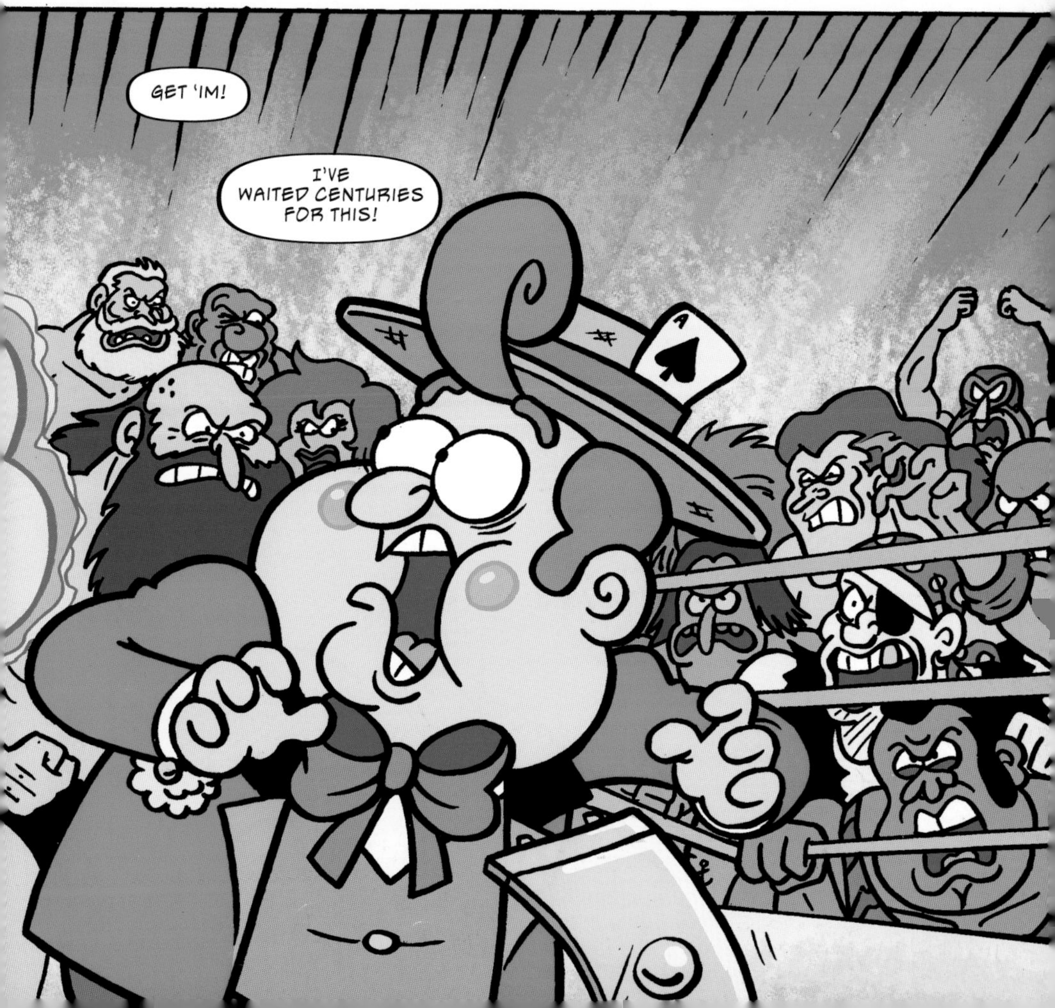
GET 'IM!
I'VE WAITED CENTURIES FOR THIS!

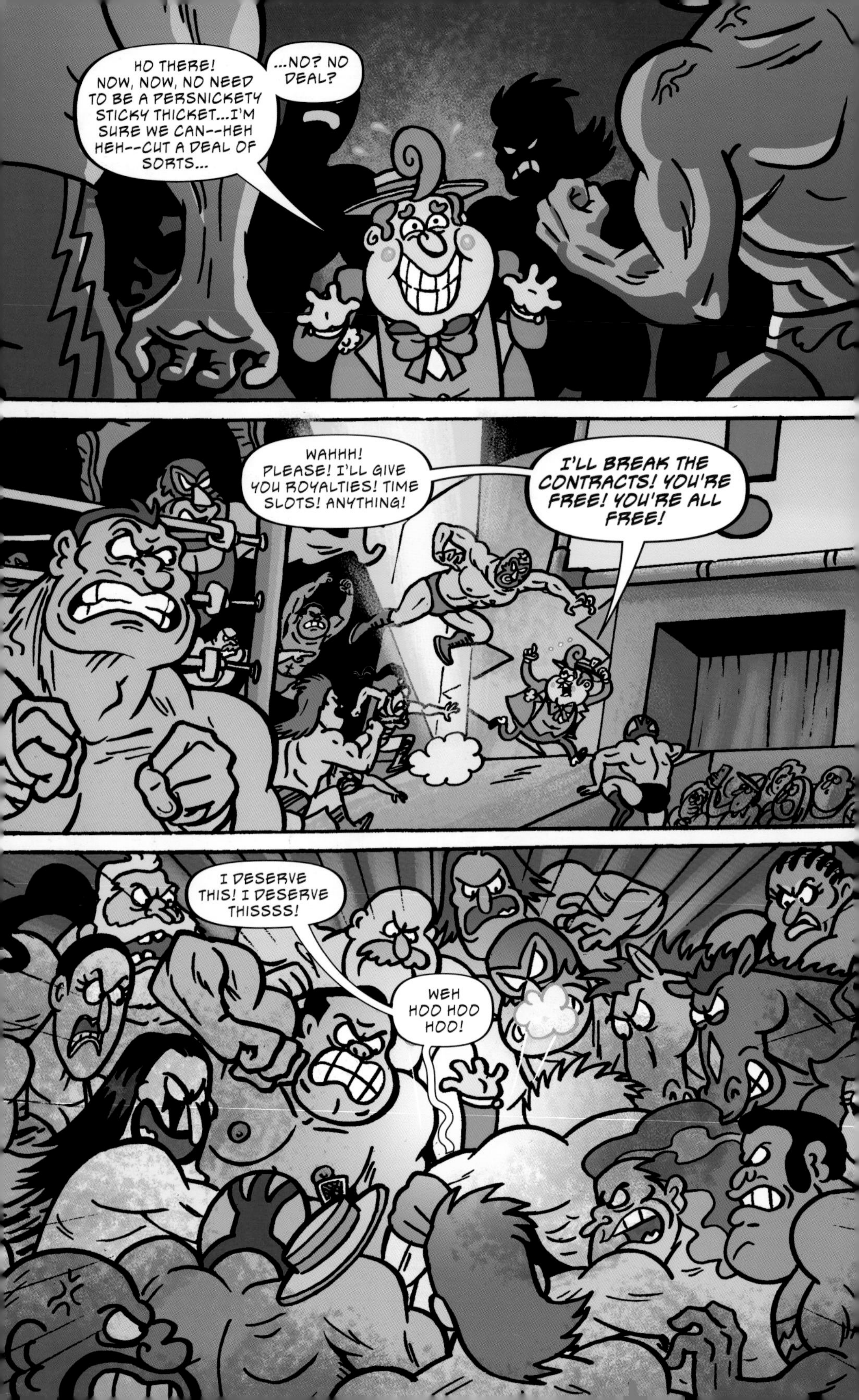
HO THERE! NOW, NOW, NO NEED TO BE A PERSNICKETY STICKY THICKET...I'M SURE WE CAN--HEH HEH--CUT A DEAL OF SORTS...
...NO? NO DEAL?
WAHHH! PLEASE! I'LL GIVE YOU ROYALTIES! TIME SLOTS! ANYTHING!
I'LL BREAK THE CONTRACTS! YOU'RE FREE! YOU'RE ALL FREE!
I DESERVE THIS! I DESERVE THISSSS!
WEH HOO HOO HOO!

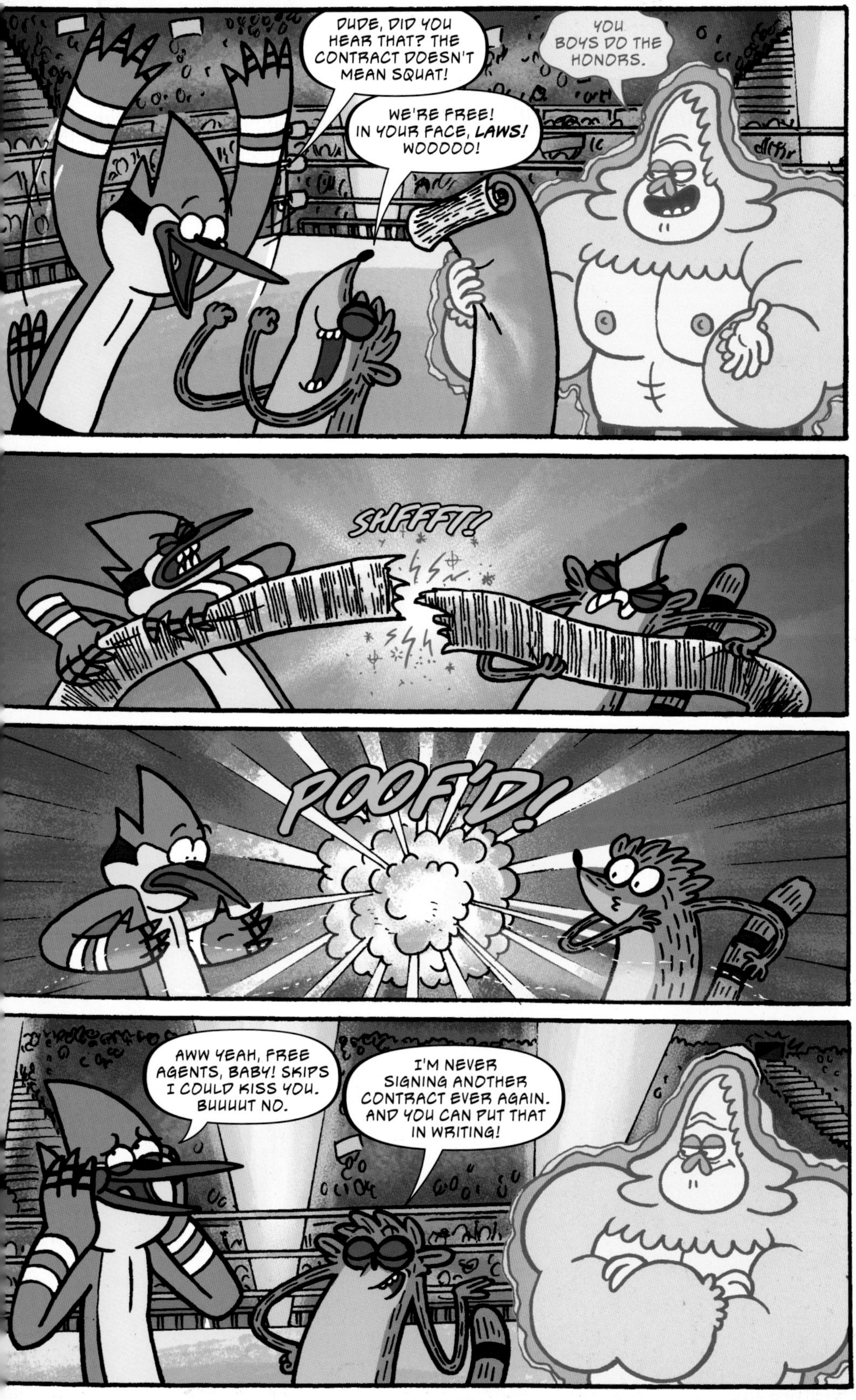
DUDE, DID YOU HEAR THAT? THE CONTRACT DOESN'T MEAN SQUAT!
YOU BOYS DO THE HONORS.
WE'RE FREE! IN YOUR FACE, LAWS! WOOOOO!
SHFFFT!
POOF'D!
AWW YEAH, FREE AGENTS, BABY! SKIPS I COULD KISS YOU. BUUUUT NO.
I'M NEVER SIGNING ANOTHER CONTRACT EVER AGAIN. AND YOU CAN PUT THAT IN WRITING!

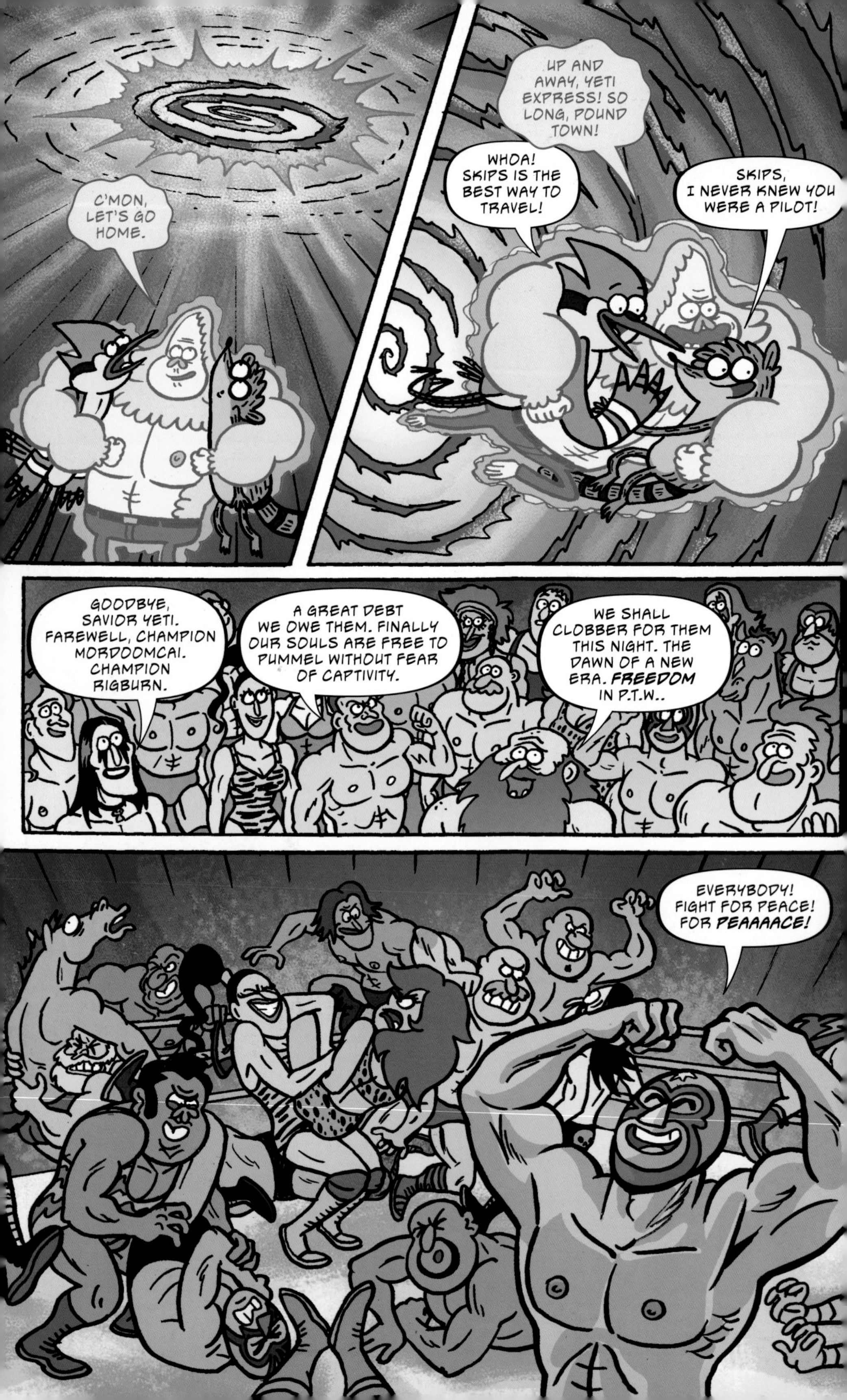
C'MON, LET'S GO HOME.
UP AND AWAY, YETI EXPRESS! SO LONG, POUND TOWN!
WHOA! SKIPS IS THE BEST WAY TO TRAVEL!
SKIPS, I NEVER KNEW YOU WERE A PILOT!
GOODBYE, SAVIOR YETI. FAREWELL, CHAMPION MORDOOMCAI. CHAMPION RIGBURN.
A GREAT DEBT WE OWE THEM. FINALLY OUR SOULS ARE FREE TO PUMMEL WITHOUT FEAR OF CAPTIVITY.
WE SHALL CLOBBER FOR THEM THIS NIGHT. THE DAWN OF A NEW ERA. FREEDOM IN P.T.W..
EVERYBODY! FIGHT FOR PEACE! FOR PEAAAACE!

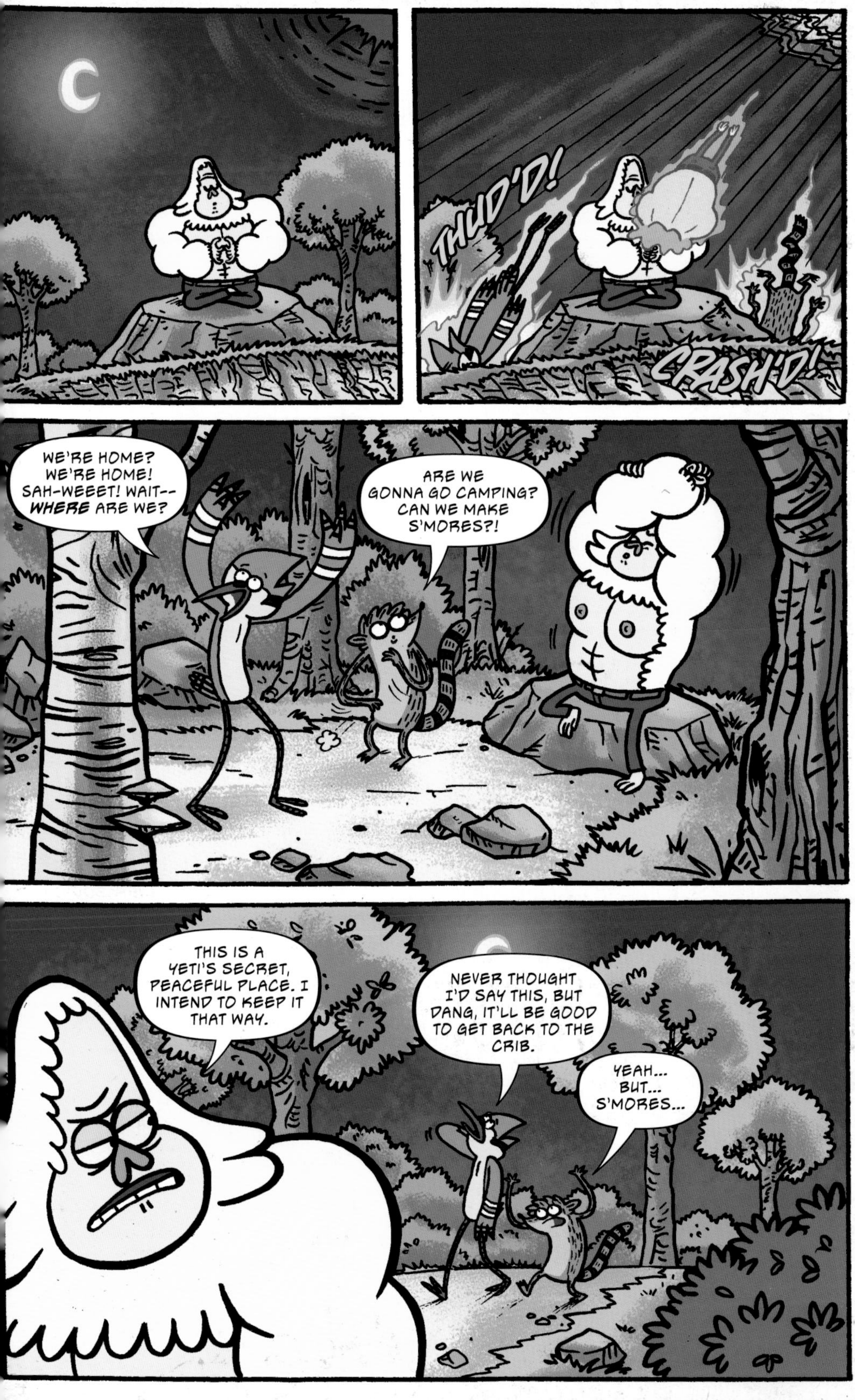
THUD'D!
CRASH'D!
WE'RE HOME? WE'RE HOME! SAH-WEEET! WAIT-- *WHERE* ARE WE?
ARE WE GONNA GO CAMPING? CAN WE MAKE S'MORES?!
THIS IS A YETI'S SECRET, PEACEFUL PLACE. I INTEND TO KEEP IT THAT WAY.
NEVER THOUGHT I'D SAY THIS, BUT DANG, IT'LL BE GOOD TO GET BACK TO THE CRIB.
YEAH... BUT... S'MORES...

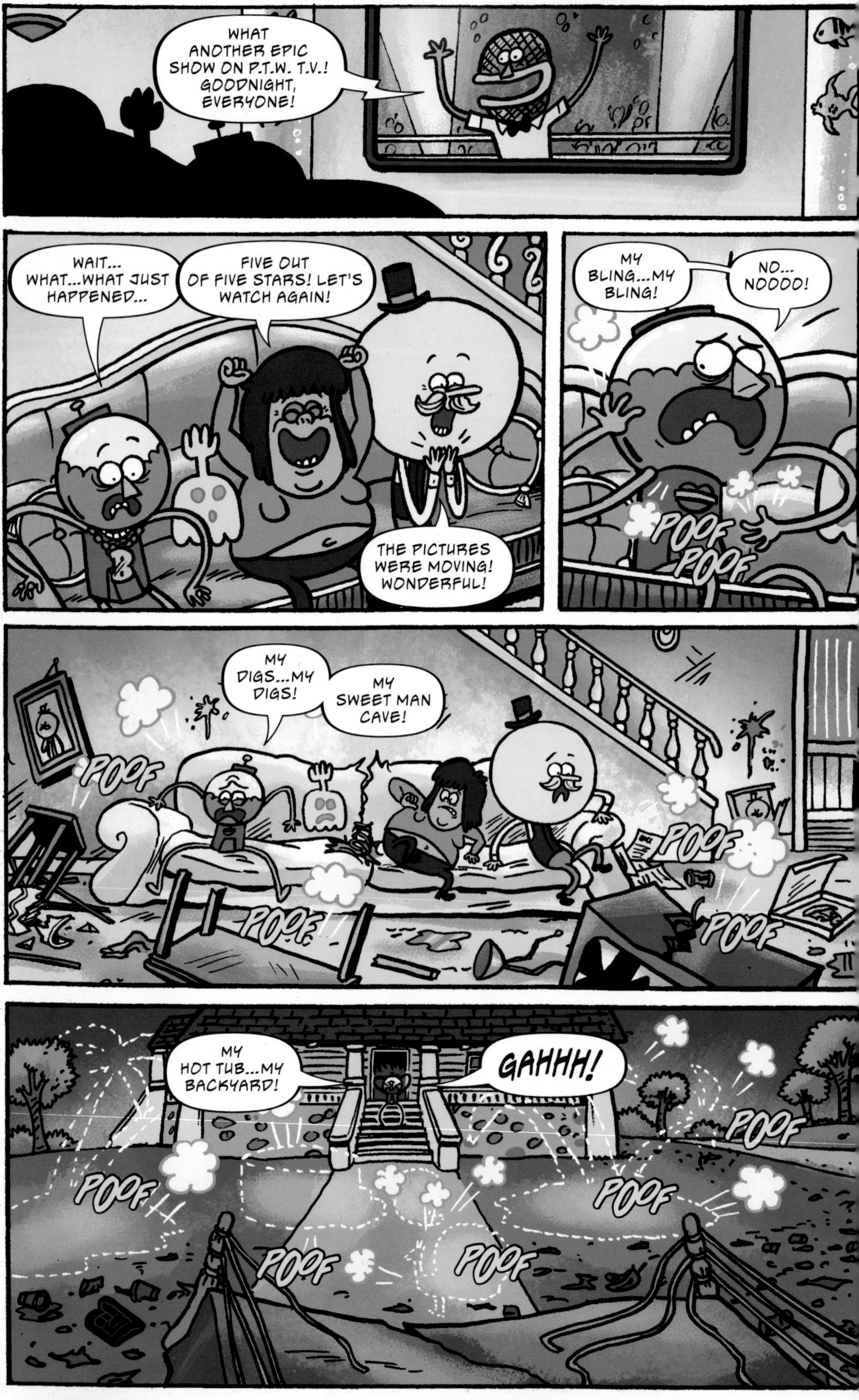
WHAT ANOTHER EPIC SHOW ON P.T.W. T.V.! GOODNIGHT, EVERYONE!
WAIT... WHAT...WHAT JUST HAPPENED...
FIVE OUT OF FIVE STARS! LET'S WATCH AGAIN!
THE PICTURES WERE MOVING! WONDERFUL!
MY BLING...MY BLING!
NO... NOOOO!
POOF
POOF
MY DIGS...MY DIGS!
MY SWEET MAN CAVE!
POOF
POOF
POOF
POOF
MY HOT TUB...MY BACKYARD!
GAHHH!
POOF
POOF
POOF
POOF
POOF

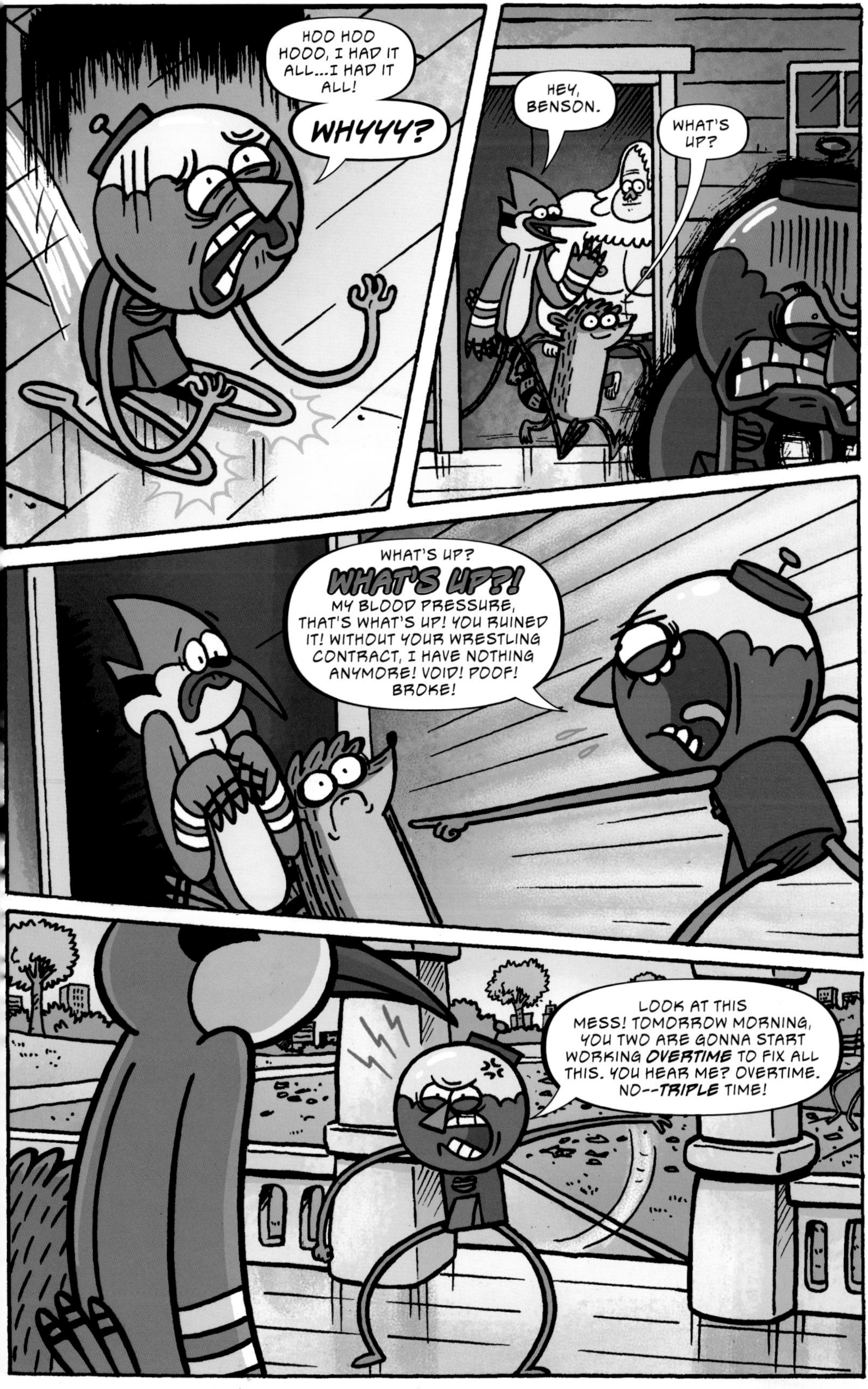
HOO HOO HOOO, I HAD IT ALL...I HAD IT ALL!
WHYYY?
HEY, BENSON.
WHAT'S UP?
WHAT'S UP? WHAT'S UP?! MY BLOOD PRESSURE, THAT'S WHAT'S UP! YOU RUINED IT! WITHOUT YOUR WRESTLING CONTRACT, I HAVE NOTHING ANYMORE! VOID! POOF! BROKE!
LOOK AT THIS MESS! TOMORROW MORNING, YOU TWO ARE GONNA START WORKING OVERTIME TO FIX ALL THIS. YOU HEAR ME? OVERTIME. NO--TRIPLE TIME!

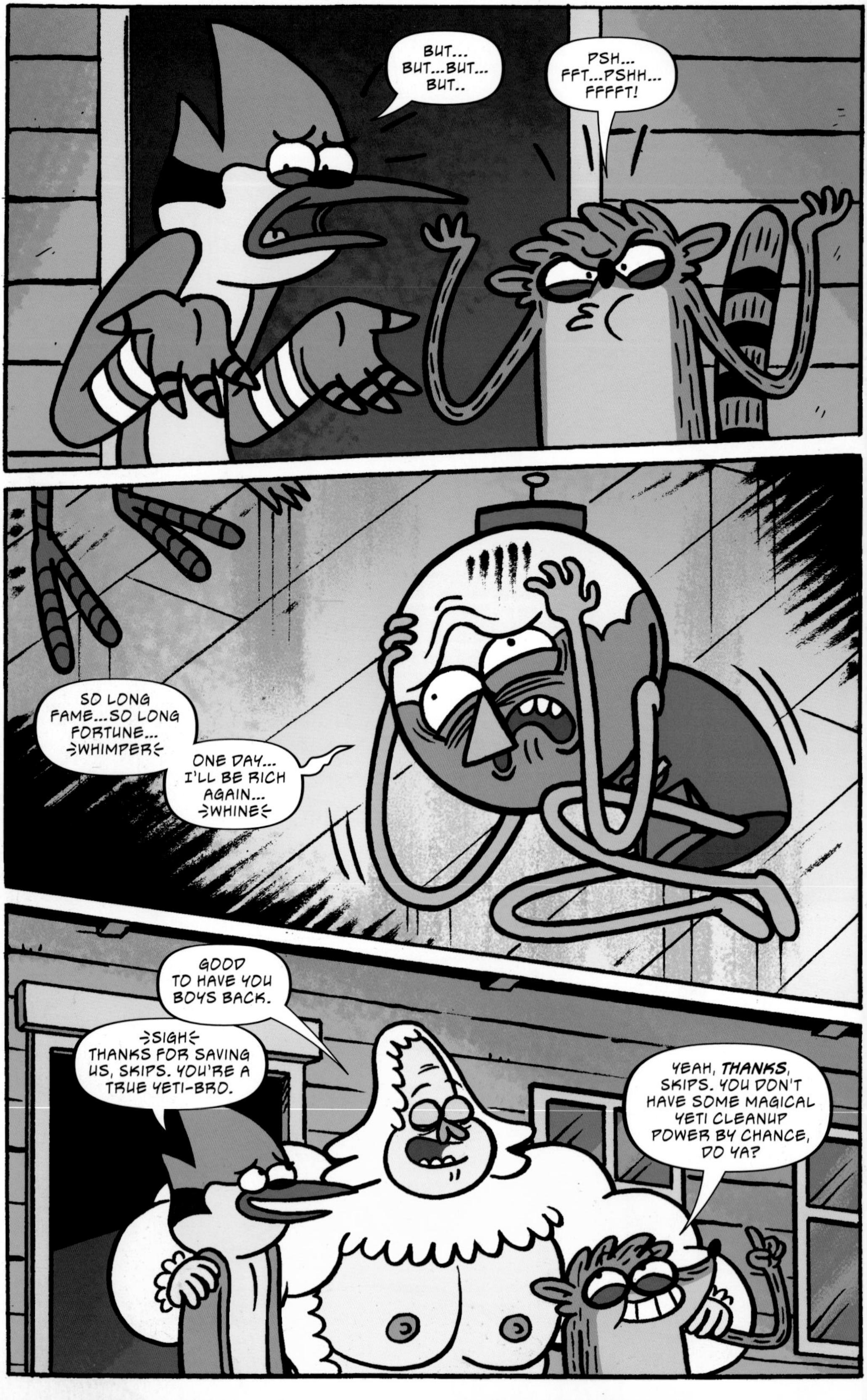
BUT...
BUT...BUT...
BUT..
PSH...
FFT...PSHH...
FFFFT!
SO LONG FAME...SO LONG FORTUNE... ⋟WHIMPER⋞
ONE DAY... I'LL BE RICH AGAIN... ⋟WHINE⋞
GOOD TO HAVE YOU BOYS BACK.
⋟SIGH⋞ THANKS FOR SAVING US, SKIPS. YOU'RE A TRUE YETI-BRO.
YEAH, ***THANKS***, SKIPS. YOU DON'T HAVE SOME MAGICAL YETI CLEANUP POWER BY CHANCE, DO YA?

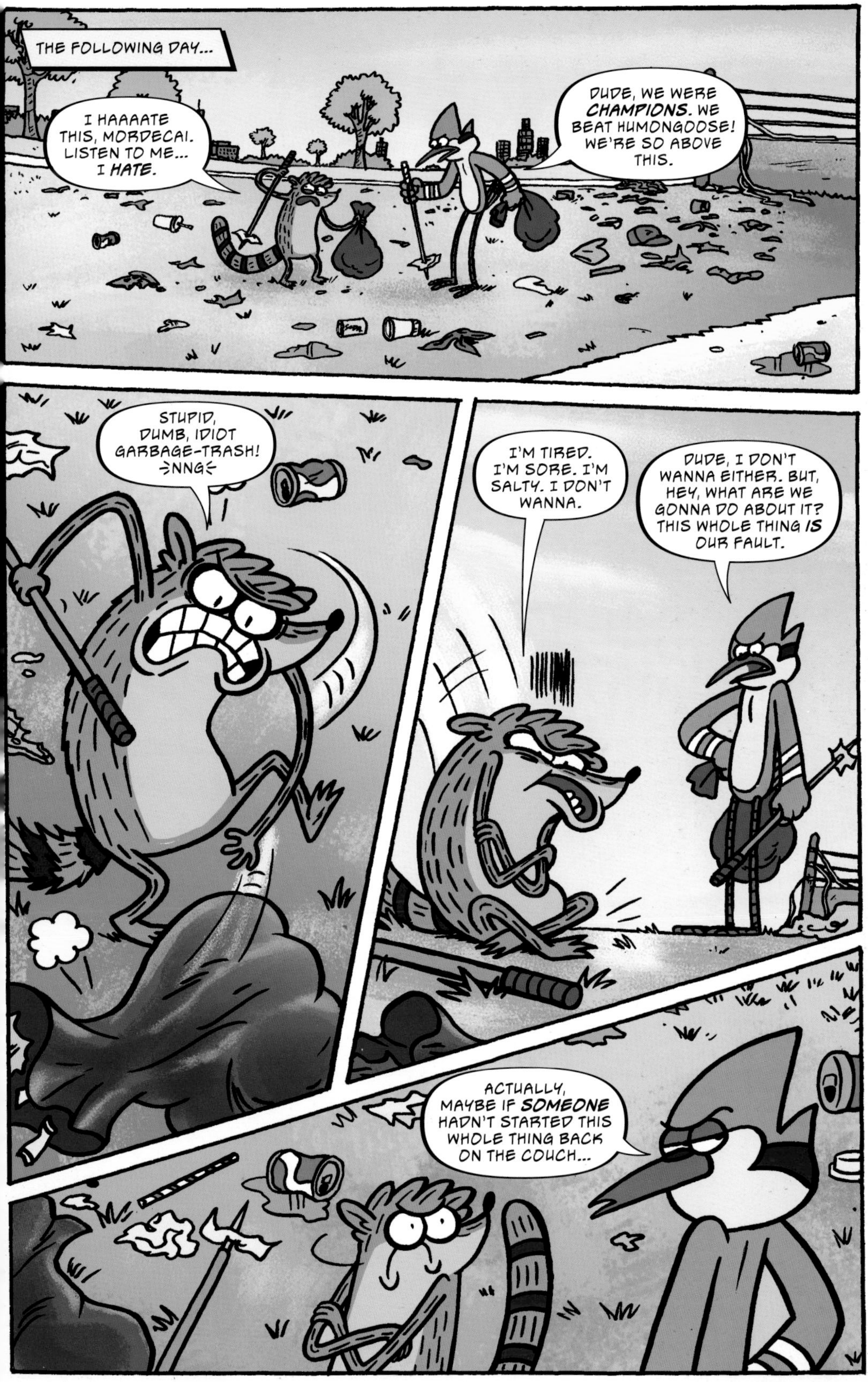
THE FOLLOWING DAY...
I HAAAAATE THIS, MORDECAI. LISTEN TO ME... I *HATE.*
DUDE, WE WERE *CHAMPIONS.* WE BEAT HUMONGOOSE! WE'RE SO ABOVE THIS.
STUPID, DUMB, IDIOT GARBAGE-TRASH! NNG
I'M TIRED. I'M SORE. I'M SALTY. I DON'T WANNA.
DUDE, I DON'T WANNA EITHER. BUT, HEY, WHAT ARE WE GONNA DO ABOUT IT? THIS WHOLE THING *IS* OUR FAULT.
ACTUALLY, MAYBE IF *SOMEONE* HADN'T STARTED THIS WHOLE THING BACK ON THE COUCH...

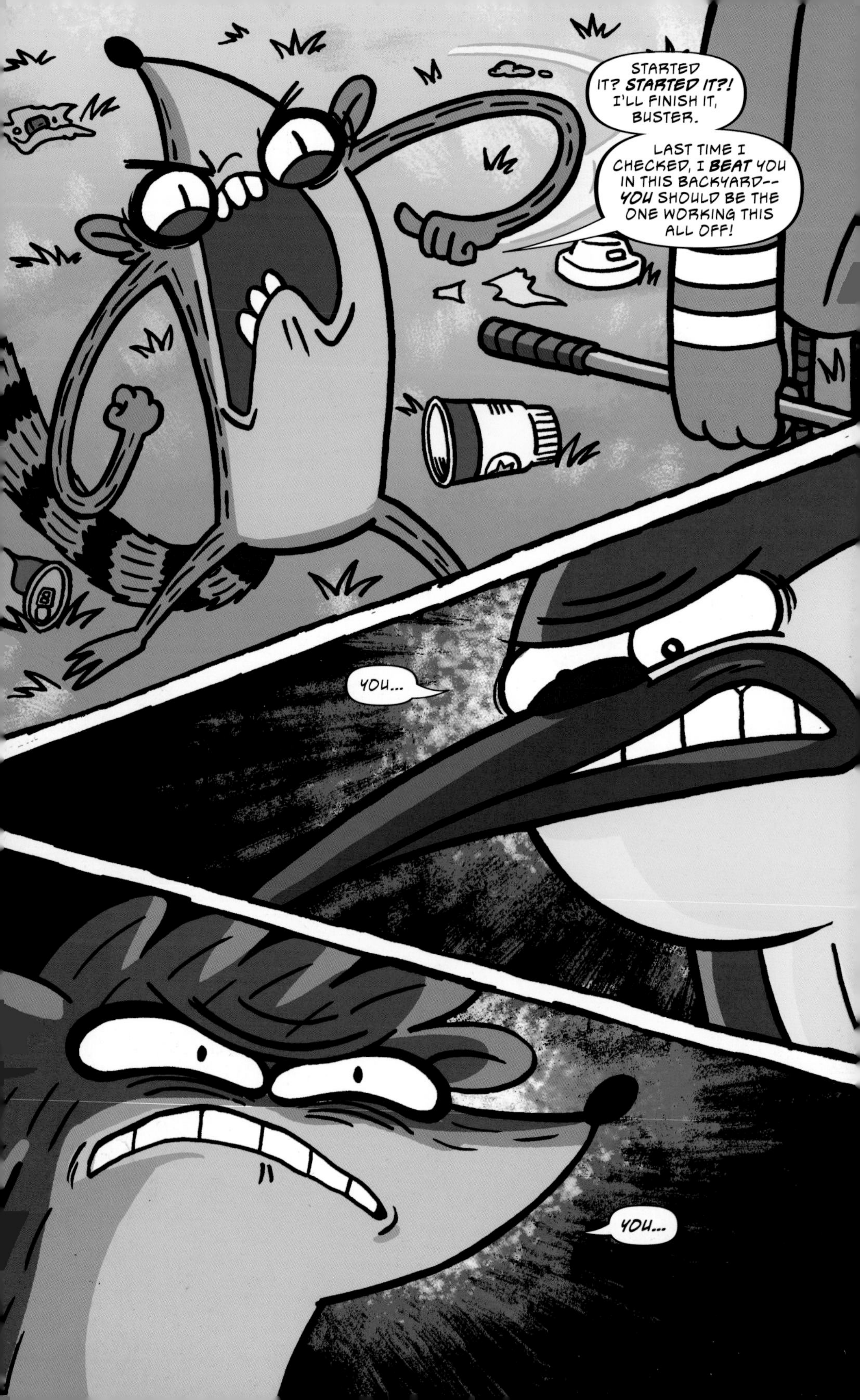
STARTED IT? **STARTED IT?!** I'LL FINISH IT, BUSTER.
LAST TIME I CHECKED, I **BEAT** YOU IN THIS BACKYARD-- ***YOU*** SHOULD BE THE ONE WORKING THIS ALL OFF!
YOU...
YOU...

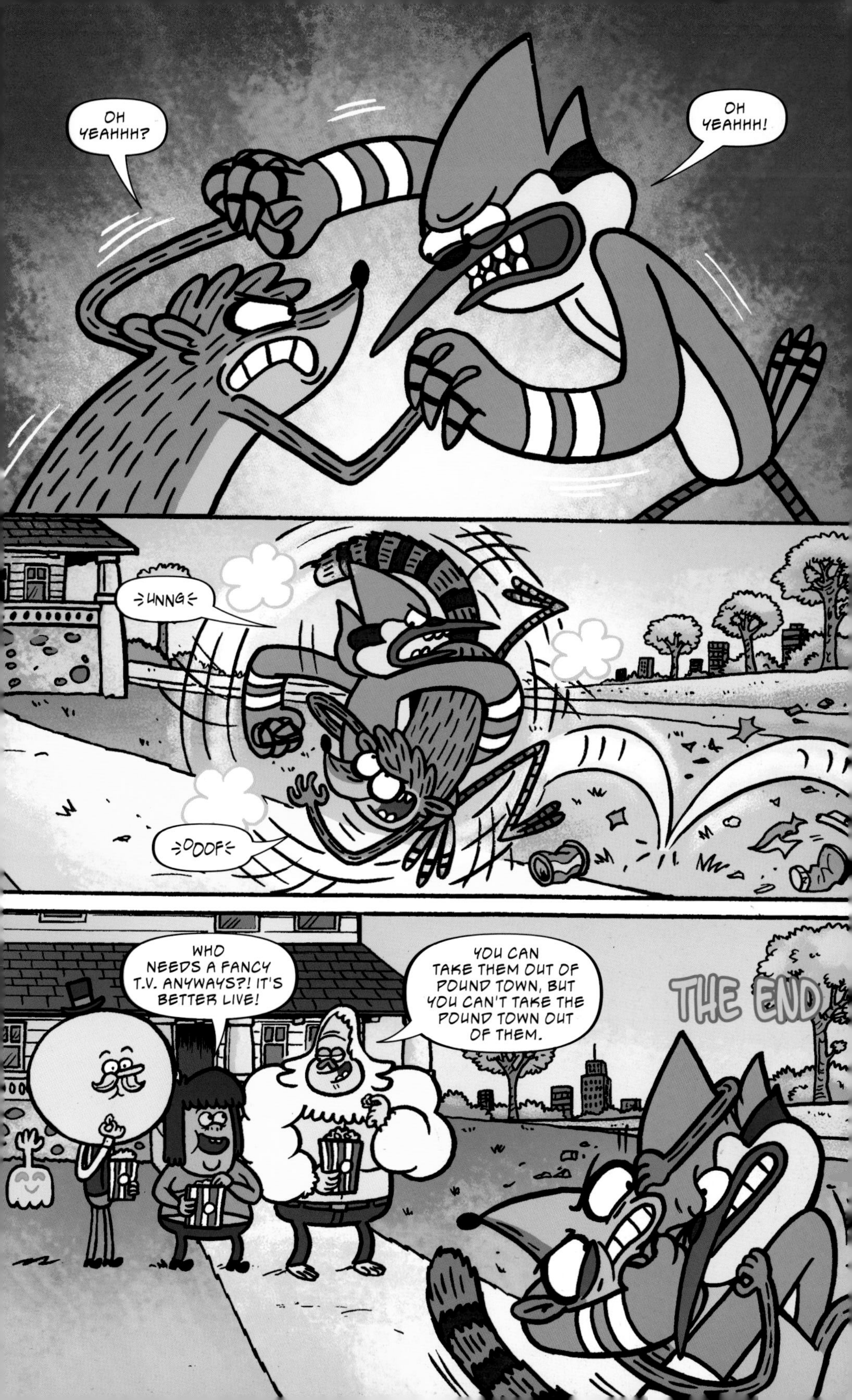
OH YEAHHH?
OH YEAHHH!
UNNG
OOOF
WHO NEEDS A FANCY T.V. ANYWAYS?! IT'S BETTER LIVE!
YOU CAN TAKE THEM OUT OF POUND TOWN, BUT YOU CAN'T TAKE THE POUND TOWN OUT OF THEM.
THE END

"THE COMEBACK"

WRITTEN BY

EDDIE WRIGHT

ILLUSTRATED BY

ELLE POWER

COLORED BY

LISA MOORE

LETTERED BY

WARREN MONTGOMERY

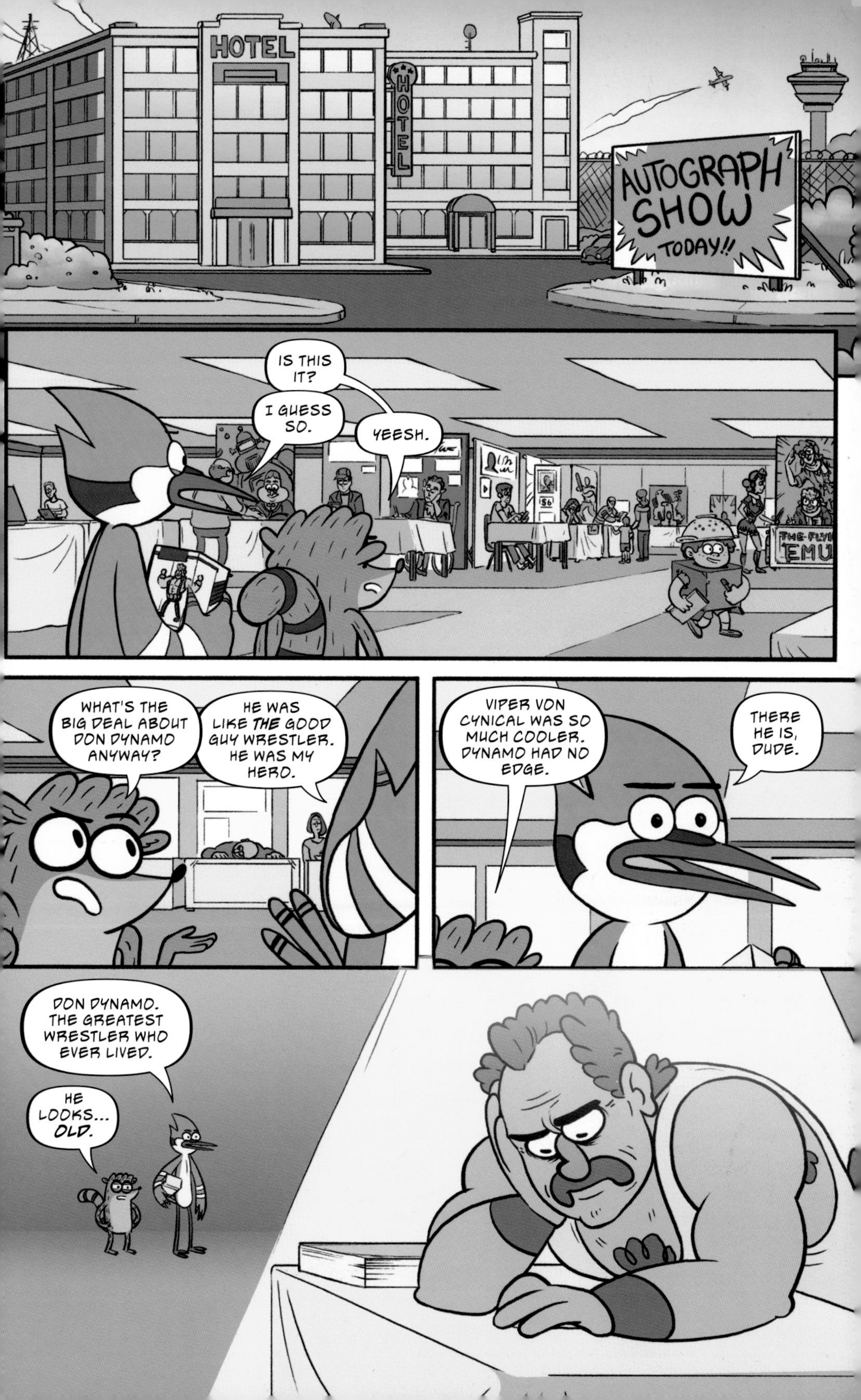
HOTEL
HOTEL
AUTOGRAPH SHOW TODAY!!
IS THIS IT?
I GUESS SO.
YEESH.
THE FLYI
EMU
WHAT'S THE BIG DEAL ABOUT DON DYNAMO ANYWAY?
HE WAS LIKE THE GOOD GUY WRESTLER. HE WAS MY HERO.
VIPER VON CYNICAL WAS SO MUCH COOLER. DYNAMO HAD NO EDGE.
THERE HE IS, DUDE.
DON DYNAMO. THE GREATEST WRESTLER WHO EVER LIVED.
HE LOOKS... OLD.

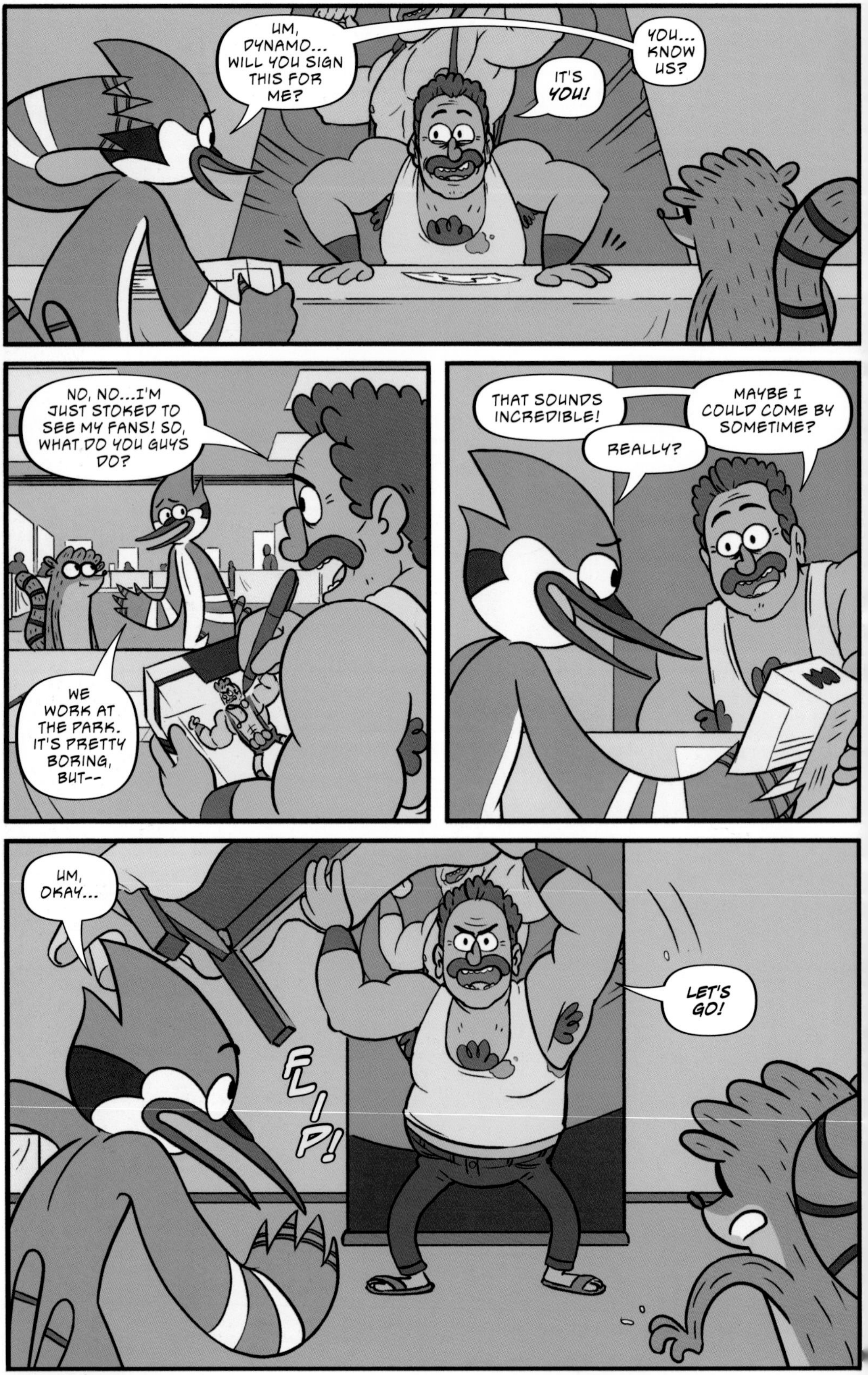
UM, DYNAMO... WILL YOU SIGN THIS FOR ME?
IT'S YOU!
YOU... KNOW US?
NO, NO...I'M JUST STOKED TO SEE MY FANS! SO, WHAT DO YOU GUYS DO?
WE WORK AT THE PARK. IT'S PRETTY BORING, BUT--
THAT SOUNDS INCREDIBLE!
REALLY?
MAYBE I COULD COME BY SOMETIME?
UM, OKAY...
FLIP!
LET'S GO!

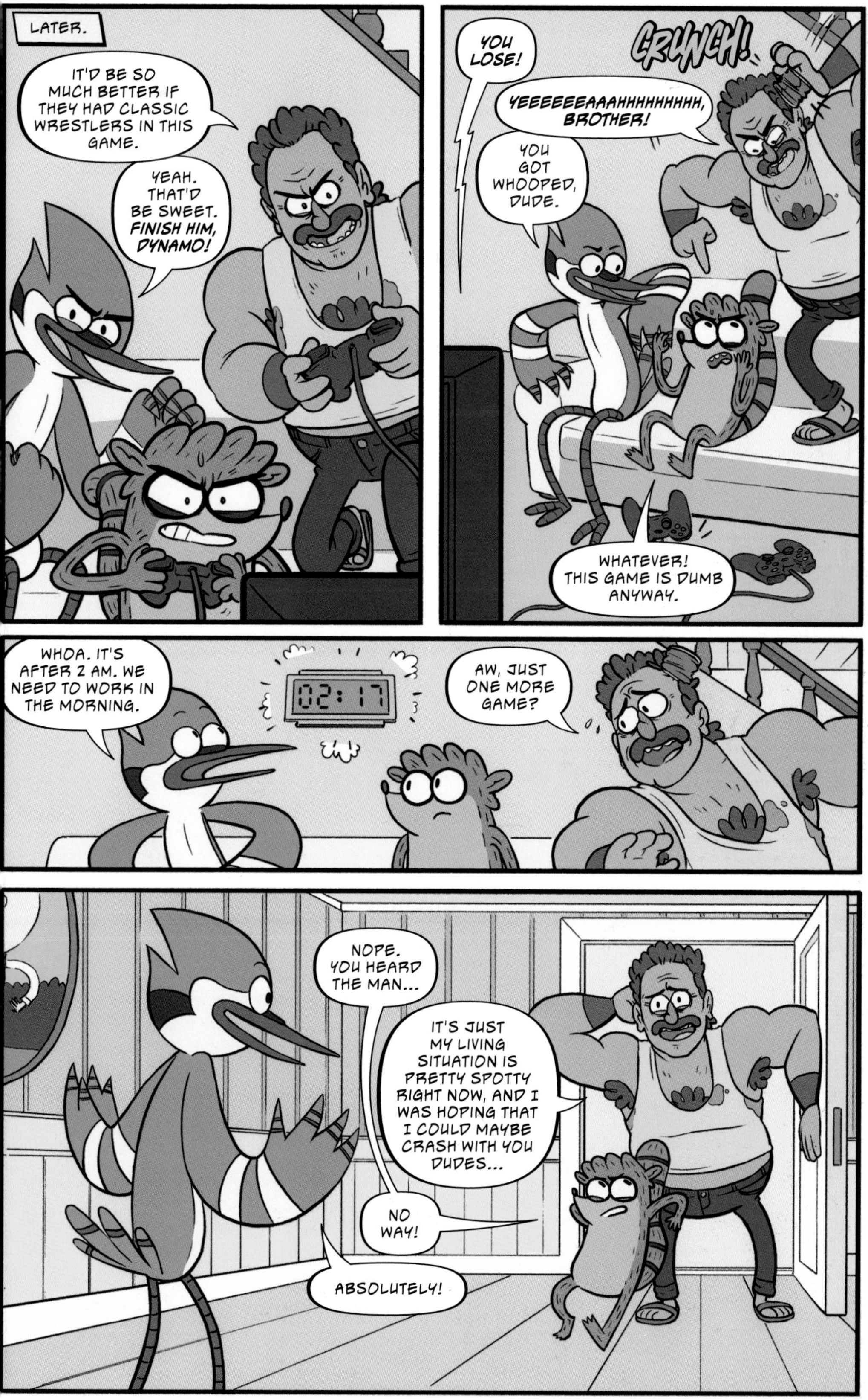
LATER.
IT'D BE SO MUCH BETTER IF THEY HAD CLASSIC WRESTLERS IN THIS GAME.
YEAH. THAT'D BE SWEET. FINISH HIM, DYNAMO!
YOU LOSE!
CRUNCH!
YEEEEEEAAAHHHHHHHHH, BROTHER!
YOU GOT WHOOPED, DUDE.
WHATEVER! THIS GAME IS DUMB ANYWAY.
WHOA. IT'S AFTER 2 AM. WE NEED TO WORK IN THE MORNING.
02:17
AW, JUST ONE MORE GAME?
NOPE. YOU HEARD THE MAN...
IT'S JUST MY LIVING SITUATION IS PRETTY SPOTTY RIGHT NOW, AND I WAS HOPING THAT I COULD MAYBE CRASH WITH YOU DUDES...
NO WAY!
ABSOLUTELY!

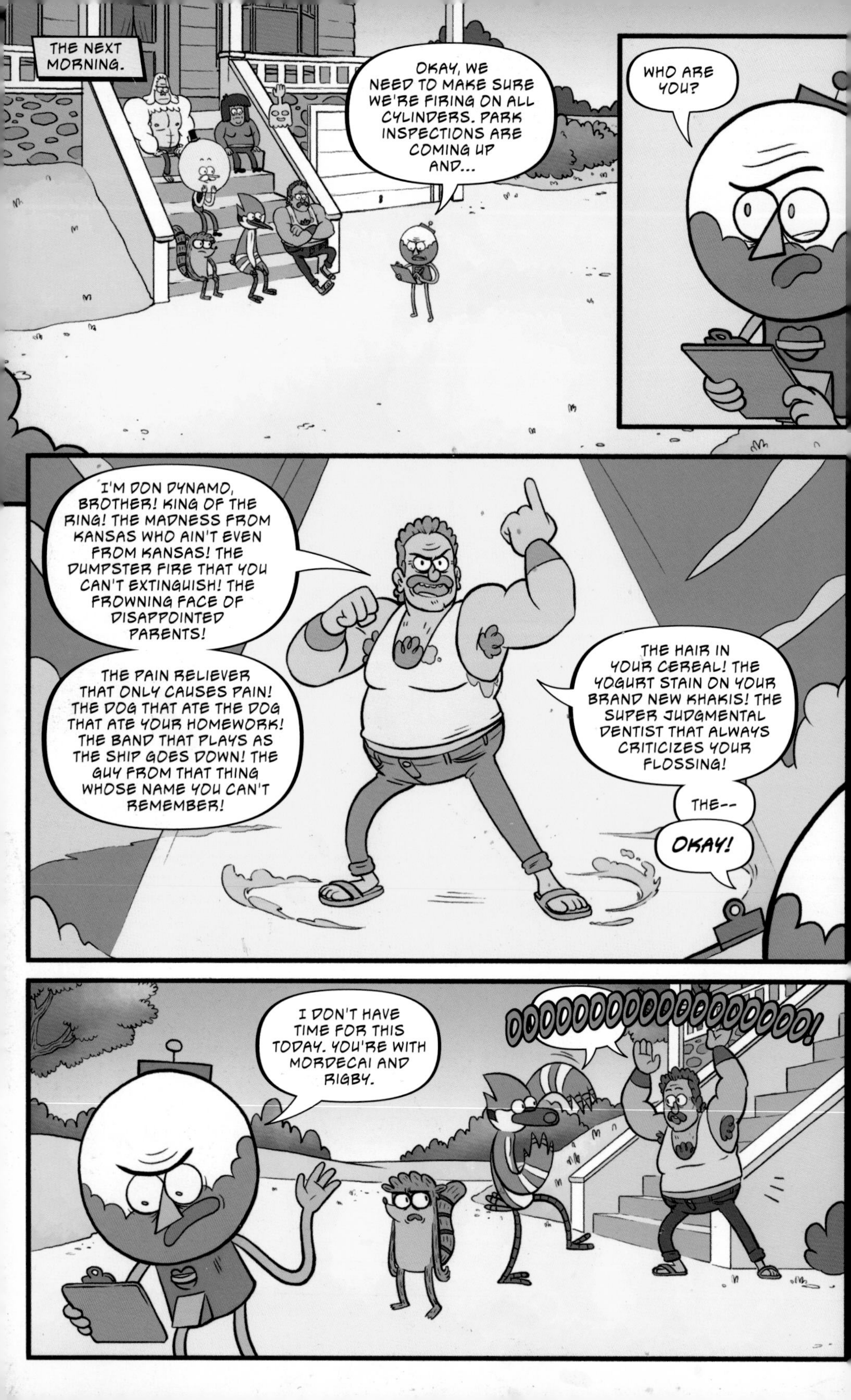

THE NEXT MORNING.
OKAY, WE NEED TO MAKE SURE WE'RE FIRING ON ALL CYLINDERS. PARK INSPECTIONS ARE COMING UP AND...
WHO ARE YOU?
I'M DON DYNAMO, BROTHER! KING OF THE RING! THE MADNESS FROM KANSAS WHO AIN'T EVEN FROM KANSAS! THE DUMPSTER FIRE THAT YOU CAN'T EXTINGUISH! THE FROWNING FACE OF DISAPPOINTED PARENTS!
THE PAIN RELIEVER THAT ONLY CAUSES PAIN! THE DOG THAT ATE THE DOG THAT ATE YOUR HOMEWORK! THE BAND THAT PLAYS AS THE SHIP GOES DOWN! THE GUY FROM THAT THING WHOSE NAME YOU CAN'T REMEMBER!
THE HAIR IN YOUR CEREAL! THE YOGURT STAIN ON YOUR BRAND NEW KHAKIS! THE SUPER JUDGMENTAL DENTIST THAT ALWAYS CRITICIZES YOUR FLOSSING!
THE--
OKAY!
I DON'T HAVE TIME FOR THIS TODAY. YOU'RE WITH MORDECAI AND RIGBY.
OOOOOOOOOOOOOOOOOOOO!

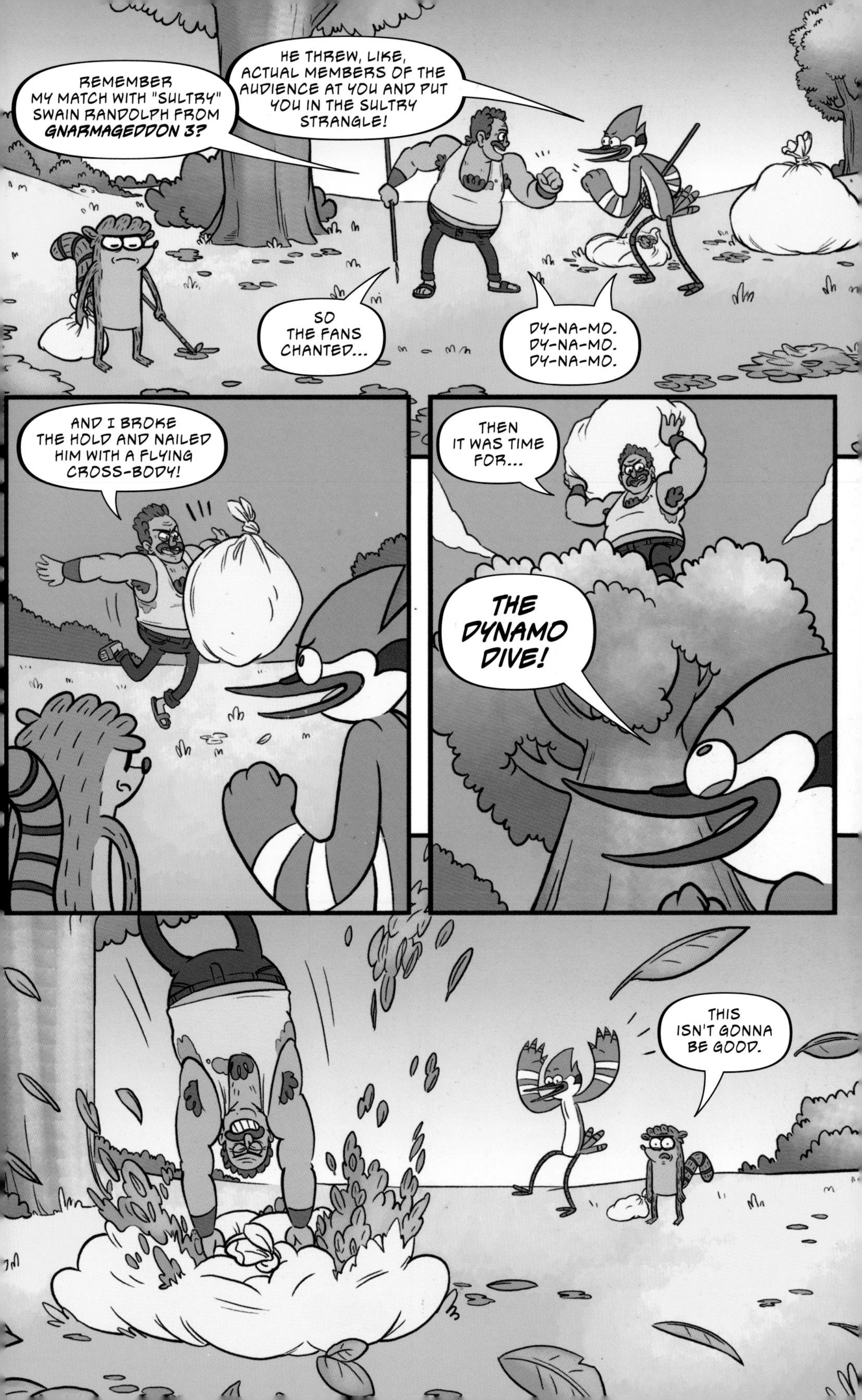
REMEMBER MY MATCH WITH "SULTRY" SWAIN RANDOLPH FROM GNARMAGEDDON 3?
HE THREW, LIKE, ACTUAL MEMBERS OF THE AUDIENCE AT YOU AND PUT YOU IN THE SULTRY STRANGLE!
SO THE FANS CHANTED...
DY-NA-MO. DY-NA-MO. DY-NA-MO.
AND I BROKE THE HOLD AND NAILED HIM WITH A FLYING CROSS-BODY!
THEN IT WAS TIME FOR...
THE DYNAMO DIVE!
THIS ISN'T GONNA BE GOOD.

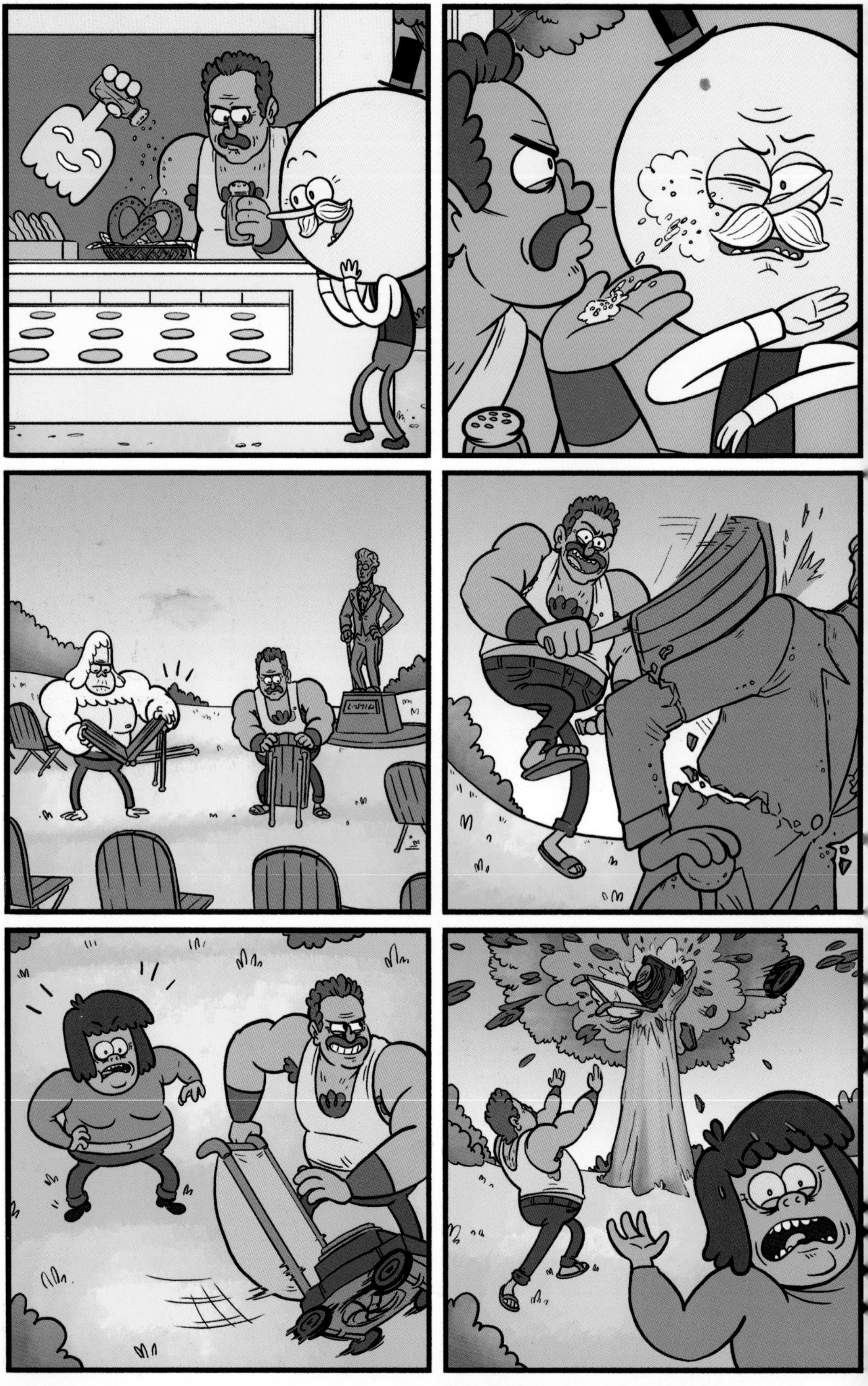

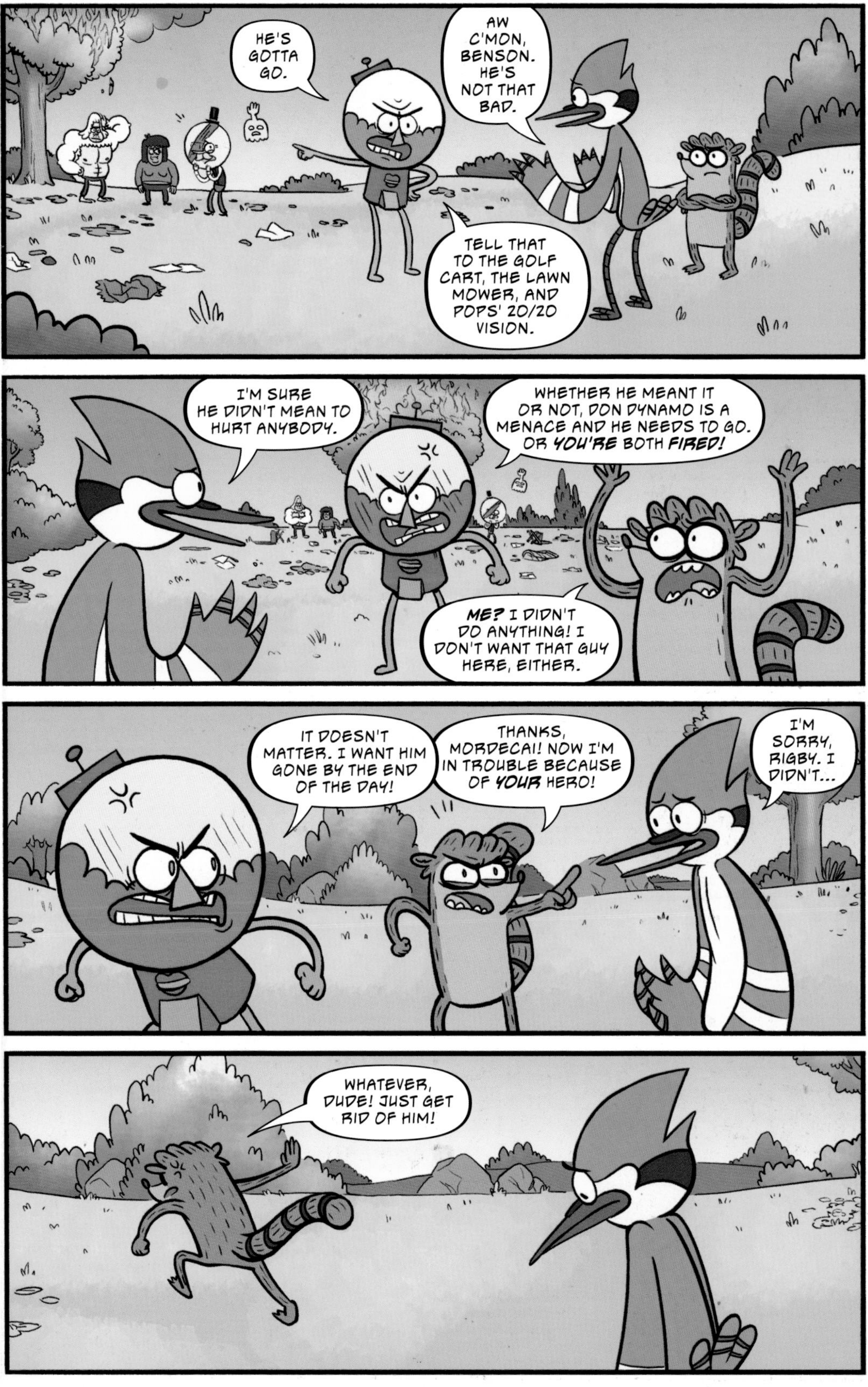
HE'S GOTTA GO.
AW C'MON, BENSON. HE'S NOT THAT BAD.
TELL THAT TO THE GOLF CART, THE LAWN MOWER, AND POPS' 20/20 VISION.
I'M SURE HE DIDN'T MEAN TO HURT ANYBODY.
WHETHER HE MEANT IT OR NOT, DON DYNAMO IS A MENACE AND HE NEEDS TO GO. OR YOU'RE BOTH FIRED!
ME? I DIDN'T DO ANYTHING! I DON'T WANT THAT GUY HERE, EITHER.
IT DOESN'T MATTER. I WANT HIM GONE BY THE END OF THE DAY!
THANKS, MORDECAI! NOW I'M IN TROUBLE BECAUSE OF YOUR HERO!
I'M SORRY, RIGBY. I DIDN'T...
WHATEVER, DUDE! JUST GET RID OF HIM!

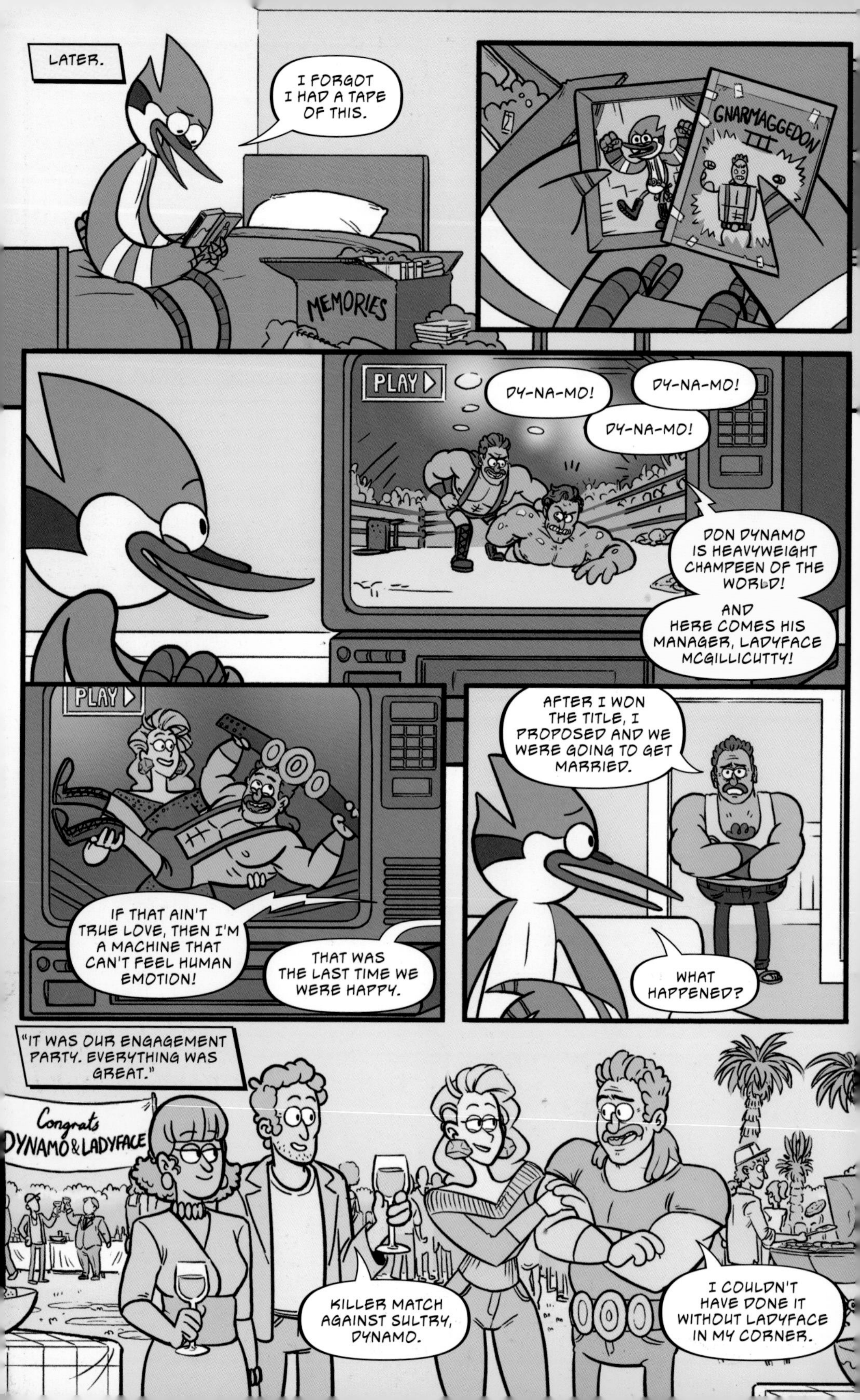
LATER.
I FORGOT I HAD A TAPE OF THIS.
MEMORIES
GNARMAGGEDON III
PLAY
DY-NA-MO!
DY-NA-MO!
DY-NA-MO!
DON DYNAMO IS HEAVYWEIGHT CHAMPEEN OF THE WORLD!
AND HERE COMES HIS MANAGER, LADYFACE MCGILLICUTTY!
PLAY
IF THAT AIN'T TRUE LOVE, THEN I'M A MACHINE THAT CAN'T FEEL HUMAN EMOTION!
THAT WAS THE LAST TIME WE WERE HAPPY.
AFTER I WON THE TITLE, I PROPOSED AND WE WERE GOING TO GET MARRIED.
WHAT HAPPENED?
"IT WAS OUR ENGAGEMENT PARTY. EVERYTHING WAS GREAT."
Congrats DYNAMO & LADYFACE
KILLER MATCH AGAINST SULTRY, DYNAMO.
I COULDN'T HAVE DONE IT WITHOUT LADYFACE IN MY CORNER.

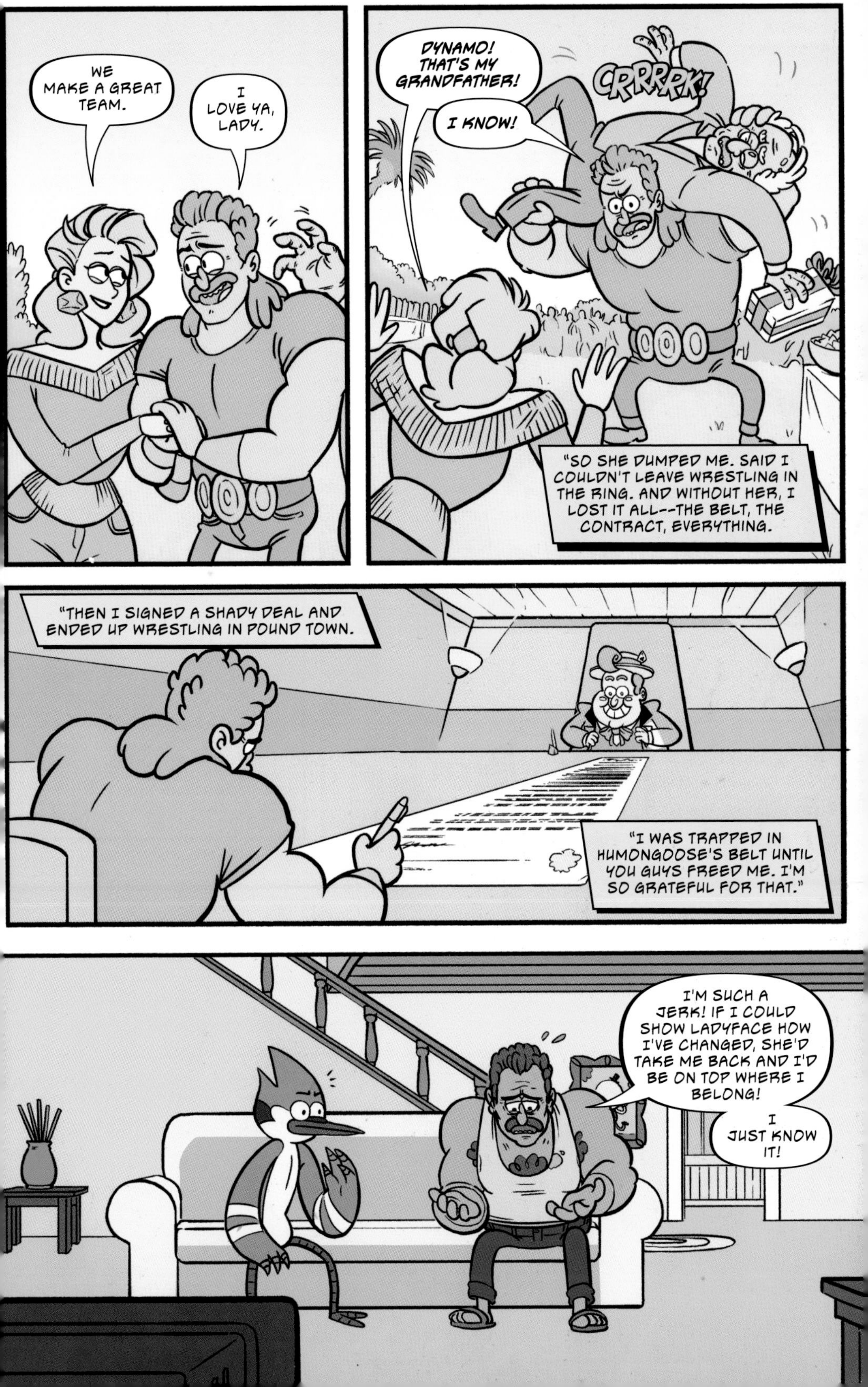
WE MAKE A GREAT TEAM.
I LOVE YA, LADY.
DYNAMO! THAT'S MY GRANDFATHER!
I KNOW!
CRRRRK!
"SO SHE DUMPED ME. SAID I COULDN'T LEAVE WRESTLING IN THE RING. AND WITHOUT HER, I LOST IT ALL--THE BELT, THE CONTRACT, EVERYTHING.
"THEN I SIGNED A SHADY DEAL AND ENDED UP WRESTLING IN POUND TOWN.
"I WAS TRAPPED IN HUMONGOOSE'S BELT UNTIL YOU GUYS FREED ME. I'M SO GRATEFUL FOR THAT."
I'M SUCH A JERK! IF I COULD SHOW LADYFACE HOW I'VE CHANGED, SHE'D TAKE ME BACK AND I'D BE ON TOP WHERE I BELONG!
I JUST KNOW IT!

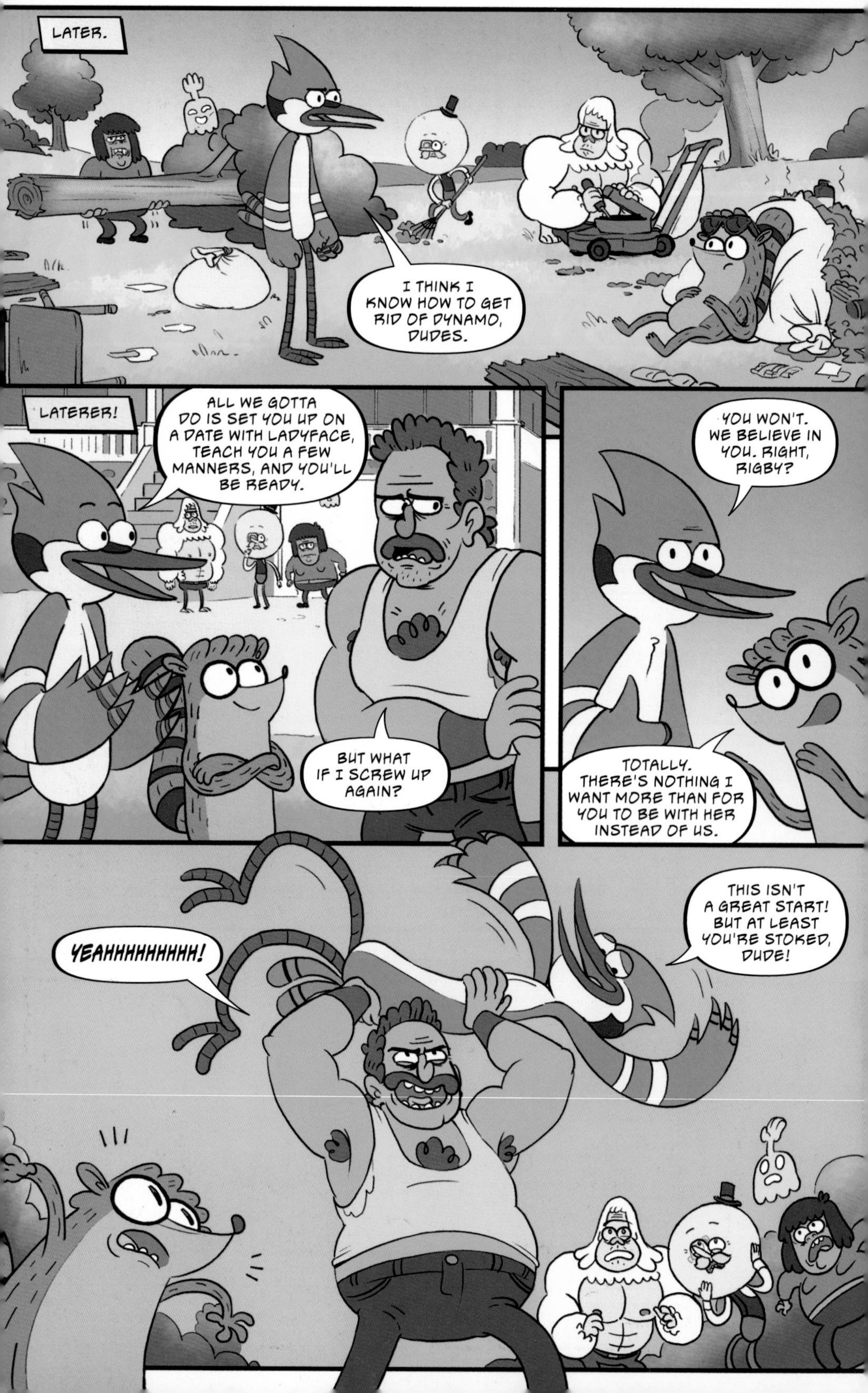
LATER.
I THINK I KNOW HOW TO GET RID OF DYNAMO, DUDES.
LATERER!
ALL WE GOTTA DO IS SET YOU UP ON A DATE WITH LADYFACE, TEACH YOU A FEW MANNERS, AND YOU'LL BE READY.
BUT WHAT IF I SCREW UP AGAIN?
YOU WON'T. WE BELIEVE IN YOU. RIGHT, RIGBY?
TOTALLY. THERE'S NOTHING I WANT MORE THAN FOR YOU TO BE WITH HER INSTEAD OF US.
YEAHHHHHHHHH!
THIS ISN'T A GREAT START! BUT AT LEAST YOU'RE STOKED, DUDE!

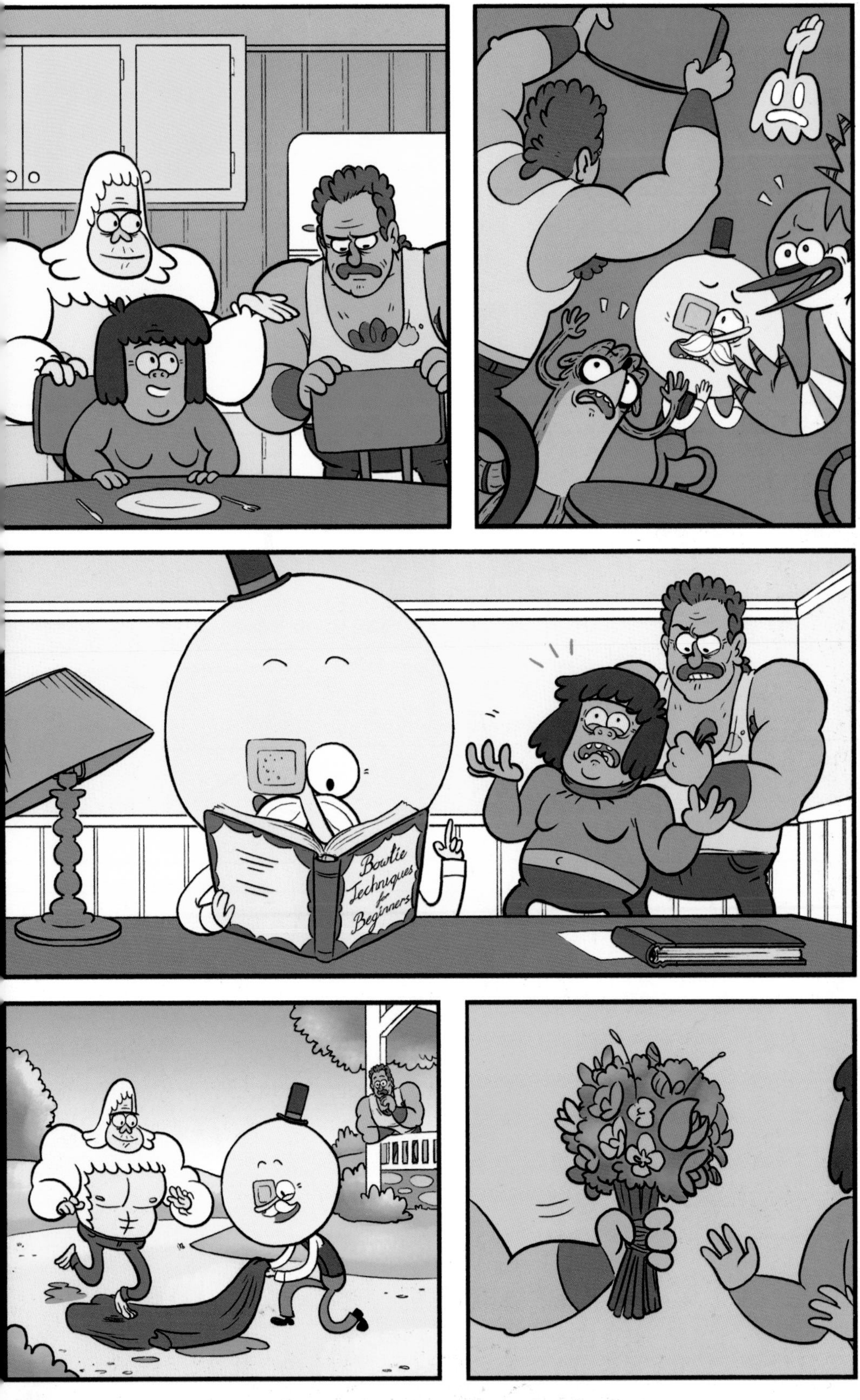
Bowtie Techniques for Beginners

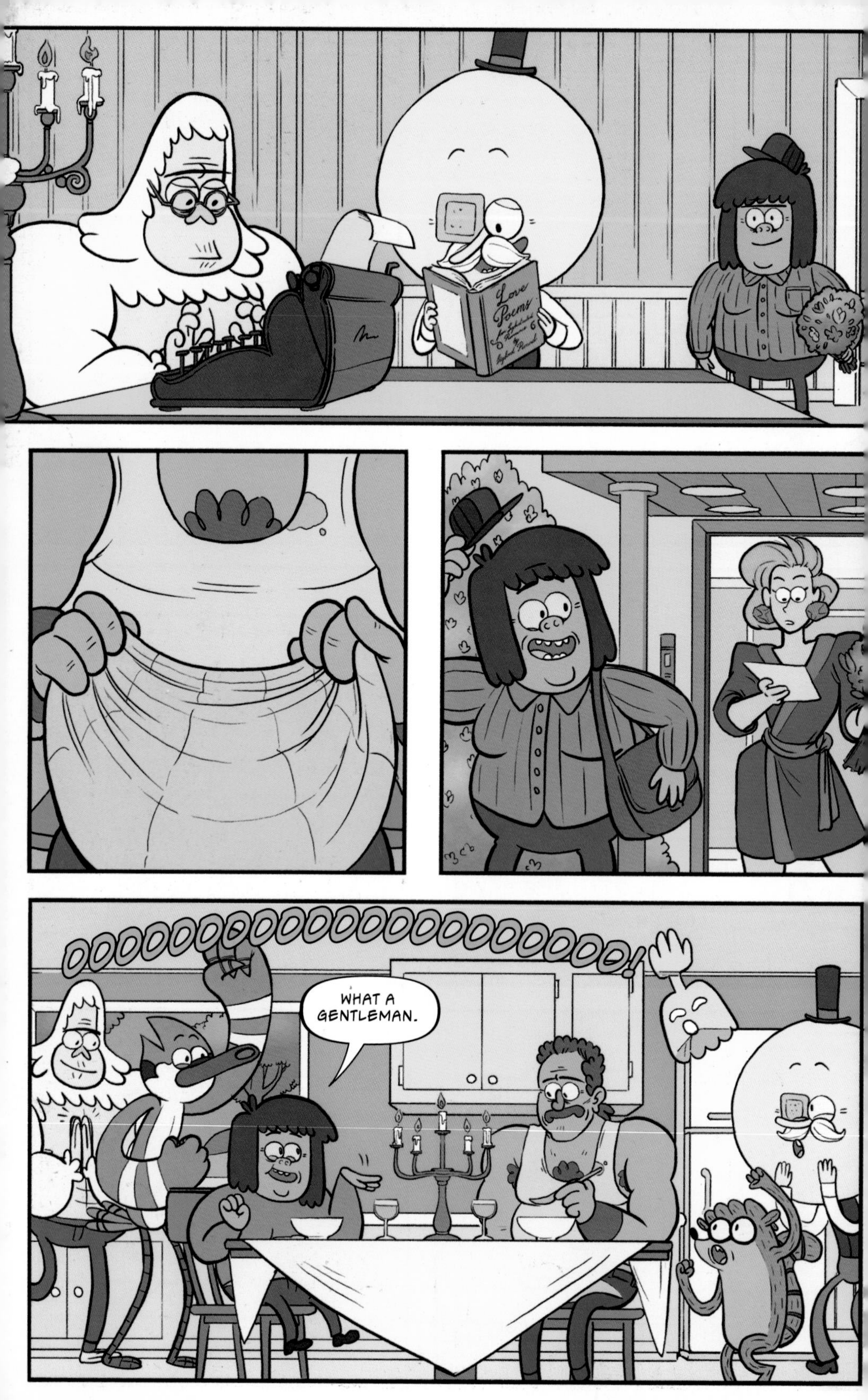
Love Poems
OOOOOOOOOOOOOOOOOOOOO!
WHAT A GENTLEMAN.

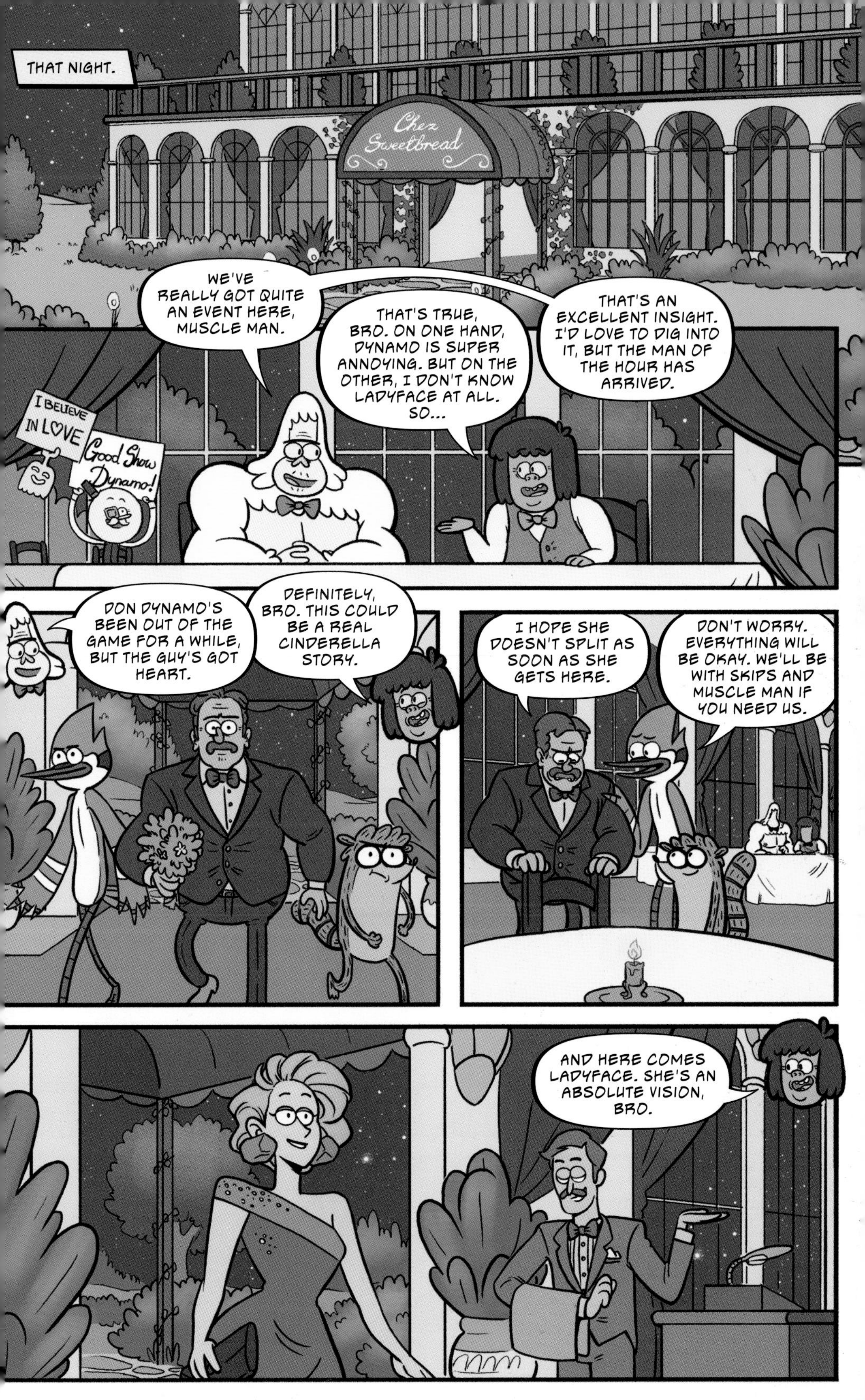
THAT NIGHT.
Chez Sweetbread
WE'VE REALLY GOT QUITE AN EVENT HERE, MUSCLE MAN.
THAT'S TRUE, BRO. ON ONE HAND, DYNAMO IS SUPER ANNOYING. BUT ON THE OTHER, I DON'T KNOW LADYFACE AT ALL. SO...
THAT'S AN EXCELLENT INSIGHT. I'D LOVE TO DIG INTO IT, BUT THE MAN OF THE HOUR HAS ARRIVED.
I BELIEVE IN LOVE
Good Show Dynamo!
DON DYNAMO'S BEEN OUT OF THE GAME FOR A WHILE, BUT THE GUY'S GOT HEART.
DEFINITELY, BRO. THIS COULD BE A REAL CINDERELLA STORY.
I HOPE SHE DOESN'T SPLIT AS SOON AS SHE GETS HERE.
DON'T WORRY. EVERYTHING WILL BE OKAY. WE'LL BE WITH SKIPS AND MUSCLE MAN IF YOU NEED US.
AND HERE COMES LADYFACE. SHE'S AN ABSOLUTE VISION, BRO.

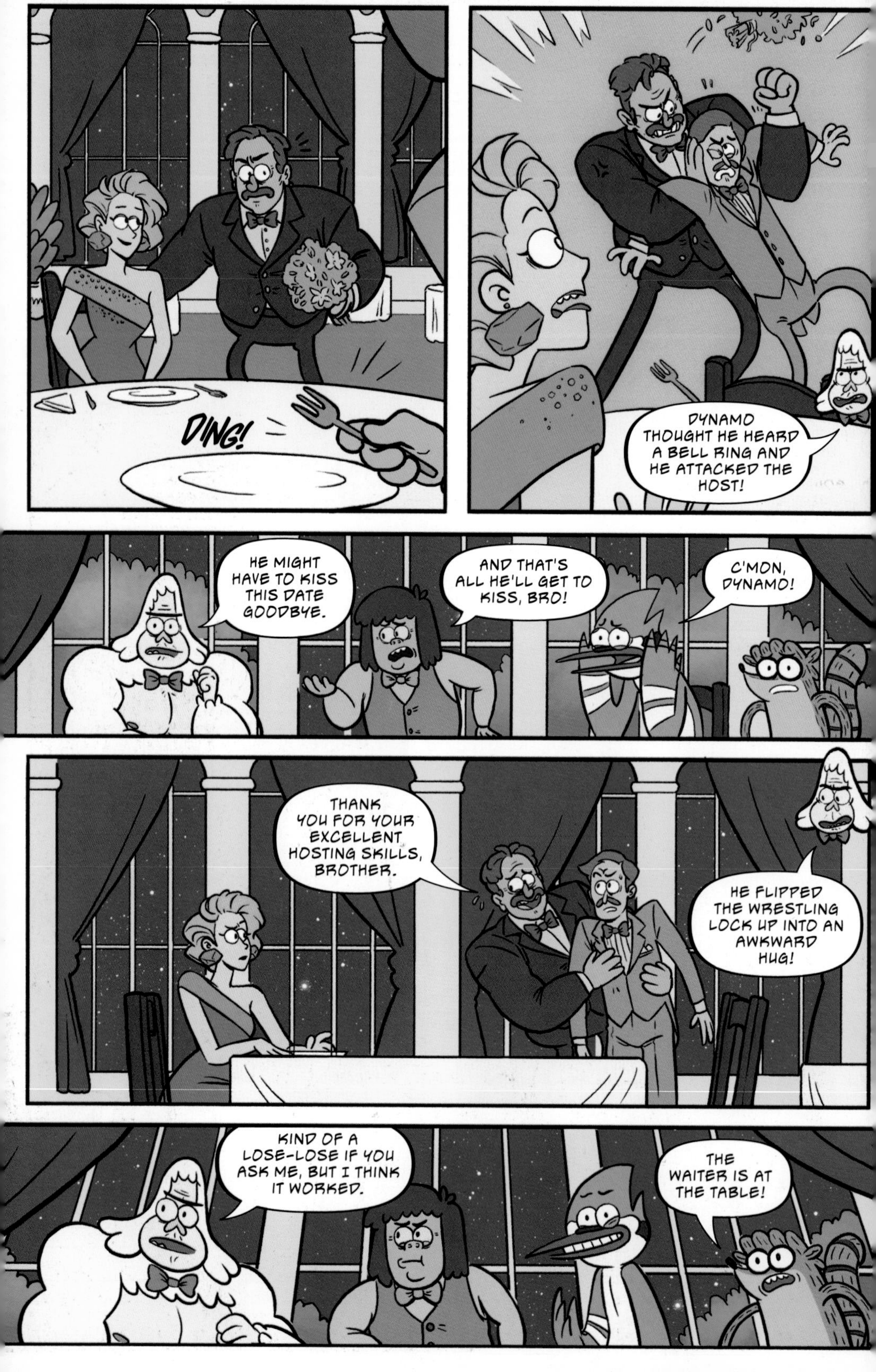
DING!
DYNAMO THOUGHT HE HEARD A BELL RING AND HE ATTACKED THE HOST!
HE MIGHT HAVE TO KISS THIS DATE GOODBYE.
AND THAT'S ALL HE'LL GET TO KISS, BRO!
C'MON, DYNAMO!
THANK YOU FOR YOUR EXCELLENT HOSTING SKILLS, BROTHER.
HE FLIPPED THE WRESTLING LOCK UP INTO AN AWKWARD HUG!
KIND OF A LOSE-LOSE IF YOU ASK ME, BUT I THINK IT WORKED.
THE WAITER IS AT THE TABLE!

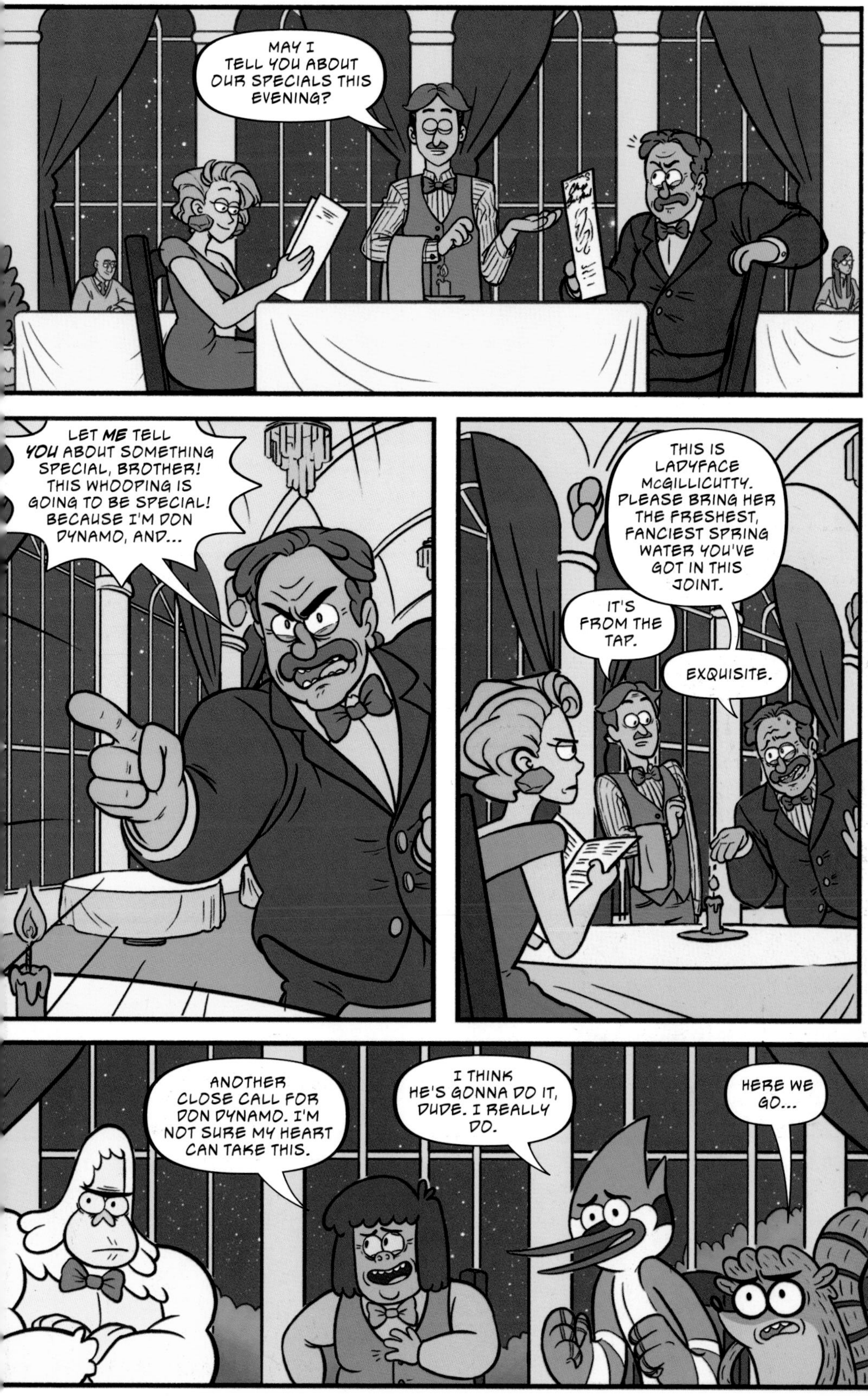
MAY I TELL YOU ABOUT OUR SPECIALS THIS EVENING?
LET ME TELL YOU ABOUT SOMETHING SPECIAL, BROTHER! THIS WHOOPING IS GOING TO BE SPECIAL! BECAUSE I'M DON DYNAMO, AND...
THIS IS LADYFACE McGILLICUTTY. PLEASE BRING HER THE FRESHEST, FANCIEST SPRING WATER YOU'VE GOT IN THIS JOINT.
IT'S FROM THE TAP.
EXQUISITE.
ANOTHER CLOSE CALL FOR DON DYNAMO. I'M NOT SURE MY HEART CAN TAKE THIS.
I THINK HE'S GONNA DO IT, DUDE. I REALLY DO.
HERE WE GO...

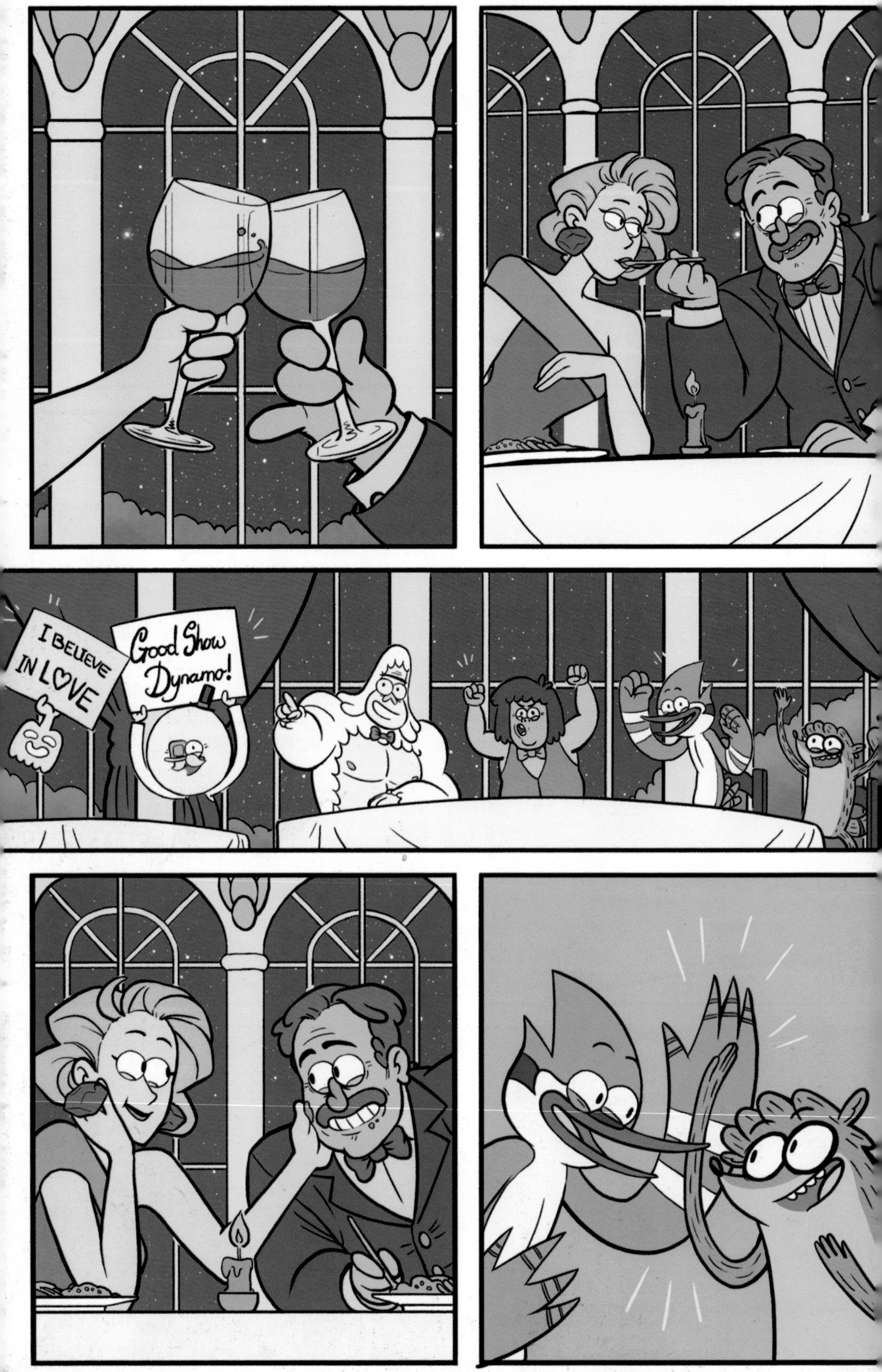
I BELIEVE IN LOVE
Good Show Dynamo!

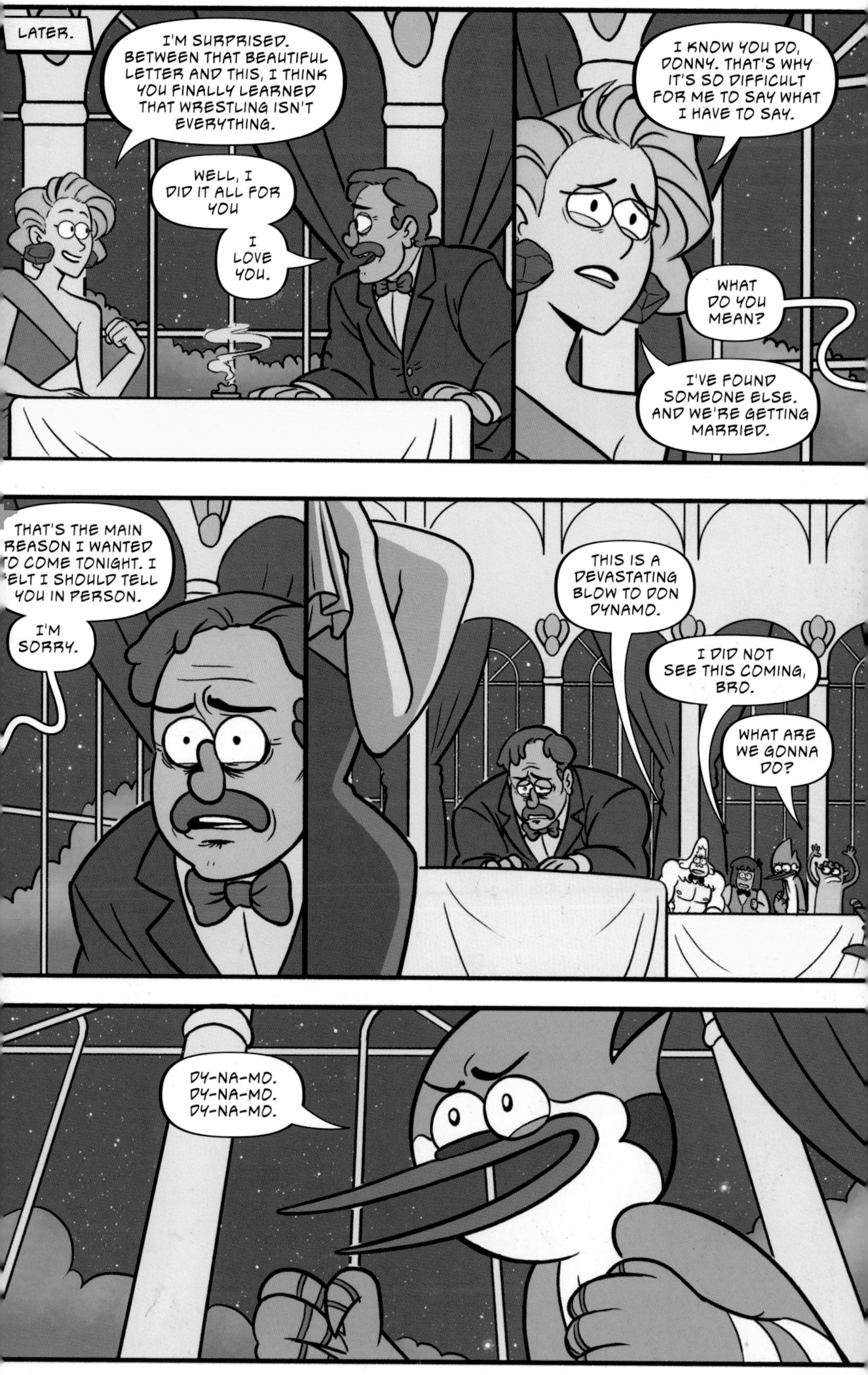
LATER.
I'M SURPRISED. BETWEEN THAT BEAUTIFUL LETTER AND THIS, I THINK YOU FINALLY LEARNED THAT WRESTLING ISN'T EVERYTHING.
WELL, I DID IT ALL FOR YOU
I LOVE YOU.
I KNOW YOU DO, DONNY. THAT'S WHY IT'S SO DIFFICULT FOR ME TO SAY WHAT I HAVE TO SAY.
WHAT DO YOU MEAN?
I'VE FOUND SOMEONE ELSE. AND WE'RE GETTING MARRIED.
THAT'S THE MAIN REASON I WANTED TO COME TONIGHT. I FELT I SHOULD TELL YOU IN PERSON.
I'M SORRY.
THIS IS A DEVASTATING BLOW TO DON DYNAMO.
I DID NOT SEE THIS COMING, BRO.
WHAT ARE WE GONNA DO?
DY-NA-MO. DY-NA-MO. DY-NA-MO.

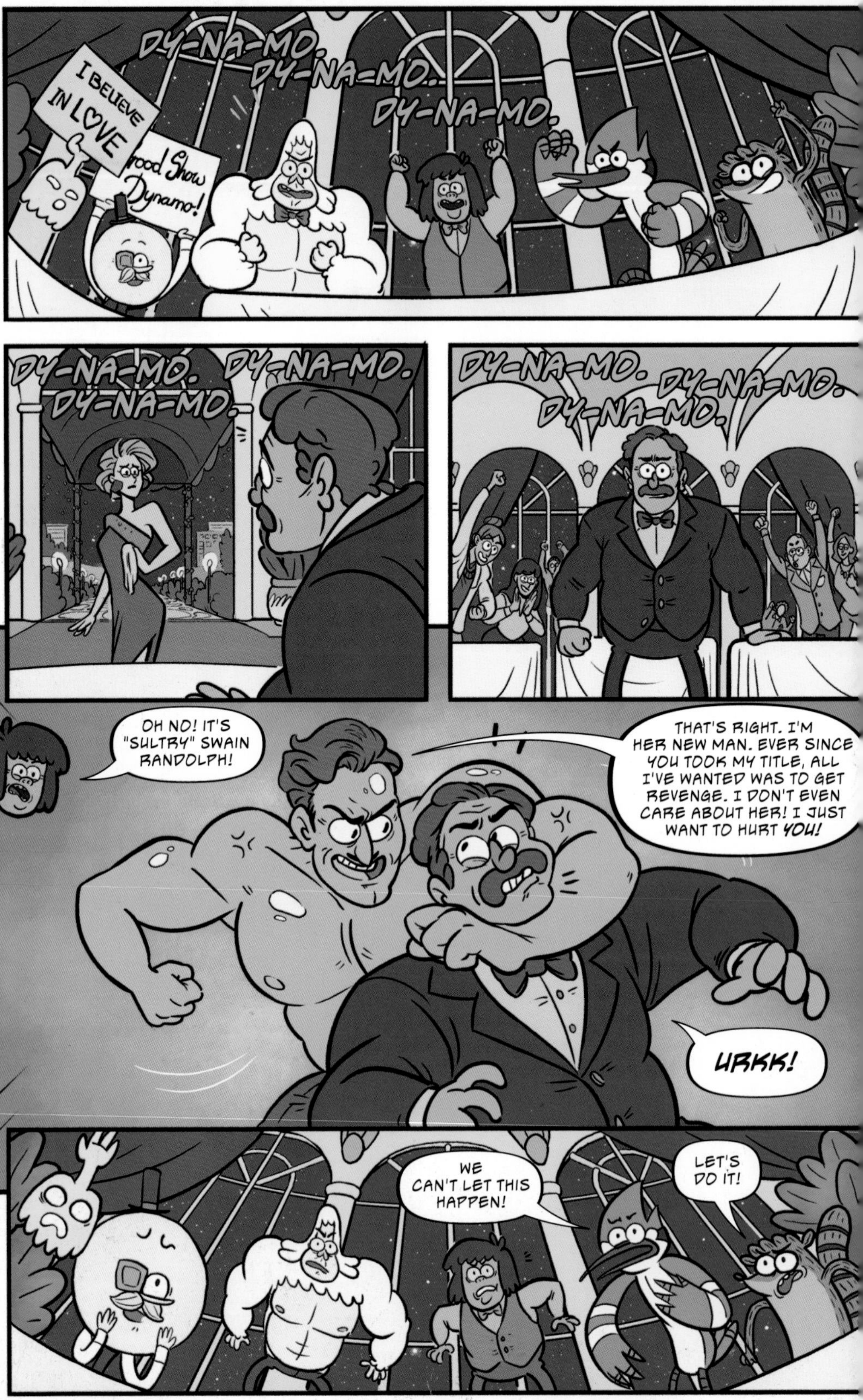
DY-NA-MO. DY-NA-MO. DY-NA-MO.
I BELIEVE IN LOVE
Brood Show Dynamo!
DY-NA-MO. DY-NA-MO. DY-NA-MO.
DY-NA-MO. DY-NA-MO. DY-NA-MO.
OH NO! IT'S "SULTRY" SWAIN RANDOLPH!
THAT'S RIGHT. I'M HER NEW MAN. EVER SINCE YOU TOOK MY TITLE, ALL I'VE WANTED WAS TO GET REVENGE. I DON'T EVEN CARE ABOUT HER! I JUST WANT TO HURT YOU!
URKK!
WE CAN'T LET THIS HAPPEN!
LET'S DO IT!

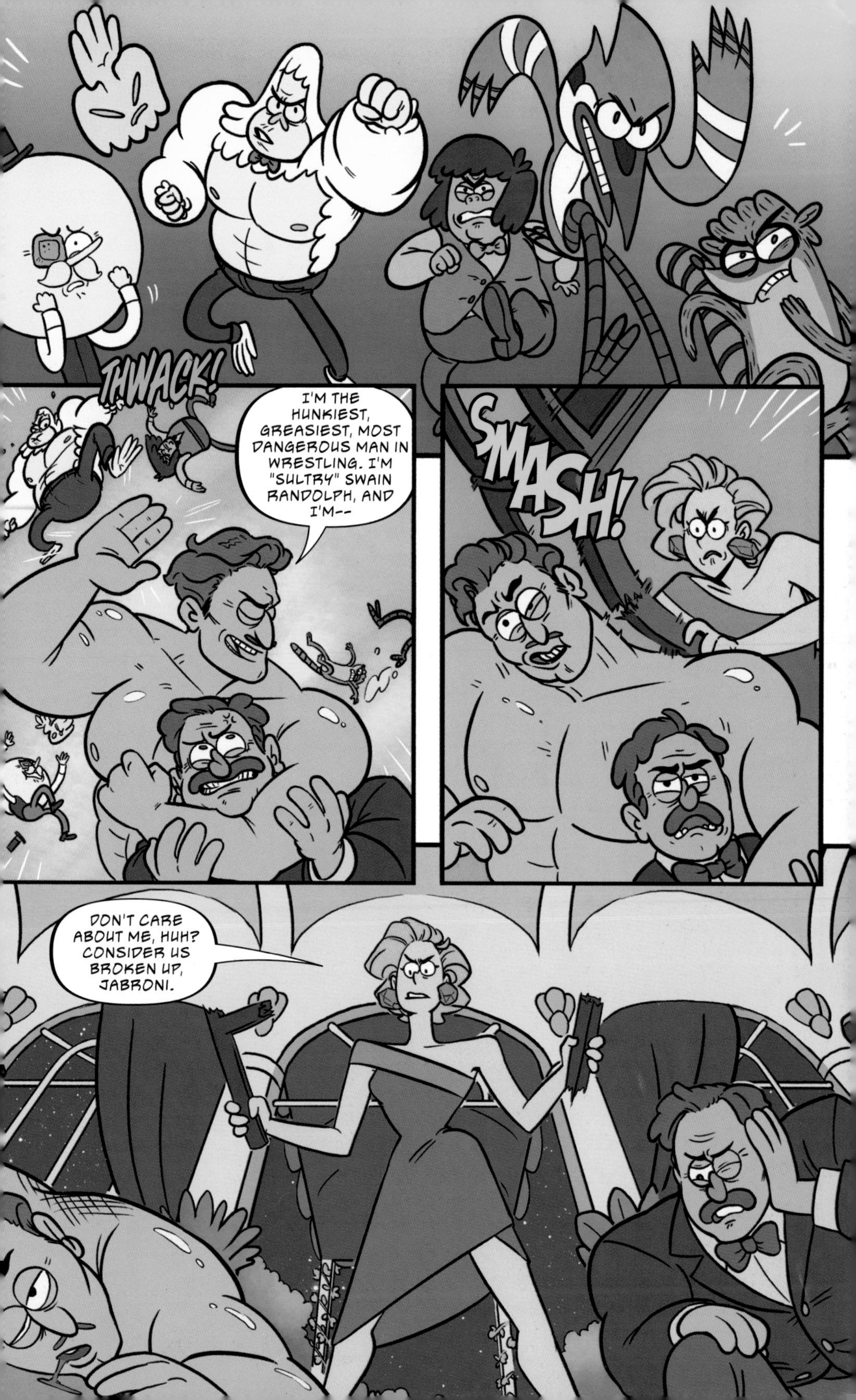
THWACK!
I'M THE HUNKIEST, GREASIEST, MOST DANGEROUS MAN IN WRESTLING. I'M "SULTRY" SWAIN RANDOLPH, AND I'M--
SMASH!
DON'T CARE ABOUT ME, HUH? CONSIDER US BROKEN UP, JABRONI.

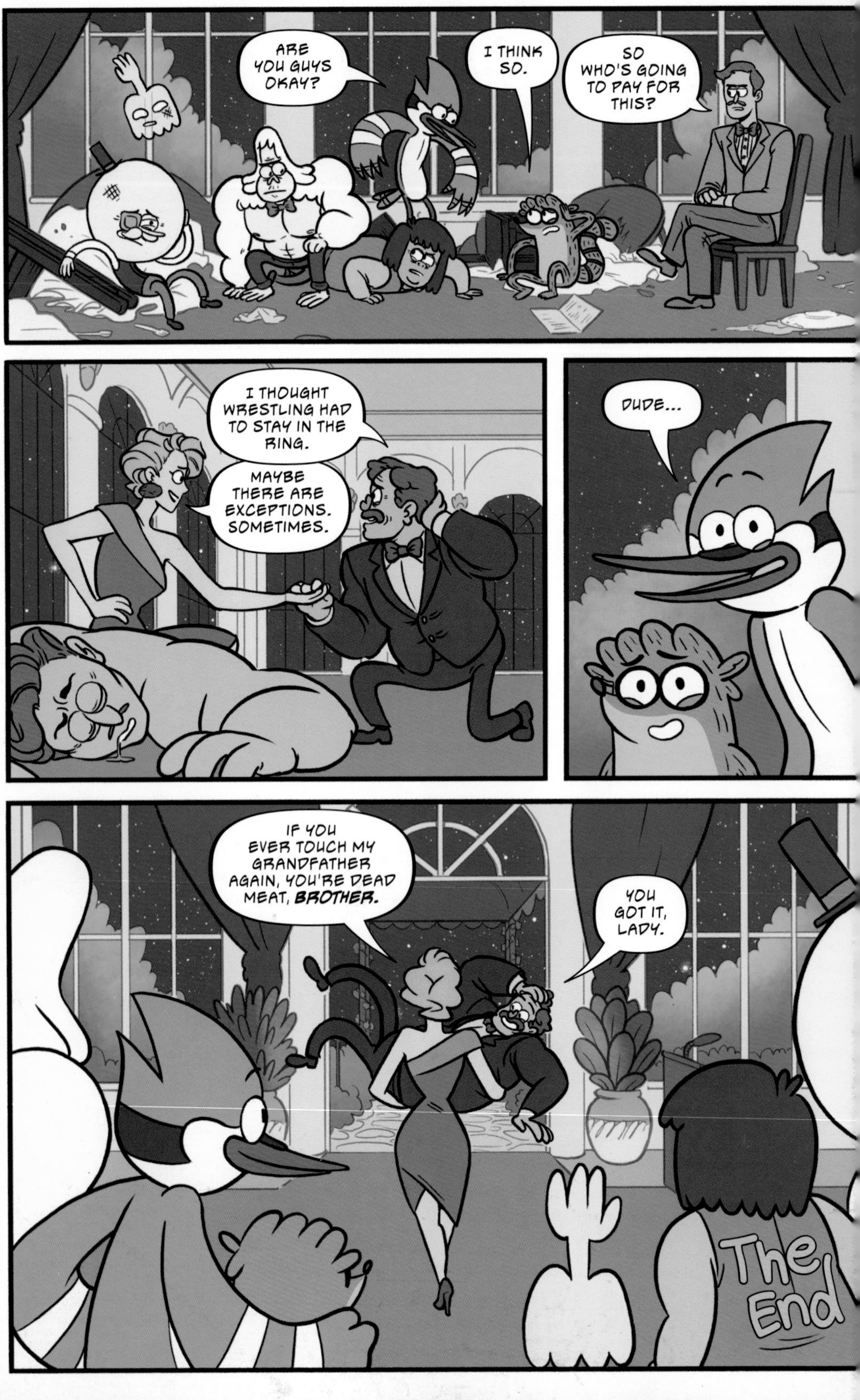
ARE YOU GUYS OKAY?
I THINK SO.
SO WHO'S GOING TO PAY FOR THIS?
I THOUGHT WRESTLING HAD TO STAY IN THE RING.
MAYBE THERE ARE EXCEPTIONS. SOMETIMES.
DUDE...
IF YOU EVER TOUCH MY GRANDFATHER AGAIN, YOU'RE DEAD MEAT, BROTHER.
YOU GOT IT, LADY.
The End

DISCOVER
EXPLOSIVE NEW WORLDS

Adventure Time

The Amazing World of
Gumball

Steven Universe
Volume One

Over the Garden Wall
"A unique, delightful read."
—Comic Book Resources

Garfield
By Jim Davis

Charles M. Schulz
Peanuts

AVAILABLE AT YOUR LOCAL COMICS SHOP AND BOOKSTORE

To find a comics shop in your area, call 1-888-266-4226

WWW.**BOOM-STUDIOS**.COM

kaboom!™

Adventure Time
Pendleton Ward and Others
Volume 1
ISBN: 978-1-60886-280-1 | $9.99
Volume 2
ISBN: 978-1-60886-323-5 | $14.99 US
Adventure Time: Islands
ISBN: 978-1-60886-972-5 | $9.99

Regular Show
J.G. Quintel and Others
Volume 1
ISBN: 978-1-60886-362-4 | $14.99
Volume 2
ISBN: 978-1-60886-426-3 | $14.99

Regular Show: Hydration
ISBN: 978-1-60886-339-6 | $12.99

The Amazing World of Gumball
Ben Bocquelet and Others
Volume 1
ISBN: 978-1-60886-488-1 | $14.99
Volume 2
ISBN: 978-1-60886-793-6 | $14.99

Over the Garden Wall
Patrick McHale, Jim Campbell and Others
Volume 1
ISBN: 978-1-60886-940-4 | $14.99
Volume 2
ISBN: 978-1-68415-006-9 | $14.99

Steven Universe
Rebecca Sugar and Others
Volume 1
ISBN: 978-1-60886-706-6 | $14.99
Volume 2
ISBN: 978-1-60886-796-7 | $14.99

Steven Universe & The Crystal Gems
ISBN: 978-1-60886-921-3 | $14.99

Steven Universe: Too Cool for School
ISBN: 978-1-60886-771-4 | $14.99

Peanuts
Charles Schultz and Others
Volume 1
ISBN: 978-1-60886-260-3 | $13.99

Garfield
Jim Davis and Others
Volume 1
ISBN: 978-1-60886-287-0 | $13.99

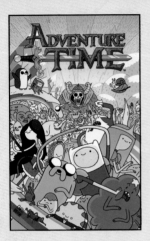

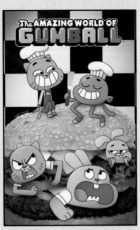

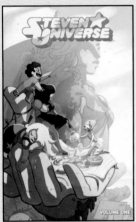

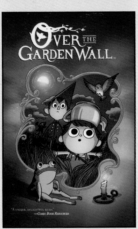

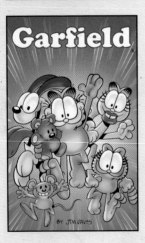

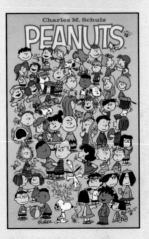

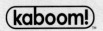